Praise for *Every* ─,─

'A beautiful, hypnotic, emotional novel. I couldn't
stop turning the pages'
CECELIA AHERN

'Sweeping, glamorous, and utterly heartfelt. I adored it'
AMANDA GEARD

'An absolute treat of a novel . . . With its immersive
storytelling, heart-wrenching emotional scenes,
this is a love story for all time'
GILL PAUL

'Rich, heartfelt, and completely unputdownable.
I flipping LOVED it!'
EMMA COOPER

'Incredible . . . manages to rip my heart out
in the best way possible'
LORNA COOK

'This is time slip at its very best – I was utterly swept up
in the story . . . Impeccably researched, cleverly plotted
and completely evocative'
LOUISE FEIN

Jennifer Ross is the pseudonym for Jenny Ashcroft, author of several historical novels, including *Secrets of the Watch House*, *The Echoes of Love*, *Beneath a Burning Sky* and *Island in the East*. She previously spent much of her life living in, working in and exploring Australia and Asia, and now splits her time between Australia and the UK.

Every Lifetime After

Jennifer Ross

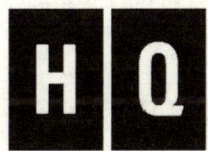

ONE PLACE. MANY STORIES

HQ
An imprint of HarperCollins*Publishers* Ltd
1 London Bridge Street
London SE1 9GF

www.harpercollins.co.uk

HarperCollins*Publishers*
Macken House, 39/40 Mayor Street Upper
Dublin 1, D01 C9W8, Ireland
This edition 2026

1
First published in Great Britain by HQ,
an imprint of HarperCollins*Publishers* Ltd 2026

ISBN HB: 9780008703363
ISBN TPB: 9780008753740

Set in Sabon LT Std by HarperCollins*Publishers* India

Printed and bound in the UK using 100% Renewable
Electricity at CPI Group (UK) Ltd

For more information visit: www.harpercollins.co.uk/green

For Matt, Molly, Jonah & Raffy

January 1989

The Theatre Royal, York

The auditorium was empty, its seats all in shadows. The house lanterns, trained on the set-less stage, were off. The city outside was bleak, the frozen cobbles noisy with crowds anxious to get to wherever they were going. But in here, it was quiet. He watched her, walking to the middle of the stage in her thick duffle coat. Knitted mittens dangled on a string from her sleeves. She flexed her fingers, raised her head, looking out into the theatre's silence.

What was she hearing? He wondered.

The whispers of players past?

The echo of every forever still to come?

Love and pain swelled in his chest.

'You look like you belong on the stage,' he called to her, his voice slicing through the dust motes in the air.

She turned, facing him. His daughter. Her round cheeks were mottled. Her hazel eyes were wide, liquid with spent tears. All he wanted was to go to her, scoop her up, cradle the precious weight of her close and convince her that it was all going to be ok. *I promise.* But they were strangers, the two of them. Just strangers. Until now, he'd never allowed them to be anything else. It had felt the kindest way. He'd known since before she

1

was born that he was going to have to leave her. His hope was that what she'd never had, she wouldn't miss.

She lived with her grandparents, her mother's parents, in a nearby village. He'd visited often these past four years, catching the bus over whenever the longing had got too much. Hidden, he'd waited for her to appear, for hours some days, then watched her for as long as he could bear to: walking to the shops, or feeding the ducks at the pond, or trotting around the green – chasing no one, listening to the air, studying the sky with her all-seeing gaze locked on empty space.

Every birthday, he'd telephoned the house, permitting himself that one small contact, desperate for every morsel of news he could glean.

He'd been working at this theatre for as long as she'd been alive. He'd started as an office temp and never left. He'd been alone today. It was a slow time of year, and the rest of the small team were away. He'd headed out at two for a walk he hadn't particularly wanted, but which instinct had told him to take anyway.

He always followed his instincts.

His intuition had propelled him up Blake Street, onto Davygate, past Bettys tearooms. And there she'd been, on the pavement outside the tearoom entrance, sobbing, her grandparents, Belinda and John, knelt before her, trying, vainly, to calm her.

Belinda and John hadn't noticed him. Caught up in her, they'd ignored the stares of all the frozen passers-by. He could easily have continued on his way, and they'd have been none the wiser.

But, 'Belinda,' he'd said. 'Can I help?'

All he'd wanted was to help.

And although Belinda and John had been stunned to see him – and John as hostile as ever – they'd also been desperate to get their granddaughter home, only they'd left the car all the way out at the Park & Ride. She couldn't have caught the shuttle there, not the way she was. So, they'd agreed that he should take her and Belinda with him to the theatre, where they could wait in the warm whilst John fetched the car.

He'd been reeling as they'd set off on the short walk back. He hadn't been able to believe it was all happening, after four years of him keeping such agonising distance. Yet, he'd also been reassured by the certain conviction that everything was unfolding as it must.

She'd been too upset to walk. Belinda had carried her, and she'd kept crying, making conversation impossible. But when they'd reached the theatre, he'd asked her if she'd like to see the auditorium, and she'd calmed down.

Whilst she'd made her way on to the stage, he and Belinda had remained in the wings. In lowered tones, Belinda had told him that there'd been another incident the day before. The worst yet. She'd run away, and by the time they'd eventually found her, she'd been in an awful state. Her psychiatrist had recommended she rest today, but she'd been so shaken, Belinda and John had wanted to give her a treat. So, they'd brought her for tea at Bettys, which they'd assumed she'd love, only when they'd arrived, she'd become inconsolable, hearing music, seeing dancers, not understanding why no one else could.

'There was plenty of dancing at Bettys during the war, of course,' Belinda had said. 'But never since.'

'Can I talk to her?' he'd asked.

'Oh, Noah,' she'd said. 'I don't know . . .'

'Please,' he'd persisted. 'You have my word I won't say anything to upset her.'

Belinda had hesitated a moment longer.

Then, 'All right,' she'd agreed. 'God knows I'll try anything.'

He approached her now, still struggling to believe he was

doing it, and she, centre stage, stared up at him with confusion, but no caution.

Maybe he was fooling himself, but he felt as though she knew she could trust him.

'Do you like it?' he asked her, gesturing at the theatre beyond. She nodded.

'Me too. I've always loved theatres.' He crouched beside her. 'I believe you heard that music earlier,' he told her. 'I'm sure there was dancing, too.'

She dipped her head, brow pinched.

This time, the urge he felt to pull her into his arms almost overwhelmed him.

'There's nothing wrong with you,' he said. 'There's never been anything wrong with you.'

She swallowed.

'Your mum's told me all about you,' he went on. 'I know that where most people see houses, you can sometimes see fields. That you hear sounds, just like that music earlier, when everyone else hears nothing, and want to play with friends you can't find. Two boys.' He eyed her. 'Is that right?'

Another nod.

'Can you think where they are?'

'I don't know,' she said, speaking at last, so quietly it was little more than a sigh. 'I've lost them.'

'No.' He shook his head. 'I'm sure you haven't. I think they probably just can't find their way here.'

Out of the corner of her eye, she looked at him. 'What do you mean?'

'I mean,' he said, 'that very few people are as lucky as you. As us.'

She blinked.

'There's a reason I've always loved theatres,' he said. 'It's because I see our world like one. The biggest theatre you can imagine.' He mustered a smile. 'You and me, and your mum, and nan and grandad, we live on a stage.' He laid his hand on the sloping floor. 'But our stage isn't the only stage. I think that all over us, and through us, are thousands more, with this life, and this time, and endless others playing out over and over again, all of them just slightly, *slightly* different.'

She frowned.

It was a lot for her to take in.

'Think of us as being in a show,' he said, trying a simpler tack. 'A show that never stops, but keeps starting from the beginning, no performance exactly the same, with all these countless layers of other shows doing just the same. Most people don't guess the other shows exist, because these –' he flicked his head at the dark lanterns – 'are lit up and pointed on them, blocking everything else out. But that doesn't mean it isn't all there.' He paused, glancing over his shoulder at Belinda in the wings. She hadn't moved, other than that she now had her hand to her throat. As their eyes met, she gave him a nod.

Keep going, she silently told him.

So, he kept going.

'Sometimes my lanterns dim,' he said. 'When that happens, I can sense the other shows I'm part of. I . . . *feel* . . . the things I must do. But I think with you, your lanterns must switch off completely, so you get to *see* other stages. I suspect you've been looking into someone else's show.'

She stared at him.

He could see how hard she was working to process his words. He couldn't imagine there were many children her age who'd even bother to try.

But she wasn't like other children.

And he couldn't stop himself any more. He reached for her hand, which she gave to him, so readily that he felt as though his heart might burst.

'Why doesn't it always happen?' she asked.

'Doesn't it?' he said.

'No. When we go on visits, it stops.'

'Like when you go to London, you mean, to see your mum?'

'Yes.'

He thought about it.

'I'm not sure,' he said. 'But perhaps there's someone here who wants to let you visit their stage. And I really wouldn't be scared of that, if I were you.' He simply couldn't stand the idea of her being scared any longer. 'Because what a wonderful thing, to be wanted so much.'

Her fingers around his tightened.

'Noah,' called Belinda, gently, 'John will be here soon.'

'Yes,' he said, but didn't get up.

He didn't want to move.

Didn't want to let her go.

How could he keep her from going?

He couldn't.

And since he couldn't . . .

'I'll come with you,' he told her, following another instinct. 'Make sure you get safely home.' He got to his feet. 'Does that sound ok?'

She nodded, keeping a hold of his hand.

He looked down at her.

She stared up at him.

The emotion in his expression was too complex for her to unpick.

Later, in the years to come, she might learn to make more sense of it.

She might decode the sadness in his eyes, the surrender, and adoration, and wish she'd known enough to say much, much more to him.

She really might do that, if she could only remember.

But she never remembered.

Her life was about to be upended, and it wasn't long before she forgot the brief minutes the two of them had just shared. Like she forgot about the dancers in Bettys, those boys she loved but couldn't find, and every ever after that, here, in her first home, she'd been able to glimpse.

It would all remain within her, though: silent, invisible, but *there*.

The last words she and he exchanged before they left the stage, remained within her.

'Can I come back and see you again?' she asked him.

'Yes, Claudia,' he said, pressing his lips to her head. 'We'll definitely do this again.'

Iris

1943

RAF Doverley, North Yorkshire

It was a moonless night, and the darkness blanketing the windswept base of 96 Squadron was almost complete. The only light came from the runway's flare path, its burning torches shimmering in the gusty air. Iris, once so captivated by these torches' sinister beauty, paid them scant attention as she came to a halt on the control tower's external stairs. Rather, it was the squadron's twenty-four Lancasters that stole her focus, all of them spewing exhaust fumes, taxiing into position for take-off: their cabins full of men, their bellies packed with flares and incendiary bombs. Pathfinders, they'd scatter as soon as they were in the air, off to lay their explosive markers for squadrons across the country to follow on yet another raid over occupied Europe.

At a fresh belt of wind, Iris reached up, holding her cap to her head. With her other hand, she gripped the stairs' handrail, so tight her knuckles burnt. Down at the foot of the stairs, the station dog, Piper, strained to escape her leash. She was watching the planes too. Barking, Iris was sure. She couldn't hear her. She heard nothing but the guttural roar of the Lancasters.

It was impossible to see their names from this distance, but

they all had them painted on their noses. *Harlow's Heroes.*
Angel's Wings. Hell's Wrath. Heaven Sent. Iris knew them, and
their alphabetised code names, by heart. She ought to. She was
one of their radio operatives. Another WAAF was on duty for
take-off tonight, but shortly, all too shortly, Iris would join her
in the control room. There, she'd place her own headset on, and
with these planes before her up and away, guide them out of
Doverley's airspace. It would be frantic work, especially in this
wind; inevitably, the less experienced pilots would be blown off
course, and she'd be inundated with requests for coordinates,
all of them coming at once. There were a couple of first timers
going up tonight, too; they always wanted to check and re-
check everything. For them, Iris would repeat her instructions,
as many times as they needed her to, until their connection, and
everyone else's, would start to fray, growing fainter the further
they flew from the reach of Doverley's transmitter.

Eventually, their voices would crackle into silence.

That silence would last for seven, maybe eight, hours.

Iris's supervisor would advise her to sleep.

She wouldn't be able to sleep.

She'd remain in the control tower, eyeing the horizon, until
the time would come for her to return to her desk, replace
her headset, and wait for the static in her ears to fracture
once more, this time with the exhausted, euphoric calls of the
returning crews requesting permission to land.

Not all of the planes now leaving would come back.
Desperately as Iris wished it could be different, she knew that
it wouldn't.

Not tonight.

And actually, it hardly ever happened that a full quota
returned. There was almost always one whose silence remained
permanent.

Iris had never before known who that would be, though.

9

She cared about every crew. She did. Even the ones who'd only just arrived.

But there was one crew that she cared about the most.

Mabel's Fury, they'd called their plane, for the flight engineer's fiancée, who'd fled her Parisian home when the Nazis had invaded France.

Iris watched them pull to a juddering halt at the head of the runway. She knew it was them. They were always the first to take off.

Eyes wide, stinging in the cold, she pictured the seven men inside the plane: the bomb aimer, Jacob, testing his safety catch; the navigator, her old friend Tim, getting his protractor out; the radio operator, Henry, adjusting his headset; Ames, the flight engineer, cracking jokes with gunners, Gus and Danny, all of them burying their nerves; and Robbie, *Robbie*, in the cockpit, his handsome face serious, running through his final checks.

Had he reminded everyone to wear their parachutes?

Iris hoped so.

'Don't let them tell you they're too uncomfortable,' she'd insisted to him, just now.

'They are too uncomfortable,' he'd replied. 'If we need them, we can get them on in no time.'

'In a tailspin?'

'I'm going to be trying very hard not to get us into one of those.'

'You're going to Germany, Robbie.'

'Yes, I know,' he'd said, drily. 'And I'm not sure I want a chute, if we go down there.'

'Don't joke.'

'I'm not joking.'

'Just wear the chutes. Please.'

'All right.' He'd smiled. That smile she'd loved from the moment he'd first thrown it her way, back when they'd still been children with Tim in the schoolroom. 'We'll wear the chutes.'

He'd made her another promise before she'd left him to climb aboard. He'd told her that, as soon as he had everyone back close enough to re-establish radio contact, he, not Henry, would make the call, letting her know that they were on their way.

'I'll be doing it before you know it,' he'd said. They hadn't been able to touch, not with so many people around, but his eyes, glinting with cold, and so blue in the darkness, had held hers. 'You'll guide us in. Get us home. Do you believe it?'

Silently, unable to talk, she'd nodded.

'No.' His brow had creased in a frown. 'Say it, please. I need to hear you say it.'

So, she'd said it.

'I believe it,' she'd forced out, knowing only that she'd wanted to. So very, very much.

He'd smiled again, reassured.

It was something, at least, that she'd been able to give him.

And now, before her brimming stare, *Mabel's Fury* jerked back into motion. Iris's colleague inside had clearly issued the command. *That's a green for go. Proceed to angels ten and vector ninety to Idaho.* Gripping the stair rail tighter, Iris followed the plane's thundering silhouette as it gathered speed on the flaming runway. She pictured Robbie again, his body taut with effort as he pulled back on his throttle, wrenching the laden craft upwards.

She still hadn't told him her secret.

She'd been keeping it from him for weeks now.

At the thought, her eyes fell shut.

And, when she opened them again, *Mabel's Fury* was airborne, rising slowly, then disappearing, fast, into the black sky.

Her tears, contained for too long, broke free, snaking down her frozen face. Hastily, before anyone could see, she wiped them away.

Then, dragging her gaze from the void *Mabel's Fury* had left, she turned, heading up the rest of the control tower stairs.

You'll guide us in, Robbie had said.

Get us home.

She pulled the tower door open, not ready, by no stretch ready, but resolved at last on facing all that this night was about to ask of her.

LIGHTS, CAMERA, AND ACTION FOR
THE BOMBER BOYS

It's happening. After months of speculation, in which the production of this hotly anticipated adaptation of Imogen Hale's word-of-mouth sensation, The Bomber Boys, *has been rumoured off more times than the relationship of its leading stars, Claudia Baxter and Nick Turner, they, and the rest of the cast, have landed in England ahead of an intense month-long shoot on the Yorkshire estate of Doverley House – the same spot where Hale's protagonists were based during the Second World War.*

For anyone who hasn't read Hale's novel yet – and who are you? Where have you been? – you need to get your hands on a copy, stat, then have some tissues ready, block your diary, too, because you won't be able to tear yourself away from this epic imagining of what really befell the vanished pathfinder crew of the now infamous ghost plane, Mabel's Fury.

Before you turn to Google, no one does know what happened to the six young men who vanished into the war-torn darkness back in 1943. They, tantalisingly close to the end of their tour of duty, took off as normal that fateful night. But when their battered plane returned to England, crash-landing on the coast, it did so empty, save for seven damaged parachute packs and the crew's badly injured navigator, Tim Hobbs (played by Felix Jade. SWOON). Tim, alive to this day, lost consciousness whilst the plane was still full of his crew mates, and has never been able to explain what befell them, or indeed how he got home with the plane's cockpit empty. His last recollection is of turbulence, dense fog, and his pilot – Squadron Leader Robbie Grayson (Nick Turner) – radioing their base's control tower, speaking to the woman with whom he was in love, Section Officer Iris Winterton (Claudia Baxter). Hobbs doesn't recall what was said between the pair, and Iris Winterton was never questioned, because she herself disappeared, that very same night.

It was her timing, and the mystery of her final radio exchange with Squadron Leader Grayson, that prompted Hale to write The Bomber Boys, *which she tells through Iris's voice, as a devastating confession: one which was rejected by scores of publishers before it crossed the desk of an editor at Acorn Press, who fell under its spell and, with a miniscule budget, set it on its way to print, so breaking my unsuspecting heart, and millions of others around the globe.*

Hale – who had her pick of studios vying for film rights – was, unusually, granted final approval on the script. The question that we at The Screen *are now all desperate for an answer to, is: will the movie stay true to Hale's shattering ending? The word is, that's still a matter of heated discussion, and a different, much happier ever after, remains on the cards.*

'We feel we have some licence,' says our inside source. 'Given the mystery that still shrouds the fate of Iris Winterton and the crew, why not use this movie to explore something different?'

Because it's not the way Hale wrote it, say we.

And what do the stars themselves think?

Claudia Baxter was giving nothing away when we caught up with her at Heathrow last week. Pictured here, fresh off the LA red eye – understated as ever in a baseball cap, puffer, and jeans – she stopped for a chat before ducking into her waiting Land Rover. Relaxed enough when we asked her to scale her happiness at being back on home soil (an eleven, obviously; she was on her way to see her mum), and how she felt about portraying the enigmatic Iris (delirious), she clammed up the moment we raised the matter of her character's final, devastating reveal.

'No,' she said, with that smile of hers, 'you're not getting me on that.'

Her smile vanished at our next enquiry, into the lay of the land between her and Nick Turner, which we can only take to mean: not great.

And what will that mean for the atmosphere on set over the coming weeks?

Oh, to be a fly on Doverley's walls . . .

Chapter One

Claudia

2 November 2018

The day before shooting begins

It's been a long time since I was last in Yorkshire. I was born here though, not three miles from Doverley, on my grandparents' kitchen floor. I haven't told anyone in publicity about that. I don't want them using it in one of their campaigns. But it's that start to my life I think about as, clearing security, Nick and I drive through Doverley's iron gates and on into lush, dripping woodland, heading for the house. I've been thinking about it for most of our drive up from London, and especially since we swapped the monotony of the motorway for the maze of stone-walled country lanes that have brought us here. It's all felt eerily familiar. I wasn't expecting it to. I'm not really sure what I was expecting, coming back here after thirty years away; a whisper of déjà vu, maybe, at the very most. Definitely not this overwhelming sense of my forgotten past, all around me.

And it is forgotten. I remember very little of the four years I spent here with my grandparents, before they died. They were the ones who looked after me back then. My father wasn't on the scene – no one knows what happened to him – and Mum was away a lot in London, finishing university, then starting work. I wish I'd held on to more of Nan and Grandad, but all I have left are snapshots: Nan chipping potatoes at the sink;

Grandad coming through the front door, smiling up at me on the stairs; both of them in a park, watching me play. And Nan's hand in mine at the door of a woman called Mrs Ellen, who Mum claims I've fabricated, but who I swear to god existed. She had a Newton's cradle that I played with, and a porcelain jar that was always full of Rich Tea Biscuits, the taste of which, to this day, gives me the strangest tug in my heart.

'You expect me to believe you still eat biscuits?' Mum would doubtless say, if I told her about that tug – which I won't, because her insistence that I've made Mrs Ellen up really, really annoys me, almost as much as it perplexes me.

Mum brought me to live in London after Nan and Grandad went. We never returned to Yorkshire after that. Not even to put flowers on their graves.

If Mum had had her way, I wouldn't be here now.

She does *not* want me to do this movie.

'You're running yourself ragged,' she said, just yesterday, the two of us up on Parliament Hill, walking her whippet, Stewart. (*Stewart.* Honestly. The only thing that makes me feel more ridiculous than yelling out that name, sprinting to catch up with his skinny grey form, is getting tagged on the inevitable videos of me doing it afterwards.) 'I'm worried you're going to end up having some kind of breakdown. You look exhausted . . . '

'I'm jetlagged.'

'And far too thin.'

'God, *Mum*.'

'Don't *Mum* me. Phil agrees.'

'Phil always agrees with you.' Phil's my stepdad, and harassed father to my two teenage sisters. 'It's how he survives.'

'He's concerned, Claude.'

I yanked Stewart's lead, restraining him from taking on an Alsatian twice his size. ('Oh my god,' said its owner, unlocking her phone. 'Claudia Baxter.')

'You're barely back from Sicily,' Mum continued. 'Before that, it was South Africa. Before that—'

'I know,' I interrupted, cutting her off before she could get to what happened before South Africa. 'I do know, Mum.'

'All right,' she said, more softly. 'But now Yorkshire, Claude? With *Nick*.'

'You want me to give up a role because of him?'

'No, my darling. I want you to give it up because of you.'

I set my teeth, not responding, because it was a pointless discussion, and one we'd already had too many times to bear repeating. I was over explaining to Mum the manifold reasons why I couldn't simply abandon a movie at this stage in the game – rehearsals, done; costume fittings, done; make-up tests, done; jitterbugging lessons, *done* – and she knew full well anyway that I'd be sued.

Plus, I don't actually *want* to abandon *The Bomber Boys*. God knows I probably should. It certainly hasn't been going well. Rehearsals were a disaster – I just couldn't get inside Iris's head, or forget that I was in an impersonal overly air-conditioned room, reading from a stack of paper, and was so stilted, I threw everyone else off with me. I know the director, Ana, is worried. *I'm* worried. Beside myself, in actual matter, at how badly I've been screwing it all up. But that doesn't mean I've been tempted to do as Mum says, risk litigation and give up on playing Iris. I haven't. Not once. I might not have found her, not yet. But she's waiting for me. I can feel it. I've been feeling it from the moment I first picked up Imogen Hale's novel.

'It would kill me to give up Iris now,' I told Mum. 'It turns me cold, even thinking about it.'

'It turns me cold, hearing you say that. She's another escape route for you, nothing more. A fresh golden ticket to a different mind, a different world, when what you really need is to face up to this one you're in.' She shook her head. 'You and Nick have barely been in the same country for months . . . '

'We've been working.'

'Running away, more like. Grief doesn't disappear just because you ignore it, you know.'

'Mum, please . . . '

'The two of you scare each other, that's your problem.'

'Is it?' I said, wearily.

'Yes. You remind each other of what you lost.'

'I don't need reminding of that.'

'No, you don't *want* reminding. That's a very different thing.' She gave me a pained frown. 'Have you considered how you and Nick are even going to cope together on this shoot?'

'It's crossed my mind.'

'An entire month together, acting out someone else's love story . . . '

'We'll get through it.'

'Will you?'

'We will, Mum.'

'Have you talked about it?'

'We don't need to. We know what we're doing.'

Her frown deepened. 'I hope you're right.'

So do I, I thought.

So do I, I think again now, looking sideways at Nick as he turns the wheel, negotiating a rut in Doverley's driveway. Mum wasn't exaggerating when she said we've barely seen one another lately. Until now, other than for the fortnight we spent rehearsing in September, we haven't been together since May, when I got home from my shoot in South Africa. Even then, I was only in LA for a few days before I left again for Sicily, where Felix Jade, not Nick, played my love interest on a steamy HBO series that ran well over schedule, obligingly consuming my every waking moment for all of June, then July, and a good chunk of August, too. (Mum's wrong: you absolutely can run from grief.) Nick, meanwhile, spent the summer doing some running of his own, going full kelter on preparation for this movie: travelling back and forth to this estate, dressing every day in uniform, eating from an RAF canteen menu, drinking warm beer. He's even learnt to fly a Lancaster, for God's sake.

The tabloids have been all over his exploits, and our long separation, too, speculating as to whether we're *on*, or *off*, and reprinting all their gut-wrenching paparazzi shots of me at the start of the year, *before South Africa*, with red circles drawn around my curved stomach. Was I ever pregnant, they've demanded. (Yes, I was. Twenty weeks, in fact.) Badly bloated? (Possibly that, too.) Can I even have children? (Apparently not any more, no.) They ran plenty of other photos, besides: of Nick, whenever he hit a bar, reliving his twenties, surrounded by crowds of gorgeous women; then just as many of me, in a bikini in Sicily, entangled with Felix – filming, but what does that matter to them?

And have Nick and I talked about those photos?

Yes, we actually have. I've tried to convince him that there was nothing in the Sicily shots, just like he's tried to convince me that he never gave a second look to any of those women he was pictured with. *Surely you believe that.* I haven't known what to believe. I'm not sure Nick has either. For the first time in our three-year relationship, I've lost faith in the trust between us, and I hate it.

I let out a sigh.

Nick hears. I see that, from the way his eyes flick towards me.

He doesn't ask me what's wrong though. He hasn't said much the entire way up from London, and we've been driving for almost four hours.

He stayed over at Mum and Phil's in Highgate last night. I wasn't planning to see him. He's been holed up here again this past week, *immersing*. But Phil suggested I invite him down, *he's probably just waiting for you to*, and in fairness, Nick did agree to come pretty much instantly when I called him. He took Phil and my sisters out flying yesterday afternoon whilst Mum and I were up on Parliament Hill. Lisa, fifteen and painfully shy, was sick, but Hannah, eighteen and loudly loving life, adored it. Phil did too. They were buzzing when Mum and I got back to the house. We found them in the kitchen, opening a bottle of wine, whilst poor Lisa was hiding in her bedroom, mortified because she'd vomited in front of Nick Turner.

'You don't always have to use his surname when you talk about him, you know,' I said, when I took her up some tea.

'It's impossible not to,' she said. Then, peeking out from beneath her duvet, 'Did he tell you I got sick on his shoe?'

'No,' I lied. 'And he's had worse, believe me.'

In the end, Nick came up too, and was the one to cajole Lisa into resurfacing, fabricating a story about how sick he'd been on his first flight, all over the instructor. It really made Lisa laugh.

He made an effort all night: helping Phil cook dinner, asking Mum about her work; even remembering the name of the school she's a counsellor at. Hannah, heading out to a club, was thrilled because he not only played taxi to her and her mates, but he got them into the club without queuing, then opened a tab for them at the bar.

'It was so good, Claude,' Hannah slurred, when she stumbled back into the kitchen at three, a half-eaten kebab in hand. Nick was out for the count upstairs, but I, sincerely jetlagged, was on my laptop at the table, conducting another fruitless search for a picture of Iris. She hasn't left anything of herself behind. Not even a death certificate. 'He's a keeper. Don't forget that, will you?'

I told Nick she'd said that as we were walking out to the car this morning. He'd been trying so hard, I wanted to give him something to make him happy.

'You've got a super fan,' I said.

'Yeah?' He grinned, his old grin, and it made me ache, because I couldn't for the life of me remember the last time I'd caused him to do that. 'Just one? Or can I count you in, too?'

And that was when our phones pinged with *The Screen*'s article. Blake, the movie's lead publicist, sent it. I was ready to delete it. After everything that's gone on, I've been trying to avoid giving that kind of thing headspace. But Nick opened it, and, as I stood in the drizzle watching him read, I saw the frown that descended on him and decided I'd better take a look.

He's tried to claim he's not annoyed that I didn't comment on the state of things between the two of us (*which we can only take to mean: not great*), or that the journalist put a *swoon* next to Felix's name but not his. And maybe if it hadn't been for those photos in Sicily, he really wouldn't have cared about that bit. That's not who he is.

The part about us, though . . .

Yeah, he's totally pissed about that.

Looking away from his brooding expression, I return my attention to the woody world outside. Again, I'm assailed by familiarity: a sense not of arriving, but returning. It makes even less sense to me now that we're actually *on* the estate. Unlike the roads we've just left, I know I've never been down this driveway before. I can't have been. Until the National Trust took Doverley over, four years ago, it was closed up for decades; derelict. I'd be tempted to put the recognition I feel down to the photographs of it I've pored over all during the war – unlike with Iris, there's plenty of that to be found on the web – but everything I've seen has been of the house and its flat, open surrounds, which we still haven't reached. All that remains hidden by these trees. And these trees, this earthy, blue-green shadowland, I'm certain I've never come across a picture of.

A bird calls, its lone song ringing out above the hum of

the car's engine, echoing into the early autumnal dusk. At the sound, I close my eyes, lean my head back, and feel a shiver snake through me.

*

It's another half mile before Doverley's woods give way to open parkland, and the house comes suddenly into view, regal and aloof beneath the heavy violet sky. I lean forward, taking in its high sandstone walls, columns and porticoes, and, as the sinking sun spikes the clouds, watch it all glimmer gold before morphing to matte again. We draw closer, and distantly I register everything else we pass – the swarms of crew out and about; the rows of trailers parked up on the meadows – but don't pay any of it attention. I'm too busy looking at the set of the base that's been built on the fields stretching out from Doverley's western wing.

There are hangars, Nissen Hut billets, and barbed wire fences. Model Lancasters stand in the rain, wheels blocked. Above them looms the control tower from which Iris exchanged her last words with Robbie, whatever they might have been.

What would she think of this set, I wonder, if she were to return and see it?

What would Tim Hobbs, *Mabel's Fury*'s navigator, say, if he were to come?

I don't suppose I'll ever find out. He was twenty-five in 1943, and has just had his one hundredth birthday. He got his message from the queen. I wrote to him too. I wanted him to know what a privilege I count it, to be a part of re-enacting such an incredible chapter of his life. I have no idea if he read my message. He's apparently getting weaker, no longer always himself. I doubt visiting a film set is even factoring as a possibility in his mind.

And I'm not convinced any of this would feel remotely authentic to him.

It definitely doesn't feel real to me.

More than anything, it reminds me of one of those theme park rides where trams funnel crowds through every ten minutes, making them jump with the same, repetitive, explosions.

'Incredible, isn't it?' says Nick, finally breaking the silence between us.

'Yes,' I say, and I'm not sure why I lie.

Maybe because it's easier than trying to explain the disconnect I feel.

The numbness.

Nick pulls up, shutting off the ignition. Holding the steering wheel, he drops his forehead against it, then turns, giving me a rueful grimace.

'Sorry, Claude,' he says. 'I've been an ass. A jealous ass.'

'It's fine,' I say, automatically, shifting in my seat, glancing again at the set. 'I should have handled that reporter better.'

'They can't be handled.'

'No, I suppose not.'

'I love you.'

'I love you too,' I reply, and this time, don't stop to question whether or not I'm lying.

I don't think I am.

I hope I'm not.

Regardless, the journey's been uncomfortable enough as it is.

We're set upon as soon as we get out of the car.

Naomi, the assistant director, is the first to pounce, jogging through the drizzle from a nearby trailer to hand us both updated call sheets for the morning. Emma Jameson – who's playing Iris's best friend, Section Officer Clare Holmes – now can't work tomorrow, so we're pushing my first scene with her out, and starting instead with a later one, between Nick and Felix.

'You get a lie-in, Claude,' says Naomi.

I nod, even though I doubt I'll sleep, and shrug on my puffer. It's biting, much colder than it was in London. To my left, on the opposite side of the house to the set, sheep graze in fenced-off fields. Their musty scent carries on the icy breeze, and, as I breathe it in, I'm hit by another wave of familiarity. A memory too, of myself running among woolly coats in frost-crisped grass. And a voice – my gran's? – calling for me to slow down. *You'll start a stampede.* Briefly, I replay it, then I shelve it, because it makes me sad, and it's not the time for that.

'Why isn't Emma working?' I ask Naomi.

'She's got gastro.'

'What?' I frown. 'Since when?'

'She took a turn at lunchtime. But she's sleeping it off, and I need you to leave her to it. No one's allowed in breathing distance.'

'Is gastro airborne?' asks Nick.

'Maybe. Probably. I don't want anyone taking any chances.' Removing her glasses, Naomi rubs her eyes. 'We're all hoping it's a twenty-four-hour thing, obviously.'

'For Emma's sake,' I say. 'Obviously.'

'Yes,' she says, and has the good grace to smile. 'Obviously.'

Jeff, the location manager, joins us, waterproofed from top to toe in a cagoule and rain pants, his posse of lackeys trailing. He directs them to fetch our luggage, park Nick's car, and hands me two card keys.

'This is for your trailer,' he says, 'and this is for your room.'

'Wardrobe needs Nick,' yells a runner, running. 'Adjustments for tomorrow . . .'

Then, 'Oh good, you're here,' comes Ana's voice, making

25

us all turn as she appears from the house, jogging down its wide front steps. She holds a clipboard over her cropped curls, and is wearing a cosy get-up of an oversized fluffy jumper, leggings and Ugg boots. It could almost make her look quite comfortable. *Mumsy.* I expect the extras congregated at the catering truck have all been fooled. Never mind. They'll realise soon enough she's an utter badass.

'All well, Claude?' she asks, in a tight, braced tone that I can only bear to give one answer to.

'Great, Ana,' I say. 'Really great.'

'Right,' she replies, and I know she hasn't been fooled. Of course she hasn't. She's Ana.

'Nick.' She claps her hands, much as Mum might to Stewart. 'Wardrobe. Go. Claude, come with me. There's something I wanna show you.'

And, as Nick goes, throwing me a frown that lets me know he hasn't appreciated Ana's clap, I also do as instructed, following Ana up the steps she's just come down.

The middle one is a different height to the rest. Ana trips, then rights herself.

'Damn thing keeps getting me,' she says.

It doesn't get me, though.

Even as Ana stumbles, I tap my toe to its edge, skipping over it without consideration.

Then we reach Doverley's front door.

'Ready to see something amazing?' Ana says, flashing me a smile.

'Always,' I reply.

'So come right this way, Ms Baxter.' Grabbing a hold of the door's brass handle, she pushes it wide. 'I'm about to blow your mind.'

26

Chapter Two

I was twenty when I met Ana. She was still assisting back then, and we were working together here in England, on an adaptation of *The Go-Between*. Felix was with us too – he was Ted Burgess to my Marian Maudsley – and for both of us, it was our big break. I was a nervous wreck, utterly in awe of the director, as well as most of the cast, and if it hadn't been for Felix and Ana, I'm not sure I could have got through it. But Felix and I had hit it off during auditions – one-upping each other with our sorry tales of failed call-backs, and bit-parts in budget advertisements – and, on set, he made me laugh, all the time; even when I was about to vomit with anxiety in the lead-up to our closed-set scenes. Ana, meanwhile, took me under her wing, sitting with me in make-up, attending my every take, and getting me into rushes each morning so that I could watch the scenes I'd shot the day before and see that I wasn't, in fact, making an idiot of myself. Thanks to her, I began to believe in myself. *Trust* myself. In the end, I wound up getting nominated for an Oscar for that movie, and winning a BAFTA. Felix won a BAFTA too, and Ana scooped both awards as part of the Best Picture team.

We had a really good time celebrating.

Nick hasn't worked with Ana before – he hasn't worked with me, come to that – and Felix hasn't been on another project with her either, until now. But Ana and I have done a ton together; this will be our seventh movie, and I'd love to say I'm instantly at ease, being back in her company, but I feel as vomity as I used to, filming those scenes with Felix. Because, in all Ana and I have worked on, I've never before let her down, and the only thing I can think about as we head into the house, is how badly I've been doing that so far with *The Bomber Boys*.

I follow her through a porch lined with National Trust pamphlets, and on into Doverley's entrance hall, which has been artfully restored to its Georgian heyday, with a mosaiced floor, and gilt-framed paintings on its walls. At the far end, a staircase sweeps up to a landing which, I guess, leads to the bedrooms.

Normally, the National Trust let out the rooms here on a bed and breakfast basis, but through November, we've taken them over. The website promises 1,000 thread count sheets, underfloor heating, and rolltop baths. According to Nick, reality delivers.

Our characters obviously wouldn't have been so comfortable, and they definitely wouldn't have seen the house looking like this. There'd have been no paintings on the walls for a start. All of those were sold when Doverley's owners fell on hard times at the end of the First World War. A lot of their furniture went then, too, and the family finally moved out in the 1930s, selling the estate to the RAF, who wanted it for its flat grounds, perfect for runways, and remote position. It was then that most of the house was locked up.

The RAF did make use of some of it, though. The desk-staff had offices here, and everyone's meals were cooked in the basement kitchen. The library was given another lease of life too, as an officers' mess, and a handful of personnel were billeted inside. Not the airmen – they were all down at the base – but the women who supported them. The WAAFS.

I think about them, as I follow Ana to the stairs.

I think about Iris.

She walked across this floor, I tell myself. *Breathed this air.*

I pause, close my eyes, and wait to feel something.

But I'm distracted by a distant banging.

'What's that?' I ask Ana.

'What's what?'

'That hammering.'

'I can't hear it.' She shrugs. 'It'll be the rigging crew, probably, getting a jump on lighting the library for tomorrow.'

'Is that where you're taking me?'

'No.' She throws me another smile. 'I wouldn't waste your time with that.'

'Then . . . ?'

'I'm not gonna say. It'll be better if you see it. Now listen.' She starts up the stairs. '*The Sound of Music* was showing on my flight . . . '

'Mine too.'

'You watched it?'

'No, I was going over the script.' Again, and again. 'I didn't watch anything.'

'Me either. I was trying to get my head around what the hell we should do about our ending. But I had a flick through the options, and as soon as I saw the thumbnail of Maria dancing her heart out in the Alps, it got me humming that song, "How Do You Solve a Problem Like Maria?", only it became, *How do I solve a problem like Claude?*'

'Wow, Ana, don't pull your punches.'

'You can take them.'

'Can I?'

'One hundred per cent.' We reach the landing and head

down a plush corridor lined with numbered doors. 'The thing I've realised about Maria,' Ana continues, 'is that as soon as she's liberated from doing as she thinks she *should* be doing, she starts nailing life. It's hit me. I need to liberate you.'

'You want to marry me off to an Austrian naval captain?'

'Not quite,' she says, and talks on, telling me that the fact I spent my entire flight in the weeds with the script rather than do-re-mi-ing is exactly my problem; I've had a year from hell, got myself too caught up in my own sense of failure, lost any confidence to act with my instincts, which is only making me fail more. 'Agree?' she says, and, miserably, I nod, really hoping that we get to her solution soon, because actually I don't know if I *can* take much more of this candour.

'You could keep doing as you are and we'd get away with it,' she says, as we come to a halt at the end of the corridor. She extracts a key card from the waist of her leggings. 'Your technique's flawless, so we could shoot this with you all in your head, and it would be . . . *fine*. But you're better than that. We need you to relocate those instincts. Find Iris.'

'How, though?'

'Patience, Claude.' She taps the card to the fob on the door before us, then clicks it open. '*Patience.*'

Brow creasing, more intrigued than anything now, I follow her into a fluorescently lit service room that holds several luggage trolleys, and a fire-door, which, with the same card, Ana opens.

As she pushes it wide, I feel a punch of cold. Curiosity growing, realising we're heading into an un-refurbished section of the house, I follow her along another corridor. This time, the floor is stone, and the doors are of old wood. Lead-lined windows rattle in the wind, letting more icy air in.

Ana heads to the closest door, creaking it open onto what I recognise immediately as a servants' staircase. I've acted on enough locations to know one. And I don't question any more where we're headed. It's certainly not to any set, which are confined to Doverley's ground and first floors, where there's easy access for the rigs. An old drawing room has been repurposed as Iris's billet, which she shared with Clare – who poor Emma is playing – but their room wasn't in the main part of the house. No, it was as far away as could be got from the men in their offices.

It was up in Doverley's attics.

'I've worked it out,' I say to Ana, as she lights her phone's torch.

'Yeah?'

'Yes.' Then, so there's no doubt, 'We're going to my room.'

'Oh, I *love* that you just said, *my* room. Too bad you guessed though.' She sighs. Then, grins. 'No matter. It's still gonna knock your socks off.'

She sets off at a jog, and, lighting my own phone, I follow, more slowly, distracted by the strange echoes our footsteps throw, and a tightening in my chest that takes me back to how I felt driving through the woods earlier. Just as then, I'm disorientated by the oddest sense of somehow having been here before.

'Be careful now,' Ana says, as I join her on the attic's landing. 'I doubt our insurance will cover any accidents. I probably should've got you to sign a waiver.'

'How did you even find your way up here?'

'Imogen gave me the route.'

I nod, making sense. Imogen's relayed her explorations of Doverley in interviews, thanking Tim Hobbs for showing her around, back when he was in better health. *My very own navigator.* I haven't yet met Imogen, but we've spoken on the phone quite a bit – mainly so I could pick her brain about Iris. Apparently, Imogen drew all her inspiration for her from Tim.

'He'd talk and talk about her when we used to meet,' she's told me. 'I'm certain he was in love with her, too. The way he spoke about her, I think he loved her very much.'

I felt no surprise, hearing her say that. She infers as much in her novel. She describes too how close Tim, Iris, and Robbie were growing up, all attending the same village primary school. It wasn't far from here. Not far at all. Just like me, the three of them were children in this vast, rugged place, and even though I've known that a while now, it still makes my spine lengthen, thinking about the coincidence of it.

'Come on,' says Ana, swivelling her phone to light our path down a narrow hallway.

As we walk, I glance at the closed doors running either side of us, and find myself imagining the bustle that must have once filled this silent space. The air shifts in a whispering draft, and, for a disorientating second, it's as though I hear it, still going on now.

Ana comes to a halt, opening a door midway down the hallway, and stands back to let me through.

Wordlessly, I go.

Then, I stop.

I stare.

The room before me is nothing like what I was expecting.

I'd *expected* it to be an empty shell.

But this room is furnished. Not extravagantly. Enough though for it to feel instantly like a home. Slowly, my hand trembling with the now almost choking proximity of the past, I move my torch, illuminating a pair of metal-framed beds wedged beneath sloping eaves. Both of them, unbelievably, still have their pillows on top of them. At their feet are two storage trunks, open and empty, but very easy to picture bursting with stockings and fair isle jumpers. To their right stands a chest of drawers with a mirror above it, and a dark dash of what might be nail polish staining the wood.

I turn back to Ana. 'It's as though they just left.'

'I know, right?'

'And you found it like this? You didn't have the furniture moved up here?'

She laughs. 'I knew you were gonna ask that. And no, I swear it. Jeff's been finding loads of stuff around the place. I guess the RAF had more than they knew what to do with, once it was all over. Props are like kids at Christmas.'

'You won't let them touch this, though?' The rush of possessiveness that comes over me, shocks me. I'm not sure why I feel so strongly about it being left as it is. Maybe because it has been, for all these years.

'Don't worry,' Ana says, 'no one's gonna touch anything.'

I nod, relieved, and edge further into the room. Gravitating to the left bed, I sit, feeling the mattress give. I'm so tired, I'm tempted to lie down, but I can hardly do that with Ana here. Instead, I bend over the bed's edge, looking beneath it, to see what, I have no idea, and there's nothing there anyway.

Ana crosses to the dormer window, beyond which night is rapidly falling – the clouds no longer violet, but deep grey – and I get up, moving to the chest of drawers, where I peer into my reflection in the mirror. I frown. My face doesn't seem to belong in this old, mottled glass. I'm too twenty-first century, with my messy ponytail, mascaraed lashes, and hooped earrings. I should be in costume: a tie around my collared neck; a WAAF cap on my hair.

Looking down, I pull at the chest's top drawer. It sticks, then gives, jolting open. On first glance, it appears empty. But then I spot a strip of metal wedged into the back seam. Reaching for it, I yank it free, and, seeing that it's a hair grip, feel a tingling in my skin. I turn the grip over, running my thumb across the grooves, and the tingling grows.

She breathed this air, I had to tell myself about Iris, back in the entrance hall.

I really don't need to tell myself anything up here.

'Come look at this,' says Ana from the window.

Setting the hairgrip down, I go. She gestures downwards, towards the set. It's much harder to make out now that it's getting so dark. The huts, tower and planes are all cloaked in shadows. Somehow, they seem more believable for it.

'Eerie, isn't it?' Ana says.

I nod in agreement.

And, from the direction of the woods, that bird calls again.

It's a distinctive sound, more a screech, than a song. Instinctively, I'm drawn to it. Yet it unsettles me too.

'Come up whenever you need,' says Ana. 'You'll work things out here.' She hands me her key. 'I know it.'

Chapter Three

I return to the attic within a few hours.

I don't plan to.

I plan to try and get some rest. Even though Nick and Felix are now going to be shooting first thing, I still need to be in make-up at nine. With Emma out of action, Naomi's frontloading some montage shots of the rest of us around the base. It'll be straightforward, but dull, and the last thing I need is to be as knackered as I've been today.

But, when Nick and I turn in at ten, I can't sleep. I lie beside him, wrapped in our 1,000 thread count sheets, listening to his stillness, thinking about the evening that's been.

Nick was still in wardrobe when I let myself into our room earlier, so I unpacked and sank into the roll-top bath. There, I flicked through my worn copy of *The Bomber Boys*, then stared, like I've stared so often before, at the photograph of the original *Mabel's Fury* crew on the cover. It was taken the afternoon before they left on their final mission. Tim and Robbie are in the middle of the group, both of them stirringly handsome – Tim, like a young Robert Redford; Robbie, in a class of his own – and Robbie's focus is direct into the camera. He has one foot forward, like he's about to set off towards the person behind the lens.

Iris?

I've wondered about that for a long time. I asked Imogen if she knew, but she said that Tim can't remember who took the photo. I think it probably was Iris, though, and it breaks my heart, looking at the smile on Robbie's face. It kills me, looking at all of them. I hate how young they are, how alive.

Dropping the book face down, I dressed, then, texting Emma to check she was awake, went to see her. Her room wasn't hard to find. It was the only one with a 'No Entry' sign fixed to the door.

'How are you feeling?' I asked her, once she'd let me in.

'So bad,' she croaked in her southern drawl, shuffling back to bed.

She'd been crying, I could tell from her blotchy face. I felt awful for her, locked away in quarantine, all miserable and alone. She reminded me so much of Lisa, burying herself beneath her duvet, that I very nearly went and gave her a hug.

I didn't though. We only met at rehearsals, and although we spent plenty of time together then, the days were packed, I was all over the place, and I guess we're still finding our way as friends. But I do like her. Honestly, she's pretty much the only person I haven't been dreading seeing here.

'Is it something you ate?' I asked, perching on her bed.

'I dunno,' she said. 'I can't think about food.'

'Can I get you anything?'

'No, but thanks for coming, Claude. No one else has.'

'Naomi's banned it.'

'Yeah, I know.' She gave me a weak smile. 'But you're still here.'

I stayed with her a while, reluctant to leave now I'd seen the state she was in. I coaxed her into drinking some water, helped her to the bathroom when she had to throw most of it back up, then sat with her until she drifted off to sleep: watching the blackness outside with half my mind, still thinking about the attic upstairs with the other. When I did finally leave, I had to race down to the dining room, a quarter hour late for Ana's welcome dinner.

'You won't stay her favourite if you keep this up,' whispered Nick, as I slipped into the seat beside him, midway through Ana's speech.

'I'm not her favourite,' I whispered back.

At which Felix, opposite, opened his mouth, as though to chime in, then promptly shut it again: remembering, all too clearly, that the way he's decided to convince Nick of how innocent everything between us in Sicily was, is to ignore me entirely.

I understood him taking that line during rehearsals. He and Nick are old friends too – they flat-shared when they were both starting out – and those photos were still everywhere, back then. But it's November now, the press has mostly moved on, and I've been really hoping we could, too. Counting on it, actually. We've grown up in this industry together. I can hardly remember what it was like being in it without him, and ever since *The Go-Between* I've taken it for granted that we'd always be in each other's corner. In Sicily, before those photos broke, Felix *was* in my corner: the best of co-stars on set, and the very best of friends off, never leaving me to my thoughts, but dragging me out for swims, and carafes of chilled wine, and bowls of pasta and gelati. It meant *everything*.

Which only makes the way he's behaving now hurt more.

It's hideous being treated like you don't matter, by someone who matters so much to you.

'You're being rude,' I was upset and tired enough to tell him, when I cornered him as we left the dining room. 'You possibly don't care, you've made it pretty clear which friendship you've decided to prioritise, but can I remind you that you don't actually need to cut me out. We never did anything wrong.'

He stared at me: blankly for a second.

Then, his swoon-worthy face moved in a frown.

I have no idea if he was planning on finally saying something.

If he was, I didn't stick around to hear it.

Losing patience, I walked away, catching up with Nick, who'd gone on ahead and was looking back at us.

'Everything all right?' he asked, as I joined him.

For once, I couldn't bring myself to pretend.

'Not really,' I said, and it was only when my voice shook that I realised how close I was to tears. 'How is it for you?'

To which he replied with a deep sigh, and an arm around my shoulders, which might have been for my benefit, but could just as easily have been for Felix's.

We undressed for bed silently once we got back to our room. I expected we'd get into bed that way, too. But, as I was coming out of the bathroom, Nick, in an armchair with his phone, reached out, pulling me to him.

'Claude . . . ' he said, and this time, it was his voice that cracked.

His face, turned up to me, was wretched.

'What is it?' I asked, alarmed.

For a hideous moment, I genuinely feared he was about to admit that he hasn't, in fact, been as true as he's claimed.

I watched him draw breath, searching for the words.

Or maybe it was courage he was looking for, to say them.

Either way, he shook his head, and forced a smile. 'I'm glad you're here,' he said. 'That's all.'

I knew there was more to it.

I could have pushed it.

But I was too afraid to, so I let it go.

And now here I am, my coat thrown over my pyjamas, my phone torch held out before me, once again letting myself into Iris's room.

I didn't come here on an impulse. I considered it for a long time before I finally slipped out of bed. The prospect of heading up to this haunting silence was hardly comforting, and actually quite terrifying, but in the end I couldn't resist. And I'm glad now that I didn't. It's better being here, doing something, than tying myself in knots downstairs.

There's a glow coming through the window. I assume it must be security lights, but when I get to the cobwebbed glass, I see that a series of flares has been lit, apart from the set, outlining three runways, just as they would have during the war: to guide the planes off, and beckon them home. The black air around their flames shimmers with heat. There must be crew down there, I realise, preparing for the night shoots we have scheduled after the weekend. I can't see anyone though. All I see, beside the flares, are the slumbering shapes of the planes, huts, and control tower, silhouetted against the distant woods.

Eerie, isn't it?

It really is.

And, as I stare at it all, the oddest thing happens.

It's fleeting, gone in a second. But the second stretches, my throat constricts, my gritty eyes swim, and the shimmering around the flares spreads, until everything is wavering. It's like the night itself has become a veil; it shivers, the flares spark, suddenly brighter, and, for a beat, the blanketing silence fractures, and I hear the static planes roar.

Then, the flares disappear, the set's security lights flash on, illuminating everything in a flood of white, and all is solid again; all is quiet.

I swallow.

What the hell was that?

I have no idea.

Exhaustion?

I should go back downstairs, I tell myself; take an Ambien, knock myself out.

But I'm too shaky to move.

So, I sit on what I seem to have decided was Iris's bed, and, at its creaking softness, am overcome by the same urge I had earlier to lie down. This time, I give into it, lowering myself sideways, resting my head on the thin pillow.

Just for a minute.

But I sleep for a lot longer than a minute.

For the first time since rehearsals, I sleep deeply, without interruption.

When I wake, it's to watery sunlight, and the sight of Ana standing over me, looking amused.

'You gone off central heating?' she says.

I blink, groggily, and touch my icy fingers to my icier face. 'What time is it?'

'Almost eight. Nick's been trying to call you.'

'Really?' I grapple for my silenced phone. It has seventeen missed calls. 'Oh. God . . . '

'Yeah. He was about ready to mobilise the search parties. I told him to give me five. What have you been doing up here? Other than snoring . . . '

I sit up, rolling my neck. 'I was looking at the flares.'

'What flares?'

'The runway flares. Effects had them on . . . '

'What?' Her face moves in bemusement. 'No, they didn't.'

'They did . . . '

'No. You must have dreamt it.'

I run my hands through my hair, dislodging a dusty feather, and don't argue.

I'm too disorientated. And cold.

But I didn't dream those flares.

40

They were real.

Weren't they?

Because what about the planes?

The noise from them felt real too . . .

I close my eyes, replaying it.

'I gotta run,' Ana says. Distantly, I'm aware of her voice. 'Everyone's waiting in the library. You need to move, too. Make sure you have some breakfast before make-up, yes?'

She doesn't wait for an answer.

And I don't give her one.

I don't watch her go, either.

I'm too busy staring at the window, my entire body shaking, wondering if it's possible that Mum's right after all, and I'm on the cusp of some kind of breakdown.

Chapter Four

Iris

February 1943

RAF Doverley, North Yorkshire

It had been a long time since Iris was last in Yorkshire. She'd been born here though, in a village called Heaton, not three miles from Doverley. As a child, she'd often trespassed on the dark, rain-sodden grounds she'd just tramped through, but had never dared to venture so far as this house. Rather, it had been to the derelict old gamekeeper's cottage, deep in the woods, that she'd always scampered, losing endless hours inside its crumbling walls. She'd been caught there once by Lord Heaton, when he'd been out walking his setters.

Get out of there this instant, he'd yelled.

What would he think, she wondered, if he were to learn that that scruffy girl who'd outrun him, all the way to his iron gates, was now a resident of his home?

She doubted he'd mind too much; she had been put up in this attic, after all: the old servants' quarters.

Probably, he'd consider that quite fitting.

It wasn't her first time in a servant's room. When she'd left school, age fourteen, she'd gone into service as a housemaid at an aristocratic pile in Surrey. Her mother would have hated it for her. Iris hadn't much liked it for herself. She remembered how, arriving in Surrey, she'd been handed her monochrome

uniform and sworn to herself, *I won't wear this my whole life.*
Back then, she had, of course, still thought of life as something
that most usually went on for decades. But that had been
1933, and whilst she'd been learning to set a table with perfect
angles for breakfast, lunch and dinner, Hitler had been getting
himself appointed Chancellor of Germany. When, in 1937,
aged eighteen, she'd used her squirreled away savings to secure
a place at secretarial college, the Spanish Civil War had been
raging. Two years later, and this world war they were all now
embroiled in had kicked off. By that point, she'd qualified for her
secretarial diploma, which had been enough to get her through
the door with the RAF, who she'd assumed would want her as a
typist, only her interviewer had been tasked with sourcing radio
operatives, so that's what she'd trained as – in another uniform
after all: just air force blue, rather than black and white, with
a peaked cap that was currently dripping rain down her neck.

She should remove it, she knew. Take her sopping overcoat
off, as well.

She was too tired to do that, though.

Instead, she dropped her head forwards, resting it against
the glass of her new bedroom's window. Behind her, Clare lay
face down on the bed she'd flung herself on, drenched too. No
one had been waiting for them at Heaton when their train had
arrived from London – delayed, as trains mostly were these
days – so they'd had no choice but to head to Doverley on foot,
lugging their belongings with them. They hadn't exactly been
given a warm welcome when they'd arrived, either. Rather,
when the base adjutant had come out to meet them in the
driveway, umbrella aloft, he'd torn a strip off them for being
so late.

'Have you seen the time?' he'd barked.

'I haven't dared look, sir,' Clare had replied. 'My watch isn't
waterproofed.'

'Are you being smart?'

'Gosh, I hope not, sir. Although I'm so tired after that walk, I hardly know.'

'And what about you?' he'd snapped at Iris.

'What about me, sir?'

'Is your watch functional?'

'I haven't checked either, sir.'

'Because of the rain?'

'Yes, sir. Plus, it's really quite dark.'

It had been. Not a seam of light had escaped Doverley's blacked-out windows, or penetrated the thick, scudding clouds above.

Still, not so dark that Iris had missed the adjutant's narrow-eyed stare.

'Now, I know you're being smart,' he'd said.

'I'll try not to be in future, sir,' she'd replied.

At which his eyes had become slits.

He'd kept her and Clare out in the rain whilst he'd run through Doverley's rules (no mischief between the sexes; no leaving the base without a pass; no bath to be run deeper than four inches; no alcohol for WAAFs, anywhere . . .); then, to make matters more uncomfortable, when he'd finally led them up to Doverley's front door, Iris had tripped on an uneven step, falling painfully to her knees.

'Careful,' the adjutant had remarked, 'you'll want to watch yourself there.'

Her kneecaps were still smarting now, and she'd ruined her stockings, which she held little hope of being able to replace. She'd have been fine at the base she and Clare had just left in Norfolk. Before Christmas, it had been taken over by the USAAF, who were always handing out packs of impossible-to-get nylons. Their airmen had them issued as part of their kit: a tool for making themselves welcome so far from home. But it was all RAF personnel at Doverley, so there'd be no more stockings, or gum; just plenty of long nights, waiting for these boys now flying thunderously overhead, to come home.

For the past minute, Iris had been watching them all take off, the attic window giving her a direct view to the base's burning flare path. She hadn't seen one like it before. All the runways at her previous postings had been electric. Those static lights hadn't crackled, or made the air around them dance with heat. These torches were hypnotic, she thought; ethereal and other-worldly.

Menacing too, though.

More than anything, menacing.

Because what was their purpose, if not to facilitate death? That's what the crews above were flying towards, after all: either their own, or those of the strangers they'd shortly find. And how many, now breathing, would be gone before the night's end? Iris couldn't bring herself to guess. She felt no pleasure, thinking of the assault these throbbing planes were about to unleash; no satisfaction that, after the relentless pounding the Luftwaffe had given Britain, Britain was now very much giving one back. She was just weary, deeply weary, that, more than three years into this hideous war, it was still all going on.

And afraid, sickeningly afraid, for Robbie.

Tim too, of course.

Stepping away from the window, she moved her gaze to the attic's sloping roof. The dark ceiling lamp swayed with the force of the planes' cacophony. And Robbie and Tim were inside one of them. Robbie was *flying* one of them. Unbelievably, after all these years that Iris had spent wondering about him, he was now just a few hundred feet from where she stood, with Tim as his navigator, piloting a Lancaster called *Mabel's Fury*, probably without a clue that she too had been stationed back here.

She hadn't asked to be. Although she and Clare had realised a transfer was on the cards when the USAAF had arrived in Norfolk, and had hoped to stay together, they'd also known they'd be given no say in whatever happened to them next. Happy as Iris had been when their matching move orders had arrived, her elation had given way to shock the instant she'd learnt that RAF Doverley was where they were headed.

She hadn't imagined that she'd find anything but sadness waiting for her when she arrived. But just this morning, she and Clare had been issued with the particulars of 96 Squadron's active crews to memorise on their journey up, and there Robbie and Tim's names had been, at the very top of the list, in typeset black and white.

'Someone you know?' Clare had asked Iris, noticing her sudden stillness.

'Yes,' Iris had said. 'Or knew, anyway.'

'It's not . . . ' Clare had begun, looking over Iris's shoulder. Then, 'Oh. *Oh.*'

And now, the sound of the planes was growing quieter. Already, Iris was having to strain to hear them.

How long would it take them to reach the continent from here?

Not that long, surely, over the North Sea.

Then it would be straight into enemy flak, and the guns of patrolling ME-109s.

Drawing a sharp breath – needing, quite suddenly, to distract herself – Iris moved to her bed and, sitting on it, leant over the edge, pulling out her case, which she'd kicked beneath.

She needed to keep busy, she resolved. Unpack.

She didn't unpack.

She looked up at the ceiling again.

The lamp's swaying had stilled.

Other than for the drumming rain, there was no longer any noise coming from above at all.

'He'll be all right,' came Clare's voice.

'Will he?' said Iris, bringing her gaze down to meet her friend's sympathetic stare. She understood this fear Iris was feeling, of course, all too well. She – in love with a pilot whose identity she'd confided in no one but Iris – had been scared for him since 1 September 1939.

'Of course he will.'

'How can you know?'

'I have powers.' Clare smiled. 'This is the beginning of your story. Not the end.'

'Robbie and I have had our beginning.'

'Fine. This can be your middle, then.'

'Our middle,' Iris echoed. 'I like that.'

'Good. Now –' swinging herself to sitting, Clare reached for her own case – 'what do you say to a medicinal brandy?'

'You've twisted my arm.'

'Excellent. If you wouldn't mind seeing to the lights.'

And, whilst Clare rooted around for the bottle, Iris got up to do just that.

She paused again at the window, before letting the blackout fall. The flares were all being extinguished now, disappearing one-by-one. It came to her that when they burned again at dawn, they'd stand for something very different: life, not death; hope, and *home*.

Let him still be here to see them, she entreated whoever might be listening, up in the silent sky. *Let Clare be right, and let this be our middle.*

I wasn't ready for our end.

She dropped the blackout down.

I never will be, not for that.

Chapter Five

She didn't expect to sleep that night. Once she and Clare climbed into their new beds – frozen from the tepid four-inch bath they'd shared, and layered up against the attic's chill in nightgowns, scarves, cardigans, and multiple pairs of socks – she *expected* to lie awake until dawn: thinking, remembering; listening for the Lancasters to return. But the sound of the rain on the attic's roof was soporific, Clare's steady breathing was too, and, in the end, Iris was too exhausted, and wrung out by the emotion of the day, to resist their joint lullaby. She wasn't aware of the moment she slipped into unconsciousness; rather, it came upon her so swiftly, she didn't realise she was sleeping at all until the clanging of Clare's alarm clock whiplashed her awake again at six.

Her eyes snapped open. In her chest, her heart pounded a hectic rhythm to the alarm's trilling bell. The blacked-out room was pitch dark, and for a second, the splintering noise, and the unnerving vividness of the dream world she'd just left, was all there was.

Then, from Clare's bed, came the creaking of springs, a crack of bone on plaster, and a gasped expletive.

Groggily, Iris deduced Clare had hit her head on the eaves.

'Are you all right?' she asked her, scrambling to the floor, wincing at the pain in her own grazed knees as she flailed among the chaos of their half-unpacked belongings for the belting alarm.

'No,' Clare choked, through a sob. 'Won't you turn that thing off . . . '

'I'm trying,' Iris replied, and felt rather than saw the clouds of ice that left her as she spoke. 'Where did you leave it?'

'By my case . . . '

'Where's your case?'

'On the floor.'

'I'm on the floor. I can't see anything.'

'Where's the light switch?'

'By the door.'

'Hang on. I'll get it . . . '

But before Clare had the chance to, the door flew open, and a woman in a quilted dressing gown appeared, torch in hand, her bottle-blonde hair curled in rags. Wordlessly, she combed the room with her torch's beam, locating the alarm *not* by Clare's case, but hopping frantically atop a pile of woollens at the foot of Clare's bed. The woman swooped, silencing the bell, then turned to Clare and Iris, daggering them with her stare.

'Did we wake you up?' Clare asked her, meekly.

'I've been on duty all night,' the woman replied, coldly. 'I only just got to sleep.'

'I'm sorry,' Clare said.

'I'm so sorry,' Iris echoed. And then (because how could she leave it unsaid?), 'Did *Mabel's Fury* come back?'

'Yes,' the woman hissed.

Iris drew a sharp breath of relief.

'Anything else you want to keep me here talking about?' the woman asked.

Mutely, Iris shook her head.

'Excellent.'

Tossing the alarm on Clare's bed, the woman turned on her heel and left, slamming the door behind her, plunging Iris and Clare back into blackness.

'You see,' came Clare's voice, after a short pause, 'I told you they'd be fine.'

Iris nodded, but didn't reply, still too overcome to speak.

Mabel's Fury was back.

He was back.

He was *here*.

It was him who she'd been dreaming about just now. She'd been dreaming of him all night: such strange, compelling dreams in which, over and again, she'd seen herself living their reunion scores of different ways: all over the house, and down at the base; inside the breakroom of a control tower she hadn't yet seen. In every one of those dreams, when Robbie had caught sight of her, and their eyes had locked, he'd grinned.

Without exception, when he'd opened his mouth to speak, he'd said the same thing, and it had made her balloon with happiness.

It had all felt so real to her, it was almost like it had already happened.

But it hadn't happened.

Of course it hadn't.

The day, this day, was still waiting to be written.

It was here though.

It was starting.

Nearly ten years after she and Robbie had so unwittingly said their last goodbye, they were finally going to see one another again.

*

50

The two of them had been just six years old when Robbie's family had moved to Heaton in the autumn of 1924.

'All the way from London,' Mr Johnson, the village school master, had announced to the class on Robbie's first day, and Iris had turned, peeking at Robbie, sat beside Tim Hobbs on the boys' side of the room. She could still picture them as they'd been then: Tim with his knee socks around his ankles, and his thick blond hair, that his mother had hated cutting, out of control; Robbie, by contrast, had had his dark hair tamed into a neat side-parting, whilst his sturdy body had been packed into immaculately pressed shorts, waistcoat, and shirt. He'd appeared older than Tim, older than them all, with a shadow lurking in his blue eyes that had seemed to speak of things seen; matters *known*. There'd been a bruise purpling his cheekbone, too, but Iris hadn't really marked that. She'd been too caught up in the wonder of Robbie having come from the mythical-seeming London.

It had felt like a foreign country to her. At that stage, the furthest she'd travelled from Heaton had been to York with her mum for birthday teas at Bettys. She'd only ever had one home, in the rented cottage she'd been born in. It hadn't occurred to her that she'd ever have cause to leave that cottage – although she had, even then, had some vague awareness that the narrowness of her horizons had made her somehow *less* in the eyes of others: those who'd owned the grand Georgian houses on the village green, and employed Iris's mother to clean for them.

'It's honest work,' Iris had once overheard her gran scolding her mother, when they'd both believed her in bed. But Iris had often used to resurface and listen to them talking in the candlelit kitchen, preferring to hover in the cottage's cold hallway, close to her mum, than remain warm, and alone, upstairs. 'You should be proud of yourself,' her gran had gone on, and Iris, hidden in the hallway, had pictured her wagging her arthritis-twisted finger. 'Proud of what you do for Iris and me.'

'I wanted more, Mum . . .'

'Too late for that. You're the one who lifted her skirts.'

Iris hadn't really understood what her gran had meant by that. But she'd guessed it had probably had something to do with her father, an army colonel who she'd known better than to ever mention, but who she'd liked to think had been a courageous war hero – albeit one who'd failed to marry her mum before he'd disappeared in the trenches.

Iris hadn't known many others with fathers who'd fought. Most of her classmates had been the children of farmers and miners, reserved from conscription. But Tim's dad had served, as a surgeon in Flanders, where he'd vanished too. And Robbie's father, like Iris's, had been in the trenches, only he *had* returned, with a lame left leg, and an abhorrence of noise that had eventually made life in London – amongst so much else – intolerable to him. That was why, in 1924, when Lord Heaton had begun his doomed fight to hold on to Doverley by selling off the first of his estate's assets – the dower house on the outskirts of Heaton – Robbie's father had bought it. Iris hadn't questioned where he'd sourced the money from. She had, after all, only been six. But eventually she'd learnt that everything he'd had, had come from Robbie's beautiful, harrowed mother, who hadn't often appeared anywhere around the village, because she'd had bruises, too.

Perhaps it had been Iris and Robbie's shared awareness of coming from homes with guarded secrets that had first drawn them together. Or perhaps it had been that Iris's tiny cottage, and Robbie's dower house, had lain at opposite ends of the same winding lane, leading them to constantly run into one another on their ways to and from school. Or maybe it had simply been that Iris's gran had always packed her jam sandwiches for lunch

(Robbie's favourite), where Robbie's cook had most usually given him ham and cheese (Iris's!), so they'd got into the habit of swapping. Looking back, Iris honestly couldn't pinpoint the moment when she'd realised that this thoughtful, funny, sometimes naughty, always brave boy from London had started to become her best friend. What she did recall was that, on Robbie's first day in Mr Johnson's classroom, Mr Johnson had noticed the way that she'd been staring at Robbie and rapped her on the knuckles for being so brazen. Furious, mortified, she'd pulled a face at Mr Johnson behind his back, then, catching Robbie's smile, beamed at him, her pain forgotten, just because that was the kind of smile Robbie had.

For five years, they'd run wild together, with Tim too.

He'd been Iris's first friend.

'Do you ever get sad about your dad, even though you never knew him?' he'd asked Iris in the playground, the day they'd started school.

'Sometimes,' she'd said, taking his chubby hand in hers.

He'd smuggled her a boiled sweet after Mr Johnson's knuckle-smacking, and nodded his approval when she'd snuck it into her mouth.

'I made it last,' she'd said at the end of that day, sticking out her tongue to show him the sliver still left.

'You didn't need to,' he'd replied, grinning. 'I'd have given you another.' Then, 'Want to come looking for conkers with Robbie and me?'

She had wanted to do that. She'd always relished playing with Tim. He'd used to dream up such elaborate dares: painting the feathers of the vicar's chickens; using the same paint to renumber Heaton's herds of sheep; removing the laces from Mr Johnson's outdoor shoes; that kind of thing. His home had been one of those on the green, but his mum had had live-in help, so Iris's mother had never worked for her. Even if she had,

Iris knew Tim wouldn't have made anything of it. Permanently muddy, always the first to race from the classroom when the bell rang – his pockets stuffed with those boiled sweets, given to him by his mother – all he'd cared about was having fun. That, and talking with Iris from time to time about their dads.

He'd carried a picture of his in his pocket, along with his sweets.

'I'm sorry you don't have a photo,' he'd said to Iris, one rainy Saturday, when they'd been waiting on Iris's front step for Robbie. 'Do you think your mum might ever tell you his name?'

'No,' Iris had said, kicking her heel at a loose rock. 'It makes her upset to talk about him.'

'My mum likes talking about my dad.'

'Maybe because he remembered to marry her. And gave you your house.'

'Who gave you your house?'

'No one. We pay to borrow it from Lord Heaton.'

'Oh.' Tim had looked towards Doverley. 'Wasn't he a colonel in the war, too?'

'Just a silly show one, my gran says.' Iris had shrugged. 'He never went to France like our dads.'

'I bet your dad would have really liked you, Iris.'

'Thanks, Tim,' she'd said, heart lifting as she'd spotted Robbie coming up the lane. 'I bet your dad would have liked you lots, too.'

Tim's mother hadn't approved of Iris much. Certainly, she'd never invited her to any of Tim's birthday parties, or on the pantomime trips she'd organised each Christmas to the Theatre Royal in York.

'Who wants to go to a pantomime anyway?' Iris's mum had used to say.

To which Iris had always responded, 'Not me.'

Only she had wanted to go.

It had made her feel less again, missing out.

'It was boring anyway,' Robbie had reliably assured her afterwards. 'You'd have hated it. I did, without you. When I have enough money and a motorcar, I'll take you with me everywhere I go.'

He'd used to save his interlude chocolates for her; they'd eaten them together, in Doverley's woods, holed up in the old gamekeeper's cottage that they'd never told anyone else about, not even Tim, because it had been theirs, just theirs.

They'd discovered it not long after Robbie had arrived in Heaton, the pair of them stalking a rabbit that had lured them through a disused gate in Doverley's boundary wall, up to the cottage's front path.

'Do you think it actually exists?' Robbie had asked Iris in a whisper, as they'd stared up at the cottage's overgrown walls. 'Or has it been magicked here for us?'

'It's definitely been magicked,' Iris had whispered back, because that really had felt like the most plausible explanation for its existence.

They'd returned to that crumbling, enchanted place as often as they'd been able, rocketing around its abandoned rooms, make-believing they were in a ranch, or a fort, or a boat, or a palace, or a boat-palace.

'What exactly is a boat-palace?' Robbie had asked Iris, dangling from one of the windows.

'This is,' Iris had replied, throwing her arms wide. '*This.*'

When their games had been spent, they'd lain flummoxed on the decrepit floors, and talked. Iris had confided in Robbie everything there'd been to tell about her own life, including more than she'd shared, even with Tim, about the mystery of her unmentionable father. ('Why do you think it's so bad to lift your skirts?' she'd asked. 'I'm not sure,' Robbie had said. 'Maybe because you could catch a cold?') Robbie, in turn, had told her about his. It hurt her, still, remembering the pain that had used to crease his troubled face when he'd talked about how silent his dad could be, until he wasn't. And how, when he lost his temper, his mother would beg him to run and hide.

'I don't ever, though,' he'd told Iris, his blue eyes raw and confused. 'I couldn't. He's so much bigger than her.'

God, how Iris had hated that man. *Mr Grayson.* She'd often used to catch him staring at her in the lane from the window of the dower house, and she'd stare right back at him, letting him know that she wasn't afraid. When she'd used to see him at church every Sunday, she'd divert herself from the vicar's sermons with fantasies about all the things she'd one day say to him, when she'd grown old enough to be listened to. She'd used to study Robbie's mother, too, on the occasions that she'd appeared at church – always with her gloved hand holding tight to Robbie's – and had found herself hating her almost as much. She hadn't been able to understand her not taking Robbie and running away. She hadn't known, then, that the courts would most likely have taken Robbie from her if she'd tried it. Hadn't grasped how trapped Annabelle Grayson must have felt.

Iris was sure now though that it must have been a relief to her when, at eleven, Robbie had left Heaton for boarding school in Windsor. Tim, sadly, had gone, too – not to Windsor, but Oxford with his mother, so that they could be closer to her brother and his family. Iris, meanwhile, had stunned herself by passing a scholarship exam to attend the local grammar school.

'No cleaning for you, my darling,' her mum had said, dancing her around the kitchen when the letter had arrived, offering her the place.

Even Iris's gran had smiled.

'Let's see her go, now,' she'd said.

Iris's mum had emptied the rainy-day savings jar, and taken Iris to buy her new uniform from an outfitter in York.

'But what will happen now if it rains?' Iris had asked her, when they'd gone for a cup of tea, but not a bun, afterwards.

'You let me worry about that,' her mum had said. 'Besides, it's rained on us enough.'

Iris had loved that uniform. Desperately as she'd missed Tim and Robbie, she'd felt so happy, leaving the cottage in it every day, satchel swinging, heading off for the bus to school. She'd never used to take it off, except for washing. She'd even used to wear it to church on Sundays.

Which is even more boring without you, she'd told Robbie, in one of the scores of letters they'd exchanged. They'd had to use a boy's name for her – his school had had a policy of confiscating any letter to a pupil from an unrelated girl – and, before Robbie had left Heaton, had had a lot of fun debating what that name should be. *Clarence* had been the one they'd finally settled on, the pair of them scrumping for cheek-suckingly sour apples in the vicar's garden. ('It suits you,' Robbie had proclaimed, juggling the fruit. 'Clarence Winterton . . . It's got a ring to it.') *Whenever Father Bannister does that thing where his cheeks wobble*, Iris had written on, *I turn to look at you in your pew, then there's just your dad . . .*

And my mum? Robbie had written back. *When did you last see her?*

I saw her this afternoon, Iris had replied, just as soon as she *had* lain eyes on her. *She was in your front garden picking holly.* Robbie's father had been watching from his usual window, but Annabelle Grayson hadn't seemed aware of him. Rather, she'd smiled at Iris – tentatively, shyly almost – and crossed over to her, handing her a sprig from her basket. *She asked me whether I was missing your ham and cheese sandwiches.*

What did you tell her? Robbie had asked.

That I do, of course, Iris had replied. *And you a bit, too.*

I miss you a bit as well, Clarence. Ten sleeps until Christmas . . .

Now just eight, she'd written back.

Now five, he'd said.

Never had she looked forward to a holiday more.

It had been on the evening before Robbie's return that his father had called at the cottage for the first time, ordering Iris to leave his son alone.

'You're not children any more,' he'd said, even though Iris and Robbie, barely twelve, absolutely had been. He'd towered over Iris, who'd been sitting at the kitchen table doing her maths. 'And you're not in his class.'

'No, I'm in Miss Rogers',' Iris had said, misunderstanding. Against her will, her voice had trembled. She'd hated herself for that: being scared of him, after all.

'He doesn't mean that kind of class, pet,' her gran had said, her own voice hard.

Mr Grayson hadn't flinched. He'd scrutinised Iris, with his eyes that had been as blue as Robbie's, but hadn't seemed to really look at her. Rather, she'd felt as though she was being erased beneath his dispassionate gaze; like her face had disappeared, her body too, and all Mr Grayson had been able to see of her was *less*.

'Get out,' Iris's mum had told him, raising the knife she'd been chopping carrots with. 'And don't you dare speak to my daughter again.'

'Watch your tongue,' Mr Grayson had told her.

'You watch yours,' Iris's gran had replied, 'and your hands while you're at it. Don't think we don't all know what you are.'

At which he'd raised his brow, letting Iris's gran know how little her opinion meant to him, and, instructing Iris to be a good girl now and know her place, limped away.

Iris had known instinctively that he'd be too proud to admit to Robbie that he'd stooped to such a visit. She hadn't mentioned it to Robbie, either. It was the first secret she'd kept from him, and she hadn't liked doing it, but when, the following afternoon, she'd returned from school and found Robbie waiting for her at Heaton bus stop – taller, suddenly broader; grinning as she'd run from the bus stairs – she hadn't been able to bring herself to make him sad. Instead, she'd thrown herself into his hug, knocking her hat sideways, and, feeling the vibration of his laugh, laughed too, *loving* that he was home.

It had since dawned on her that he must, of course, have already known that their friendship had become a prohibited thing. His father would, undoubtedly, have had his own conversation with him. Robbie had never betrayed a hint of that to Iris, though: protecting her, just like she'd wanted to protect him. She could imagine now, all too easily, the scenes he must have endured that Christmas, behind the dower house's thick sandstone walls. But, every morning, he'd come knocking for her, a smile on his face, ham and cheese sandwiches in his pockets, ready for another day in the old gamekeeper's cottage, where they – still children – had played much as they ever had, but with an unspoken awareness shadowing them: that their closeness had become a thing to hide.

Mr Grayson hadn't given up on trying to get between them. He'd never got wise to their correspondence, *Dear Clarence*, so hadn't known to put a stop to that, but for as long as Iris had remained in Heaton, he'd kept on at her to keep away from Robbie, intercepting her in the laneway, and after church, and at her bus stop – even, once, at her school gate – berating her for trying to drag his son down to her level.

'I don't understand why he thinks I'd want to hurt him,' Iris had said to her mum, after the long summer break of 1931, the autumn she and Robbie had turned thirteen. 'I never could. He's my *friend*.'

'You're both getting older, Iris,' her mum had replied, patting her cheek. 'Friends have a funny habit of turning into something else.'

Iris had pulled a face. 'What do you mean?'

'No.' Her mum had laughed. 'You're not old enough for me to tell you that.'

By the following Christmas, when Iris and Robbie had reached fourteen, Iris had begun to understand.

It had been bitterly cold all through the holiday, but they'd spent as much time as ever in the gamekeeper's cottage, no longer playing their games of make-believe, but talking, of so many things, and especially what they might do after their school certificate. Iris had drifted apart from Tim by that point. They'd tried to stay in touch too, when Tim had first left Heaton, but he'd always been a much better talker than writer, and, as the years had passed, their letters had, without either of them intending it, petered out. But Robbie had remained close with him, visiting him on exeats, and told Iris that Tim always asked after her, just as she always asked after him. He'd moved house again, apparently, into the centre of Oxford, and Robbie had cooked up the idea that they should all apply to study at the university together.

'We can ride bicycles on cobbled lanes,' Iris had said, on the third frozen day of 1933. It had been the afternoon before Robbie was due back at school, and the pair of them had been kneeling in the cottage's old kitchen, building a fire.

'And row,' Robbie had said, stuffing leaves beneath her sticks.

She'd nodded. 'I'll give that a go. And after, we can read poetry on riverbanks . . . '

'Beneath a willow tree?'

'Exactly.'

'What kind of poetry?'

'Any kind.'

He'd smiled, turning to her, and, in the half-light of the cottage's shell, she'd been struck by how grown up his face had become: stronger, like his body, the boyish curves of his features given way to a new, far from displeasing, definition, that had, out of nowhere, caused heat to rise in her own skin.

'I can picture you with a book beneath a willow tree,' he'd said.

'Can you?'

'Yes, Clarence.'

'Well, you know you'll be welcome to join me.'

'You know I will,' he'd said.

And, at the idea, she'd felt her flush deepen.

Robbie had noticed; she'd been certain of that from the questioning slant that had entered his smile. But he hadn't appeared embarrassed, or asked her what was wrong. He'd just held her gaze, his own bright, and, beneath her thick pullover, her heart had thumped. She recalled how, high above them in the winter's sky, a goshawk had sounded its call; for those few moments that that bird had sung, and they'd continued staring at each other, it had been as though time had shifted, dropping a curtain on their shared yesterdays, whilst lifting another, revealing a tantalizing glimpse of their adult tomorrows.

Leaning into that glimpse, into each other, they'd tilted their heads, until just a whisper of air had been left between them. Their lips had almost, *almost*, touched.

Then, 'Is there someone in there?' had come an incensed shout, making them both leap in their skins. 'There is. There's someone bloody in there.'

Barks had followed: Lord Heaton's setters.

'Quick,' Iris had said, scrambling to her feet.

'Come on,' Robbie had said, at the same time.

'Get out of there this instant,' Lord Heaton had yelled, his head poking through the hole that had once served as the kitchen's window. 'My god, is that you, Iris Winterton?'

And, exploding with laughter, children once more, Iris and Robbie had run for the door and out of the cottage, racing, lungs burning, through the frosted woods, not stopping until they were safely back in their laneway – where, amid the white hedgerows, they'd reluctantly said their goodbyes, promised to write, and mentioned not a word of their almost kiss.

They hadn't mentioned it in any of their letters either. For the next month, they'd ignored what had nearly happened so completely, that Iris, replaying it constantly, had almost started to wonder whether she'd imagined the entire thing.

Then, at the start of February, she'd stopped thinking about it at all, because her whole world had crumbled, her heart with it, when her mum, her beloved, wonderful mum, had died, suddenly and without warning, of an embolism, walking home across Heaton Green from another day's cleaning. Father Bannister had been the one to see her fall, and had run out to her from the rectory, then carried her inside. Vaguely, Iris recalled him arriving at the cottage to break the news of her death to herself and her gran, but she remembered little of what he'd said. She had no recollection of the funeral either – which had once again emptied the rainy-day jar – other than that Robbie hadn't been there, because his father had refused him permission to come. (*I'm sorry*, Robbie had written, *I am so sorry*.) Looking back, she'd held on to almost nothing of that dark, desperate time; her mum had been gone, just like that, and she hadn't been able to bear it – she still couldn't – so she'd buried it instead.

But her death had been the end of Iris's dreams of Oxford

(they had, after all, been make-believe), because, without her mum's support, she'd had no choice but to give up school and earn a wage. She could have stayed in Heaton to do that, but she'd been desperate only to leave, run as far as possible from her mum's headstone, the room they'd shared, the sight of her school bus, and the eyes of everyone – Robbie's father especially – who'd watched her catch it, so proudly. And although she would still have remained in Heaton if her gran had asked her to, her gran, shrunken by grief, had insisted on leaving too. Saying that the cottage held too many memories, and would inevitably need to be sold by Lord Heaton anyway, she'd had Father Bannister arrange her a place in a Harrogate church rest home.

'It's what I want,' she'd told Iris. 'I won't have you fight me on it.'

Iris hadn't had any fight in her. Numbly, she'd packed up the cottage – donating almost everything to the rest home, in lieu of her gran's first month of board – and, using a copy of *The Lady* loaned to her by Father Bannister's housekeeper, she'd applied for domestic positions far and wide, accepting the first one she'd been offered, as a housemaid for a Lord and Lady Somers in Surrey.

'Don't lose heart,' her gran had instructed her, the last evening they'd spent together by the cottage fire. 'You've got places to go. It's your path that's changing, not your destination.' She'd fixed Iris with her beaten eyes, and, unusually for her, reached over, resting her twisted hand on Iris's arm. 'You save every penny you can in Surrey.'

'I'll be sending my pennies to you,' Iris had said.

'I won't need much,' her gran had replied.

Iris would have gladly given her everything she had.

But the fight had been gone from her too, and before March had been out, the unthinkable had happened, and she'd joined

Iris's mum in whatever world she'd vanished to, leaving Iris numb with devastation in hers.

Her gran had been buried in Heaton, next to Iris's mum. Father Bannister had paid for that funeral from the church's collection fund. Iris had attended the bleak, colourless service – Lord and Lady Somers, not unkind people, had advanced her the money for the fare – but hardly anyone else had been there. Robbie had still been at school, unable to get away (*I'll never forgive my father for this*, he'd told Iris), whilst most of the rest of the village, Robbie's parents included, had remained at home, not deeming Iris's gran worthy of their goodbyes.

I can't go back again, she'd written to Robbie, on her return to Surrey. *It hurts too much. Mum and Gran should be there, and they're not. And when I'm there, I remember I'm not really me any more, either.*

You are you, he'd replied. *You'll always be you.*

My mum wanted me to be more, she'd told him. *I wanted to be more.*

You are you, he'd repeated. *You can't be more than that.*

For the three years that had followed, they'd kept writing. Iris hadn't made any close friends among the rest of the Somers' staff, all of whom had been much older, but she hadn't minded that, so long as she'd had Robbie. His letters, devoured by candlelight in her cubby bedroom, had been a lifeline to her, with their funny accounts of exams, and rugby games, and cricket captaincies, and, eventually, a place won at Cambridge, not Oxford. *Not without you, Clarence*. Iris had kept them all stacked in her bedside cupboard – right next to the slowly re-filling rainy-day jar – and, whenever her loneliness had become too much, she'd taken them out, making herself feel better by reading them again.

It had been in the June of 1937, as Robbie's time at school had drawn to a close, that the Somers had seen the political writing

64

on the wall and decided to get ahead of the looming war by moving to New Zealand. Their decision hadn't been greeted with much enthusiasm by Iris's colleagues, who'd suddenly had to find themselves new posts ('At my age!' Cook had huffed), but Iris hadn't minded. She'd by then saved enough pennies to enrol in a Pitman course, and Lady Somers – really not a bad sort, but definitely feeling like one since making her household redundant – had given her a glowing reference, helping her to secure a place at the Holborn college, commencing in July. Not only that, but she'd also leant on her considerable social circle to source Iris part-time employment in nearby Fitzrovia, acting as a companion for an elderly Miss Bower in exchange for her board.

Iris hadn't written to Robbie about any of it. She'd been waiting to *tell* him. With the end of his exams, he'd finally had freedom from school bounds, and they'd arranged to meet on the eve of his return to Heaton, on the final Friday of that June, for a day in London. Iris should still have been working, but Lady Somers had released her from her duties ('It's the least I can do,' she'd said), and Iris – set to start her Pitman course the following Monday – had imagined taking Robbie with her to the college, and perhaps even walking by her new home in Fitzrovia. Eating ices in Green Park.

I'll take you to a show, Robbie had written, imagining plans of his own. *Buy you chocolates in the interlude.*

I can't wait, Iris had replied, and, for the first time since her mum had died, she'd felt excited. A life that felt like her own had started to feel possible again. *I'm counting the sleeps.*

But when she'd arrived at Waterloo that sunny Friday morning – buzzing with anticipation and nerves, all dressed up in her best blouse and skirt – Robbie hadn't been there to meet her beneath the station clock, like he'd promised to be.

She'd waited for him to appear. She'd waited for hours,

only leaving her spot beneath the clock to comb the packed platforms, then hurrying back to it again, her heart in her mouth that she might have missed him. By noon, she'd started to accept that he wasn't coming. It hadn't been until four, though, that she'd finally returned to Surrey: hot, grubby, and fighting tears.

'What a cad,' Cook had said, when Iris had reached the kitchen.

'Do you think he saw me and ran off?' Iris had asked. It hadn't felt like something Robbie would do, but she'd still tortured herself with the possibility the entire way home.

'Only if he's an idiot,' Cook had replied. 'Look at you, for heaven's sake.' She'd handed Iris a wedge of Victoria sponge (her solution to most things). 'You're better off without him.'

'I'm not,' Iris had replied, staring forlornly at the cake. 'And he's not a cad.'

'He does a good impression of one,' Cook had sniffed. 'You write and tell him that.'

Iris had written to Robbie, at the Dower House: not to tell him he was a cad, but to give him her new address in Fitzrovia, and also to ask him what had happened. *I hope you're all right.*

'Could you try telephoning him?' Cook had asked, when, on Sunday, Iris had departed Surrey for good. 'I can give you a penny for the call box.'

'Thank you, but there's no point,' Iris had said. 'Heaton's not on the phone.'

'Well, I'm sure Robbie will write to you in London,' Cook had said, handing her another slice of cake, for the train.

But Robbie hadn't written to Iris in London.

Nothing had arrived for her at the mews house that was to be her home for the following two years.

Confused, dismayed, worrying her own letter might have gone astray, Iris had sent Robbie another.

And, once again, he hadn't replied.

Growing fearful that something awful might have befallen him, Iris had dug out the name of his house master, Mr Waters, and written to him at the school, asking if he could help her to reach Robbie.

Dear Master Clarence, Mr Waters had replied. *You're lucky to have caught me before I leave for the summer. I'm afraid, though, that I'm not at liberty to divulge the private circumstances of our pupils. But let me assure you that Robbie is indeed at home with his family. May I suggest you continue attempting to correspond with him there.*

So, Iris had. She'd written to Robbie constantly over the course of that summer, in which she'd come to know Miss Bower as a quiet, solitary employer, familiarised herself with London's Tube system, begun to learn short-hand, and grown absolutely beside herself over Robbie's continuing silence.

I must have upset you, she'd written to him, *but I can't think how. Please just tell me, so I can make it right.*

He hadn't told her anything.

Nor had she been able to comfort herself with the possibility that he might yet have been trying to reach her at the Somers' estate. She'd known that, even if all her letters to him *had* somehow gone missing, she'd have received anything he might have written to her. Lord and Lady Somers had paid the Guildford Sorting Office to forward all the staff's mail until the end of the year.

Iris couldn't have afforded the service herself. Even with Miss Bower financing her board, she'd barely been able to run to stamps after the cost of her tuition, books, and Tube tickets. She certainly hadn't had the means to purchase a fare to Heaton to seek Robbie out in person. Even if she had, she wasn't sure how she'd have coped with such an expedition. Looking back, she hadn't been in a state to cope with much at all. The way Robbie had disappeared from her life, as completely and suddenly as her mum and gran both had, had made it feel almost as though they'd died all over again, only worse, because this time they'd taken Robbie with them. He'd been her last person. Her *only* person.

Without him, she'd been lost.

As October had approached, she'd written to his mother, explaining how frantic she was, but had received no response to that letter either. Trying another tack, she'd written to Robbie at his new Cambridge college, Christ's. That letter she had had a reply to, albeit not one she'd been happy to receive, because it had come from one of Christ's porters, letting her know that Robbie had withdrawn from his place there back in August.

Family matter, as I understand it. I'm afraid I can't give you any more information than that.

And, silently, Iris had screamed.

She'd have written to Tim, but she didn't have his new address, and knew from Robbie that he'd deferred going to university, preferring to travel instead. Thinking Robbie might have joined him, Iris had written again to his school – care of the headmaster this time, because what had she left to lose? – asking if he might shed any light on his whereabouts. But the headmaster's secretary had replied, refusing to do any such thing. *You must understand, at an establishment such as ours, we have to protect the privacy of our families. But even if I was permitted to help you, I couldn't. We haven't heard from Master Grayson since his departure. Please don't trouble yourself enquiring again.*

Can you help me? Iris had eventually resorted to asking Father Bannister, at the start of 1938. She'd held little hope that he *would* be able to help her, given that, to her knowledge, Robbie had only ever spoken to him to be told off for painting his chickens. But she'd had no one else to turn to. *It's awful, not knowing . . .*

I'm afraid to say I've lost track of young Robbie, Father Bannister had replied, in a kind letter that had talked of how pleased he'd been to hear from Iris, making her feel a heel for not writing sooner. *I haven't seen anything of him since his mother became so unwell*, he'd continued, letting Iris know that Annabelle Grayson had. *Mrs Grayson was removed to a facility in York, and Mr Grayson sold the Dower House to a brewery, who've turned it into a public house, of all things. I don't know where he, or Robbie, went. I'm sorry, dear, not to be more help.*

Sorry too – extremely, horribly sorry – Iris had disconsolately added Father Bannister's letter to the pile of other dead ends she'd received since beginning her search.

She'd stopped trying to find Robbie after that.

She simply hadn't been able to think where else to look.

But not a day had gone by when she hadn't, at some point, missed him, not a bit, but a lot.

When the war had started, she'd hoped that he'd be all right.

She'd never stopped hoping since.

With little choice though, she'd resigned herself to never knowing.

That was, at least, until now.

Chapter Six

She had no opportunity to go in search of him that morning, which, after a breakfast of congealed porridge in the WAAF's dining room – itself housed below stairs in the old housekeeper's cubby– Iris and Clare spent almost entirely in the adjutant's office.

He'd shown them the way the night before, and ordered them to be there waiting for him at zero seven hundred hours *sharp*.

'Preferably in a more presentable state than you are now,' he'd said, humourlessly looking their sodden selves up and down.

Resolving that it probably wouldn't be sensible to risk irritating him any more than they already had, not if they wanted him to ever approve their leave requests, Iris and Clare had made themselves parade-ground ready – polishing their shoes, dressing in their spare, dry sets of uniform, pinning their hair neatly beneath their caps – and were so determined not to be late again, they arrived at his door ten minutes early.

Where, in the draughty hallway, beneath a flickering light, he kept them waiting for a further hour. There was no one else around. All the other doors lining the corridor were, like the adjutant's, closed. No telephones rang. No typewriters clacked. Aside from the occasional static from the light's bulb, and a scratching beneath the threadbare carpet that spoke discomfortingly of rodents, all was silent.

'Everyone must still be at breakfast,' said Iris.

'He definitely said seven?' Clare asked.

'Definitely,' said Iris, leaning back against the damp wall. 'Do you think he's trying to make a point? Tit for tat?'

'Probably.'

'I hate him.'

'So do I. We could have had an extra hour in bed.'

'That woman could have too.'

'Oh, I'm not worried about her,' said Clare.

'No?' said Iris.

'*No*. She can't have been that tired. She took the time to rag her hair.'

'I don't know,' said Iris, picturing her again: the sheen of cold cream on her face. 'I suspect she might be the kind who can't ever sleep until she does.'

Clare smiled. 'Would we be better people, do you think, if we always ragged our hair?'

'Unquestionably.'

'And wore slippers that matched our dressing gowns?'

'Also that.'

'I wonder what her name is,' said Clare.

'Prunella?'

'What about Prudence?'

'Much better,' said Iris. 'But no one's allowed to shorten it to Pru.'

'Obviously.'

'Or, there's always Primrose,' said Iris. 'And if we're shortening that . . . '

'*Prim*,' said Clare.

'*Prim*,' echoed Iris, and they both started laughing.

'Something funny?' enquired the adjutant, who naturally chose that moment to appear, shouldering his way through the corridor door, a cup and saucer in hand.

'No, sir,' they chorused.

'No, I didn't think so either,' he replied, and, without apology or explanation for his lateness, strode towards them, handed Iris his tea, unlocked his door, reclaimed his tea, and ushered both her and Clare in.

A crushingly tedious morning followed, in which the grey dawn slowly lightened, the corridor outside grew more bustling, and the three of them trawled through the endless paperwork that reliably accompanied any wartime posting. Once that was all duly dotted and crossed, the adjutant set to looking for Iris and Clare's rotas from among the folders piled on his desk: a protracted, and ultimately fruitless search that resulted in him telephoning for someone called Twinton to reproduce the said rotas, directly, and bring a fresh pot of tea, too.

Twinton – a bespectacled WAAF – did as ordered, throwing Iris and Clare a pitying smile, and supplying three cups with the pot. Not that the adjutant offered to pour for Iris or Clare. No, he took up just one of those cups, filling it, and draining it, then filling it again – either truly oblivious to his own rudeness, or making a concerted effort at it (Iris suspected the latter) – all the while briefing Iris and Clare on their shifts.

There was to be no easing in for them. Rather, with all the crews who'd just returned marked for ops again that same night ('Where to?' Iris asked anxiously. 'You'll find out when you need to know,' said the adjutant, 'like everyone else.'), they were to report to a Sergeant Browning in the control tower for their first shift at seven, and would then be on standby for the foreseeable.

'I'm assured you know what you're doing,' the adjutant said, reaching for a cigarette from his tunic pocket. 'I hope that's the case.' He treated them to another of his narrow-eyed glares. 'I've never worked with female radio operatives before. But,' lighting the cigarette, he exhaled smoke through his thin nose, 'I must take what I'm given.'

'I hope we won't disappoint you, sir,' said Clare, with impressive sincerity.

'As do I,' said the adjutant, not impressed; rather, raising a sceptical brow. 'Now,' he tapped ash in his saucer, 'there's a deal I need to bring you up to speed with before I set you loose, so listen carefully. I won't say it twice.'

Iris quickly wished he hadn't troubled to say it once: 'it' being an entirely extraneous history of the life and times of RAF Doverley, from its earliest incarnation, back in the thirties, as a training camp, through the war itself, during which it had variously played host to Fighter Command, special operations, and, briefly, a regiment of paratroopers. The adjutant detailed the planes that had called Doverley home, the volume of airmen who'd passed through its gates, finally working his way up to the year before when, due to the pressing need for more bomber bases, the estate's runways had been strengthened to bear the weight of Lancasters. The newly formed 96 squadron had itself moved in just a month prior.

'We're a large station,' he said. 'We have more than fifteen-hundred men based here, and try to keep twenty-four Lancasters operational, the crews cycled on and off to enable rest. There are fourteen of you now,' he waved his cigarette in Clare and Iris's direction, '*WAAFs*. Twinton, obviously. She helps me. Then we have three in the kitchen, five drivers, a parachute rigger, one intelligence officer, and one plotter.'

Was Prim a plotter, Iris wondered?

It would make sense, given she'd been up *all night*.

The adjutant gave her no opportunity to probe. He continued talking, drinking his cooling tea, briefing herself and Clare on Doverley's rest times, its mealtimes, the protocol for bomb deliveries (everyone was to keep *well clear*, was the gist), and the names of all 96's senior staff, from the station commander, Group Captain Frederick Lacey, downwards. At no point did he enquire whether Iris and Clare had any questions, or might even require a break to visit the latrine. He just kept on, and on, until Clare – legs crossed – glazed over, catatonic with boredom, and Iris, in a similar state, started to despair that he'd ever run out of things to say.

*

It was noon before he finally released them, *setting them loose*, and left his office too, at pace: desperate, Iris guessed, for the loo himself. All that tea.

'It's coffee I need,' said Clare, down in the basement, once she and Iris had made use of the WAAF's lav. 'Strong coffee.'

'Good luck with that,' said Iris, who could hardly remember what such a thing tasted like.

'And all the very best of the British to you,' said Clare, heading in the direction of the kitchens. 'See you for lunch.' She threw a smile over her shoulder. 'Maybe.'

'Yes, maybe,' said Iris.

The bell would ring at one, according to the adjutant's schedule. It left her an hour to accomplish what she'd been desperate to do all morning long.

She pressed her hand to her stomach: fluid with apprehension, now that her moment was at last here.

'I'm scared,' she found herself calling to her friend.

Clare stopped, turning to face her, her smile taking on a pained slant.

74

'What of?' she asked.

'That he won't want to see me. Or that he's married. A father, even . . . '

'No.' Clare shook her head. 'Not a chance.'

'You can't know that.'

'I can. I've got powers, remember.'

'Seriously . . . '

'I am being serious,' said Clare. 'Put it from your mind.'

'It's not only that,' said Iris, putting nothing from her mind. 'I've got this . . . ' She broke off, struggling to name the heaviness she'd felt hanging over her since she'd been watching the flares the night before. '*Sense*, I suppose, that it's going to . . . Well . . . ' She stared into Clare's gaze. '*Hurt.*'

'Oh, Iris,' said Clare, moving back to stand before her, taking her hand. 'What good thing doesn't hurt, these days?'

Iris nodded, acknowledging it.

Because what happiness was there anywhere, any more, that wasn't shadowed by the terror of it being ripped away?

'I loathe it,' she said.

'We all do,' said Clare, thinking, Iris knew, of her own Robbie, whose ring she wore around her neck, but whose name couldn't be mentioned, except in whispers, because it was Hans.

She'd told Iris, in whispers, of how the pair of them had met, in the summer of 1934, when she'd been seventeen, and her diplomat father had been posted in Berlin. She'd gone to a dance, and a mutual friend had introduced her to Hans. 'There was a swing band,' she'd said, 'that hadn't been banned there yet. Hans swept me off my feet, quite literally, and that –' she'd smiled – 'was that. The next morning, he came to the house and asked me to go swimming. That evening, he took me dancing again. The next morning, for another swim. I couldn't believe my luck. He was fun, and handsome, and whip-smart, and made me laugh until it hurt.' She'd shrugged. 'It hurt much more, of course, the deeper I fell for him, and the worse everything got.'

It was in the spring of 1939 that Hans's father, a left-leaning politician, who Clare never spoke of without a catch in her throat, was executed by the SS. Hans was invited to join the Luftwaffe then, as a fighter pilot, to demonstrate loyalty to the Reich on behalf of his mother and sisters. He went, because he had to, but asked Clare to marry him before he left.

'I cried,' she said, 'so did he. His father was gone, and mine was telling me we'd have to leave too. We were being watched constantly by that point. Hans couldn't hold the ring steady when he put it on my finger. We both knew it was a pipe dream, but we set the date anyway, for his first leave, in September. I was back here by then, obviously. We left in such a rush when the Nazis moved against Poland, I barely had time to write Hans goodbye. I don't even know if he got the letter.'

She still wrote to him, every day: pages and pages that she couldn't post, but which she said brought him closer, helping her hold faith he was alive. *I haven't lost faith*. Iris wished there was something she could say or do to make it easier for her, but of course there wasn't. So, she did the only thing she could: she listened, whenever Clare needed her to.

And now, squeezed her hand.

'Go,' said Clare, squeezing her back. 'You're wasting time.'

'Yes,' Iris agreed, and, chilled by another wave of disquiet – at just how little time she and Robbie might have – she went, in search of him.

The house was all but empty in the lead-up to lunch. Iris did see a couple of airmen when she returned to the entrance hall – both heading to the officer's mess in the library ('Utterly off limits to you,' the adjutant had told her and Clare) – but they didn't look at Iris with startlingly blue eyes, nor did their inquisitive smiles make her heart sing.

They weren't Robbie.

It came to her, as she looked for him – moving from the hall, to the billiards room, out to the misty front steps (she was ready for the uneven one this time, tapping her toes to its edge and skipping past) – that she was revisiting all the places she'd pictured them meeting in her dreams. If only he'd cooperate by appearing. Casting a frustrated look around the carriage circle, she headed back inside, following those other officers up to the library – where she was just raising her hand to knock on the door when another airman who wasn't Robbie opened it.

'Well, hello,' he said. He had fair floppy hair, and wore tartan slippers. Iris wondered if his mother had given them to him for Christmas. 'Can I help you? Please say, yes.'

'Yes,' she obliged, and didn't salute him – he was a flying officer, from his single stripe: the equivalent rank to her – just told him she was looking for Robbie Grayson, and hoped he didn't notice the strain in her voice.

'Ah, Robbie is it?' he said, the skin around his bloodshot eyes creasing in a knowing smile. (Clearly, he had noticed the strain.) 'Sly dog. He never told me he had a girl.'

'I'm not his girl,' said Iris, sounding, if such a thing were possible, more strangled yet. But Robbie didn't have a girl. He didn't have a *wife*. 'We grew up together.'

'Ah, just friends, then?'

'Yes.'

'Thank goodness,' said the officer, placing his hand theatrically to his heart. His fingers jittered, just perceptibly, belying his carefree act. 'In that case, I don't mind telling you he's definitely not inside.'

'You're sure?'

'I am. I suspect he's catching some shut-eye. That's what

I should be doing.' Another smile. 'But then I wouldn't have met you.'

'Imagine that.'

'Quite.' He cocked his head. 'You're new, aren't you?'

'Yes,' she replied, distractedly.

'My name's Lewis.'

'Hello, Lewis.'

'And you're . . . ?'

'Iris.'

'What a pretty name. But I'm concerned you're about to run away, Iris.'

'I'm afraid I am.'

'Damn.' He sighed. 'Well, so you at least run in the right direction, Robbie's in billet 4B. You can have a drink with me later to say thank you.'

'I'll say thank you now,' Iris told him, hastening for the stairs. *Billet 4B.* 'Thank you so much.'

But Robbie wasn't in Billet 4B.

'I'm not sure where he's got to,' said *Mabel's Fury*'s bomb aimer, Jacob, who Iris met when she arrived at the hut. He was sitting outside, despite the bleak weather, slumped in a deckchair at the foot of the hut's stairs. He wore a dressing robe over his uniform, and had a newspaper on his lap. He didn't seem interested in reading it. Rather, he'd been lost in thought when Iris had come upon him just now, staring into the icy mist.

A Border collie lay at his feet.

'Her name's Piper,' said Jacob, seeing Iris looking. 'She keeps coming to call.'

'She looks like she should be chasing sheep,' said Iris, thinking of the farms, all around. She could barely see the flocks grazing in the neighbouring fields, the fog was so thick, but she could smell them: still there, just as they'd always been, in the midst of this madness. She might almost have smiled, recollecting how she, Robbie and Tim had used to renumber their coats, had she not been so deflated by Robbie's absence.

'We think she's probably retired,' said Jacob, leaning down to ruffle Piper's head. 'One assumes she's got an owner, but who knows.' He shrugged. 'She likes the bacon we give her, anyway.'

'Maybe that's why she keeps coming back,' said Iris.

'Possibly,' Jacob concurred.

'Do you know where Tim is?' she asked.

'Sleeping,' said Jacob, looking not at the curtained hut behind them, but once again into the swirling fog.

Iris turned, following the direction of his gaze, and saw that it was the Lancasters he was staring at, pulled up at their distant dispersal points. There were groundcrew working on some of them, melding flak holes and patching up bullet-tears. Iris could smell that too: the scent of molten metal.

'Were you hit last night?' she asked Jacob, chest tightening on her suspicion that they must have been, for him to be fixating on the planes' repairs like this.

But, 'No,' said Jacob, frowning. 'That never seems to happen to us.'

'Isn't that a good thing?'

'I'm not sure. We've been flying together for fifteen months. This is our third squadron. The odds can't be on our side.'

'I don't think that's how odds work,' said Iris, as much for her own benefit as his. 'I'm sure they reset, every night . . .'

'Do they?' He sounded less than convinced. 'My fear,' he said, still eyeballing the planes, 'is that when our luck runs out, it's going to do so in spectacular fashion.'

'Don't say that,' said Iris, appalled. 'Please.'

'You're right, I shouldn't.' With a ragged laugh, he pulled his focus from the planes, back to her. 'I'm being morose.' His eyes were as red as Lewis's in the library, swollen with exhaustion. 'Don't tell on me, will you?'

'Who to?'

'Rob, when you find him.'

'That doesn't feel very likely at the moment,' she said. 'Can you really not think where he might be?'

'Afraid not. But I'll tell him you came by.'

'Thank you,' she said, and didn't ask whether Robbie had ever mentioned her to him.

She wanted to do that.

She wanted to do it very much.

But she was too afraid of hearing Jacob say no.

She'd already trawled the base looking for Robbie's billet, but did so again anyway, just in case she'd missed him. Retracing the steps of her dreams all over again, she covered its every fog-shrouded corner before eventually setting back for the house. A light drizzle had started, a biting breeze with it, lifting the mist. She wished it would stop. She'd been hoping for the visibility to worsen and ground everyone that night.

My fear is that when our luck runs out, it's going to do so in spectacular fashion.

If only she could shake Jacob's laconic voice from her mind.

The lunch bell rang, carrying through the spongy air. She didn't pick up her pace, hearing it. She wasn't remotely hungry. And, as she saw the men that began to spill through Doverley's porch, headed for the base's canteen, she realised how little appetite she had for meeting any more strangers. She and Clare had been alone in the WAAF's dining room for breakfast – they'd got there so early that no one working a day shift had yet arrived, and those on nights had already left – but lunch would inevitably be busier.

Prim would undoubtedly be in attendance.

Iris couldn't face her.

She grimaced at the rapidly advancing men, and decided she couldn't face anyone.

She stopped walking, considering where she should go.

Then: another sound, piercing through the blanketing cold.

A sound so instantly familiar that it dizzied her, whisking her backwards, across the years, stealing her breath with memories.

It went on: the high, penetrating call of a goshawk.

She turned towards it, peering into the sky above Doverley's woods.

She couldn't see the bird circling, but it kept calling, its short-sharp song filling her ears.

And, as her feet moved, taking her into the meadow's long grass, she didn't question any more where she wanted to be.

She knew.

She'd never had to find her way to the cottage from the house before. When she'd run to it as a child, it had always been through that old gateway on Doverley's boundary, which Robbie had used to heave open. But even now, after all these years, this woodland felt like home to her. Instinctively, she sensed where she was going.

The dour day became darker yet, the deeper she pressed into the trees. The fallen leaves of Doverley's great ashes and oaks formed a cushion beneath her feet; their branches, a dripping lattice canopy. Firs vied for space, spindly peaks poking upwards, reaching for the sky. She inhaled their pure scent and found herself once again catapulted back in time, picturing herself in a faded pinafore: sprinting, laughing; chest bursting in delight. The image came to her so vividly, it seemed that if she could only turn quickly enough, she might catch her child's shadow, flitting across the earthen floor: these woods of Doverley a Neverland of sorts, holding a version of herself that would never grow up.

The hawk had fallen silent. The woody silence surrounding her was fractured only by the rustling branches, her crunching footsteps, and the sound of her breaths, quickened by the cold. She moved hurriedly, impatient, now that she could feel herself so close, to get there.

As, quite abruptly, she did, breaking through a thicket of branches to find herself in the cottage's clearing.

She stalled, heart hammering, reabsorbing its crooked, overgrown form: there, exactly as it had always been, all wild, and broken, and beautiful.

Has it been magicked here for us? Robbie had asked, the first time they'd come.

It's definitely been magicked, Iris had replied.

'Definitely,' she breathed again, now, making her way to the cottage's weeded front path.

There, she crouched, pushing ivy back from the gate's swollen, splintered post, and smiled, running her thumb over the engraved names that she and Robbie had left, one long-ago summer.

Letting the ivy drop, she stood, carried on up to the front door, which the wind and time had blown ajar. She pushed it wide, her hands shaking in anticipation, sudden nerves, over what, she gave herself no pause to consider, because she was slipping into the hallway, which smelt just as it always had – of damp plaster, and old smoke – and looked exactly as she'd always recalled, too, with its low ceiling, and peeling walls. But it wasn't its perfect sameness that stilled her feet. Because the small, dilapidated space she'd entered held so much more than memories, and she wasn't nervous any more.

She wasn't alone.

A man in air force blues stood facing her, filling the archway that led to the kitchen.

He was taller than he'd lived in her mind.

Older.

His eyes, that even in childhood had seemed to have seen so much, were weighted with a gravity that spoke of him having borne witness to much, much more.

But they were as blue as she'd always known them.

Every bit as warm.

And when he smiled – as he did: slowly, disbelievingly, *happily* – they sparked, which absolutely, unequivocally, made her heart sing.

Slowly, he shook his head, and took a step towards her.

She remained rooted to the spot.

It was every one of her dreams, all over again.

He opened his mouth to speak, and she knew already the words that were coming.

She didn't say that, though.

She still wanted to hear him say them.

So, she remained silent, waiting.

His smile grew, like he knew she was doing that.

She felt her own cheeks move in response.

Then, in a voice that was lower than she recalled, huskier, he let go those words she'd been waiting for.

'Hello, Clarence,' he said.

Chapter Seven

Claudia

3 November 2018

Day 1 of shooting

'Hello, Iris,' Nick says, and, on cue, I freeze, set down the cup I'm holding, then turn to face him. But as I do, raising my eyes to meet his dark gaze (*deepest brown*, is how Robbie's eyes are described in the novel, *almost black*), the entire thing still jars, feels wrong, even though this is now our one-hundred-and-forty-second attempt at this torturous scene.

'Cut,' comes Ana's call, saving us from having to push on and fail at the rest of it (like we already have, one-hundred-and-forty-one times). 'Let's take a break.'

And, as the camera rolls back, it's like the room exhales. The silence that's been blanketing the set evaporates, replaced by a buzz of conversation as everyone moves, heading to the Portaloos, or the refreshment table, as relieved as I feel to not be *going again*.

It's gone nine. We've worked through dinner. We've been at this scene ever since lunch, when the weather closed in, forcing us to abandon Naomi's montage sequences outside. They'd all been going so smoothly, too. Not even I managed to screw up walking through Doverley's meadows, or jogging up and down its front steps (a tap, a skip, of the uneven one); and afterwards around the base, when Nick and I set to exchanging loaded stares across crowds of uniformed extras, Ana declared the tension between us sliceable.

'Maybe I should go missing more,' I joked to Nick, in a vain attempt to lift the mood between us, not that I really expected him to laugh.

Which he didn't, still one hundred per cent pissed about the way I disappeared to the attic last night.

'Without a word,' he said, earlier this morning, seeking me out in my trailer just as soon as he'd finished his scene in the library with Felix. I was in costume, all made up and ready to go, trying, without success, to push what I'd seen at Iris's window from my mind. He was in uniform, too, neither of us quite who we were any more. The dislocation of it unsettled me, even more than I already was; his eyes, so dark and aggrieved above his air force blues, disorientated me. It was them that I focused on as he continued talking, saying how worried he'd been when he'd woken at 4 a.m. and discovered me gone. 'Why didn't you leave a note?'

'I didn't mean to be that long,' I told him.

'I didn't know what to do. I went all over the house looking for you. Except the attic, obviously. Your and Ana's secret . . .'

'It's not a secret.'

'Well, I definitely didn't know about it. I wound up walking the entire damn estate.'

'What?' I said, stunned. 'Outside?'

'Yeah.' He let go a humourless laugh. 'Outside.'

'You shouldn't have done that.'

'You were missing. Not answering your phone. What else was I going to do?'

'Wait?' I proffered.

'Yeah, I guess that's what you'd have done in my shoes.'

'Nick, come on. It was just a few hours.'

'Not to me it wasn't,' he said, and went, slamming from my trailer, too angry to want to hear anything else I might say.

85

And now here we are, one-hundred-and-forty-two takes closer to insanity, the tension between us still very much sliceable, just not, apparently, in the right way.

We're on the outskirts of the reconstructed base, inside one of three super-sized hangars, all of which have been built as soundstages. This one holds the set for the interior rooms of the control tower, and the airmen's canteen. Next door is a cutaway of *Mabel's Fury*, where Nick, Felix and the rest of them will film their flying sequences. Next door to that is the inside of The Heaton Arms, a dance hall, and Bettys cocktail bar. Not all of the movie's going to be shot here on site – the sequences at Bomber Command HQ, and during Iris, Robbie and Tim's childhood, will, for example, be filmed in other locations, with a different cast, in the new year – but the plan is to film the bulk of the wartime action here, and down the road in Heaton. Timing-wise, it's super ambitious, but it's been near impossible to align everyone's schedules, so we need to make the most of having everyone in the same place. Ana's also hoping we can get the ending done ahead of Christmas – when the ending is finally agreed on – and we will need to move for that, although where to is still, obviously, in hot dispute. Imogen's finale in the novel has Iris on a Yorkshire beach, wading into the rolling sea and disappearing beneath it. Honestly, I'm hoping that's not the one we go with. I don't want to immerse myself in the North Sea, ever, and definitely not in the middle of winter. Besides, I hate that ending for Iris.

It's just so unbearably *sad*.

But for the present, that's still weeks away, and this scene that Nick and I are currently butchering is in the control tower's recreated breakroom, where Iris and Robbie meet again. Iris is about to start her first shift, and Robbie – who's just learnt from his bomb aimer, Jacob, that she's been looking for him – runs up to see her before taking off. He's in full flight gear, with time for only the briefest exchange with Iris before leaving. It's a gorgeous passage in the novel, full of words unspoken, and emotion unspent. Written on the page, it rings absolutely true, but here, now, it's the nightmare of the rehearsals all over again, only a thousand times worse, because for every failed take, we're not only haemorrhaging time, we're wasting money too, and the movie's nearly been called off twice as it is because of its stratospheric costs. It's only going ahead now because all overheads have been kept to a minimum – no entourages, personal make-up artists, or diva requests of any kind – and because Ana, Nick, Felix, and I have agreed to work for a cut of profits rather than an upfront fee.

'I feel like crying,' I say to Nick, as we take the bottles of water a runner brings us.

'Don't do it, Claude,' calls Ana, reminding me that my microphone's still on. 'You'll ruin your make-up.'

I reach down, switching my mic off, and Nick does the same with his.

'Don't cry,' he says. 'We'll get there.'

Wearily, I raise my bottle to my lips, drinking. I'm sweltering under the lights in my thick uniform, and know it must be even worse for him, layered up in his bomber jacket and flight suit. He hasn't complained about it, though. He hasn't let go so much as a sigh of frustration at how long this is taking. He's on best behaviour. We both are. The set is packed, the eyes of the entire crew on us, and neither of us want to give them a sideshow.

I shift my weight, studying Nick sideways as he stares sightlessly down at his bottle. His set face looks really tired, above his sheepskin collar, and I feel a punch of guilt thinking of him out walking the *entire damn estate* this morning, before the sun was even up.

It was just a few hours, I told him.

Not to me it wasn't, he said.

But I didn't listen to him properly. Didn't appreciate how frantic he must have been.

Not like I do now.

'I'm sorry,' I say, way too late. 'I should have left you a note.'

'It's all right.'

'No, it's not.'

'Ok, then,' he agrees, and for the first time today throws me a smile that is tight and heavy, and, like his laugh earlier, not really a smile at all. 'But it's done.'

'I genuinely didn't plan to fall asleep.'

'No, I get that.'

'And I would have told you about Iris's room.'

He gives me a disbelieving look. 'Yeah?'

'*Yes.*'

'Look,' he says, 'you can tell me what you like. It's your business. I just wish you'd . . . I don't know . . . ' he searches for the word ' . . . *felt* . . . like talking to me about it. It's obviously meant something to you. But you sat all through dinner, and never mentioned it. You told me you'd been with Emma . . . '

'I had been with Emma.'

'Claude,' he says, frowning, 'come on.'

'I'm just saying, I wasn't lying about that. And I couldn't talk about Iris's room. There were too many other people there. I didn't want them all going up. Plus, Felix was being such an arse.'

'Yeah.' He fills his cheeks with a breath, then lets it go. 'Has he apologised?'

'No.'

'He said he was going to.'

'Well, he hasn't. He told me everything was my fault.'

He called by my trailer earlier, too, to do that, arriving barely a minute after Nick had stormed off.

'Those photos didn't just happen to you,' he said, without preamble, letting me know he'd come with them ready to go. 'And it was you who shut me out first.'

'That's rubbish,' I said.

'No, it's not. All I wanted when we got to Sicily was to try and make things better for you. Then the photos broke, and you couldn't even look at me.'

'I *could* look at you . . . '

'You couldn't. You were . . . appalled . . . '

'Well, Felix, it was all fairly appalling . . . '

'Yes, *Claude*, agreed. But it hurt me as well, ok? It really hurt, that I'd become part of the problem for you. And that you turned so cold, so fast.'

'I did not . . . '

'You did. It's your defence. Something's too hard, so your barriers come up and you close yourself off to feeling . . . '

'Wow, Felix, congratulations on your psychology certification.' I was so angry, I practically spat the words. But he'd hit a nerve. I've calmed down enough now to be able to admit that. 'I had no idea you were studying for one.'

'I don't need a certification. I know you. And you *shut me out*.'

'So, what, you want me to say sorry for you ignoring me the past three months?'

'That's not what I want at all,' he said, and, furious too, left, just as Nick had.

I haven't spoken to him since.

It really has been a spectacularly crap day.

Beside me, Nick unscrews his bottle, taking a drink, and, restlessly, I let my eyes wander the crew. Almost everyone is clustered in groups, snacking, chatting. Only Naomi and Ana stand apart. Naomi's talking into her phone, looking harassed. Ana's bent over her screen – jumper tied around her waist; curls pulled up in a knot – reviewing what we've shot. Back in the old days, she'd have had to wait for everything to be transferred to film: those rushes she used to let me in to see when we were shooting *The Go-Between*. I don't for a moment question whether she's about to show me anything now. She looks way too concerned for that. And perturbed: like she's trying to work something out.

Whether to fire me, maybe.

Shit, I think, more sweat breaking out beneath my tunic. *Shit, shit, shit.*

'What was it like?' Nick asks, cutting through my escalating panic.

'What was what like?'

'Iris's room.'

'Oh,' I say, and take a breath, wrenching myself from my inner spiral. 'Incredible, actually. All the furniture's still there . . . '

'From the war?'

'I think so.'

'Ana didn't put it there?'

'No.' I have to laugh. 'I checked.'

He laughs too. An actual laugh.

For a second, we laugh together.

Then we trail off, out of practice.

'You planning on sleeping up there again?' Nick asks.

'No,' I say, and don't mention how scared I am of what else my imagination might create in its shadows. I'm still trying, very hard, to forget about that. 'But if I change my mind, I'll tell you first.'

'Thanks.'

'It's ok.' I look up at him, into those dark, *almost black*, eyes, and I don't know if it's his stare, or the heat, or this unbearable day, or the simple strangeness of being on a set with him at all, *acting out someone else's love story*, as Mum said, but I feel so abruptly overwhelmed, by everything, that I quite genuinely fear I might cry. 'I really am sorry about earlier,' I say, fighting to control myself. 'I hate that you were that worried.'

'Claude,' he says, with an exasperated sigh. 'Of course I was worried.' He shakes his head. 'I'm always worried about you.'

I'm always worried about you.

Those words, the unmissable catch in Nick's voice as he said them, prey on me as we get back to work. I realise that's what I've become to everyone – him, Mum, Phil, my sisters, Ana . . . Felix, even: a worry.

I don't want to be a worry.

I want to be me, but even as I think it, I see myself as a past tense, and that scares me, because that can't be good, can it?

Not really, my darling, Mum's voice tells me.

And I'm back to spiralling again, battling to conceal it as I move around the set to Ana's instruction, saying my lines over and again.

The tenor's off, Ana says. The pitch is awry. We try different blocking, variations on timing, the lines themselves ('Hello, Iris . . . ' 'Hello again, Iris . . . ' 'Iris, hello . . . '), and even though Ana declares herself happy with where we finally get to when, at midnight, she calls an end to the entire sorry exercise, we all know she's lying. Everyone's muted, leaving the set: the crew heading exhaustedly to their assigned trailers; me, Nick, Jeff, Ana, and Naomi returning to the house.

Nick and I barely talk as, zombified, we shower, brush our teeth, and fall into bed. Nick has to be up again first thing, even though it's a Sunday. We're filming six days on, one day off, and since Emma's unfortunately no better, but has now been diagnosed with an E. coli infection (not a twenty-four-hour thing after all: that was the news Naomi was getting on the phone earlier), Naomi's once again reshuffled her meticulously planned schedule so that Nick, Tim, and the rest of the *Mabel's Fury* crew will spend tomorrow and Monday filming inside their plane's cutaway.

Knowing how shattered Nick is, I expect him to go to sleep instantly when our heads hit our pillows. But his breathing doesn't deepen. His body doesn't take on that tell-tale heaviness. He remains tense and alert, and I can tell without looking that his eyes are open, fixed on nothingness, staring into his unspoken thoughts.

I can guess all too easily what those thoughts are.

My own keep pulling me the same way: back to who we were; what we so nearly had. I can't keep my mind in check, like I normally do. It's impossible, now I'm spending all this time with him.

You remind each other of what you lost, Mum said to me, up on Parliament Hill.

She's right, we do.

I suspect she'd try to convince me that that's a good thing. That we both need reminding. To face up to things.

But it doesn't feel good.

It feels really painful.

It's at maybe one, or perhaps two – I can't bring myself to check the time – that Nick moves, on to his side, looking down at me. He shifts his arm, the sheets rustling, and I feel his hand, hovering in the blackness above my shoulder. I hold myself still, biting my lip, waiting for his touch.

But it doesn't come.

It's only when he moves again, back away from me with a heavy sigh, that I realise he was waiting for me to turn to him; reassure him that I wouldn't push him away.

I think about doing it now.

Reaching out to him.

I tense, almost, *almost* ready to.

Then he sighs again, and it's somehow easier to remain where I am.

Thinking about myself as a past tense.

Remembering our tiny little boy.

With the tears I've been containing all afternoon, leaking silently from my eyes.

*

Nick wasn't in Los Angeles the night I miscarried. He was in New York, working. I drove myself to the hospital when the pain started, and didn't telephone him, or Mum, because I knew what was happening and I was terrified to make it real by involving them. But my OB had Nick's number. She summoned him back.

'He's on his way,' she told me, as they wheeled me into the delivery room.

At twenty weeks, you have to go through labour.

It's the loneliest and most scared I've ever felt.

All I wanted, was Nick.

It's a long flight to LA from New York, though.

It was all done by the time he arrived.

I lost a lot of blood. They put me under. I don't remember that happening.

But when I woke, there Nick was, by my side, holding my hand in both of his. It was our hands that he was looking at when I opened my eyes. He didn't immediately realise that I'd come around, so he didn't know I was looking at him.

It was the only time I saw him cry.

'I'm sorry,' I said, my voice cracking, because I couldn't bear it. I just couldn't bear it.

'No,' he said, pressing my hand to his lips. 'None of this is your fault.'

'It is.'

'No. I should have been here . . . '

'You couldn't have done anything.'

'I should have been here,' he repeated.

'You're here now,' I said, and had been grateful for that at least.

I'd still been able to need him, then.

We'd still been able to need each other.

But the next day, I spiked a fever, started bleeding more, and had to go back into theatre. The day after that, my OB broke it to us that it was unlikely I'd ever be able to carry a baby to term – scarring, misshapen uterus; I couldn't listen to her words – and Nick told me that he didn't mind, all he cared about was that I was all right, but I didn't believe him. I *couldn't* believe him. How could he not mind?

My heart was shattered.

I think it was then, even before we left the hospital, that I started to pull away from him. Because it made me angry, it made me so bloody furious, that he was pretending like everything was going to be all right, when, to me, our whole world had ended. He didn't ask me about the labour, and I can see now that that was probably because he was afraid to make me relive it, but at the time, I resented his silence. Resented that I'd had to endure it when he just got to ignore it, which I know wasn't fair, or right, but it was just so much easier being angry, than being sad.

Nick was patient with me, at first.

'Fine, Claude,' he said, 'you need a punching bag. Use me. I'm here for it.'

But it wasn't long before he fell back on anger too, and we rowed, a lot, screaming rows, neither of us listening, just raging at the single unchangeable loss that was tearing us apart. Until quickly, way too quickly it got so it was easier to be silent, than say anything, and better to be apart than together, because the being together was just too painful.

That was when the running started: to South Africa, then Sicily, for me; into all those bars for Nick. And the faces of the women he was pictured with weren't always different. There was one in particular who kept cropping up. The tabloids never failed to highlight her, drawing comparisons between her pretty, smiling features, and Nick's long line of exes.

Who is she? I've asked Nick.

I've got no idea, he's told me.

I've wanted to believe him.

I've *tried* to believe him.

I used to trust absolutely that he left his good time ways behind when we got together, but god it hurts, taunting myself with how far his need to escape might have taken him backwards.

I've hurt him too. I do know that.

We keep hurting each other.

And yet, when we each got the call about doing this movie, our agents making it clear that the studio was only interested in securing us as a double-act, we both agreed without hesitation.

We drove up here to Doverley together.

We're lying together now, beneath the same 1,000 thread count sheets.

I really want to think that means there's some hope left in us.

Through my tears, I shift on my pillow, ready to turn to Nick after all.

But he, oblivious, is already moving, pushing the sheets back and reaching for his phone, sitting on the edge of the bed with his back to me.

So, I stay where I am.

He fixates on whatever's got his attention on his screen, and I keep pretending to sleep, until, at last, sleep comes.

When I wake again in the morning, emerging with a jolt from the dreams that abruptly release me – such strange, compelling dreams in which, over and again, I see myself with Nick, reshooting Robbie and Iris's reunion in scores of different ways, all over the house, and down at the base – my first instinct is to tell Nick about them.

But our bed is empty.

The room is silent.

It's not yet light outside, and he is already gone.

Chapter Eight

I'm on my own most of the morning. Emma remains in her room, sipping Dioralyte and popping antibiotics, whilst everyone else is busy shooting. I don't go down to the set to watch. I'm pretty glad to have this reprieve from it all. And although I do drop in to check on Emma, I don't stay with her long, because it's obvious how much she needs to sleep.

'Call me if you need anything,' I tell her as I leave.

'Ditto,' she says. 'And no beating yourself up, ok?'

I've filled her in on the mess that was yesterday. I didn't plan to bother her with it, but she asked how it had gone, *distract me, please*, and, before I knew it, out most of it came. Not what happened at Iris's window (I still can't talk about that), but everything else.

'Felix won't stay mad,' she assures me.

'Won't he?' I say, with an uneasy frown.

You shut me out, he said. *Turned so cold, so fast.*

I truly haven't remembered it like that. But now that I've gone back over it all through the lens of his words, it is looking . . . different. He was so great, all summer, and I was so devastated by the violation of those photos – *appalled*, like he said – that I think he probably is right.

I think I couldn't look at him, after they broke.

We only had a few days of shooting left. I'm not sure I even said goodbye to him before I flew off.

I must have though.

Didn't I?

'I screwed up,' I say, as much to myself as Emma.

'You get a pass,' she tells me. 'Felix knows that. He'll come round. And you'll sort everything else out. But you could use some rest too. So, take it, yes?'

'All right,' I say, since she's sick, and I want to placate her.

Rest isn't on my agenda though.

I've got way too much to do.

First, walking back to my room, I pull out my phone, texting Felix before I can change my mind.

I never wanted to shut you out, and if I could do it all again differently, I would. I'm really sorry for you not talking to me for the past three months. I'm sorry for all of it. No excuses. I miss you.

Hitting send, I feel instantly lighter.

I have no idea how he's going to respond. I hope Emma's right, and that he'll come round, but regardless, it's such a relief to have taken this step back towards him.

My initial intention, when I reach the room, is to grab Nick's car keys and drive to Heaton. My grandparents didn't live in the village itself – their house was just outside it, on one of those post-war estates built by the government to replace all the homes that had been destroyed by the bombing – but I'd obviously have been in and out all the time. It might well even have been in Heaton that I used to visit Mrs Ellen with her jar of Rich Teas. I can't be sure, and haven't asked Mum, knowing we'd only end up in another argument about Mrs

Ellen's existence. What I am certain of is that I feel a whole bag of emotions at the prospect of returning there – apprehension, curiosity, anxiety – so don't want to be doing it for the first time in costume, about to shoot. I need to at least try and get my head straight first.

I've told Nick that I'm planning to go. Unlike the movie's publicity department, he knows all about my past here, just like I know he was born and raised in Montana, by a mum called Lola and a dad called Brad, who are both great, and kind, and fun, and cried, *happy tears*, when we told them we were having a baby, and who I have no doubt cried again when Nick broke it to them that he now never will. At least, not with me.

Nick's their only child. They still live in the house he grew up in, whereas I've never had one of those. Mum did her best for us when she first brought me down to live in London; she was actually a bloody superhero, barely twenty-three, grieving her parents, and working full time in a law firm, before retraining in psychotherapy, all the while moving us from rental to rental, regrouping each time a landlord sold our flat, or hiked the rent too much, somehow always managing to keep me in the same school catchment. She met Phil when I was nine, but I was fourteen before we moved in with him in Highgate. Phil says convincing Mum to do that was the hardest he's ever had to work at anything. Mum's told me she was scared of letting me depend on him, in case he vanished, like my father.

Which Phil of course never did. He's been the kindest and best dad I could have hoped for; I've never felt like he's loved or treated me any differently to Hannah or Lisa – neither of whom were born on a kitchen floor, but in the maternity wing of the Whittington.

They've asked me, over the years, about Mum's parents, our grandparents: what they were like; what Mum was like, when they were around.

'I'm not sure I really saw her that much,' I've told them truthfully, and don't blame Mum for that. Like I say, she did her best, and her best was pretty amazing.

I can't remember much about the January afternoon that Nan and Grandad died, skidding on black ice, head on into a tractor, driving the three of us home from a trip to York. I have no recollection of what we'd been doing in York, or the crash itself. What I do recall, vividly, is that it was the tractor's driver who extracted me from my backseat booster, with arms that shook, and blood pouring from his head.

'You're safe,' he said, wrapping me in his coat. 'Someone was watching over you.'

I didn't have a scratch on me.

Everything's hazy after that. I don't know who called the ambulances, or how long it took them to appear, or whether I went alone to the hospital, or with the tractor driver. Mum says a woman from social services looked after me while the hospital staff tracked her down. It took them hours, apparently, and I'm not sure what I did while I waited for those hours to pass. It's all a blank until the moment Mum arrived, rushing into the room I was in, her pale face wet with tears. She came straight to me, bundling me up to her, and hugged me for so long, and so tight, that in all I've forgotten, I've never forgotten that.

'You mightn't have forgotten much else either,' said Mum the other night at dinner. 'It could well be waiting, ready to resurface when you get back there.' She turned to Nick, her expression imploring; scared, almost. 'You will look after her, won't you?'

'If she'll let me,' said Nick.

'I don't need looking after,' I said, and at the time, two hundred miles away in Highgate, I didn't believe that I did.

I still don't want to believe it.

Don't want to be a worry.

But as I stand by Nick's side of the bed, his keys in my hand, I discover I don't want to go back to Heaton.

Not yet.

And maybe, actually, not alone.

Instead, I spend most of the morning down in Doverley's empty dining room, resolutely *not* waiting for Felix to reply to my message, but parked at a table with my worn copy of *The Bomber Boys* novel, combing over the scene Nick and I massacred last night. Because it hasn't felt miraculously better for the light of a new day. If anything, it feels worse, now I'm looking back at it: too fraught, and stiff, and overdone.

Can I please see it? I texted Ana, when I woke.

Nope, she replied.

So, it's as bad as I think? I said.

Nothing's as bad as you think, she told me, with a smiley emoji that did nothing to reassure me. Ana never uses emojis.

It's definitely as bad as I think.

But no matter how many times I reread the passage in the novel, I can't find anything there to help me work out how we should fix it. There's no dialogue – that much I already knew – but now I return to the pages, I realise there's also weirdly a lot less description than I've held in my mind. In my *mind*, this first meeting between Iris and Robbie has lived so vividly that it stuns me how sparing Imogen's portrayal of it actually is.

The scene, like all of the novel, is written in Iris's retrospective voice. She's already dead – not that Imogen reveals that until the end of the book – and narrating what is in effect a novel-length letter of contrition to Robbie's unreachable ghost.

When you said my name, it sent me still, she tells him. *As I met your stare, I saw you as you were, and a thousand other ways, too. Present pixelated with past, and every moment we've known coursed through my mind. It was a glorious show, but one that played out as a subtext, no match for the reality of you, there, with me . . .*

I read on, skimming over the remaining couple of paragraphs – how Iris and Robbie start talking, then stop, because there's too much to say, and don't kiss, because they daren't, *not yet* – and find myself frowning, irritated by how unconvinced I suddenly am by this now too. Probably because I'm viewing it through the lens of my own and Nick's stilted performance. I throw the book down, stare at it for several seconds, then pick it back up, flicking to the author's note.

Whilst this story is, of course, inspired by true life events, Imogen writes, *it is nonetheless a story. My story. I've been extremely fortunate to spend the time I have with Tim Hobbs, listening to his memories, but there was plenty he didn't bear witness to, well beyond the final disappearance of Iris, Robbie, and the rest of* Mabel's Fury's *crew. He was a friend to Iris and Robbie, but by no stretch their constant companion, and, as with all great love affairs, theirs largely played out in private. Tim wasn't with them. Nobody was. So, whilst I've done my utmost to stay true to the facts, where I have them, this novel should not be taken as a history. I never forgot, when I was writing it, that Section Officer Iris Winterton and Squadron Leader Robert Grayson were two very real people, whose lives were cut tragically short. Although I feel like I do now know them, the reality is that I didn't know them at all, and it would be a huge presumption to suggest that they – and especially Iris – should be judged on the basis of these fictional pages. This novel is an imagining of what led them to their deaths, nothing more. The truth about that, and so much else, belongs to them, and them alone.*

I set the book down again, less stroppily this time, and lean back in my chair, focusing on Tim's face on the cover.

Like Robbie, he's looking into the camera, but none of the other boys are. They're either looking at each other, or, in the case of Jacob the bomb aimer, down at the Border collie, Piper, who's sitting at his feet. It's occurred to me before now that they probably weren't ready for the shot to be taken. What I've never really thought about though is that Tim's attention is on the photographer anyway. Just like Robbie's is. And if that photographer really *was* Iris, then wouldn't that add weight to Imogen's theory that Tim was in love with her, too?

I lean forward, peering into the focus in Tim's black-and-white gaze, mulling over his claim to Imogen that he can't recall who was behind the camera. For the first time, I wonder if it's the truth.

He was the one who told Imogen that Iris and Robbie first met again in the control tower, and that it was Jacob who gave Robbie the message that Iris had been looking for him at their billet. I know that, because all of us on this production have been told which elements of the novel are rooted in Tim's recollections. The screenplay doesn't mess with any of them, and, contractually, we're not allowed to, either. Any changes to those scenes, however minor, have to be run by Imogen first.

'It's one thing altering what's come from me,' Imogen said, when we spoke on the phone, 'but I can't have anyone rewriting Tim's memories.'

No one bothered to call her about the new lines we tried last night, because none of them worked, but if they had, then Naomi would absolutely have had to request Imogen's approval.

Impulsively, I reach for my phone, deciding to call her myself.

She picks up almost instantly, and the sound of pumping

Little Mix and what might well be five thousand rampant children comes down the line.

'Are you at a concert?' I ask her.

'A soft play,' she replies, laughing. 'I wish I was at a concert.'

'Should I call back?'

'No, no, I'm fine to talk. As long as you don't mind the cacophony.'

'Not at all,' I say, which I don't. It makes me smile, actually, that it's all going on at barely 9 a.m. I have no issue with being reminded that other people have children. I just wish I could have known mine. 'As long as I'm genuinely not interrupting anything.'

'You're genuinely not.'

'And you don't mind this banging here.' The rigging crew have started up again, hammering away in the sets above me. 'I can move . . . '

'Stay where you are,' Imogen says, with another laugh. 'I can't hear a thing. How's it all going there?'

I hear the eagerness in her voice. The excitement.

I can't bring myself to puncture it.

'Brilliantly,' I lie. 'I'm just doing some prep, actually, and was hoping to run something by you.'

'Run away,' she says.

So, I do, not mentioning last night's disaster, just saying that Nick and I have been running our lines for Iris and Robbie's reunion, and could use some more context, if she has any.

'I feel like we might be missing something,' I say, honest about that much. 'I don't know if it's the script, or the way we're portraying it, but I thought I'd pan for gold with you.'

She doesn't immediately answer.

The pause is long enough that I start to panic I've offended her.

But then, 'Oh my God,' she says, with an agonised groan,

'that scene. That bloody scene. I can't tell you how it's *tortured* me.'

'Really?' I say, laughing, simply at the relief that it's *not just me.*

'Really,' she says, ruefully. 'I wrote it so many different ways. In the control tower, down by the plane, up at the house, by the attic stairs . . . Honestly, I had Iris and Robbie bumping into one another *everywhere.*'

'You did?' My laughter fades as I'm reminded of my dreams last night: myself and Nick re-enacting the scene, *everywhere.* Quickly, I dismiss the coincidence as just that – a *coincidence* – much more intrigued in any case by Imogen's admission. 'How come you did that?' I ask. 'I thought Tim told you they met in the control tower.'

'He did,' said Imogen. 'At first.'

'At first?'

'He got confused sometimes.'

'I keep looking at the cover photo,' I say, returning my attention to Tim's stare. 'Are you sure he's definitely forgotten who took it?'

'He definitely told me he has.'

'You believed him?'

'I saw no reason not to. I mean, when you consider what he went through, just a few hours later . . . '

Silently, I nod. She's right, of course. And, as I replay everything Tim endured that night – his terrifying journey, navigating *Mabel's Fury* across Germany; the crew's final flight home; how close Tim, so badly burned, came to dying when the plane crashed, *with only him inside* – it seems suddenly incredible to me that he's remembered anything. Look at how much I've forgotten about my grandparent's crash, and that was in 1989, not 1943.

'It was all such a long time ago, too,' says Imogen, echoing

105

the line of my thoughts. 'Although, it never actually seemed to feel that way to Tim. And he was always completely convinced by whatever account he was giving me, even if he'd told me something totally different the week before.'

'Did he realise he'd told you something different?'

'Oh yes. It would panic him. He'd call me up, ask to meet, and make me write down his new version, word-for-word. He'd watch me do it. It was extremely important to him that I got it right. And once he was settled on a version of events, he'd relax, you could see it in him. It was like he was just so relieved to have it all ordered in his mind.'

'Hence you not wanting any of it changed in the movie.'

'Exactly. Obviously, I'm not going to pick at the minutiae, but I need the big stuff to chime with what he told me. I don't know whether he'll still be alive when this is finished, or if he'll even want to watch it, but if he does, then I can't have him confused. I can't have him regret this.'

'I get it,' I say, and don't ask her what Tim's view is on the ending, because I really don't want to ruin her Sunday, which I have no doubt I would, bringing up that thorny issue. Plus, Ana's told me it's the one element of the book Tim's always refused to discuss with Imogen. It upsets him too much, apparently.

Again, I get it.

Imogen's ending upsets everyone who reads it.

'If I'm honest,' she goes on, 'I think it probably means more to me than him, that we keep his scenes locked. I just feel it's something I owe him. But I'm not sure he'll even remember now what we agreed on.'

'But he did *agree* that the control room was where Iris and Robbie met?'

'Absolutely. He was there too. He'd gone up with Robbie, desperate to see Iris himself. He didn't want me to put that in the book, though. "It's their story, not mine," he used to say. "Let me give them their story."' Even above the pulsing pop music, I hear her sad sigh. 'The rest of it though is just as he told me, the first time we spoke about it. Iris and Robbie played cat and mouse all day looking for each other, then Robbie finally tracked Iris down in the control tower, running there straight from his flight briefing. I like it, I think it works, but as I say, Tim gave me a smorgasbord of options, all over Doverley, out in the woods . . . '

'The woods?' That piques my interest.

'Yes, apparently Iris and Robbie had this secret place that they used to go to as children. An old cottage of some sort.'

'Oh, that's gorgeous.' In my mind's eye, I picture it: an abandoned overgrown hideaway. 'How come you don't mention it in the book?'

'It was another thing Tim made me promise not to write about. He said Iris and Robbie were both very protective of it, which used to make him terribly envious when they were little. I gather he used to take himself on all these expeditions, trying to find it. Now, he just wants to make sure it remains hidden. Sacred.'

'Have you seen it?'

'No, I've never been able to find it either. Those woods are *vast*.'

'And you weren't ever tempted to have Iris and Robbie's reunion there?' Instinctively, it feels much more atmospheric to me than the control tower breakroom.

'Not really,' says Imogen. 'No more or less than anywhere else. Every time I rewrote the scene with a different setting, the essence of what went on between Iris and Robbie was the same, anyway.' She breaks off, and when she speaks again, her tone is musing. 'I suppose that's what shone through for me, writing it all those different ways. It was such a miracle that they got to see each other again. They were in the midst of a war. Either of them could have been killed, long before they met. They could have been stationed at god knows how many other places. But they were thrown together, in their childhood home, after nearly a decade of separation. It gives me goosebumps even now, thinking about it.'

I get them too, hearing her say it.

'I think that was why I was never too precious about which of Tim's settings we used,' she says. 'I realised it doesn't matter where Iris and Robbie met. It just matters that they did.'

I nod, struck by the perfect truth of it.

'Does any of that help?' she asks.

'Yes,' I say, and it really does.

I might not have my nugget of gold yet, but I'm getting closer, I can feel it.

Thanking Imogen, I leave her and her daughter to their morning, and, cradling my silent phone, once again pick over everything Nick and I shot last night.

I replay Ana's directions ('*This isn't some meet cute*,' she said. '*Don't forget the plane waiting for Robbie outside. The terror of where he's about to go . . .* '), and remember the weight I felt, staring into Nick's eyes.

I recall our every move and turn of expression, and realise, with a jolt, that neither of us smiled.

For everything we tried, we never tried that.

It comes to me that we were so focused on portraying Iris and Robbie's foreboding, we forgot what must, in that moment, have trumped everything else for them.

It's the emotion that Imogen captures so perfectly in her writing, and which I experienced over and again in my dreams last night, but haven't consciously registered until this second, because it just felt so instinctive, and now that I finally see it, really, blindingly obvious.

Because although I have no doubt that dread was a near-constant feature of Robbie's and Iris's too-short love affair, I'm not actually convinced it would have got a look in at their reunion.

Not in that moment of them first locking eyes on one another.

It's like Imogen said, it really must have felt miraculous to them.

So, they'd have been full of wonder, surely?

Happy, too.

More than anything, happy.

I'm pretty confident they'd have smiled.

I'm in no rush to share my epiphany. I've messed up so much lately, I want to be really certain I'm on to something before I involve anyone else.

Gathering my things, I return to my room, grabbing the key card Ana gave me, then leave again, heading into the old section of the house, up the echoing servant stairs to Iris's room.

You'll work things out here, Ana said. *I know it.*

I must know it too, because why else would I have come?

It unsettles me that I have. I wasn't lying to Nick when I told him I had no plan to return. If anything, the memory of my hallucination (because what else could those flares and roaring planes have been?) frightens me all the more, now that I'm here, pushing Iris's door wide.

Yet, as I step into her room, and soak in its ghostly stillness – that sense that she and Clare have only just this moment walked out – I realise that I was always going to find my way back here this morning.

I think I've probably been wanting to do it ever since I woke.

Iris's bed is still rumpled from my body. On the bureau, her hairgrip remains lying where I left it, next to the nail polish stain. Instinctively, I go to it, raising it to my own loose hair. It slides in easily, its touch triggering a tingling that radiates outwards, closing around my scalp. I flex my neck, feeling the tingling spread, and keep my stare fixed on my pale reflection in the mirror. It still doesn't fit, not in this glass. I look harder, and, as I blink, the tingling in my skin surges, my face seems to evaporate, and I see another reflection entirely.

I yank the grip from my hair.

'Stop.' I breathe. 'Enough.' My shaken voice fills my ears. 'You're doing this to yourself.'

I'm tempted to leave. Run back to the secure, soulless luxury of my room.

It's what I tried to tell myself to do after I heard those planes.

But, just as then, I don't go anywhere.

I move to the window, compelled to know whether everything outside will look as it should.

And, to my shuddering relief, it does. I see the catering truck, pulled up outside the hangar where everyone's filming, and a smattering of crew, darting around in the mist. Huge security and studio lights are positioned across the base which, in the cold light of day, once again appears reassuringly synthetic. *Disneyfied.* High above it all, a helicopter circles, doubtless carrying some pap photographer, waiting to snap a sellable shot. I wish them luck in this weather. Except I don't. Not at all. I hate them, and their obsessive diarising of my body and my life. I hate them, I hate them, I hate them.

A sound comes, cutting through the helicopter's throbbing. It's that bird again: the one with the haunting call that gave me shivers the day I arrived, and who now makes me turn, searching for it in the heavy sky over the woods.

I can't see it. It must be too far away.

But, as its call goes on, I shift my focus downwards, to the trees, thinking of Iris and Robbie meeting within them, in their *old cottage of some sort.*

And suddenly, I no longer want to be in Iris's room.

I don't want to be in the house.

I want to be out in the woods, searching for Iris and Robbie's cottage myself.

So, without hesitation, or pause to consider how improbable it is that I'll find it, that's what I set off to do.

Chapter Nine

Rusty, the dog who's been cast as Piper, is out in the meadows when I cross them, playing ball with her wrangler. She should be a Border collie, but she's a groodle, because groodles score higher with audiences in the cuteness stakes. Imogen isn't happy about the switch, but hasn't kicked up a fuss. ('It's not the hill I want to die on,' she's told me.) In fairness, Rusty is extremely cute. I watch her, bounding ecstatically after her ball, and suspect she'd make Stewart feel woefully inadequate. That bird's still going, but she isn't giving it a scrap of attention. Stewart would have been off by now, chasing it down, *in for the kill.*

Poor Stewart, doomed to a lifetime of toeing the line on Parliament Hill. I feel quite protective of him, now I'm comparing him to this shaggy A-list beacon of virtue.

Leaving her and her wrangler behind, I press on, not dropping my pace until I reach the treeline. I've headed towards the bird's song, for no better reason than it seems as good a place to start as any, in these woods which absolutely are vast.

The air softens once I'm beneath the trees' canopy, muffling Rusty's bark, and the world outside. The mist clears a little too, caught like cobwebs in the trees' branches. I walk across fallen ash and oak leaves, through firs grown tall and lean, and, as I inhale their scent, am dizzied once again by a sense of belonging in this timeless place. It's even stronger now that I'm outside, rather than cocooned in Nick's car. So perhaps, after all, my grandparents did bring me walking here as a child. They must have, I think.

What other explanation could there be for this nostalgia I feel, tightening around my heart?

I walk on, for what might be miles, listening to the rustling branches, my crunching footsteps, and the sound of my breaths, quickened by the cold. I don't worry about getting lost. I trust, somehow, that I won't.

I trust these woods.

The bird's no longer calling; I'm not sure how long it is since it stopped, but I tilt my head, searching for it in the canopy above, where I sense it's lurking, looking down.

My face stings, swollen with cold. When I breathe, I make clouds, and, as I watch those clouds rise, morphing with the mist, my whirring head swims with memories: elusive, intangible, impossible to *see*, but there, whispering to me that I have been here, done *this*, before.

A breeze blows, making the icy air quiver, and, fleetingly, I hear what sounds like more whispers: of distant shouting; a child's laughter.

I pause, straining to hear it again.

I don't.

But, in the lengthening silence, I can't help but remember those voices I *almost* believed I heard up in the attic's corridor, when Ana first took me there.

Those planes, too.

And, still, that face in the mirror.

It's your imagination, I tell myself, feeling shakier yet, because why does it all seem so real?

I don't know, and I can't think about it.

It's scaring me too much.

So, I walk on, clenching my numbed hands into balls, fighting to keep my fear at bay, and my attention on the trees, waiting, *waiting*, to spot something in their gaps.

As, eventually, I do: a solidity, all but concealed by foliage, which, the longer I look at it, takes on the shape of a wall.

Impatiently, I pick my way towards it, through a thick, tangled path of roots and branches.

I've found it, I'm certain: Iris and Robbie's cottage of some sort. It's here, right before me, and, as I push on, wrestling branches aside, I don't lift my stare from the wall, half-afraid it might disappear.

But it remains just where it is: palest yellow, crumbling on all sides, surrounded by piles of overgrown rubble.

'Oh,' I say, a pressure of pure sorrow building in my throat as I take that rubble in. 'Oh . . . '

Never have Iris and Robbie's deaths felt more personal, or more tragic, to me, than now, in this moment.

They loved this place.

It was theirs.

Theirs.

And it's in ruins.

I wasn't expecting it.

I wasn't expecting to find my way here at all.

But if I did, I'd pictured something whole: a place with lopsided eaves, and a crooked chimney; a hallway with faded floral paper decorating its walls.

I move forward, picking my way around fallen beams and stone, until I come to a gatepost, hidden beneath a shroud of thick ivy. Crouching, I reach out, shakily pushing the ivy apart, revealing the post's surface beneath.

My eyes find the engraving immediately.

It's the first thing they go to.

And, as they do, my cheeks work, the mass in my throat builds, and I reach out, running my frozen thumb over the two names I see.

Robbie, reads one.

Clarence, says the other.

I don't question who Clarence is.

I know.

Imogen has Robbie use the nickname all the time in the novel.

'Tim said it always made Iris smile,' she told me.

It makes me smile now, through the tears rolling down my cold face.

I'm really crying.

It stuns me, this overwhelming emotion I feel.

I have no idea how long I sit with it, my trembling hand pressed to these names, letting my sobs free.

But when I do finally rise again, my legs are stiff, my heart feels emptied, and I know what we need to do.

*

We reshoot that same night.

It didn't take me long to convince Ana and Nick that we should go yet again when – once I'd returned to my room, washed my face, and wrestled myself under some degree of control – I carried on down to the *Mabel's Fury* set, catching them on a break from filming. We all want to get the scene right, and, when I put the change I want to them, they both agreed with it immediately.

I was still very shaken, reeling from my onslaught of feeling in the woods.

Your barriers come up and you close yourself off, Felix said to me yesterday.

But I hadn't closed myself off.

I hadn't been able to.

Felix was in the hangar too, over with all the other bomber boys at the refreshment stand. He hadn't yet replied to my message – he still hasn't – but when I caught his eye, he gave me the first smile I've had from him in months, which was far from easy, but nonetheless made me feel a bit better.

It helped, actually, to be back in the thick of everyone. It was a relief not to be alone any more, and to have the distraction, however short-lived, of a purpose.

'This could really work,' said Ana, finally dropping her pretence that last night's attempts were anything approaching ok. 'Check you out –' she shot me a wink – 'all Maria von Trapp. Hey Naomi, Jeff –' she raised her arm, summoning them over – 'I got another curve ball for you guys. I know how much you love them.'

They don't love them, obviously, but they're also among the best in the business at handling them and so got right down to setting everything up.

There at least wasn't a huge amount for them to do logistically; we're shooting in the control tower breakroom again, so nothing's changed there. I didn't consider proposing that we shift filming to Doverley's woods, even though those woods will, for me, always now be where Iris and Robbie's reunion belongs. I knew no one would agree to something so major. And besides, how could I have asked them to without giving away that I'd discovered Iris and Robbie's cottage? I couldn't, and, as Imogen herself said, all Tim Hobbs wants is for that cottage to remain hidden.

Sacred.

I want that too. Now that I've seen it, I couldn't bear for

it to be descended on, even if it is in ruins. All these years, it's belonged to Iris and Robbie: theirs, just theirs.

I won't rob them of that.

So, the line I've taken is that it was purely down to my call with Imogen that I've dreamt up the change we're about to run with. I don't feel great about deceiving everyone. I feel awful. Especially about lying to Nick.

'Why did Ana call you Maria von Trapp?' he asked me, once Ana, Jeff and Naomi had left us on the soundstage floor.

'It's just this thing she came up with on her flight,' I said. 'She thinks that to stop failing, I need to be more Maria.'

He frowned. 'That makes no sense.'

'It did the way she said it. And I have been failing.' My voice faltered as I thought not about work, or this movie, only us, and our son, who we never named, because it hurt too much, only now I wish we had. I really wish we had. 'I've been failing at everything.'

'You've failed at nothing,' he told me, his own voice softening. 'And you don't need to be Maria. You need to be you.'

'On recent evidence, I'd say I need to be more.'

'You need to be you, Claude,' he repeated. 'You can't be any more than that.'

And I don't know what it was about those words, coming from him, but they took a hold of me, deep in my chest, with an intensity that I've carried ever since. I'm carrying it still now as I stand here in my WAAF uniform, looking across at Nick on the opposite side of the set, feeling worse than ever for not having trusted him with the truth about the cottage. It already feels too late, though, to do anything about it.

Oblivious to my stare, he tips his head back, using the eyedrops that Ines from make-up has brought him.

'Better?' he asks her, tossing the bottle back.

'Better,' she pronounces, even though his eyes don't look any different to me.

They're still very red, and very puffy.

He's exhausted. I don't think he can have had more than an hour's sleep last night, if he got any at all, and has, like everyone else, already worked twelve-hours straight today, getting three minutes and twenty-two seconds of air footage successfully in the can.

But he's here.

He's present.

'Ready?' he says, turning to me.

'Ready,' I say.

'Reckon we can do it in a take?'

'Just the one?' It feels such an implausible suggestion after the debacle of last night.

'Just the one.' He clicks his fingers. 'Bam. No looking down.'

'All right,' I agree. 'No looking down.'

'Super,' says Ana. (Our mics are on again.) 'Then let's go.'

I take my position at the tea counter.

Nick takes his at the set door.

'Action,' Ana calls.

And, unlike last night, Nick says nothing.

But, as I hear him open the door behind me, and *feel* the weight of his gaze on my back, I do set my cup down on the counter.

Then, chin to my shoulder, I tilt my head in his direction.

I still can't see him, and for a second more, I wait, stilled by the energy that shoots, like thousands of arrows, through my skin. I pull a slow breath on the sensation, transported to how I felt in front of Iris's mirror, and her window, when I saw those impossible things.

Vaguely, I'm aware of myself moving, turning to face Nick properly. Our eyes lock, the camera, lights and crew receding, and I think of Robbie, whose carved name I traced on that cold wooden post. I feel the engraving still, imprinted on my skin. I picture Robbie, his face on the cover, *present pixelating with past*, only not static, but alive: his smile filling Nick's smile; his eyes in Nick's eyes.

The vividness of the illusion dizzies me.

The memory of that face I saw beneath mine in Iris's mirror, dizzies me.

The thought of that flare path, and those planes, the voices in the attic, and the laughter in the woods, does.

I have no idea where it's all coming from.

And I can no longer subdue my fear.

It petrifies me, how uncontainable my own mind seems so suddenly to have become.

But, in a blink, Nick becomes Nick again, looking at me with *his* eyes that are puffy, and tired, and the wrong colour, but snapping with a love that, just like the vibrations of sensation in my skin, feels too true to be a pretence.

I realise I don't want it to be a pretence.

I *want* to believe that he isn't acting, that he *hasn't* strayed, but loves me, *me*, as much as he says he still does.

I need, very much, to trust that he still can.

That revelation dizzies me, too.

Everything does: me, him, the doubt and silence straining the air between us, and my growing confusion over whether this love I see in him now is genuine, or Oscar-worthy.

He takes a step towards me.

I remain rooted to the spot.

It's every one of my dreams, all over again.

He draws breath, and even though I know the words that are coming, I still bite my lip, waiting for them.

He smiles.

He knows what I'm doing.

For a beat more, he leaves me waiting.

For that beat, we remain us.

I still remain me.

Then, in a voice that is low, and husky, no hint of Montana, Nick lets the words go.

'Hello, Clarence,' he says.

And, as my world spins again, I feel my cheeks move in a smile to match his, but it's not my smile.

My hammering heart is not my heart.

I don't think about that though.

I don't consider anything I do.

Because I'm in.

I'm finally in.

Hello, Clarence.

I'm all Iris, now.

I have no sense of the scene passing.

I don't think of it as a scene.

Caught up in the heady, giddy joy of this miracle that isn't mine, but feels completely like it is, I live rather than act this reunion with Nick, who's Robbie, and could go on doing it with him for hours.

But we don't have hours.

We have a minute.

Just a minute before Ana calls, 'Cut,' wrenching us out of it.

It's too short.

As I jolt back to reality, I'm left with a certain sense of having been forced from a conversation that was far from over.

I'm still looking at Nick, who's back by the set door, which he was just about to leave through.

See you in the morning, was what I was meant to have said to him.

'Don't do anything stupid now, will you?' is what actually came out.

So, we'll have to clear that with Imogen, too.

No one seems to mind, though.

Nick's grinning at me. And I've just heard Ana telling Naomi to circle what we've done, so know she must be pleased too.

We won't go another time.

We really have done this in a single take.

Bam.

Filling my cheeks with air and letting it go, I look around at the crew, who appear pretty jubilant themselves: some of the Americans exchanging celebratory high-fives; a couple of Brits running to an awkward one. My legs feel weak, like I've stepped from a keeling ship back onto solid ground. I swallow, fighting to reorientate myself in reality. It's not a completely unfamiliar struggle; this is hardly the first time I've felt the lines blur on set. I've spoken in scores of interviews about how consumed I can become by my character whilst filming. It's what Mum's taken to calling my escape route, *a fresh golden ticket to a different mind, a different world*, which isn't entirely unfair. But it's also at least fifty per cent bullshit.

Because I've never *actually* left behind who I am before, however much I might have wanted to.

Not like I just did.

So, *god*, has my need to escape become so intense that my mind is now quite genuinely giving in, giving way, and setting me loose?

Is *that* what all these illusions, these *hallucinations*, have been about?

The idea horrifies me.

It's too wild.

Too uncontrollable.

121

I don't want to be set loose.

I return my attention to Nick, and don't want to escape him.

Was it just an act earlier when he was looking at me the way he was?

I wish he'd look at me again so I could be sure, but he's been descended on by Ines, with her drops, and Jeff, who's slapping him on the back.

I turn from him, turn from them all, and catch Ana's thumbs up from over by the camera. She really is happy.

Everyone's so happy.

I want to be, too.

All I want is to be happy.

But I'm just so, so *scared*.

Sad, too, broken-hearted actually, for Iris and Robbie. Because revelatory as it was to be swept up in their elation just now – to be immersed, however fleetingly, in the delirium of their love story, rather than feeling so battered by my own – it's beyond awful to remember that their story, their beautiful story, ended so very quickly.

And although I don't know how that happened, what I feel suddenly quite certain of, with a clarity that spikes through my panic, fear and grief, is that Imogen's version of events is, most definitively, wrong.

Iris couldn't have been responsible for them all dying.

I won't believe it.

Not of her.

Not of the person I just felt.

I bite the insides of my cheeks, and don't want any of them to have died at all.

They must have, though.

They really all must have.

Yet, as my mind moves back outside, to the dark woods, I picture Iris and Robbie together, full of fragile hope in their old cottage – not as it is now, but as it must have been then – and cannot make peace with the idea that they simply vanished.

I can't accept the defeatism of Imogen's author's note that the truth about what happened belongs to them, *and them alone*.

Because it surely has to be lurking *somewhere* still, doesn't it?

I stand straighter.

I'm right. I know I'm right.

Truth doesn't vanish.

It just gets hidden.

And, in a rush, it comes to me how much I want to uncover this truth.

I don't pause to unpick my motive, or consider whether it's about clearing Iris's name, or my own curiosity, or simple desperation for another of Mum's golden tickets: a distraction, any distraction, from everything else I'm too terrified to think about. I just know that doing this will help me, because I'll have no peace until I've uncovered what really happened to Iris, Robbie, and the rest of *Mabel's Fury*'s crew.

The task feels overwhelming.

I have no idea how I'm going to manage it.

But, with a fresh shot of adrenalin, I realise where I should start.

Or rather, with whom I should start.

Tim Hobbs, of course.

Tim, who's claimed to have forgotten so much of his crew's last hours, including who took that photograph of them all, but who I now know from Imogen has misremembered plenty about his recollections in the past.

Tim, who's a hundred years old, and living in a nursing home in York.

Tim, who here and now, under these burning studio lights – on this Hollywood set of a very real world that he himself walked and breathed – I resolve I need to visit.

Just as soon as I can.

Assuming, of course, that he'll let me.

Chapter Ten

Iris

February 1943

Iris and Robbie spent much more than a minute together in the old cottage that afternoon.

They spent hours there, not leaving until the early winter dusk descended, leaving them no choice but to return to the house, and the base, and the war that they had, all too briefly, managed if not to forget, then to separate themselves from.

But those afternoon hours passed in the space of a minute, whilst that first minute they shared – with those words, *Hello, Clarence*, reverberating in the frozen air between them – stretched across seconds that turned into hours that swiftly became an eternity.

To Iris, still half in her dreams, it was as though she was living it in an echo chamber, looking across at Robbie with swimming eyes that saw him both here and now, in the cottage's crooked hallway with its peeling floral wallpaper, and all the other countless places she'd imagined them meeting, too: layers upon layers of alternative paths that they might so easily have chanced onto.

And was time really a constant? Or did it flex and bend?

Iris thought it probably did.

Especially in this old cottage, where it had always travelled at such strange speed.

Now she was within its walls again, encircled with Robbie by this motionless moment, it was impossible for her not to remember the last time the clocks had shifted for them here: back in that January of 1933, when the pair of them had knelt by the kitchen fire, and shared their almost kiss.

Was Robbie remembering it too?

Even as the question sounded in Iris's mind, she watched his eyes, glassy with cold, shine, as though in answer.

Yes, he seemed to say, *yes*.

I've never forgotten.

Her smile grew.

So did his, lifting, but not disguising, the fatigue shadowing his face. There were lines around his eyes that hadn't been there before, and which shouldn't by rights have belonged to him for years to come. It was almost as though age had travelled backwards to find him, knowing how slim the chances were of them now meeting in the future.

But Iris couldn't think about that.

'Robbie,' she choked, focusing on what was real, what was now, which was that she'd found him. 'Where did you go?'

'Where did I go?' he said, incredulous. 'Where did *you* go?' His accent hadn't lost its trace of Yorkshire.

'London,' she said, tears brimming, because she loved that she could still hear that boy she'd known. Loved that he'd held on to him. 'I told you that. I wrote . . . '

'*I* wrote.'

'No . . . '

'Yes . . . '

'What?' she said, in bewilderment, and so much relief. He hadn't meant to disappear. 'Where?'

'The wrong place, I think. Please don't cry.'

'I can't help it. I've missed you a bit.'

'I've missed you a bit, too,' he said, no longer still, but

closing the distance between them, scooping her up in a hug, just as he had countless times before. Only now, he didn't swing her playfully around and release her. He held on to her, as she held on to him, her heart no longer singing, but swelling, until she felt it might burst. 'I've missed you,' he repeated, his lips to her ear. 'I've missed you every single day.'

'I tried so hard to find you.'

'I tried to find you.'

She said no more. There was too much to say, and explain, and try to make sense of, and she didn't know where to start with any of it.

She didn't want to start.

Not yet.

She just wanted to go on holding him.

So, she did, losing herself in his embrace, his warmth.

Him.

He said nothing either, just tightened his arms around her.

It was enough.

For that minute of time standing still, it was more than enough.

But eventually, that minute did end.

He set her back on her feet, and together they turned for the kitchen, where they set to unpicking the past nearly six years that they'd lived as strangers.

Then time started moving again.

Then, it raced.

*

It didn't take them long to establish what had gone so wrong for them, back in the summer of 1937, when Robbie had failed to meet Iris at Waterloo, and their letters had failed to reach each other. By the time they'd finished laying a fire in the old grate, their hands skimming over each other's as they stacked dry leaves and sticks, they'd got to the bottom of it.

It wasn't a complex tale.

Just a sorry one.

Robbie hadn't been able to come to Waterloo that day because of his mother. The revelation saddened, but didn't surprise Iris. She'd suspected as much ever since Father Bannister had written to her about Annabelle Grayson becoming unwell.

Only, Annabelle Grayson hadn't been unwell.

She'd fallen, with the help of Robbie's father, down the Dower House stairs, breaking her spine. She'd never walk again, and to this day lived in a York nursing home, paid for from the proceeds of the Dower House sale, which Robbie had forced his father into.

'He knows not to set foot near her again,' he said. 'I've told him that I'll go to the police if he does. It's only because of my mother that I haven't done it already.'

'She doesn't want him prosecuted?'

'No.' He cracked a stick, throwing the pieces into the grate. 'She says he suffered enough in the trenches.'

It was his dispassionate tone. The set of his jaw.

'You don't think he did?' said Iris.

'I'm sure he did,' said Robbie. 'But everyone suffers in war.' He reached for another stick. 'He's the only one who's put my mother in a wheelchair though.'

He went on, saying that his father had told everyone, Robbie's headmaster included, that the fall had been an accident.

'My headmaster called me to his office,' he said, 'just as I was about to leave for Waterloo to meet you. My father had telephoned from the hospital in York, saying I had to come straight away, that Mum might die. My headmaster drove me.

128

It was the longest journey of my life. Well –' he raised a wry brow – 'at that point, anyway.'

'I'm so sorry,' said Iris, her cold hands full of leaves, aching at how terrified he must have been. Aching for his mother, too, with her shy smile and basket of holly.

'No, I'm sorry,' he said, taking the leaves from her. 'I hate that I left you waiting like that.'

'What choice did you have?'

'I should have found one.'

'You couldn't have.' She watched him push the leaves into the grate. 'There was nothing you could have done.'

'But I did do something.' He looked back at her, and his face – his strong, handsome face, that was older, and tired, and still the one she liked more than any other – strained with regret. 'I did the wrong thing.'

She frowned, uncomprehending. 'What do you mean?'

'I mean . . . ' He exhaled a ragged sigh. 'I *mean*, Iris, that I told my father about you. Clarence.'

'Oh,' she said, and that was all the time it took her – just the length of that single syllable, *oh* – to realise, with a cold jolt, why he'd never received her letters.

As she stared into his eyes, picturing his father's arctic replicas – the disdain in them when he'd used to watch her in church; his sneer when he'd towered over her in her gran's kitchen . . . *you're not in his class* – it all made crashing sense.

Silently, she listened as Robbie told her the rest: how he'd lost his temper when he'd got to the ward and found his father next to his mother's bed, and dragged him away from her, letting go all his fury, a lifetime of it, telling him that his control over both of them was done with.

'All those years after you left Heaton, he stopped me seeing you,' he said. 'He kept me from your mum's funeral, your gran's. I needed him to know that he hadn't won, that *we* had, by

129

staying in each other's lives anyway. I wanted him to feel weak, a fool, so I told him everything.' He stared at her. 'I was the fool.'

'No.' She wasn't having that. 'You can't blame yourself for who your father is.'

'I should have known better. Shouldn't have lost control.'

'Anyone would have . . . '

'But I asked a nurse to send you a wire, right in front of him. I gave her the money.' He shook his head. 'He must have stopped her.'

'Yes,' said Iris, boiling inside, because how dare he have done it?

To them.

To his own son.

He was the one who wasn't in Robbie's class.

He was the one who was less.

'My mother didn't properly wake up for days,' Robbie said. 'At first, I didn't leave the hospital. I was terrified she was going to die. And that my father would try to come back into her room. Which he did. Often. Until I threatened to go to the police. After that, I stayed in a local pub. I couldn't go home with my father there. But he went back every night. He'd have been there each morning for the post.'

Iris closed her eyes, visualizing all those letters she'd written arriving at the Dower House, straight into his hands.

Had he read them, before he stole them?

She was sure he must have.

It made her feel sick.

'I guessed something must be wrong,' Robbie continued. 'I knew you wouldn't just ignore what had happened to Mum . . . '

'Of course not.'

'I wrote to you. I wrote . . . God . . . I don't know . . . *so* many letters.'

'But I should have got them,' she said, still not understanding that bit. 'Lady Somers paid to have all our mail forwarded.'

'Are you sure?'

'Well, no.' She emitted a sound, much less than a laugh. 'Not any more I'm not.'

'Did you ever get anything forwarded from anyone else?'

'You're the only person who wrote to me there.'

'I tried to see you. I went to the house.'

'What?' Her eyes widened. 'When?'

'The start of August, after Mum moved to her nursing home. My father had left York, I have no idea where he went, and all I wanted was to get to you. It . . . *broke* me, when I found the Somers' house all boarded up.'

It broke her, thinking about him doing it.

'I called in at a farm,' he said, pulling a box of matches from his coat. 'They told me the house had been put up for sale.' He extracted a match. 'Apparently, the Somers had sold a lot of the estate off already. Like Heaton with this place.'

'I had no idea,' said Iris, her reeling mind now struggling to absorb that, too.

The Somers had always seemed so affluent to her, with their house parties, and motors, and weekends away.

'They told us they were building a house in New Zealand,' she said. 'That they were leaving to get away from this war.'

'Well, that certainly worked out for them,' said Robbie, lighting the match and flicking it into the grate, his face glowing in the sudden crackle of flames. 'I suspect though that they were most interested in saving face, and getting away from their debts. Their neighbours seemed to think they were carrying a lot of them.'

'So they lied to us,' said Iris. 'They lied to *me*.' She took a breath, digesting just how much their pride, their arrogant pride, had cost them both. 'If they'd just been honest, said they couldn't afford to pay the post office . . . My *God*.' She placed her hands to her face, digging her fingers into her cheeks, thinking of everything she might have done differently, if she'd only known. 'I want to scream.'

'Don't do that.'

'Don't you?'

'Want to scream? No.'

'Why aren't you angrier?'

'I am angry. I'm furious.'

'But you're *smiling*.'

He was.

He was smiling at her.

And now she was doing it too, just because that was the kind of smile he'd always had.

She pelted him with the heel of her hand, very much as though they were still eight years old.

'Why are you smiling?' she demanded.

'Because I finally know what happened,' he said, his exhausted eyes alight with amusement at her regression back into childhood. 'It can't torture me any more. I'm free of it. And you're here.'

'I am,' she agreed.

'With me.'

'Yes,' she said, agreeing with that, too.

'So, I don't care about the Somers,' he said. 'I don't care about my father.' His gaze, tinted amber by the reflection of the fire once again became serious. 'I care about you.'

I care about you.

She felt the wonder of those words, all through her.

She didn't reply.

Not straight away.

The leaves hissed in the grate, the sticks smoked, and time once again stretched.

Then, 'I care about you, too,' she said. 'There's no one I care more about.'

And it was his turn to be silent.

He leant forward, towards her.

She didn't move.

She thought he might be going to kiss her.

But he didn't kiss her.

Not yet.

He asked her a favour.

'Let's not look back,' he said. 'I don't want us to waste time on things that can't be changed.' His shining eyes entreated her. 'I don't want us to waste any time at all.'

'No,' she said, no longer smiling, but remembering what a precious commodity time had become. She'd forgotten there. Briefly. 'I don't want to waste it either.'

They wasted none that afternoon.

They made the most of every speeding second, talking, constantly, as the day's meagre light outside faded, pulling them inevitably towards the looming night.

He was going to Italy, he said; he shouldn't have been told that until his pre-operation briefing later, but all the pilots in 96 had clubbed together to bribe the station's confidential clerk into keeping them informed on their upcoming movements.

'And where were you last night?' Iris asked.

'Cologne.' He stood, shrugging off his great coat. 'I knew you were on your way before I went up. Fred, our group captain, told me after briefing that we were getting new radio operators.' He grinned. 'Never have I been more determined to come back.' He crouched, making his coat into a cushion, and she shifted on to it, leaving room for him beside her. 'I headed straight to the house after interrogation this morning,' he went on, sitting back down. His arm brushed against hers, and he didn't move it away. 'But you were locked in with Ambrose . . . '

133

'Ambrose?' said Iris. *That* was what the adjutant was called? He'd only told her and Clare his surname, which was Brown. *Flight Lieutenant Brown.* He was a rank down from Robbie, which was actually quite gratifying. Almost as much so as his incongruous first name. 'I don't think I've ever met anyone less ambrosial.'

'I gather from Beth Twinton that Ambrose thinks much the same of you and your friend.'

'Clare. You'll like her.'

'I'm sure I will.'

'I wish you'd come in and rescued us.'

'I thought about it. But Beth said it would only get Ambrose's back up more. And I didn't want to see you for the first time with him there.'

'No,' Iris agreed, realising, now he'd said it, that she wouldn't have wanted that either.

It struck her how glad she was that they hadn't had any audience at all.

'Beth told me you should be done with Ambrose by eleven,' Robbie went on, 'so I went back then, but you were still in there.'

'He didn't let us out until twelve.'

'I went back again just after, but you were already gone.' He narrowed his eyes. 'It was extremely frustrating.'

'I'm sorry.'

'I went looking for you . . . '

'I was desperate for the loo.'

'Well, I didn't go looking for you there. But I tried everywhere else.'

'I looked for you everywhere too,' she said. 'I met Jacob . . . '

'That must have cheered you up.'

'He introduced me to Piper.'

'I think he might be making her depressed.'

134

'Then I gave up and came here.'

'Snap,' he said. 'I come here most days, actually. It's felt very quiet, until now.'

'How long have you been back?' she asked, at once saddened by the idea of his lone visits, and moved, beyond words, that he'd kept coming.

'Five weeks,' he said. 'We were one of the first crews to arrive.'

'Have you been into Heaton?'

'Yes.'

'And your house? Father Bannister told me it's been turned into a pub.'

'The Heaton Arms,' he said. 'And yes, I've been. I couldn't avoid it. Everyone goes.'

'What's it like?'

'Better with beer.'

'I'm dreading going back,' she confessed. 'It's been so long.' She looked into the fire, thinking of her old cottage.

'It hasn't changed,' he said, reading her mind.

He'd always been good at that.

'Does anyone live there?' she asked.

'A family,' he said. 'I've seen the children playing.'

'That's nice,' she said, liking that it hadn't been left empty. '*Did* Lord Heaton sell it?'

'He must have. I don't think he held on to anything. He's back in uniform, apparently, running a barracks in Preston.'

'Poor Preston.'

He smiled. 'What was it your gran used to call him?'

'A silly show colonel,' Iris said, smiling too. Then, she bit her lip. 'What about my gran and mum's graves?' The question, which she'd taunted herself with ever since they'd died, was hard to ask. 'I don't suppose you've . . . '

'I've been, Iris,' he said, softly. 'I looked after them when you went. Don't worry. I've looked after them since I got back.'

'You've looked after them?' she said, and the words tremored.

'Of course I have.'

'So . . . ' She swallowed. 'They're not all overgrown?'

'No,' he said. '*No.*'

And she flung her arms around him again, in so much relief, and gratitude, and *love.*

'Thank you,' she said. 'Thank you.'

'You don't need to thank me,' he said, holding her fast. 'You never need to do that.'

When the fire dwindled, they went outside to fetch more kindling, and filled each other in on their wars, learning that they'd both been with the RAF from the off.

Robbie, who never had gone to Cambridge, had been with them since before the war even started. He'd only intended to defer his degree for a year after his mother's fall, but early in 1938, Tim had returned from his travels around Europe, and – appalled by what he'd seen of the Nazi's growing power – had talked Robbie into applying for pilot training with him.

'He didn't actually last that long,' Robbie said. 'The night flying got him.'

'Poor Tim,' said Iris, who'd heard the same story from plenty of others. It was meant to be terrifying at first, flying purely by instruments. She could well imagine it. The idea of whizzing through a void of blackness, trusting entirely what a rickety dashboard was telling you, and not looking out, or down, because the dark was too huge, too empty, was, to her, the stuff of nightmares. 'Did he panic?'

'He nearly killed himself,' said Robbie. 'He refused to go up again, and transferred to navigation instead.'

'But you carried on, obviously.'

'I couldn't have stopped. It gets addictive, very fast.'

'Yes,' said Iris, who'd heard all about that, too.

She'd yet to encounter a pilot who didn't love to fly. However much they feared what they flew into.

'Tim can't wait to see you, by the way,' Robbie said.

'I can't wait to see him either.' She pictured him, with his socks around his ankles, and that picture of his father, held tight in his fist. 'Does he still have all his tufty hair?'

Robbie gave her a bemused look. 'Tufty hair?'

'Yes, those blond locks. His mother never liked cutting it.'

'Didn't she?'

'No. You must remember . . . '

'I don't remember thinking about his hair at all. Unlike you, apparently.' He kept his expression level, but there was amusement in his voice.

He was teasing her, she knew.

As her friend?

Or something more?

She knew what she wanted him to be.

She was almost certain of him wanting it too.

She'd been almost certain of it from the first moment she'd seen him again, and had grown ever more so with each moment that had passed since.

But she still wasn't quite certain enough to do anything about it.

And perhaps it was the same for him, because, in unison, they looked away from each other, and got on with collecting more sticks.

'Have you always flown bombers?' she asked, to distract herself, but also because she wanted to know.

'No, I was in a spit at first.'

That made her look up. 'You flew that summer?'

137

'Yes,' he said, and didn't elaborate.

But, as he picked up then tossed a broken branch to the ground, Iris saw the sudden sobriety in him, and knew he was remembering those long cloudless days, eighteen months before, when Winston's few had taken to the skies for the Battle of Britain, and fewer yet had survived to see autumn.

She, in a station in Sussex at the time, had watched them all, every day: their vapour trails, and frantic dodging; the sparks of their guns, then sudden plummets to earth.

Even knowing the danger Robbie was facing now, it turned her cold that he'd been part of that.

'I wasn't happy when I got reassigned to bombers,' he said, moving the conversation along.

She didn't try to stop him. In his shoes, seeing what he must have seen, losing the friends he must have lost, she'd want to change the subject too.

'Reassigned?' she said. 'It wasn't your choice?'

'It was a choice I was strongly encouraged to make. They needed pilots.'

'They always need pilots.'

He sighed. 'True.'

'You must have been glad to get in a crew with Tim, though.'

'I was furious with Tim. You remember his uncle in Oxford?'

'Yes.'

'He's high up in Bomber Command. Tim gave him my name . . .'

'What? Without talking to you?'

'He claims he was drunk at the time. Don't *laugh*, it's not funny . . .'

'I'm not laughing . . .'

'You actually are.'

She actually was.

He was a bit, too, and she was glad of that.

Glad to see the shadow that had descended over him, lift.

'It's just he was always so cheeky,' she said, wrestling herself under control. 'And I assume you've forgiven him?'

'Just about.'

'How do you feel about flying bombers now?'

'I like being in a crew. I love my crew.'

'Even Jacob?'

'Even Jacob,' he said, with another brief smile. 'But I hate what we do. And Lancasters are heavy, much harder than a spit to manoeuvre in a fight.'

'You seem to have been managing well so far. Jacob told me this is your third squadron.' She didn't mention what else Jacob had said, about the odds they were facing. *My fear is that when our luck runs out, it's going to do so in spectacular fashion.* She didn't want to think about that. 'You must have flown scores of ops.'

'Sixty-three,' he said, 'as of last night.'

'That's quite a number.'

'It will be sixty-four tomorrow, when we come back from Italy, and you give us our permission to land.'

'I'll look forward to that.'

'So will I.'

'Are you scared, though?' she asked, because she had to.

'Not especially,' he said. 'Italy's not like Germany.'

'No,' she said, and again, she'd heard the same from other pilots. The Italian defences were thinner, their flak fields lighter; they had fewer night fighters to scramble than in Germany.

Nonetheless, there were still always crews that didn't come back from raids there.

'Don't worry,' said Robbie. 'It'll be straightforward. We might even bring you some ice cream.'

'It might melt.'

'I don't know.' He smiled. 'It can get pretty cold up there.'

'Then don't worry about the ice cream,' she said. 'Come back quickly and warm up.'

*

'Do you not need to sleep?' she asked him, once they were inside again, feeding the fire.

'I don't want to sleep.'

'What about lunch?'

'I think that ship's sailed. But –' he reached into his pocket, producing a chocolate bar – 'you've reminded me. I've still got this from last night.'

'Aren't you meant to eat your rations on the flight?' she said, eyeing the treat.

'That's the traditional approach.' He handed her the bar. 'I saved it for you, though.'

'Just like your interlude chocolates,' she said, breaking it in two, and handing half back to him.

'Exactly the same,' he agreed. 'I often think how similar sorties are to pantomimes.'

'You said you've flown sixty-three?'

'That's right.'

'Does that mean you've only flown three so far, here?'

He grimaced. 'Yes. We've had a lot of stand-downs. The weather . . . '

She nodded, and didn't have to work too hard to calculate how many more flights he'd have to survive as a pathfinder before he could hope for a safer posting in training, or on the ground. It was a simple sum, and forty-two was the answer: fifteen more than it would have been if he'd been doing another tour with an ordinary squadron. Pathfinding was still a new practice, and the pilots spearheading it had been handpicked from the cream of their previous squadrons ('*Think of them as bomber command's cricket first XI*,' Iris's CO in Norwich had told her and Clare; he'd been fond of euphemisms); they were given higher pay, and a jump in rank, but in return were expected to do the most dangerous work, leading attacks, flying low and laying targets that were a beacon to their own presence, for longer.

She eyed Robbie's badge on his chest: the hovering eagle, glinting in the firelight, that was given to all pathfinders. They weren't allowed to wear it on operations, because of the interrogation they'd face if they fell into the gestapo's hands. Assuming they survived that long.

Raising her hand, she placed her fingertips to the eagle's metal, and watched Robbie look down, his eyes on her touch.

'Why did you agree to this?' she asked him. 'You could have said no.' She dropped her hand. 'Everyone's allowed to say no.'

'Then someone else would have had to do it instead of me,' he said, lifting his gaze back to hers. 'And at least this way, I'm doing something to get the bombs landing where they're meant to be, not on schools, or hospitals.' The lines around his eyes deepened in a frown. 'It's something.'

Iris nodded.

It was.

They left the cottage at a quarter to five. Despite the blanketing dark, they were careful to rejoin Doverley's driveway out of sight of the house, not wanting to risk anyone spotting them leaving the woods together. They both knew the rules prohibiting what the adjutant had referred to as *mischief*. Senior as Robbie was, he wasn't exempt from them. Iris certainly wasn't, and she had no interest in running the gauntlet of a dishonourable dismissal. Especially when she still hadn't done anything to deserve it.

They were quieter for their walk back to the house; sober, now that the night ahead had become so suddenly imminent.

Iris didn't have to report to the control tower for another two hours, but it would be all activity for Robbie from this point on, checking his plane, attending his intelligence briefing, changing into his flight gear, readying his crew.

They bade one another goodbye in the carriage turning circle, standing a careful distance apart. Iris shivered. The sky had cleared, and the temperature plummeted even further. The rising moon, unblanketed by cloud, was dangerously full.

'You should head in,' he said. 'Thaw out.'

'It's even colder inside,' she reminded him.

And he smiled.

But tightly.

Distractedly.

He needs to be gone, she thought.

I need to let him go.

'Good luck tonight,' she told him, looking to the airbase.

'Good luck to you, too,' he said. 'I'll be listening for your voice.'

'I'll be listening for yours,' she said. 'Or your wireless operator's . . . '

'Henry.'

'Henry,' she echoed.

'All right.' He drew a sharp breath, seeming to brace himself to leave. 'All right.' And, with a nod, he turned and went.

For several paces, she watched him walking away, shivering more, from the cold, and fear too. It was so much worse, now that he was going, to think of where he was heading to. Because Italy might not be Germany, but it was still Italy, and even as she stood here, on this frozen Yorkshire gravel, breathing in this frigid British air, there were people on the ground over there, preparing their guns and searchlights with the sole objective of shooting planes like his down.

He knew that.

Of course he knew that.

How often must he have had to dodge their flak?

So, he must be scared.

Terrified, for all his talk of ice cream.

'Robbie,' she called out, and didn't know what she wanted to say, only that she had to say something to help him with his fear.

Something to alleviate it, if only for a moment.

He stopped, turning back to her.

Desperate to run to him, she remained where she was.

He didn't move either.

And, in a rush, the words came to her.

'Don't do anything stupid now, will you?' she said.

To her delight, he laughed.

He was still laughing when, shaking his head, he once again turned from her, and carried on walking away.

The thought of that laugh kept her going through the long night that followed.

She held it very close, all the way until dawn.

Chapter Eleven

Zero four hundred hours: that was when the squadron was expected to begin returning from Italy. The station commander, Group Captain Frederick Lacey – *Fred*, as Robbie had called him – arrived in the glass-walled control room to look out for them all, just as Doverley's groundcrew had finished relighting the flare path to beckon them home.

A railway marshalling yard near Milan was the target they'd been given. The squadron, which had left at full strength – twenty-four planes – had been trailed by many hundreds of other crews from around Britain. Their route had taken them across the sea and occupied France, up and over the alpine ranges – where the weather was always unpredictable, and more than cold enough to cause an unlucky plane to ice up and drop from the sky – then on to that yard, which they'd been ordered to obliterate before turning around and doing the entire perilous journey in reverse.

The control room's clock ticked above the doorway.

It was already seven minutes past four, and so far only one of 96's planes had come back: *Lady Lucy* – coded T for Tiger – who, thanks to an electrical fault in their wireless transmitter, had been forced to abandon the mission before they'd reached

France. They'd discharged their bombs into the North Sea, and sent up a flare on approach to Doverley, but, with their broken transmitter, hadn't been able to radio the switchboard for permission to land. Right up until they'd arrived, Iris had hoped that they were *Mabel's Fury*.

But *Mabel's Fury*, like everyone else, was still gone.

And now it was eight minutes past four.

From her seat at the switchboard, Iris stared out into the vast night sky. The moon was still very bright. It angered her that an operation had been ordered in these conditions. No one liked flying on a clear night under a full moon. It made them too easy to spot. She hoped the strategists in Bomber Command were very sure of this railway yard being worth the danger they'd put everyone in.

She dropped her eyes to the glimmering torches. Four ambulances were parked at the head of the main runway, manned and on standby.

Waiting.

To her right sat Clare, headset on, staring out at the night too. Waiting.

Their Supervisor, Sergeant Browning, stood to their left, by a chalkboard bearing the names of all twenty-four planes that had gone up. He had his hands stuffed in his pockets, and his eyes on the sky. Waiting too.

Group Captain Lacey, *Fred*, stood over at the windows, also with his hands in his pockets. Also watching the sky.

Also waiting.

He'd been to Cologne with everyone the night before, but had stayed behind tonight. Robbie – who'd served under him at his previous squadron, back in Kent – had told Iris that he, who could fly when he chose, only ever flew on the most dangerous missions, to keep morale up. He hadn't felt the need to do that tonight. Not to Italy.

145

And now it was nine minutes past four.

No one spoke.

The clock ticked, both too slow, and too fast.

Time was playing its tricks again.

Other than for that ticking, there was no other noise in the room, aside from the odd grunt from Piper, who Sergeant Browning had brought in from the weather, and who was lying at his feet.

Watching the sky.

Waiting.

Just a few hours earlier, the base had been all activity. When Iris and Clare had arrived for their shift, everyone had been preparing to go. The planes had lined the runway perimeter, spilling light from their open bomb bays as ground crew had loaded them up with flares and incendiaries. Fuel trucks had racketed around, screeching alongside the Lancasters, filling the last of their tanks. Engineers had clambered over wings, making final adjustments to propellors and flaps, conducting yelled conversations with their pilots who'd stood beneath them. (And had one of those pilots been Robbie? It had been too dark for Iris to tell.) Over at the parachute store, crews had collected their packs from a WAAF called Lydia Jenkins who'd wished them luck and checked them off on a clipboard.

Iris had met Lydia, and all the rest of Doverley's WAAFs, before she'd left the house earlier. Clare had insisted on dragging her to the basement for dinner ('You need to eat,' she'd said. 'You'll keel over if you're not careful.'), and everyone had been there, picking at portions of stodgy potato pie and over-boiled greens.

Not wanting to keel over, Iris had done her best to force down that pie too whilst she'd made everyone's acquaintance. Prim – who, disappointingly, wasn't actually called Prim, but Eleanor – hadn't said much to her, or anyone, but had sat apart, her hair coiffed in blonde waves, flicking through a copy of *Time* magazine. The rest of them, including Lydia, had been much friendlier. Especially Beth Twinton, who'd given Iris and Clare those teacups in the adjutant's office, and had saved Iris from having to meet Robbie again in front of him.

Already, Iris liked her.

'He'll be all right,' she'd said to Iris with a nudge, as they'd cleared their meal trays into a waiting trolley. 'He has to be. I've got a soft spot for his bomb aimer, Jacob.' She'd pulled a face. 'Clearly, I'm a glutton for difficult men.'

She'd be asleep now, up in the attic.

She'd told Iris she preferred it that way.

'I couldn't bear to be sitting in that tower with you, watching the sky,' she'd said. 'Much better to wake up and find out everything's fine.'

Iris was inclined to agree.

And she was really regretting that potato pie. She could feel it bubbling, lardy and indigestible, in the pit of her stomach.

She, not Clare, had been the one to take charge of take-off earlier. Sergeant Browning – a wiry, moustached Scot in his late forties – had given them the choice, and Iris, knowing Robbie would be listening for her, had quickly volunteered, while Clare had gone off to the breakroom to fetch them all some tea. Unlike the adjutant, Sergeant Browning had worked with female radio operatives before, and (also unlike the adjutant) was very amicable, and grateful to have Iris and Clare's help in the tower. He'd said that he'd been all right until now, with ops so often cancelled for the weather, but there'd still been a lot of practice flights taken, and he'd been worried about how long he could go on managing.

'I'll take this opportunity to put my feet up,' he'd said, smiling, and doing just that as Iris had set to issuing each taxiing plane with their order to take-off, starting with *Mabel's Fury*.

'Hello, Oscar,' she'd said, since that was their code signal: O for Oscar. 'Do you read me? Over.' She'd been addressing Henry, the radio operator, but it hadn't felt like that at all.

'Hello, Tower,' Henry had replied. 'We read you. Awaiting instruction. Over.'

'That's a green for go,' she'd said, just as soon as she'd seen the flash go up. Then, double-checking Sergeant Browning's written instructions, which told her that number one plane was to climb to two thousand feet before taking a route out to the coast over a farm some thirty miles away, she'd issued Henry with that order, too. 'Proceed to angels twenty and vector one ten to Baltimore. Over.'

And, ending the transmission, she'd moved directly on to the next plane, which had been *Bucks Boys* – Q for Queen, that Lewis with the tartan slippers piloted – who were to climb a fraction lower before ascending. 'Hello, Queen,' she'd told them. 'Proceed to angels seventeen, vector one ten to Baltimore, up to angels twenty.' Then, it had been straight on to the next plane.

Then, the next.

By that point, *Mabel's Fury* had been long gone. Neither she, nor Clare, had heard from them again. Unlike several of the other plane's operators, who'd called back to check their instructions, Henry hadn't requested any help. Iris could only hope *Mabel's Fury* hadn't needed it. They were a well-seasoned crew, after all. Tim was an experienced navigator. He'd already directed them through sixty-three missions.

Please let him make it sixty-four, Iris silently entreated the empty sky now. *Please, please, please.*

It was close to twenty past four before the darkness finally fractured with the wing lights of the first returning plane.

'Here we go,' said Fred, raising his binoculars, his voice light with relief. 'They look intact.'

'Hello, Tower,' came a voice through Iris's headphones. A young voice. Elated. Not Henry's. 'Romeo here.'

'*Young Guns* are back,' Iris said to Sergeant Browning, who turned to the chalkboard and ticked them off, whilst Clare issued *Young Guns'* operator with the instruction to land.

'Hello, Romeo. Pancake, over.'

And, as she did, more wing lights appeared, and Fred raised his binoculars again, and another voice that wasn't Henry's sounded in Iris's ears.

'Hello, Tower. Queen here.'

'*Bucks Boys*,' said Clare to Sergeant Browning.

He marked them home, too, and Iris, relieved at least for Lewis and his slippers, gave them the instruction to circle at thirteen hundred feet to await landing. 'Aerodrome thirteen. Over.'

'Hello, Lima,' Clare was already saying to the next arrival, *Night's Knights*. 'Aerodrome fourteen. Over.'

With a roar, *Young Guns* landed, bouncing along the tarmac, so Iris called back to Queen, instructing them to pancake, over, then switched to Lima, telling them to take Queen's place in holding at thirteen hundred feet, whilst Clare asked the next incoming plane to circle at fourteen hundred feet.

And so they went on.

For half an hour, they continued bringing the returning planes safely back down to the ground, whilst Fred kept his vigil at the window, and Browning ticked the names off, one by painstaking one, on his board.

Several of the squadron returned with flak damage. Three radio operatives called in with emergency transmissions that they had wounded men on board, so Browning scrambled the ambulances, who sped those men off to hospital. Fred ran down to see them before they went, and returned with the news that the Luftwaffe, making the most of the full moon, had sent up night fighters to intercept the stream on their way home over France.

'A couple of planes from another squadron bought it,' he said, not without feeling, but also not without that disconcerting pragmatism with which every airman seemed to speak about death. 'I don't know about our blokes.' He returned to the window, raising his binoculars back to his eyes. 'They all got split up.'

By five that morning, they were still missing two planes.

Mabel's Fury was one of them.

Hamps Heroes – V for Verity – was the other.

Don't worry, Robbie had told Iris, back in the woods.

But she was worried.

Her stomach was by now liquid with terror; her ears felt ready to burn with the strain of listening to her silent headphones.

Hamps Heroes were newcomers, like herself and Clare. They'd arrived just that morning, sent to replace the only crew that hadn't come back from Cologne the night before. According to Browning, that crew had flown under V for Verity too.

Iris had never used to be superstitious, but this war had changed that for her. Back in Norwich, P for Peter had been the code letter everyone had feared. Any plane given it had lasted one, at the most two, operations. Eventually, the station commander had struck it from use. It had been the same with one of the billets. For a spell, no one had slept in it for longer than a week before disappearing.

Was V for Verity to be the same?

Please not, she silently entreated the empty search beams roving the sky. *Please let them come back.*

Please let him.

And, as though in answer, the static in her ears fractured, sending her heart into her throat.

Clenching her shaking hands into fists, she waited for a voice.

From beside her, Clare reached out, touching her wrist in a gesture of solidarity. Iris knew how hard she must be thinking about Hans – whether he'd been piloting one of the fighters that had sent those two planes down – but didn't for a moment doubt that she was rooting for Robbie and the rest of them, too.

The static cleared, and the radio operator spoke.

'Hello, Tower, Verity here.' He sounded ecstatic. Jubilant.

And why shouldn't he be?

Iris didn't begrudge him it.

But nor could she bring herself to answer him.

'Hello, Verity,' said Clare, doing it for her. 'Pancake, over.'

And Browning marked them off on his board, too.

He didn't smile.

Nor did Fred at the window.

Not with *Mabel's Fury* still missing.

Clare removed her headphones. She hardly needed it explained to her that, if another call did come, Iris would be the one to take it.

A minute passed.

Then another.

It was somehow ten past five.

'We'd better get down to interrogation,' Browning said to Clare, heading for the door, beckoning Piper with him, but leaving Iris where she was.

'Keep the faith,' Clare whispered to her, before she went.

Fred didn't leave with them.

He remained with Iris.

Waiting again.

He was married, Robbie had told Iris. His wife, Miriam, had moved to Heaton when Fred had been stationed here. They had a baby daughter called Margaret.

I've told him about you, Robbie had said. *I told him months ago, back in Kent. I wanted to. You've always been the person in my life I'm most proud of having.*

Iris watched Fred's frown as he looked down at his watch, then checked it against the clock.

'Let's give it another five minutes, shall we?' he said to her.

'Yes, sir,' she agreed, her voice hollow to her own ears. 'Let's.'

They waited nine.

And, at precisely twenty-five minutes and thirty-two seconds past five, the switchboard flickered, Iris's headset crackled, and, in the sky, distant wing lights appeared, blinking into view.

'Hello, Tower,' came Henry's voice. 'Oscar here, over.'

'Hello, Oscar,' Iris said, and it wasn't just her hands that trembled any more. Her entire body did. 'You took your time.'

'Rob made us stop for ice cream. Over.'

She laughed, then nearly cried.

She'd been so scared.

'In fact,' Henry said, 'we had to escort another plane home. Someone got angry with them. We're quite low on fuel so would like a pancake please.'

'Pancake,' she said. 'Absolutely pancake. Over.'

Exhaling a shuddering breath, she leant back in her chair, and, fumblingly, removed her headset.

Then, looking up, she caught the expression on Fred's face.

'Absolutely pancake?' he said.

'Sorry.'

'You know, I suppose, that the airwaves are meant to be kept as clear as possible?'

'I'm sorry,' she repeated.

152

But she knew he wasn't annoyed.

He was smiling.

He turned back to the window, watching them come in, and she followed his stare.

Their wing lights were getting bigger now. Lower. The morning was still like night, the sun wouldn't lighten the horizon for another hour, but they'd be here to see it when it broke.

They were home.

'Might I ask a favour?' said Fred.

'Of course,' she said, not lifting her eyes from *Mabel's Fury*, landing now, without a bounce.

'That lot –' he nodded at them, speeding to a stop on the runway – 'are a shade late for interrogation, and so am I.' Leaving his post at the window, he moved to the door. 'You wouldn't run out to them, would you? Hurry them along?'

She looked at him, wondering if she'd heard him right.

On-duty WAAFs weren't meant to go racing out to the runway to welcome crews home.

It wasn't *done*.

But Fred's lips twitched in another smile.

'Go on,' he said, 'that's an order. Best not mention it to Ambrose. He's a stickler.'

'Thank you,' she said, pushing herself to her feet. 'Thank you so much.'

They didn't have long together.

And they weren't alone.

When she caught up to him – crossing the meadow's frosted grass as the runway flares were extinguished – he was surrounded by his crew, the seven of them already making their way to the motor waiting to take them to interrogation, their parachutes slung on their shoulders. They of course hadn't needed any hurrying along.

153

'Iris Winterton,' called Tim. 'Just look at you, all grown up, and still doing what you shouldn't.'

'I'm not doing what I shouldn't,' she called back, laughing, because he – tall and boyishly handsome, in the way he'd always had in him – had grown up too. And it was so very, very good to see him again. After all these years. *Safe.* 'I was sent.'

'By Fred?' said Robbie, coming to a halt before her.

In touching distance.

Meeting his blue gaze, she nodded.

'I've a present for you,' said Tim, tossing her something small and round.

She caught it, then laughed more, seeing it was a boiled sweet.

'From your mum?' she asked.

'From me,' he said. 'It felt like a lucky charm in my pocket, knowing I'd be back here, giving it to you.'

'Are you absolutely pancake?' asked another, older man, joining them. She placed him instantly as Henry from his gritty voice.

'I'm afraid so,' she said, with a grimace.

'Don't be afraid about it,' he said. 'You made my night.'

And, with a chuckle, he walked on, trailing the flight engineer, gunners, and Jacob, who, casting Iris a weary smile, waved Robbie and Tim onwards.

'Come on,' he said. 'I want to make sure they know that yard's no more. I don't really fancy getting sent back there again tonight.' He glanced up at the moon. 'I don't fancy getting sent anywhere. Maybe you could get your uncle on the blower, Tim. Remind him that it's not actually much fun flying in a plane with a torch shining on you.'

'Don't worry,' said Tim. 'I intend to.' Then, with a salute to Iris, and a last look from her, to Robbie, he went.

Robbie remained where he was.

'Are you all right?' he asked Iris.

'Am I all right?' She shook her head. 'Are *you*?'

'I'm fine.' He stood very still, seemingly fighting the urge to move closer to her. 'We were attacked, but they didn't get us. We couldn't leave the other plane, though, in case they had to bail out, or were attacked again.' His face, all in shadow, moved in a frown. 'It's been a long night.'

'It has,' she agreed. 'When was the last time you slept?'

'I don't know . . . '

'You should sleep. You need to sleep.'

'I'm sure you do, too.'

'Yes.' She didn't want to sleep, though.

Nor did he.

'Will you meet me back at the cottage?' he said. 'After interrogation.'

'Yes,' she said, without consideration.

'Good.' He smiled. 'Straight there?'

'Straight there,' she agreed.

'All right,' he said, 'See you then.' He set off to join the others, but walked backwards, still looking at her. 'Who knows,' his smile grew, becoming a grin, 'maybe we'll do something stupid.'

*

But they didn't do something stupid.

What happened between them, a little under a half hour later – after he'd given his report to intelligence, and she'd been dismissed by Browning – felt, to Iris, the least stupid thing possible.

She'd done plenty of thinking over the course of the night she'd just spent, waiting for him to come home. In her fear

155

that he mightn't, it had struck her just how easily this gift that the two of them had been given of finding one another again, might be snatched away, in this world run amok, where minutes might bend, and seconds might stretch, but they nonetheless always passed.

I don't want us to waste any time, Robbie had said to her yesterday.

I don't want to waste it either, she'd told him.

She'd meant it.

She'd been determined about it.

But she was even more determined now.

So was he.

He was already waiting for her when she reached the cottage, standing at the gate, still in his flight gear.

She was still in the uniform she'd worn all night.

They didn't say hello to one another.

They didn't again mention how tired the other must be.

They didn't speak at all.

Iris simply went to him, and he reached out to her.

Looking into her eyes, he pulled her close, and, touching at last, she leant into him, resting her head for a moment against the beat of his pummelling heart.

Then she moved, raising her face to his, looking into his intent stare.

A light wind rustled, shivering through the trees.

High above, a formation of fighters soared, soundlessly.

From closer to earth came that goshawk's call.

At the sound, she watched his expression move in recollection.

Get out of there this instant, Lord Heaton had shouted at them, almost a decade before, interrupting their almost kiss.

No one shouted now.

No one interrupted.

156

He dipped his head in the same moment that she reached up to him.

As their lips touched, the hawk called again.

But neither of them were listening.

Not any more.

They were too wrapped up in one another.

Not doing something stupid.

A STRAINED START FOR
THE BOMBER GIRLS

Doverley House has felt frustratingly reminiscent of Soviet Russia pre-glasnost this past week, with its iron gates heavily secured, and all cast and crew prohibited from giving unauthorised interviews. And – spoiler alert – no interviews have been authorised.

We at The Screen *know that this kind of radio silence tends to mean someone's trying to keep something from getting out, and we love nothing more than ferreting out what that something is. So, we've been doing lots of digging (you're welcome), and can now disclose that Doverley has been proving almost as cursed for Emma Jameson as it was for ill-fated Clare Holmes, who Emma is playing. According to our new inside source – who wishes to remain anonymous – Emma has been down and out with severe food poisoning most of the week, causing massive scheduling headaches, and budget spikes. Without giving anything away to those of you who haven't yet read the book (and again, who even are you?), Emma hasn't been contracted for the same length of time that Claudia and her bomber boys have.*

'The original plan was to frontload Emma's scenes, then free her up,' our source said, 'but that's fallen by the wayside. It will be a major concern for the studio, who are already worried about the huge costs involved with this production. Ana (Ashley) didn't want them panicking, so has been trying to keep it under wraps.'

Whoops!

Emma is at least on the mend now, as you can see from these aerial shots of her and Claudia Baxter out and about in uniform yesterday, accompanied by the dog who's been cast as Piper. (A groodle. We'll allow it.) They've reportedly put a whole stack of overtime in, playing catch-up, and their first scenes together have been shot without a hitch.

'Ana's got us all under the pump,' said our source, 'but the results are speaking for themselves. This thing is going to blow everyone away. I was sceptical about Nick (Turner) at first. His casting with Claudia felt like a publicity stunt. But he's something else, and so's Claudia. It's a bit disturbing, watching her work. It's as though she disappears.'

She's apparently been disappearing plenty off-set, too, taking herself on long solitary walks in the woods.

'They're clearly not doing her any good,' said our source. 'She seems more fragile by the day. Like with one nudge, she'd shatter.'

We can only hope that she hasn't shattered, given the media storm that's just broken, in which many less scrupulous sites than ours have printed extracts from leaked clinical documents confirming that her long-rumoured pregnancy last year was not only real, but ended tragically in a late miscarriage. And if you're hoping for more intel on that here, we're happy to disappoint you. That kind of thing's not our jam.

And to anyone reading this who's got themselves involved in the speculation over whether Felix Jade rather than Nick Turner was the real baby daddy, shame on you.

There's a line, people.

Chapter Twelve

Claudia

9 November 2018

Day 7 of the shoot: the first day off

Nick's gone absolutely ballistic.

Ana's gone ballistic.

Felix has too.

But Nick . . .

I've never seen him this angry. Not even during our worst rows last year.

It's just gone ten on Friday morning, a week to the day since we started shooting, and everyone is meant to be taking a breath before we dive back into another six-day run of filming tomorrow. I should be sleeping. I haven't managed a decent night of it since the one I spent up in Iris's room. Each time I've climbed into my and Nick's bed, I've felt like I'm heading into battle against my own insomnia, and the more tired I've grown, the more intimidating that battle has turned, whilst my mind – my unruly, wild mind – has become increasingly uncontrollable, the less sleep I've got. And I really don't want to dwell on how deeply unhinged I by now feel, so I'd be glad to have this excuse not to, if everything happening wasn't such an utter, sickening nightmare.

It was yesterday lunchtime, first thing LA time, whilst Emma and I were on the control tower soundstage shooting

Iris and Clare's first shift, waiting for *Mabel's Fury* to return from Italy, that the tabloids started going live with the clinic's leaked files. In fairness, there's been plenty of disgust directed at those tabloids since – with journalists from the BBC, to Sky News, to the Associated Press, issuing statements condemning the publication of such private details, right down to my son's weight – but none of that can change the fact that the worst loss of my life has been laid bare for the world to see. Extracts of my records have been dissected all over social media (*what the hell's a misshapen uterus?*), whilst scores of polls have sprung up on Twitter, with users across the globe voting on whether Nick or Felix was really the father, and who, out of the two of them, might have made the cuter kid.

Nick spent most of last night on the phone to his lawyers in LA, who are even now building a case against the clinic for gross negligence. His parents have kept trying to call him from Montana, but he's refusing to pick up to them.

'Not until I've got something useful to say,' he's told me, but I don't think he's waiting for that at all.

I *think* he's terrified that if he talks to them and lets their concern in, for even a moment, he'll break down. Because incensed as I don't doubt he is about the clinic's leak, I know he has also, without question, been crushed by the suggestion that anyone but him could have been our tiny little boy's daddy. I'm crushed by that.

I've gone ballistic about that.

It's what I've been on the phone to *my* lawyers about: getting all those hideous polls, and their accompanying comments, taken down.

'So, you're fighting each other's battles, keeping yourselves from thinking about your own,' said Mum to me on the phone yesterday evening. Unlike Nick's parents, she's within driving distance, so I had to pick up to her. She'd only have descended on me here otherwise, probably bringing Phil and my sisters with her. The three of them have all called too, Phil petrifying me by saying how much he wants to get commenting himself, remind everyone that Nick and I are both human beings with human hearts. ('Under no circumstances do that,' I told him. 'You'll only give them more ammunition. And we're not human, not to them. You know that.')

'Does anyone know who's behind this leak?' Mum asked me.

'Apparently not,' I said. 'They're not even sure it was someone inside the clinic. It could have been a hack . . . '

'Well, that would certainly be convenient for the clinic. No blame on them that way. I hope your OB's apologised.'

'Of course she has.' Fiona called me within minutes of the first headline hitting. I was oblivious, filming. Everyone on set was oblivious. Nick, who arrived looking grim, was the one who asked Ana to call a break and took me aside, behind the cameras and lights, breaking to me what was unfolding.

'I'm so sorry, Claude,' he said, and didn't hug me, even though it felt, in that moment like it was all either of us were thinking about him doing. There were so many people there, though, most of them with their phones out, catching up on the news, glancing our way. Their attention made me think of Imogen's note at the end of *The Bomber Boys*, about Iris and Robbie's relationship. *As with all great love affairs, theirs largely played out in private.* How nice that must have been for them.

'I'm sorry too,' I told Nick, but I spoke numbly, still not really feeling . . . anything.

I didn't *want* to feel.

I realise now that that's why I insisted to Ana and Emma that we continue working.

'Are you sure?' said Ana, when, turning from Nick, I called out to her that we should carry on.

'I'm sure,' I said, making for the stage.

'You don't have to do this,' said Emma, joining me. Unlike Nick, she did reach out, laying her hand on my arm. Her touch was gentle, her round eyes full of compassion. All of a sudden, I felt my own burn. It was like her sympathy resensitised me, because in a rush, the full enormity of what had happened started to hit me.

I couldn't let it in.

'I do have to do this,' I told Emma, my voice swollen with the pressure of my mounting tears. 'I can't face being me.'

'What about Nick?' she said, looking over at him, making for the exit with his head bowed, avoiding everyone's stare.

It was even harder not to cry, watching him go.

'What about him?' I said, averting my eyes.

'I think he might need you to be you.'

'I can't,' I repeated, hating myself for how selfish I was being, yet unable to help it. The temptation to retreat back into Iris was too strong. 'Please, can we just get going?'

She hesitated.

'Please, Emma . . . '

'All right,' she said, with a slow nod. 'If it's really what you want.'

'It's really what I want.'

'Ok.' She squeezed my arm. 'So, let's go.'

And we went.

I went.

It's as though she disappears, that source who spoke to *The Screen* said.

That's not what happens, though.

I don't disappear – how could I? – but I do feel myself slipping, more completely every day, from the realms of my

163

own grief-weary consciousness. When Emma and I were filming yesterday – adjusting our headphones, issuing instructions (*absolutely pancake;* I love that line) – I remained aware of the cameras and crew and bluescreens, of course I did, but I didn't focus on them. I looked through them, at memories that *can't* be memories, of a slowly ticking clock, static in my ears, and an endless night that was dark and frozen and lit by a full moon. Those memories, or illusions, or whatever they were, are with me still now, nestled in my mind's eye: yet another layer of lunacy in my teetering stack. And that source was right about it being disturbing. It's got so there are times that I don't feel so much that I'm breaking down, as breaking apart. And I haven't even told anyone, which is making me feel madder yet. But I can't talk about it. I *can't.* I'm still clinging to the hope that it will all somehow stop.

Except yesterday, I chased the madness, for as long as I could, because as much as it frightened me, the idea of returning to the present scared me even more.

I had to come back to the here and now at some point though, and when I did, I went straight to my trailer. I'm honestly not sure how long I stayed there, shaking, crying, googling stress-induced hallucinations – and, before I could stop myself, my miscarriage. But eventually I got a hold of myself enough to return Fiona's call. I had to talk to her. She was incredibly kind to me when it all happened, and very upset on the phone.

'In pieces, actually,' I told Mum.

'Probably worried about what this will do to her reputation.'

'Fiona's not like that.' She wasn't. I've been in this business long enough to know when someone's being genuine, and Fiona's guilt felt raw and sincere. 'I don't actually want to sue the clinic. She's the one who'll pay, and it's not her fault.'

'The clinic will have insurance,' Mum said witheringly. 'Don't worry about them. Worry about you. And Nick.' She paused: frowning, I could tell. 'I wasn't trying to say that you *shouldn't* worry about him before. That boy's as lost as you.'

'He's a thirty-five-year-old man, Mum,' I said, but with a sigh, because I knew she was right.

He's been lost since his hopeless race to get from New York to LA in time to be by my side in the delivery room.

I've never properly faced up to that before now. I knew he was sad, of course I did. If he hadn't been, he'd never have spent all those nights trying to escape his feelings in bars, or by going to the lengths he did to prepare for this movie. But I realise now I haven't let myself absorb just how broken he's been. I don't know why it's taken all this time, and all of this hideousness, for me to finally do that. Maybe I was too angry before – that old crutch I've been using of fury in place of grief. Or perhaps I was just too scared of how much it would hurt to feel Nick's pain as well as my own.

It's hurting me now, doing that.

It's hurting very much.

And the worse I hurt, the guiltier I feel, because no matter what he, or Fiona, or Mum might say about none of this being my fault, it was in my body that it all happened.

'Be kind to yourself,' Mum said to me, before she hung up. 'No more of these lone walks in the woods, please. And don't forget that the hateful voices might be loud, but it's the kind ones that are strong. There's much more goodness in this world than bad, Claude, I promise.'

Is she right?

It hasn't felt much like it, these past twenty-four hours.

'Don't look,' I kept telling Nick, every time he picked up his phone to track the latest on Twitter.

'I'm not looking,' he kept replying, throwing his phone aside. For five minutes.

I look across at him now, in his twenty-first century uniform of jeans and a loose jumper, and, seeing the defensive way he's standing in the doorway of Doverley's library – his arms folded, his face set – once again ache for him. Twitter did take that grim cuteness poll down in the end, but not before it had notched up several million votes: 48% to him, 48% to Felix. 4% 'on the fence'.

'You're the only one whose child I've ever wanted,' I choked out to him at some point between sunset and sunrise last night. We weren't in bed, but slumped on the floor at the foot of it, our phones in our laps, our heads tipped back against the mattress.

He turned, looking at me.

'You're the only one whose child *I've* ever wanted,' he said.

But I can't give you one, I thought, but couldn't bring myself to say. Not that.

Not again.

I've said it more than enough.

Just as he's tried to convince me it doesn't matter to him.

I can't be convinced, though.

I won't be.

Never have I felt surer of that than I do now, seeing – properly *seeing* – his pain.

Honestly, I don't think he'll ever be convinced, either.

So where does that leave us?

The question is too huge, and too awful, to think about, so I park it, and move my attention from Nick to Felix, who's standing beside him, also with his arms folded, and also scowling. None of us want to be here for this emergency meeting that Blake, the movie's head publicist, has called, and Felix, unshaven and rumpled, is making no secret of it.

166

I don't think he can have slept much last night either. He posted on his own Twitter feed at 3 a.m.

Claudia and Nick are my friends and two of the best people I know. They've been through enough, so please leave them alone and stop this abhorrent intrusion on their privacy.

He got a lot of likes.

He's still getting them.

That poll still notched up more votes though.

I catch his eye, and, fleetingly, his face softens in a smile.

He finally replied to my apology text on Monday, the morning after Nick and I reshot Iris and Robbie's reunion.

I miss you too, he said, filling me with relief. *I've written this message about five thousand times already, with too many words, when only a few are needed. So I'll cut to the chase. I'm sorry as well. You deserved a more understanding friend than you got. I guess we're both idiots.*

I'm the bigger one, I typed back.

No, he replied. *You don't get to call that.*

Things aren't completely back to normal between us. There's this lingering strain we can't seem to shake, no matter how many times I drop by his trailer to say hi, or we attempt to chat like we used to between takes. But his smile now means a lot.

His Tweet last night did.

In the midst of all this, it really does matter, knowing that he's back on my side. *In my corner.*

Other than him, Nick and me, there's just Blake and Emma here for this meeting. Emma's beside me on a sofa by the cold fireplace. Opposite us, Blake's in an armchair, his laptop open before him.

You wouldn't know, looking around the library now, that it's been used as a set this past week. All the rigs have been taken away, the windows have been stripped of blast-proof tape, the officers' bar has been dismantled, and the notice boards – variously adorned with propaganda about careless talk costing lives, and advertisements for local dances – have been removed. There'll be no more filming here. Thanks to Emma's food poisoning, all the mess scenes, *male* scenes, have now been shot. Another air sequence is in the can, too. There are plenty more to go – not least the boys' final flight – but nonetheless, Nick, Felix and the rest of their crew have spent hours on *Mabel's Fury*'s cutaway, re-enacting the fear and devastation that was life for Robbie, and Tim, and tens of thousands of other World War Two bomber boys, night after night after night.

The intensity of the flight filming has shaken Nick, I can tell. It's got under the skin of everyone involved, I think. I have now tried to watch some of it myself, but couldn't. It was too upsetting. And of course I realise that none of it was actually real. I do *know* that we're all of us actors, playing at war from within this safe, secure pocket of our increasingly volatile world. But this war that we're playing at wasn't a game, it wasn't a movie. It was a tragedy, of unfathomable proportions, and the more time I spend immersed in recreating it, the more overcome I feel by how much was given, and how much was lost. That was real.

It *is* real, and it's breaking my heart.

I shift in my seat, and Emma turns, giving me a wan smile. She's still very pale, and is obviously far from being back to 100%, despite the long hours she's championed through since returning to work (and, probably, because of them), which only makes me more thankful for the way she kept filming yesterday. Not that you'd have guessed she was struggling. She gave everything, and was so compelling that, at times, I forgot who she was, too.

That's happened quite a bit this week. In spite of everything, I really have liked that part of things: being with Clare when the cameras are rolling, finding Emma again on the cuts. And between us, we've got a lot done. On top of our first shift, we've also now shot our arrival in our recreated bedroom, cracking Clare's *medicinal brandy*; after that, we filmed a blustery walk with Rusty (which *The Screen* printed its photo of); then, a montage sequence in the WAAF's dining room, along with a handful of extras – none of them named, since the screenplay, like Imogen's novel, leaves the other WAAFs at Doverley very much in the background.

'Maybe I'd have done it differently if I could have interviewed one of them,' Imogen's said to me, 'but all those I found records for were already gone. I think the others must be, too. I'm sure they would have come forward by now if they were still alive.'

Sadly, I think she's probably right.

She texted me last night, saying she was thinking of me. I replied, saying how much I appreciated it, and – realising she probably wasn't having the best day herself, given *The Screen*'s article was followed by scores of others catastrophizing about the likely fate of this movie – hypocritically advised her to stay offline.

It's all just clickbait. We're on track.

It wasn't a lie. Although very little has happened when it should have – and we've still done no night shooting at all – we've got close to one quarter of the scenes scheduled for this Doverley part of the shoot finished.

No one's exhaling, though. We won't until it's over. And for the present, the reason that Nick, Felix, Emma and I are all here in the library with Blake is because Blake emailed us first thing – subject header: Damage Control – saying he needs our help.

169

Ana was copied on the email too, but hasn't come along. I assume she's busy with Naomi and Jeff, the three of them doing some damage control of their own. The studio execs are, unsurprisingly, none too happy about *The Screen*'s outing of Emma's food poisoning, and have hauled Ana over the coals for keeping it from them. She, being Ana, didn't seem particularly fazed when she called by my and Nick's room earlier, checking on how we were, but nor was she thrilled about the studio's demand that she send them the raw footage of everything we've so far filmed, plus the new schedule for approval, and forecasted overspend, given the extension of Emma's contract and everyone else's overtime.

'They'll calm down once they've taken a breath,' Ana said. 'And I've convinced them we don't need to replace Emma. Now we just need to make sure no one gives them anything else to freak out about. God –' she gave a hollow laugh – 'I'd love to know who this anonymous source is that spoke to *The Screen*.'

'My money's on Blake,' said Nick.

'So's mine,' said Emma, when we ran into her and Felix on our way here.

And so, in fact, is mine.

It was that bit about this movie blowing everyone away. What publicist wouldn't want that in the press?

'Sceptical about me, were you?' Nick says to Blake now.

'Did you want to get me fired?' demands Emma.

'No,' says Blake, removing his horn-rimmed glasses and rubbing his eyes. I guess he hasn't slept much either. 'And I've never been sceptical about you, Nick. I'm not the source. It's like I keep saying, that's not how I work. And think about it, why would I tell *The Screen* that your casting, or anything come to that, is a publicity stunt?'

'To bury the lead?'

'I didn't do it, Nick. I don't know what else to say.'

'How about filling us in on what you need our help with?' suggests Felix.

So, Blake does, beginning with his concern that the public might be starting to lose faith in this movie, no matter what *The Screen*'s anonymous source might have said about how great it's shaping up to be. 'A lot of the commentary since hasn't even mentioned that, and we're running a real risk of being written off before we've hit the screens.' He gives us a, *can you imagine*, look. 'People who aren't excited don't buy movie tickets, and right now, what's anyone got to be excited about? We've got a director who's been accused of trickery, and a lead actress who's rumoured to be on the edge of a mental health episode.' He throws me a grimace. 'Sorry to be brutal, Claudia, but I have to say it like it is.'

'Do you, though?' asks Nick.

'It's ok,' I say.

'No, it's not,' says Nick.

Which it isn't, of course.

'Added to that,' Blake continues, regardless, 'everyone's just waiting for the news to break that the three of you,' he raises his hand, gesturing at first Nick, then Felix, then me, 'have come to blows and walked away. And as for you,' he turns to Emma, '*you* need to convince everyone that you're up to this. Ana might have talked the studio around for now, but we all know these things can turn on a dime.'

'But I am up to this,' Emma says, with unveiled irritation, for which I really don't blame her.

'Blake,' I say, 'she has, quite literally, *been* up to this.'

'People need to see that though.'

'*The Screen* published that photo of us . . . '

171

'We need to show them more.'

'What?' asks Emma.

'Lunch,' he says. 'I've booked you all in today at The Heaton Arms. Robbie's old house.'

'I don't want to do that,' I say, for a hundred reasons, not least that I still haven't actually *been* to Heaton. Loath as I was to do that for the first time in costume, about to shoot, I'm even more reluctant to do it now for some forced show of camaraderie, knowing that everyone there will most likely be thinking about how I had an epidural at 4cm dilated, and that my son never grew heavier than 318g.

'It will be all right,' says Blake.

'You're only saying that because you don't have to do it,' says Felix, and again, I'm grateful to him.

Grateful to Nick, who, turning to go, instructs Blake to think of some other way to control this damage.

'No,' says Blake, stopping Nick short.

'No?' says Nick, raising his brow.

'*No?*' says Felix.

'Wow,' says Emma.

'This has to happen,' says Blake, and, in another set of circumstances, I might almost admire his nerve, holding his ground against our collective front. 'You need to be at The Heaton Arms for twelve. They're excited. There'll be a bunch of photographers there to catch you going in and out. Ones we can trust. A few others will probably turn up, too.'

'A few?' says Nick. 'Come on, Blake. We all know it'll be a circus.'

'It won't,' Blake insists. 'I'm managing it.'

'*How?*' says Nick.

'I'm not going,' I say. 'Absolutely not.'

'You need to, Claudia,' says Blake. 'I don't want to play this card . . . '

'Then don't.'

'But contractually . . . '

'Seriously, Blake?'

'For Christ's sake,' says Nick. 'You don't think she's been through enough?'

'Of course I do,' says Blake. 'But contractually, you all have to do publicity that's deemed in the best interests of the movie. And I very much consider the world holding faith that the four of you aren't about to keel over or combust as being in the best interests of this movie. *The Screen* called me this morning asking for a comment on whether there's anything behind the rumours that the studio are about to call it all off. I told them no, obviously, but those rumours are coming from somewhere. Where there's smoke . . . '

'I still don't see why I have to have lunch,' says Emma. 'I could just go for a walk, take Rusty again. Do anything, actually, that doesn't involve eating.'

'No, you need to be there,' says Blake. 'It will look too staged if it's only Nick, Felix and Claudia.'

'That's not what's going to make it look staged,' says Nick.

'And,' says Blake, ignoring him, 'we want everyone to see you enjoying your lunch, Emma.'

'Well, that's not going to happen,' she says.

'You can pull it off,' Blake says. 'How many Oscars do you have?'

'Just the one.'

'Wouldn't you like to make it two?'

'Frankly, I'm more interested in spending today horizontal.'

'You can spend this afternoon horizontal,' Blake says. 'Just have lunch first. Maybe a quick chat with the locals. Don't worry, I'm sure there won't be a horde. A handful probably, out and about.'

I sit up straighter at this mention of Heaton's locals.

It's not the first time I've worried about them.

I've been anxious for a while that someone might be waiting to come forward and put it out that I was born nearby. Mum's been concerned about it, too. Neither of us want my grandparents' deaths splashed over the newspapers. So far, it's remained quiet. If anyone in Heaton has remembered that John and Belinda Cuthbert, killed in 1989, had a granddaughter called Claudia – who took the surname Baxter when, in 1999, her mum married her new stepfather, Phil, and he enquired whether she might consider letting him adopt her – they've either been too discreet, or too disinterested, to say anything about it. Up until now, I've been hoping that that will remain the case. But this past couple of days has been a rude reminder of just how deeply, and unscrupulously, some people are willing to dig for the sake of a prime position on the news cycle.

Ana's the only person on the movie, besides Nick, who knows about my roots here. Before all of this mess started, both she and Nick advised me to confide everything in Blake too, so that if there were any warning signs of it all coming out, he'd know enough to spot them and get ahead of the story. Bury it, if possible.

I've kept brushing them off, insisting there was no need for me to tell Blake anything.

'It's fine,' I've said, because I've wanted it to be.

But it's not fine.

Nothing is.

And I really don't want it to all get worse.

So, 'Blake,' I say, 'there's something I should mention,' and, before I can think better of it, I fill him in, as sparingly as possible, on the fact that I was born in the self-same postcode as Iris Winterton, in 1985, sixty-seven years after Iris herself was born in 1918, and forty-two years after she disappeared in 1943. Not only that, but my grandmother – originally from Heaton herself, and very much alive in the war – might, quite feasibly, have met Iris. And Robbie. And Tim.

For several seconds, Blake says nothing. Just gives me this blank stare.

Emma and Felix both stare too, similarly shocked.

Nick, meanwhile, doesn't so much stare at me, as look, *see*, with his eyes that, free of make-up's interventions, once again belong purely to him.

I try to read his expression, but can't settle on whether it's one of sadness, or sympathy, or even, maybe – perhaps – that love I really do wish I could believe he not only still feels, but feels in a way that's enough, given it's all I can give him.

'Are you kidding me, Claudia?' says Blake, rediscovering his voice. 'You really didn't think it might have been useful to mention this before? It's incredible. You and Iris probably went to the same school.'

'I didn't go to school here,' I say, pulling my gaze from Nick's. 'I was too young. Even if I had, it wouldn't have been to Iris's. You know that.' We *all* know Iris's school was closed years ago, and the building turned into a bank. It's one of the reasons the movie will have to shift locations in the new year, when the little people playing Iris, Robbie and Tim as children will run in and out of an old schoolhouse in Derbyshire, where there's no ATM at the front. It irks me that Blake's forgotten that.

Clearly, he's got himself way too excited.

'I don't want this getting out,' I insist to him.

'But . . . '

'No,' I say. 'My grandparents were killed before they were sixty. My mum can hardly bring herself to speak about them, to this day. I *cannot* have that all over the press. Mum's never signed up for that.'

'We could make sure it's handled sensitively—'

'No, Blake.'

'You could even write a piece—'

'No.'

'Or we could arrange an interview, with someone great—'

'*No.*' The word cracks. But I've had enough.

I am *done* with my personal life being treated like a commodity.

'All right,' says Blake, with a put-upon sigh. 'If you're not comfortable with it, then of course we'll keep it under wraps. But you still should have told me.'

'I thought you'd try to use it.'

'You've asked me not to.'

'I still thought you'd do it.'

'God –' he gives me, then the others, an appalled frown – 'what kind of monster do you all think I am?'

*

Monstrously, he insists we walk the nearly three miles to the pub, even Emma. It will look more spontaneous, he says, than us turfing up in a car. He does, however, agree to send a driver to fetch us after our lunch.

'No later than half one,' I tell him.

'Why the hard stop?' he asks. 'Have you got something on?'

'Nothing you need to know about,' I say, which it isn't.

I've given my word to Roger Westin, the head of Tim Hobbs's nursing home, that I won't risk anyone from the press getting wind of my appointment to visit Tim this afternoon.

But Tim has agreed to it.

Apparently, he *wants* to meet me.

'He's a huge fan,' said Roger, when we spoke on the phone, back on Monday.

It was Imogen who gave me his number. I could easily have found it online, but I didn't want to approach him behind her back. She's been so open with me, it would have felt wrong, keeping this from her. And, to my relief, when I told her how desperate I've become to get to the bottom of what really happened the night *Mabel's Fury* disappeared, she wasn't remotely put out.

'I wish you better luck than me,' she said. 'Just don't expect too much of Tim. It's been a while since I last saw him, but like I've said, even then, his memories had grown very confused.'

'He does have a favour to ask,' Roger told me, on the phone. 'He'd like you to bring Felix and Nick with you, if you can. He's intrigued to shake the hands of the men who'll be immortalizing him and Robbie.'

'Of course,' I said, since how could I have turned down a request like that?

They were both pretty pumped, when I invited them along. And, actually, I'm glad that they're coming. I'm glad Nick is. I don't want this to be another secret between us. I've been letting far too many of those build up.

Plus, with everything else going on, I couldn't bear to leave him alone again. Not like I did yesterday.

I don't want to be alone.

But I am getting fairly keyed up myself about seeing Tim.

Don't expect too much, Imogen told me.

I'm not expecting anything.

Yes, as I set off with Nick, Emma, and Felix for Heaton – the four of us wrapped up against the frozen weather in coats, scarves and hats – I think about Tim, waiting in his home, and feel a surge of anticipation.

Because he knew Robbie and Iris. He was a child with

them. He fought with them. He *lived* with them. He talked and laughed and, almost certainly, loved with them. He used to look them in the eye, every single day, and now I'm going to look into his, and perhaps, *maybe*, discover something new.

But first, I've got to get through this damn lunch.

Chapter Thirteen

We're quiet as we progress up the driveway, Nick, Felix and I matching our pace to Emma's, all of us preoccupied with our thoughts.

It's a clear morning, with a glaring winter sun that bounces off the deep frost that's set in overnight, icing the surrounding meadows with white. The sheep, clustered together for warmth, are motionless. Everything feels very still. Not even a breath of a breeze disrupts the frigid air, and the cold feels like a solid, immovable thing.

Emma's brought a KeepCup of herbal tea with her. I eye her, resting her lips on the rim, breathing in the steam that rises over her face, and feel really angry that Blake's insisted she do this. But then I guess we've all been forced through worse in our time. Much worse. And Emma's tough. Far tougher than I suspect a lot of people give her credit for, with her doll-like appearance and track record of playing the nice girl.

She started out in this business as a Disney Mouseketeer, and already had three movies under her belt by the time Felix and I met on *The Go-Between*: teen romances, which she made into box office smashes, playing the pretty, ditzy heroine. That's not easy work, not at all – I've personally tried and failed at it – but I can see how it could get old, when you're doing it on repeat.

'Which I of course did for the best part of fifteen years,' Emma said to me, back in September, when we were getting to know one another during rehearsals. 'I wanted to change things up, so bad, but my agent kept telling me I needed to stay in lane, be grateful I was still getting cast. You know, *at my age*.'

He apparently blew up last year when she changed lane anyway, accepting a part Ana referred her for, playing one of five people left on earth in a dark dystopian love story.

'Career suicide, apparently,' she said.

It was that movie, though, that she won her Oscar for, as best actress in a supporting role.

And Imogen saw it, loved it, and went straight to the casting team for this one, strongly suggesting they consider Emma for Clare. ('That's a hill I was willing to die on,' she's told me. 'Just as you had to be Iris, Emma had to be Clare.') Emma's agent was happier about that. The buzz around this adaptation was at fever-pitch, even then.

He's less happy now, however.

Emma told me earlier that he called last night, having spoken to the studio, and suggested she ease their cost concerns by reducing her fee.

'He said it would be a nice gesture,' she said. '*Nice*. Like I care about any of them thinking that way about me. I asked him if he's ever asked one of his male clients to make a nice gesture like that, and he got all indignant, so now I guess I really do have to find a new agent.' She shrugged. 'Whatever. It's overdue.'

I've recommended her my agency.

They've never advised me to be nice.

Turning from her, I look ahead to the woods, thinking of Iris and Robbie's cottage. But then, I'm always thinking about their cottage on some level. And now I'm thinking about *The Screen*'s article again too, narrowing my eyes on the woods' trees, wondering who, if not Blake, has been observing me heading in and out of them. Clearly not anyone who gives a damn about me – or certainly not enough of one to think to check if I'm ok before running to *The Screen* with their supposed concerns over my mental health.

'What have you been doing in the woods?' Nick asked me, last night.

'Just getting away from it all,' I said, and didn't mention the cottage, because I still haven't told him about it.

I wish I had.

More than ever, I wish I'd just been honest with him about it from the get-go, but if it felt hard to do that back on Sunday when I first found it, it feels impossible now I've kept it from him for the best part of a week.

And I truly don't know how I'd even begin trying to explain how often I've been drawn back to its ruins, going whenever I've been able to snatch a moment, just to sit by that gatepost, with tears pouring down my face, and my fingers touching the grooves of Robbie's name.

It's too . . . irrational.

Too deranged.

Honestly, I can barely admit to myself that it's something I've been doing.

He knows I'm keeping something from him, I have no doubt about that. I've seen his anxious looks. It's come to me, since *The Screen*'s article, that a lot of people have been throwing them my way this week – Felix and Emma included – and I hate it. Hate that I've let myself become a worry.

Again.

I have tried to stop going to the woods. Every time I'm there, I hear those murmurs, carrying through the trees' swaying branches: the voices, and that laughter, which doesn't seem to belong entirely to this world, and might almost, if such a thing were possible, be echoes from another.

But such a thing isn't possible.

Rationally, I know that.

Yet, more and more, to my own despair, I've found myself questioning the truth of it.

Especially when I'm in Iris's bedroom. I keep finding myself back up there, too. That much I *have* told Nick about, because I promised him I would, but he thinks I'm there running lines, when what I'm really doing is watching Iris's window, listening to the air, and standing in front of her mirror, holding her hairgrip, waiting for another glimpse of that face, which, in my very maddest moments, I think might actually have been hers: young, and bright, with rouged lips, dark hair, and a direct gaze that penetrates mine.

'Will you take me up?' Nick's asked me. 'I'd like to see it.'

'Then I'll take you,' I've told him, but haven't proposed a time, or said that it will have to be in daylight because I'm too afraid to return again at night.

So, how many secrets does that bring my tally up to?

I don't attempt the sum.

I don't actually want to know.

And I've got more, anyway.

Like, that banging I keep hearing in the house, but which I can't find the source of, even though I've now scoured every one of the sets – from the library, to the station commander's office, to my and Emma's bedroom.

I can't hear it, Ana said, when I mentioned it to her.

I can't hear a thing, said Imogen, on the phone.

And, probably, I should ask someone else about it, but I can't bring myself to.

Because what if I've been imagining it, too?

What if I've been imagining that bird?

It's silent now, but I peer upwards into the pale, empty sky anyway, replaying how completely Rusty ignored its call when she was out with her wrangler. I've been agonising over her oblivion ever since, and the more I've agonised, the surer I've become that Rusty's exemplary behaviour makes no sense. That bird's screech is piercing.

Surely, Rusty's ears should have pricked up for it, at the very least?

'What are you looking at?' asks Nick, bringing my attention back to earth.

I turn to him, and, seeing his frown, realise I'm worrying him.

Yet again.

'Nothing,' I say. 'Fresh air.'

'You sure?'

'I'm sure.'

'All right,' he says, but he's not convinced, and his frown doesn't go.

He's still worried.

So am I.

I'm beyond worried.

I just have no idea what to do about it.

So, for now, I do the only thing I can do. It's the same thing I've been doing all week.

I do my level best to bury what I'm feeling – willing it, so hard, away – and keep putting one precarious foot in front of the other.

Unlike the rest of us, this won't be Nick's first visit to Heaton, or the Heaton Arms; he's come in plenty on his research trips, and leads the way there, out of Doverley through an old servants' gateway that he discovered a while ago – avoiding the main entrance and any lurking reporters, since none of us want to be hounded the entire way to the village – then across a patchwork of icy fields, where a herd of hypothermic-looking cows are, thankfully, our only company.

'Think they remember you?' says Emma, nodding at the cows with a smile.

'Of course,' I reply, smiling too, but distractedly, preoccupied with the déjà vu I've once again found myself swimming in, from the moment Nick heaved open that servants' gate, and which has deepened with every step we've taken towards Heaton.

It all but overcomes me when, emerging from the fields, we reach the village itself, its glistening rooftops coming into view. The pub's on the outskirts, at the end of a lane called Bramble Rise, so we don't go all the way into the centre. I still get a good look at it though as we pass by, my pace slowing as I take in its frosted houses, stone church, glassy pond, village green, and war memorial.

I know this place, I think, just as I did when I first arrived at Doverley, *I have been here before.*

And *here*, of course, I have. I've run across the green. Thrown stale bread for ducks in the pond. Sat in the church. There was a man there who used to stare at me, with hard, blue eyes. His face rises up from deep within my memory, making me tense with hatred. Then, just as quickly, it vanishes again, sinking back into my subconscious.

Gladly, I let the man, whoever he was, go, and settle my focus on the war memorial. It's Remembrance Sunday this weekend. We all have poppies fixed to our coats. There'll be a service here in Heaton on Sunday morning, but none of us on the movie will come to it; we don't want to turn it into a press frenzy. Instead, we'll pause filming to lay wreaths at Doverley's memorial. Justin Holmes – who's playing Jacob, *Mabel's Fury's* bomb aimer – is an incredible musician, and will play the last post. No photos or recordings will be allowed, and that feels right.

Decent.

Really, it's the least we can do, given how much everyone's hoping to profit from the loss being marked.

A duck takes off from the village pond, its wings batting frantically. At the splashing, it comes to me how soundless the morning otherwise is. There's no one about at all, no cars nor bikes on the road, and although I suspect Bramble Rise is going to be much busier – a *circus*, like Nick said – I don't think about that.

I think about Nick, and the fact that he's just reached for my hand, taking it in his as we continue walking behind Emma and Felix. Easily, our fingers weave together, just as they have hundreds of times before, only not recently – not until last night, when, recalling Emma's words, *I think he might need you to be you*, I was the one to reach for Nick, telling him his was the only child I've ever wanted. And now here we are, holding hands again.

It's funny how much easier it can feel to do something, once you start doing it.

Tightening my grip on his, I move my attention to the church's cemetery, which is full of leafless trees, and crooked headstones that poke from the iced earth. My grandparents are buried beneath that earth somewhere, in their graves that neither Mum nor I have visited. I asked her why once, years ago, when I was a teenager, and she got really defensive.

'We've got them with us here,' she said, pressing her hand to her heart. 'That's all that matters.'

She's right about that, I know. But I do also think that she, who's lectured me . . . *how* many times? . . . on the importance of facing up to my grief, is too afraid to come back here and

185

face up to hers. I'm pretty sure that's part of why she's been so worried about *me* coming back. It's made this place too real to her again. Too close.

Now I am here, though, it feels really wrong that we've never come.

With my hand still in Nick's, I feel tears, always so ready, rise up inside of me, threatening to break free.

Hastily, I wipe them away with the back of my free hand, and resolve to return and visit this cemetery, just as soon as I can.

I'll bring Nan and Grandad some flowers, at last.

It doesn't take us long after that to reach Bramble Rise, no matter how slowly we walk, all as reluctant as each other to get there. I'm braced, even before we do, for what it looks like, and the fact that Robbie's old home is the only part of it that remains from before the war.

Just as with Heaton's old school, its redevelopment has meant that we can't use it for any outdoor filming. For the most part, the screenplay has avoided having any, but there is a montage of Iris and Robbie in the lane as children – with different aged actors showing them growing up, step by step – for which everyone involved will once again have to relocate, this time to a bucolic laneway near Thornton-Le-Dale, which is apparently a perfect match for the rugged one that Imogen paints in her novel.

I've never imagined it as particularly rugged myself; more soft, peaceful, and *bramble-lined*, with a stile leading to fields of grazing livestock, and the scent of woodsmoke in the air. But, I've seen Nick's photos, and all the others that Bomber Boy enthusiasts have posted online, so really am aware that, whatever Bramble Rise used to be, it's now a tarmacked strip of road, with Heaton's replacement primary school at its head (built in 1952, to cater for the influx of residents who moved into Heaton's post-war housing), The Heaton Arms at its end, and rows of identical, red-bricked terraces in between. Iris's cottage is long gone. Any stile that might once have existed is, too.

I *know* that.

It still jars though when we reach the lane, and, by the gates of Heaton Primary, I take in everything that's before me: all neat, and ordered, and double-glazed. It doesn't feel right. The road's tarmac is too smooth. The houses are too modern.

Just like my reflection in Iris's mirror, none of it seems to fit.

And, unlike in Heaton just now, nothing feels remotely familiar to me, even though my grandparents' estate is really close by. Much closer than I felt inclined to share with Blake earlier, who was wired enough as it was. Close enough, in fact, that it's called Bramble Edge, and, when I look up, I can see its chimneys poking above the school's buildings.

I feel no pull to it. No temptation to set off in search of Nan and Grandad's front door. The last thing I want to do, actually, is that. Because Mum's right, they're not there, they haven't been in almost thirty years, and it belongs to someone else now.

Not that I imagine that they – whoever they are – are currently home.

I don't think there can be many people left on the estate at all.

I doubt there are any children inside the school's classrooms, either.

And I know now why the village was as empty as it was.

It's because all of Heaton is here.

Not *a handful* of locals, like Blake said.

But a lot.

A *horde*, in actual matter: the kids all cheering at their school gate, clutching pieces of paper that I guess their teachers have doled out to them for autographs, then crowds of others who, now they've spotted us, rush down the road with big smiles, their phones out, snapping photos. Press photographers push ahead of them, aiming their wide-angled lenses in our direction, whilst reporters forge ahead of the photographers, calling out our names, shouting their demands to know our inner-most feelings.

'I'm going to end Blake,' breathes Nick.

'Get in line,' says Felix.

'I actually don't know if I can do this,' says Emma.

Nor do I.

But, as I once again glance at the school gate, I lock eyes with a little girl in a Peppa Pig hat, whose face is all flushed and hopeful and shy, and I know I will do it.

Summoning my smile, I *do* do it, going to that girl, and asking her name (Jaymee), then her age (six), and whether she has any brothers or sisters (just an older brother; he's annoying. 'No, I'm not,' exclaims an only slightly bigger boy, in a Hulk hat, making me laugh). Holding up her paper, Jaymee asks if she can have my autograph, please, and, telling her that of course she can, I crouch, taking her pen, resting the paper on my knee to sign it.

'*Cinderella* is my favourite movie,' she says, so quietly I have to strain to hear her above the racket.

'Oh, mine too,' I say, and don't embarrass her by saying it was actually Lily James who played Cinderella. I just write her a message, telling her what a thrill it's been to meet her, and hand her the paper back.

It's taken maybe forty-five seconds of my time, that's all, but it's made her so *happy*.

Giggling, she turns to wave her paper at her little pals, all of whom are waving theirs at me – and Nick, and Felix, and Emma, who, *doing it*, have joined us.

We all keep doing it, not for the press – who the headmistress instructs to remain outside the school gate, and who we ignore entirely – but for these really sweet, polite kids, and their teachers, and everyone else, who, on this freezing Friday morning, has turned out, just because they heard we were on our way, and wanted to say hello.

None of the other adults who've come are allowed past the school gates either, so they remain there with the press, waiting for us to get to them. No one complains though, or tries to push it, and we take it in turns to flit back and forth between them and the children: signing, grasping hands, posing for selfies, smiling, smiling, *smiling*.

To my amazement, Nick knows the names of quite a few of the children, and greets them with fist bumps like they're the only people he could possibly have hoped to run into this morning. Clearly, he's met them around the village before. And not only does he remember their names, but also their favourite football teams, and songs. He even notices that a boy called Hugo has lost another tooth since they last saw one another.

'I hope you got good money for that, buddy,' he says, eyeing his gaps. 'You're not going to be eating anything solid for like a month, at least.'

'I ate a corn on the cob last night.'

'That's pretty impressive.'

'And I got five pounds from the tooth fairy.'

'*Five?*' Nick throws me a look. I'm over at the gate again. 'Was that the going rate for you?'

'I used to get twenty pence,' I say, handing a woman back her copy of *The Bomber Boys*, which I've just signed for her daughter, Isla, who's fifteen, and at secondary school in York, and a huge history buff, and who'd apparently never let her mum hear the end of it if she failed at getting the book autographed.

'I used to get a quarter,' says Emma.

'Twenty pence too,' say Felix, who grew up in London. 'I think we're all showing our age. What did you get, Nick? A nickel?'

189

'No,' Nick ripostes, deadpan. 'A dime.'

'That's ten cents,' I supply, to the children.

And they all find it really funny.

Gradually, the reporters give up on their questions, seeming to realise that they're not going to get anything from us, and are running the risk of ruining everyone's fun.

We're running the risk of missing our lunch, but even after the children are marshalled back into school for theirs, a lot of the adults remain out with us on the road, despite the cold, quizzing us on the movie, and how it's going, and whether there's any chance we can give them a hint as to what might happen with the ending. We tell them we can't, that we only wish we could, but are as clueless as anyone.

'I've got a theory that it's Claude who's behind all this talk of a change,' says Felix, throwing me a wink (a wink!). 'She really doesn't want to have to get into the sea.'

That gets a lot of laughs, too.

And, when Nick says he doesn't much want me to have to get into the sea either, he's rewarded with an *ahh* that makes us both smile, setting the press cameras off, which I'm sure will make Blake very happy.

'You wouldn't really have to *do* it though, would you?' a white-haired woman in top-to-toe Sweaty Betty asks me.

'I'll absolutely have to do it,' I tell her. 'Special effects have come a long way, but not that far.'

'You'll make yourself ill,' she says, aghast.

'Par for the course on this movie,' says Emma.

At which everyone laughs again.

It's almost a quarter to one before the landlord of The Heaton Arms appears, jogging down the road and jovially enquiring as to whether anyone's planning to come in for lunch, or if he should send the kitchen staff home. It turns out that a lot of the people out with us also have reservations (more laughter), so we head off as a group for the pub, and – against all the odds, in spite of all my worst expectations – it feels really friendly and nice.

There's much more goodness in this world than bad, Mum said on the phone.

It's easier to believe that here.

I haven't forgotten everything in the news, though.

I know, without needing to ask, that neither Nick nor Emma nor Felix have either.

I'm certain that Nick and Felix must also be thinking about those photos in Sicily, and wondering how many of these people have scrolled through them over their breakfast.

I know I'm wondering which of them has read about my miscarriage.

But there's only one woman who mentions it.

She approaches me as I'm about to follow the others into the pub.

'Claudia?' she says, stopping me with a tentative smile.

She's about the same age as me, and is wearing a dark-green duffle coat that I noticed a while ago. (It's that kind of coat.) She's caught my eye a few times since, hovering at the back of everyone like she was trying to summon the courage to come forward.

I can hear from her voice how nervous she is now that she's made herself do it.

Trying to put her at her ease, I tell her how much I love her coat, and she smiles again, thanking me.

We're not alone. Nick's just ahead of us, waiting for me in the pub doorway, and there are still a lot of people milling around in the lane behind us, not ready for the party to be over. The photographers are still with us, too, cameras poised, seemingly sensing something might be about to happen.

Go away, I wish I could tell them.

Just bloody go.

I can't do it, though. At least one of them would get a picture of me looking furious, and the photo would be everywhere in hours, probably accompanied by some pithy caption about me losing it.

The woman eyes the photographers uncertainly.

'Ignore them,' I tell her quietly. 'It's what I do.'

Again, that uneasy smile.

With a breath, she opens her mouth to speak, only to shut it again.

I'm curious, but not apprehensive, about whatever it is that she's trying to get out.

Instinctively, I warm to this woman.

She's another bit of goodness, I can tell.

'What is it?' I ask her.

'I,' she begins, then pauses, biting her lip, before forcing herself on. 'I wasn't sure whether I should do this,' she continues. 'I've been worrying about it. But I'm off work today, so I thought I might as well come along. And I called my sister, and my husband. They both said I should. That you might appreciate it.'

'Appreciate what?' I ask, but even as I do, I feel my heart go out to this woman, and I realise I already know.

'It happened to me too,' she tells me, confirming it. 'Two months ago. I was twenty-one weeks.' This time when she smiles, I can tell she's trying not to cry. 'I just wanted to tell you that I understand, and you're not alone.' She blinks, taking a quick breath. 'You're really not alone. And I'm so sorry for everything extra that you've had to go through.' She turns to Nick. 'I'm sorry.'

'Thank you,' he says. 'I'm sorry for you, too. I really am.'

'I can't imagine how you're both coping.' Her eyes are

brimming. 'I couldn't bear having it all so public. I can't bear it anyway,' her voice catches, 'but I couldn't bear that.'

I don't plan to hug her.

But, before I know it, that's what I'm doing.

And she clings to me, like it means as much to her as it does to me, to share this, if only for a moment.

I don't question whether we're being observed.

I don't care if we're being photographed.

I don't think about Blake.

I think about this woman, and her bravery in coming forward to say this to me.

I think of how grateful I am to her for doing it.

And how right mum is.

The hateful voices are loud.

But the kind ones are strong.

Chapter Fourteen

I feel like going into lunch even less after that, but I don't do it alone, because Nick once again takes my hand – or I take his; I'm too distracted to register which, and I don't suppose it really matters anyway.

The meal is at least short. By the time we've all sat at the corner table the landlord leads us to, we have less than forty minutes to get through before Blake's car arrives to collect us, and, in the packed, buzzy dining room, it goes quickly.

I try, as we place our orders with the landlord (dry toast for Emma; 'Screw Blake,' she says), to picture the pub as Robbie's home, but it's been modernised so much that it's impossible to imagine it as anything but what it is: a Chef & Brewer that looks exactly the same as every other I've eaten at, down to its open fire, wine bottle candles, wooden spoons bearing table numbers, and chalkboard menu. It's perfectly pleasant, but – like the road outside, and Doverley's pamphleted porch, and luxe bedrooms – devoid of any sense of a past. Frankly, I'm more than ok with that. Given how tired and emotional I feel, I'm not sure I could handle coming up against any new trigger that might set me off into another trip down memory lane – real, or imagined.

Everyone else leaves us to it now that we're inside, getting on with their own meals. Most of the diners are retirement age – it is Friday, after all, lots of people working – and the oldest by far sits alone by the fire in a silk blouse and tailored slacks, taking her time over a pot of tea and Ploughman's. I don't remember her being outside, but nonetheless keep finding myself glancing her way as I pick at my own plate of pasta; I have this sense that she's observing me, but every time I turn to check, she doesn't seem to be looking my way at all.

'Do you think she remembers my grandparents?' I ask the others.

'Possibly,' says Emma. 'But I wouldn't worry, she doesn't look the sort to shout about it on her story.'

'Why don't you go and ask her?' suggests Felix.

'I don't know,' I say, drily, 'maybe because I don't want to tell her about them if she doesn't.'

And he flicks me with the froth of his pint, just as he would have done before Sicily, which, like his wink out in the road, relaxes me a bit, but not nearly so much that I don't register that he's done it.

We talk on, a bit about everything that's just happened outside and what a surprising tonic it all was, but mostly about the movie, and the coming week. Unsurprisingly, it's going to be another hectic one, especially for Emma who, until she heads back to the states, will be in pretty much everything we do. Over the next six days, we'll shoot an evening out for all of us on the set of this very pub, then another in our recreated Bettys Bar ('God, jitterbugging,' shudders Emma); then, three more scenes in the control tower, another in the canteen, and, at the end of the week, we'll finally start our night shooting, down on the base, when the remodelled Lancasters will be in motion, re-enacting one of 96 Squadron's departures for the Ruhr during the spring battles of 1943, which far too many of them didn't survive. Frankly, all our concerns about budgets and schedules feel . . . obscene . . . compared to what they experienced. It's pathetic that I should be allowing myself a moment's anxiety about taking part in our sanitised recreation of it, I know it is. Yet, I can't help myself.

I'm nervous.

For the first time since I saw what I saw from Iris's window, and heard what I heard, all the planes' engines really will be roaring. Effect's flare path *will* be alight. I have no idea what that's all going to do to me, but already I'm bracing for a fight to cling on to my composure. I can't afford to lose it, especially now I know that there's someone on staff talking to journalists. Plus, everyone on the cast will be there: the boys and extras out on the tarmac, Emma and me, seeing them off.

'Proving I'm *up to it*,' says Emma, breaking apart her toast. 'I'm kinda tempted to not be, you know. Now I'm here, I want to stick around a bit longer. I'm gonna hate leaving you all to it when I go. And I guess . . . Well . . . ' She gives us all a sorry look. 'I wish I could stay for Clare. Keep her alive, for as long as I can.'

'Yeah,' says Nick, understanding.

We all understand.

Of the four of us, only Felix is playing someone who actually survived the war.

It's as we call for the bill, and the landlord brings it to us, along with a complimentary sticky toffee pudding (that none of us have an appetite for, but eat anyway, because it would be too rude, and Hollywood cliched, of us not to), that we get on to the subject of Tim Hobbs. Emma knows about our appointment to see him – I've filled her in, swearing her to secrecy – but with everything else going on, I haven't had the opportunity to discuss it with her properly, and it's only now, at her probing, that I elaborate on my determination to discover what really happened to Robbie, Iris, and the rest of the *Mabel's Fury* crew.

'I'm certain Imogen has it wrong,' I say. 'Iris couldn't have killed them all. She was too smart, too good. She loved Robbie too much.'

No one disagrees. I am, after all, not saying anything that thousands of Goodreads and Amazon reviewers haven't already said, passionately – just as thousands more have countered them, passionately. (Imogen's ending is, in essence, marmite.)

But Emma does frown.

'You think Tim might know what happened?' she asks, sceptically.

'I think there are things he hasn't let on. A plane *can't* fly itself.'

Again, it's hardly an epiphany-like proclamation. Imogen acknowledges as much in her author's note, suggesting that the crew might have rigged *Mabel's Fury* to fly in a straight line for the coast before baling out – so giving Tim, unconscious and full of shrapnel, a chance at survival.

I've never really bought into that, though. To me, it just feels too far-fetched that the six of them would have been able to pull off such a thing, especially in high winds, with their engines shot to bits. Nick agrees, as does his flight instructor – and they've both spent a lot more time in a Lancaster's cockpit than Imogen.

Other theories about what might have happened abound online, but I'm not convinced by any of them either. I don't believe it was Robbie's ghost who steered his friend home, and I definitely don't think it was Robbie himself. He was no coward, and if he'd managed to get the plane close enough to England to crash land it, he'd have remained with Tim to try and see him safely down. His body would have been found.

'Who was in the cockpit then?' asks Emma.

'It had to have been Tim,' I say.

'Not a chance,' counters Felix.

'He started out in the RAF as a pilot.'

'Not for long. He only lasted five minutes in training.'

'A bit longer than five minutes . . . '

'Still, he never trained in a Lancaster. Nick, come on, could you fly one off the bat, in the dark, with failing engines?'

'Could *I*?' says Nick, discarding his spoon on the plate. 'Yeah, absolutely. Could *you*? No. No way . . . '

'Sod off.'

'Seriously, though,' says Emma. 'Could you?'

'Seriously –' he raises his broad shoulders in a shrug – 'who knows what anyone might find themselves capable of, fighting for their life.'

'He was practically dead,' says Felix. 'He'd been bleeding out since Berlin.'

'Only according to him,' I say. 'But what if he only got like that in the crash? Or what if his shrapnel wounds were minor?'

'Why would he lie about that?' asks Emma.

'I don't know. But someone flew that plane. And if Tim was well enough to do that, then he must have been able to hear what Iris said to Robbie on the radio. He heard her say *absolutely pancake*, didn't he? He *remembered* that. He's remembered so much . . . '

'But surely if he remembered what Iris said that night, and it was nothing that got them all killed, he'd have told Imogen,' says Emma. 'Why would he have let Imogen make Iris into their murderer?'

'I'm not sure he did,' I say. 'The way she tells it, he left her to it with the ending . . . '

'Yes,' says Felix. 'Because he's never known what the ending was.'

'Or,' I say, 'because he never imagined she'd pin it on me.'

'Iris,' says Nick.

'What?'

'Iris,' he repeats. 'He pinned it on Iris, not you.'

'Right.' I frown. (Did I really just say *me*?) 'Yes. Iris.'

'He still could have asked Imogen to change it,' says Emma. 'I mean, she ran the book by him before it went to print, and he gave it the nod.'

I can't argue with that. That Tim signed off on Iris's *devastating reveal* has been the card Imogen's played over and again with the studio, resisting their endeavours to rewrite it.

Still, 'Maybe he was worried to push back,' I say. 'Maybe he's hiding something, and was afraid to let it go.'

Emma pulls a disbelieving face. 'So he threw Iris under a bus?'

'Hardly. She doesn't exactly come off as a villain. Just really . . . *sorry*. Maybe Tim thought it would be all right to leave her like that . . . '

'Or maybe,' Felix says, '*he has no idea what happened.*'

'I think he might.'

'Even if he does,' Emma says, 'you do realise none of this will *actually* change anything, right? They all still went.'

'But *where?*'

'Into the sea,' Felix says with a sigh, 'like thousands of others.'

'What about Iris though?'

'Maybe she really did drown herself.'

'No way.' I'm resolute on that. I've been turning it over, all week long, and the more I have, the more certain I've become that there's no way she could have killed herself. 'Think about it,' I say. 'The crew were certified missing presumed, but never confirmed, dead. Iris wouldn't have taken her life, not while

199

there was a chance of Robbie coming home. She'd have been hoping to hear from him, every moment.' My voice shakes on the words, but I can't help it.

I feel very, very strongly about this.

I think Felix must realise, because he doesn't argue back.

In fact, he gives a slow nod of agreement.

'I still don't think you're gonna get anything out of Tim,' says Emma. 'Maybe you are right about him hiding something, but I don't see why he'd suddenly decide to open up.'

'Nor do I,' I admit. 'But I have to at least try to get him to.'

'Well, it shouldn't be too hard to weave into conversation,' says Felix, draining his beer as the landlord approaches with a credit card machine. 'It's a straightforward enough question. Hey, Tim, have you been lying about how your friends all died?'

'Funny,' I say, 'that's exactly how I've been planning to put it.'

'Excellent.'

'How was the pudding?' asks the landlord, reaching us.

'Delicious,' says Nick, handing him his card.

And, whilst he processes the payment, we all get up, gathering our things, saying nothing further about Tim now we have someone else in earshot.

Nor is it Tim who I mainly think about as we set off across the pub for the exit.

It's that woman by the fire, with her tea and ploughman's.

She turns to look up at me as I pass her by, and, as our eyes connect, I feel a jolt, but I don't know why.

I still don't recognise her.

I'm sure I don't.

And yet,

I know this woman, I think.

I have met her before.

Perhaps I should talk to her, like Felix suggested.

Introduce myself. Ask her name.

I don't, though.

Blake appears at the pub door, clearly impatient for a debrief, so I keep walking towards him, and the car waiting outside, ready to speed us all away.

*

Tim's nursing home is on the opposite side of York from Doverley. Nick drives, and although we clear Doverley's gates without running into any press – they thankfully seem to have had enough of us for the day – the traffic on the York ring road is Friday afternoon heavy, and we only just make it to our appointment on time, pulling into the home's paved forecourt on the dot of half past two.

Gratefully, I leave the car. The journey, just the three of us, was less fraught than it might have been a week ago, but the atmosphere definitely felt more strained without Emma around to dilute things. Mainly, we debated the identity of *The Screen*'s anonymous source, frustrating each other by getting nowhere ('Remind me again why we're wasting our time with this?' said Felix), and I think we're all ready for a breather from our collective effort at being *ok* – even if I have also grown quite nervy now about meeting Tim. My own questions aside, I don't want to disappoint him. Fail him, by failing to come up to par with Iris.

Drawing a stingingly cold breath, I look around at the home's low-rise buildings, purpose-built in a Georgian style, and surrounded by ice-crusted lawns that shimmer pink-grey in the diminishing light. There'll be another frost tonight, without doubt. It's -3, according to the thermometer in Nick's car, and I can well believe it.

The temperature doesn't stop Roger Westin coming out to meet us though. He – a stocky man in slacks and a collared-shirt – emerges from the main building within seconds of us parking. I deduce from his promptness that he's been looking out for us in the lobby. He flushes as he welcomes us, asking about our drive, commenting on the weather, stumbling over his words in his eagerness to get them out, and I wish – as I've wished with so very many strangers over the years – that I could wave a wand for him, dissipate the absurd illusion of our celebrity, enable him to talk to us like he would anyone else. *We're no different, I promise. Possibly just a bit more screwed up.* But since I can't, I give him my biggest smile, and thank him again for having us along. Nick, meanwhile – in the absence of his own wand – apologises for cutting it so fine, whilst Felix cracks a joke about Nick's driving, and asks what he can smell cooking.

'Scones and chocolate torte,' Roger says. 'I hope you've brought an appetite.'

'I always bring an appetite,' says Felix, not mentioning the huge portion of sticky toffee pudding we've just eaten.

'Then please –' Roger holds out his arm in the direction of the home's sliding door entrance – 'come this way. Tim's in good spirits, and eager to meet you.'

Tim's only recently moved into this home. When Imogen first met him, five years ago now, he was still living in his own house, nearby. He was there alone, but that's all I know about his past, beyond his service in the war; apparently, he was very closed up with Imogen when it came to his own life.

'Probably best not to probe,' Imogen cautioned me on the phone. 'It might upset him.'

She obviously feels very protective of him. No surprise,

given all the time they've spent together – and how much their conversations have transformed her life.

That they met was no serendipitous thing. Imogen tracked him down after seeing him interviewed in a 1970s documentary on Bomber Command in which he spoke about his role as a navigator, and, briefly, the disappearance of his crew. At that stage, she was still unpublished, with six rejected manuscripts gathering dust in her metaphorical bottom drawer, and determined, seventh time around, to come up with a premise hooky enough to entice a publisher. It was while she was trawling the internet, looking for inspiration, that she came across the phenomenon of World War Two ghost planes: aircraft which either disappeared without explanation, like Glenn Miller's, or were found, but with no trace of their crew inside. The most famous of those used to be the B-24D, *Lady Be Good*, but then Imogen discovered Tim's interview, wrote him an imploring letter asking him to share more of his memories with her, and now it's *Mabel's Fury* that everyone knows about.

'He called me as soon as he got my letter,' she's told me. 'He said it would be an honour to talk about it all. I had no idea if I'd find a story in his recollections, but then I met him, in a Costa Coffee, atmospherically enough, and within about a minute, started getting excited. All he wanted to talk about was his friends, and Iris and Robbie especially. I think they left him with huge survivor's guilt. Seventy years must have felt a very long time to carry that.'

I think about those words as Roger shows Nick, Felix and me into the lounge adjoining Tim's bedroom, and Tim – by the window in an armchair – tremblingly pushes himself to standing, his gaze hungry as he meets first mine, then Nick's, then mine again, moving across our faces eagerly, like he might discover some trace of his lost comrades in our features.

I'm no longer worrying about how I compare to Iris. I'm too distracted drinking in my first sight of him. He's changed, of course, from the young man I've obsessed over on the novel's cover, and I can see the scars left by *Mabel's Fury*'s flames clearly on his cheeks, neck, and lips. But his white hair is still thick, his jaw strong and square, and his intent eyes are unquestionably *his*.

I'd have known them anywhere.

I find them impossible to look away from. Just as with that woman in the pub earlier, they really don't feel like a stranger's eyes. They're dark in colour, *deepest brown*, much like Robbie's in the novel, and I wonder, now I see them, if it was Tim who Imogen was subconsciously thinking about when she wrote her descriptions of Robbie. She told me just this week that she has no idea what colour Robbie's eyes really were. It came up because I mentioned how much Nick's contacts have been torturing him.

'Poor Nick,' she said. 'If only I'd known he'd be the one playing Robbie, I would have written him differently. Other than for that photo, I had a free pass when it came to the boys' appearances. Unsurprisingly for a man of his generation, Tim didn't bank the finer details.'

He did, however, remember that Iris's eyes were hazel. Mine are too, but that's never felt like too big a coincidence, not like our shared birthplace. Plenty of people have hazel eyes. 18% of all Americans, in fact. (I've googled it.) But to me, the fact that Tim mentioned such a thing to Imogen – that he *recalled* the colour of a woman's eyes, seventy years after he lost her – feels like further proof that he was in love with her.

Don't we all remember those eyes we stare into?

I glance to Nick's, such a bright blue, then turn back to Tim, because he talks to me.

'So, you're Iris,' he says, and it gives me a shiver, just hearing him speak her name. The easy way he says it, his deep voice dropping on the *is*, you can tell he's done it thousands of times before. I think he must be picturing her in his memory, and wish so much that I could see her face that he's seeing, and discover whether it does – as I half hope, and half fear – bear any resemblance to the one *I've* seen, standing before her mirror.

'And you're Rob,' he goes on, nodding at Nick. 'And you,' he switches his attention to Felix, 'you're me.'

'I am, sir.'

'Couldn't they have found someone more handsome?' he says, a glint illuminating his eyes.

'He's teasing,' says Roger.

'Don't worry,' says Felix with a grin. 'I already assumed as much.'

And Tim laughs – a low, rolling laugh that's fun, and good – and blindsides me by being as instantly familiar as his stare, triggering a rush of such strange, instinctive affection in my heart.

Then pain, when I see how rapidly Tim's laughter exhausts him. Within seconds, he starts wheezing, and Roger goes to him, helping him back into his chair.

'Sit down, sit down,' Tim tells us, once he's settled, waving at the room's single settee, 'then I won't feel so conspicuous doing it.'

So, taking off our jackets, we sit, cramming together on the settee's cushions, our jackets stuffed between us, me ending up in the middle.

'Comfy?' Tim enquires.

'Yes,' we all lie, 'thank you.'

In an effort to distract myself from both Nick's and Felix's legs, touching mine, I glance around the room. It's very snug, with a thick carpet, and roaring gas fire. In front of us is a coffee table, laden with our promised afternoon tea, and next to the fire is a sideboard that bears several framed photographs.

'If you'd come a bit sooner, you'd have seen your birthday card there,' says Tim, following the direction of my stare. 'Someone's taken it though, Taken them all . . . '

'We haven't taken them,' says Roger, soothingly. 'We've put them away in your bedroom, remember?'

'Oh yes.' Tim's brow furrows. 'Yes, of course.'

'I'm glad you got mine,' I say.

'I was very glad to get it,' he says. 'Thank you.' He nods. 'Good, I wanted to say that.' He looks to Roger. 'You won't need to remind me.'

'No,' agrees Roger, 'I won't.' Then, to Nick, Felix, and me. 'Will you have some tea? Chef won't want to see leftovers.'

Thanking him, we help ourselves to the spread on the table, exclaiming on how incredible it all looks as we load up our plates (whatever, really; I've long since given up on the calorie counting and body-watching that made me so miserable in my twenties), and wedge ourselves back onto the settee.

'Iris had a sweet tooth too,' says Tim, as I take a forkful of torte. 'When we were little, and my mum used to take Rob and me to the pantomime, Rob would save his chocolates for her.'

Silently, I nod.

Neither Felix nor Nick say anything either.

We already knew about the interval chocolates, of course. They're in the novel. But it really is . . . *surreal* . . . to be hearing about them from Tim. It's amazing to be sitting here with him at all, *Tim Hobbs*, talking about Iris and Robbie as real people, not characters in a book.

'I wish I'd worked harder at making my mum ask Iris along to those pantomimes,' he continues. 'She said it wasn't proper, having a girl out with us, but what she really meant was she didn't want to be seen with a scruffy girl.' He sighs.

'I hope Iris can see you all, making a film about her. I hope her mum and gran can. And Rob.' He considers that for a moment. 'He wouldn't be surprised. He always knew Iris was the cat's pyjamas.' His eyes meet Nick's. 'You understand that I think.'

'I do,' says Nick, but not without a pause.

A pause that might be down to nothing more than him being as taken aback as me by this out-of-the-blue observation.

But a pause that nonetheless prompts me to think *not* of his hand reaching for mine earlier, but, before I can help myself, of the child I know he still yearns for, but which I can never give him.

A pause that reminds me once again of how hard he hit it in all those bars this year, whilst barely being able to pick up the phone to me.

A pause that makes me question whether he really does understand what Tim's just said.

Because really, what else could he have said to him in response?

We don't have long with Tim. Just a little over a half hour. Roger remains with us for all of it, perched beside Tim on the windowsill, holding an oxygen mask ready for whenever Tim needs it to get him through another wheezing fit.

Tim doesn't eat.

He doesn't drink.

He claims he's not hungry or thirsty, but I worry, from the way his pale, papery hands tremble, that he's scared to risk spilling anything in our company.

But despite his frailty, and despite his forgetfulness, he still has plenty to say, and it quickly becomes clear that he's come to this meeting with an agenda of his own: one that goes well beyond thanking me for my card.

207

He's obviously discussed it with Roger, because although Roger didn't have to remind him about my card, he does prompt him on other things.

Like, Nick's accent.

'Oh yes,' says Tim. 'Yes. I'd like to hear it please, young man.'

'Absolutely,' says Nick, in his Robbie voice, without missing a beat. (No pause for this.) 'It's my absolute honour to oblige.'

'Ha,' says Tim, beaming up at Roger, 'he's got it.' He turns back to Nick. 'Perfect.'

'Thank you,' says Nick, with a smile of his own, happier than I've seen him all week.

'You've even got the bit of Yorkshire,' Tim says. 'Rob never lost it. It annoyed the hell out of his father. But he held on to it anyway.'

'*To* annoy his father?' says Nick.

'A bit of that, I'm sure,' says Tim. 'But I think he was also holding on to Iris.'

He's got plenty to say to me about Iris. That much at least he has no need for Roger to remind him about. He wants me to know how intelligent she was, how sharp and quick-witted, and kind and thoughtful. 'And fun. Lots of fun. You should have seen her dance. Will you be dancing in the picture?'

'I will,' I say, enjoying his use of the word *picture*. 'I've learnt to jitterbug.' I've loved it, actually. It was the only part of rehearsals I didn't mess up. 'We're shooting some of that this week.'

'With a band?'

'Absolutely.'

'And have you discovered Iris's bedroom yet?'

'What?' says Felix, hearing about it for the first time.

Briefly, I fill him in.

'I've been spending some time up there,' I say.

'She spent an entire night up there,' says Nick.

'You *slept* there?' says Felix.

'Yes . . . '

'Weren't you cold?' Tim wants to know. 'The girls always said how cold it was.'

'I was pretty cold, yes.'

'I can't believe I didn't know about this,' says Felix. 'I want to see it . . . '

'So do I,' says Nick.

'Oh, you mustn't,' says Tim, wagging a jittering finger at them both, his eyes twinkling as they come to a rest on Felix: this relaxed, assured, *swoon-worthy* man who's been cast in his shoes. 'No airmen allowed up there . . . '

'Didn't you go, though?' I ask. I've always assumed he must have snuck up, to have been able to show Imogen the way.

'Not during the war, no. It was a long time afterwards that I went. The house was all shut up. We broke in. She showed me—' He breaks off.

'Who?' I ask.

'What's that?' he says.

'Who showed you?'

'Showed me what?'

'Iris's room,' says Roger. 'You were just saying someone showed you up there.'

'Was I?' Tim frowns. 'I don't recall, I'm afraid.'

It's the way he shifts in his chair. My senses prickle with the suspicion that he might not be being quite truthful.

But then he continues, repeating himself – 'It was years ago. After the war. The house was all shut up.' – and I decide I'm being unfair.

'Now,' he presses his fingers to his scarred forehead, 'what else was it I wanted to mention . . . ?'

'The navigational instruments,' says Roger.

209

'Ah, yes.' He turns back to Felix, quizzing him on the tools props have given him, then, the reconstruction of *Mabel's Fury*, especially the navigator's blacked-off nest. 'You can't just be hopping in and out,' he says, leaning forward at the importance of it. 'No light could escape. You mustn't forget that. It would have been suicide for us.'

'I've got it,' says Felix, 'I promise.'

'All right,' Tim says, relaxing back in his chair. 'I'm glad. It's important to get these things right. People will believe what they see. Now,' he grapples for his mask, breathing deep as Roger places it to his face. 'What else?'

'Doverley,' says Roger.

'Ah, yes,' he says, and, pushing the mask away, goes into how desperately uncomfortable conditions were there, for everyone. 'It really was damnably cold,' he says, 'and there were rats all over the place. Wood rot too. Half of the first floor disintegrated around the time of the Ruhr. Or was it Hamburg?' He shakes his head. 'I don't know. But it had to be replaced, so don't let your people have it look all just so and tidy . . . ' Talking on, he describes the bland food Doverley's kitchen staff served up, except on ops nights, when the crews were given much nicer, richer food ('Which we of course all struggled to eat.'); then, the relief everyone felt when ops were off, when they'd pile into motorcars for nights out, heading to York for good times in Bettys Bar. ('They had cocktails that could have fuelled a plane to Berlin and back,' he says. 'Oh, we had some nights there . . . ') He reminisces about the songs the band at Bettys played, and the hangovers everyone suffered afterwards, drinking far too much, because none of them knew if they'd be around to drink the next night.

'You wanted to mention the fear,' Roger reminds him. 'How young the crews were.'

'Yes, everyone was very young.' Tim nods soberly. 'Children, some of them. We had gunners come in who were seventeen, then they'd vanish, gone.' He blinks, rapidly.

For a terrible moment, I fear he's going to cry.

But he doesn't cry.

He keeps talking.

'Every mission felt like a death sentence,' he says. 'Then you'd get a reprieve, flying over the white cliffs at dawn, and feel alive again, until you were taking off for the next one.' He blinks more. 'There's a lot that gets made of how brave we all were, and of course we did keep going up. But we had no choice, and we were terrified.' His eyes burn. 'You mustn't wash over that. You can't . . . *glamorise* . . . it.'

'We won't,' says Nick. 'We're not.'

'You have our word,' says Felix.

'Right.' Tim exhales. 'Good. That's done then.'

Spent, he rests his head back against his chair and, as his laboured breathing fills the room, I feel regret course through me – not because we haven't yet spoken of the lone item on *my* agenda, but because he's so frail, and has seen, and lost, and suffered so much, and really can't have much longer left, but has put himself through all this anyway. He's done it because he's afraid of us doing his lost friends a disservice by romanticising their history – that's clear – and although I hope that we won't, it suddenly feels like an unforgivable imposition that we're shooting this movie at all.

I try to say that to him.

But he cuts me off, insisting that he's glad we're doing this, he doesn't want any of them to be forgotten, and this way they never will be.

'She wanted me to share their story,' he says.

'Imogen?' I say, assuming that's who he means.

'What's that?'

211

'You were just telling us Imogen wanted you to share their story,' says Roger.

'Oh yes.' Tim nods. 'Such a lovely lady. Such an . . . imagination.'

I could probably ask him about her ending now.

It feels a good opportunity to bring it up.

But I don't.

Neither Nick nor Felix jump in to do it either.

Well, it shouldn't be too hard to weave into conversation, said Felix earlier in the pub. *Hey, Tim, have you been lying about how your friends all died?*

I was never going to actually phrase it like that, obviously. But I think we've all realised that none of us can phrase it any way, certainly not without upsetting Tim more.

If anyone's going to mention *Mabel's Fury*'s final flight, it has to be him.

I don't expect him to do it, though.

I absolutely don't.

It astounds me when, first letting go a long rasping sigh, he *does*.

'I'm afraid she got confused about some of the things I told her,' he says. 'She mixed up where they happened.' He pauses, and I wonder if he's thinking about Iris and Robbie's reunion, and all the different venues he gave Imogen for it. *Honestly, I had Iris and Robbie bumping into one another everywhere.* But then he talks on, more to himself, I feel, than any of us, saying, 'We weren't over the North Sea when Rob radioed Iris. We'd never have been able to get through from there. Rob had us back over land already.'

I stare.

Dimly, I'm aware of Nick and Felix doing the same.

And how still the three of us have turned.

I'm not sure we breathe.

Felix is the first one to break the silence.

212

'Did you tell Imogen that?' he asks.

'What's that?' says Tim.

'Did you tell Imogen?' Felix repeats.

'Tell her what?'

'That you were already over land when you radioed Iris,' Nick says, rediscovering his voice too.

'Were we?' Tim frowns. 'When?'

'The last time you flew in *Mabel's Fury*,' I say, my heart pounding in my throat.

Slowly, Tim shakes his head. 'I don't remember anything about that.'

'But you just said Robbie would never have been able to establish radio contact from the distance of the sea . . . '

'Oh yes.' He nods. 'That would have been difficult. Very difficult . . . '

'But do you remember him doing it?'

'Doing what?'

'Radioing Iris?' says Nick, sitting forward, his hands clasped before him.

'When?' says Tim.

And I honestly can't tell if he's genuinely struggling to keep track with what we're talking about, or regrets having raised it so is now taking evasive action, but his sudden vagueness makes me think of the way he dodged my question before, when I asked him about that woman who showed him up to Iris's room.

Was he pretending then, after all?

I suspect he might have been.

I can't just let this drop too.

'We're wondering if you remember anything about Robbie speaking to Iris on your last flight,' I say to him. 'You seemed to be saying just now that you might recall it.'

'No, that can't be right. I was unconscious. We'd got hit.

213

That never happened to us, but it happened that night.' He closes his eyes. 'It took me weeks to come back to my senses. By the time I did, the squadron had moved south for D-Day. I lost touch with them.' His voice cracks, heavy with grief. 'I lost them all . . . ' He breathes, too quickly.

'Here we are,' says Roger, helping him with his mask. 'Nice and deep now. Best not to get upset. It was all such a long time ago.'

'No,' says Tim, through the mask, 'not long. It's always happening. Always.'

'Only in your memory.'

Tim doesn't reply.

He closes his eyes, retreating into himself, and within seconds his breaths start to deepen, they lengthen, and it becomes clear that he has, quite abruptly, fallen asleep.

Our meeting, I realise, is at an end.

We're all deflated as we leave, thanking Roger for having us, and repeating how delicious the food was.

As we walk out to the car, puffing clouds of white into the darkening afternoon, Nick and Felix concede that I was right all along, Tim clearly does know more than he's let on, but their agreement gives me zero satisfaction. Because what does it matter what Tim knows, if he keeps on keeping it to himself?

'It's like Emma said,' I say, shrugging on my coat. 'Why *would* he suddenly open up now?'

'But he *did* open up,' says Felix. 'He told us they all made it back to England.'

'I don't think he intended to do that,' says Nick.

'He definitely didn't,' I agree.

'But he still did,' says Felix. 'So maybe he wanted to, subconsciously . . . '

'What, like a Freudian slip?' I say, and still thinking of Emma – remembering the debrief I promised to message her – reach for my phone.

'Exactly,' says Felix.

'Shit,' I say, realising my jacket pocket's empty. I give myself another pat down. 'I don't have my phone. I must have dropped it down the settee.'

'Did you do it deliberately, Juniper Jones?' asks Nick.

And, in spite of everything, I laugh. Juniper Jones is the name of a spy I once played; there was a scene where I left my phone – a Motorola – beneath my target's bed, just for the excuse to return and find it. I can't believe Nick's remembered it. I haven't thought about it for years.

'I did not do it deliberately,' I say.

'No?' He raises a cynical brow.

'No.'

'A likely story.'

'It's the truth.' I turn on my heel, heading back inside. 'Warm the car up for me, please.'

'Or I can go and find your phone?' proffers Felix.

'Or I will,' says Nick.

'No, I'll do it,' I say, and although I really didn't drop it on purpose, I'll admit I'm pretty happy to be heading back in to see Tim.

At the very least, I'd like a chance to say a proper goodbye.

But he's still sleeping when I reach his room.

I've come alone. Roger – busy talking with another resident when I returned to the lobby – told me I should.

'A nurse will be along to help Tim to bed in a minute,' he said.

'I'll only be a second,' I told him.

'Was that Marian Maudsley?' the resident asked him as I went.

'It was, Gwen,' he said. 'But mum's the word, ok? We don't want it getting out.'

It doesn't take me much more than a second to locate my phone; it's lying on the carpet directly beneath where I was sitting, half-hidden under the settee's skirt. Scooping it up, I scan my messages – there's one from Phil, *just checking in*, and Mum too, doing the same, *xxx* – then I turn to Tim. He doesn't look comfortable, sleeping with his head against the side of his armchair, and I almost go to move him, but stop myself, remembering that we're practically strangers, and it's not my place.

His eyelids flicker in a dream.

I wonder what he's dreaming about.

The war?

My eyes move to the side table, and the framed original of the novel's cover photograph that I've been stealing glances at ever since I spotted it earlier. It's different in real life. Larger. More authentic, somehow.

Sadder.

Going to it, I pick it up, touching my finger to the side of Robbie's face. I stare at him, with a focus that makes my eyes blur, and in yet another dizzying, lunatic moment, my vision flickers, and it's as though I can see him, truly *see* him, alive and breathing; wind blowing his hair, his smile growing, his lips moving in the formation of a word . . .

'Look after that boy, won't you?' says Tim, startling me by being suddenly awake.

Very nearly dropping the photo, I spin around to face him.

He hasn't moved his head from its position against the armchair, and still looks half asleep: his eyes, heavy; his blinks, slow.

'Which boy?' I ask, shaky to my own ears.

Anxiously, I look back down at Robbie, and he smiles up at me, entirely static. Frozen by the camera.

Locked in the past.

'Phillip,' says Tim.

'Phillip?'

'Yes, that one who's playing me.'

'Felix?'

'Felix.' He nods. 'He loves you so.'

'Oh, no.' I glance again at Robbie. Did I really just see him move? What had he been about to say? 'We're very old friends.'

Tim doesn't press it.

He's also looking at the photograph in my hands.

'Jacob didn't want that to be taken,' he says. 'He thought it was tempting fate.'

'Really?' The revelation, so unexpected, makes my pummelling heart heavy. I look at him now, too, his head bowed towards Piper.

Poor Jacob.

Poor, *poor* Jacob.

'Maybe it was tempting fate,' I say, and my throat feels strangled.

I don't know what's come over me.

'This photograph didn't change anything,' says Tim, softly. 'A photograph could never do that.'

It's almost like he's consoling me.

Slowly, I look back up at him, certain, suddenly, that he's said these words before; that he once consoled the photographer too.

'Who took this, Tim?' I say, raising the frame.

He closes his eyes.

'Was it . . . Iris?' I ask, and only just stop myself from saying, *me*. 'I think it must have been Iris. Did you see her, after the crash?'

Silence.

'Tim . . . ?'

'She said you'd come. She told me . . . '

He's trying to change the subject, I think: distract me by talking about Imogen again. She must have telephoned him, mentioned my plan to visit.

I don't ask him about that though.

I can't let him change the subject.

'Was it Iris?' I repeat.

'Your eyes,' he says, reopening his, 'they're the same.' He holds my gaze, and a smile pulls at his scarred lips. 'Windows to your soul.'

It's my turn to be silent.

I don't know what to say.

I feel nauseatingly lightheaded.

My hands shake.

My entire body does.

'It was Jacob's camera,' he says, his words slurring. 'We all clubbed together, gave it to him for his birthday.' His voice fades to nothing.

His eyes once again droop shut.

They don't reopen.

He's dreaming again, but this time, I don't wonder what he's dreaming about.

He's with his friends, I'm certain, back in the spring of 1943, jitterbugging in Bettys Bar for Jacob's twenty-third birthday, making the most of a scarce night off from fighting the Battle of the Ruhr.

I draw a breath, fighting to get my tremoring under control, and, in the space of that breath, the gas fire crackles, very warm, the room swims, my vision flickers again, shifting, *morphing*, and I find myself inside Tim's dream, standing in that packed, pulsing bar, which I somehow recognise: my ears roaring with music I'm certain I've heard before, my skin slick with sweat.

A hand closes around mine.

I feel it.

I feel it.

It belongs to a man who would never actually *use* the expression the cat's pyjamas, but who'd also never pause before agreeing with anyone that I am.

It belongs to a man I love, very, very much.

A man who stops me shaking.

A man whose touch is warm.

A man who I'm deeply afraid to ever let go.

Chapter Fifteen

Iris

April 1943

In the packed, pulsing heat of Bettys basement bar – *the dive*, as everyone called it – his hand took a hold of hers, and she turned to him, kissing him through the fear that, from nowhere, assailed her, because he was here, they were both here, and for tonight at least she wouldn't have to tell him to climb to angels anywhere, or vector anyhow without her.

It was late April. This time the night before, he'd been flying to Essen. This time tomorrow, who knew what he, or any of them, would be doing. Maybe the squadron would fly again, maybe they wouldn't. Regardless, it wouldn't be long before they were ordered on another operation, and Iris would take her position in the control room, send them all off with a green for go, and helplessly watch Robbie accelerate away.

When I have enough money and a motorcar, I'll take you with me everywhere I go, he'd promised her, back when they were children.

But he couldn't take her to Germany, and Germany was where the squadron always got sent these days. There'd been no trips to Italy for weeks. That endless full-mooned night of Iris's first shift at Doverley, when all of 96 had returned from Milan, felt as though it belonged to several lifetimes ago. Far too many lifetimes had been ended since. Most of February had been quiet, with ops frequently scrubbed for bad weather, and she and Robbie had managed to steal much more time together than they'd been forced apart. But then March had arrived, and with it an inundation of orders from Bomber Command for attack after attack on the Ruhr region and beyond, with streams of up to a thousand planes leaving England some nights, following their designated pathfinders on raids over some of the most heavily defended cities in the Nazi empire: Munich, Stuttgart, Berlin. In the past six weeks, countless civilians must have been killed – mothers, grandparents, *babies* – whilst 96 had lost fifteen crews, seven of them flying under the codename V for Verity. *Hamps Heroes*, whose operator had been so elated that February night he'd broken radio silence returning from Milan, were long gone, and although Lewis in his tartan slippers was still around, Group Captain Fred Lacey with him, scores of others weren't.

They were all here too tonight. Iris could sense them everywhere: the ghosts of the present, dancing and drinking alongside the ghosts of the future.

Placing her free hand to Robbie's face, she leant into him as their lips touched, fighting to quieten the voices of those ghosts in her mind, and focus instead on the here, the now, *this moment*. She didn't want to dwell on whatever new targets the strategists in Bomber Command might be busy identifying. Or all the lives that had been taken, and would continue to be lost. She didn't want to think about how, *in this moment*, fresh recruits were arriving at training camps all over Britain to learn the dark arts of bombing, whilst women in dungarees and headscarves were clocking in for night shifts at factories, rolling up their sleeves and getting down to work soldering together new Lancasters and Halifaxes and Stirlings for more terrified airmen to die in.

She couldn't think of the sickening waves of fear that kept taking her unawares – like another just had now – filling her with foreboding so strong it felt almost like a warning: bleak, but certain, that this middle she and Robbie had found wasn't going to last, because their end, that she'd never be ready for, was already waiting for them, not so far away at all.

So, now, here, *in this moment*, she didn't think of that.

She kissed Robbie, wrapping him in her arms – laughing as the band struck up 'A String of Pearls' and he swung her around – and thought only about how they were in Bettys, together, under the jurisdiction of nobody's rules but their own, certainly not the adjutant's, and were celebrating Jacob's twenty-third birthday, with everyone who was still here safe, and alive, and happy, for one more night at least.

The adjutant, *Ambrose*, hadn't come out that night – no one had invited him – but plenty of others had made the journey from Doverley, speeding along the pitch-black country lanes in a convoy of borrowed, gifted, and inherited motors. Practically every WAAF and airman was there, including Prim (who Iris just could not condition herself into thinking of as Eleanor), and Beth Twinton, and the group captain Fred, who'd brought his wife Miriam, leaving their baby daughter back in Heaton with a sitter. Lewis was out too, along with the rest of his *Bucks Boys*, as were all the crew from *Mabel's Fury*. Ames, the flight engineer, was ecstatic because his French fiancée, Mabel, the plane's namesake, had surprised him a few hours before by turning up at Doverley, fresh off the boat from a spell in France, working for whom she wasn't at liberty to say, doing what she couldn't say either, only that it had been *très, très productif*.

She was staying at the Heaton Arms whilst she was in town, along with all the other wives and fiancées and girlfriends of Doverley's airmen who snatched whatever opportunity they could to visit. Plenty of them were at Bettys that night too, drinking and jitterbugging, clinging to their own here and nows.

Keeping her grasp firmly around Robbie's, Iris went with him, pushing through the teeming throngs for the booth that everyone else was already getting themselves settled in. They'd only just arrived but she was already perspiring in the bar's cloying heat. *Glowing*, Prim would doubtless correct her. Iris glanced across at her, well apart from the others and ensconced with her American beau, Clint, at a table for two. Unlike him, and all the other men present that night, Prim wasn't in uniform, but done up to the nines in a silk dress. Neither Iris nor any of the WAAFs from Doverley had worn uniform either – they didn't have to, they weren't on duty – and had collectively turned the icy attic pungent with hairspray, perfume and nail polish before they'd left.

'Ambrose won't be happy if he finds out about that,' Prim had remarked, pausing at Iris and Clare's open door, eyes on the red polish stain spilling across their drawers from the bottle Clare had just knocked over.

'Tell on me why don't you?' Clare had replied, mopping the polish up.

'I won't tell,' Prim had said huffily, flouncing away. 'I'd never do that.'

'Only because you've got your own secrets to keep,' said Clare.

Which Prim did.

A favourite of Ambrose's, she'd never had any of the issues

Iris and Clare had encountered securing leave passes from him, but that would doubtless change if he were to get wind of the *mischief* she was indulging in out of bounds, with an American of all things.

Ambrose held a very dim view of the Americans.

'As you know I have a low tolerance for tardiness,' he'd told Beth, 'and they were inexcusably late to this war.'

Prim wasn't the kind to be late to anything, and Iris suspected Ambrose wouldn't be averse to getting up to a bit of mischief with her himself. Beth agreed. She said he always became very flustered whenever Prim – not a plotter, as Iris had initially guessed, but one of the station's intelligence officers – delivered her post-interrogation reports to the offices for transmission to HQ.

'He always offers *her* tea,' she said. 'And biscuits. I fear it might break his skinny little heart if he were to get wind of Clint.'

Prim had met Clint at the end of February, after the USAAF had opened up a new base on the other side of Heaton from Doverley. He was a clerk rather than an airman, which Prim could get quite prickly about, insisting he'd have got his wings if he could, but was short-sighted, and flat-footed, and colour-blind. ('Christ,' Robbie had remarked soberly when she'd told him all about it, 'that's quite a list.') Iris suspected, actually, that Clint's lack of wings was part of his appeal for Prim. Beth had been stationed with her the year before, down in Cambridgeshire, and had told Iris and Clare that she'd lost three beaus there, one after the other. None of them had been serious, she'd only ever had the chance to go on a couple of dates with them, but after the third had gone down, the other men had decided she was too unlucky to associate with. Like V for Verity.

'It was pretty awful,' Beth said. 'I wouldn't have wished it on my worst enemy.'

Neither would Iris.

And truly, Prim wasn't her worst enemy.

She was just . . . *prim*.

Clint at least seemed to make her happy. She certainly loved to talk about his family's acres of land in Colorado, and he kept her well supplied with nylons and chocolate.

Not that she'd offered to share those luxuries with the rest of them. Iris still hadn't managed to replace the nylons she'd torn on Doverley's front steps and, like most other women that night, had come out bare-legged. No one wanted to wear woollens to the dive.

'Do you wish I was an American, Clarence?' Robbie asked, dipping his head towards her as they passed by Prim and Clint.

'Every day,' she said. 'Every, single, day.'

And he grinned.

They'd come to Bettys often since February. Whenever they did, she thought of her mum and their teas upstairs, which had hurt, to start, but these days felt more comforting than anything. It was the same whenever she'd returned to Bramble Lane for evenings out at The Heaton Arms (Robbie had been right, you really couldn't avoid it); initially, everything about being back there had caused her pain: passing her old home; seeing the brass knocker her mum had used to polish on the door; the milk bottle stand on the step; that crooked stile out to the sheep-filled fields, where, before Iris's gran's arthritis had got so bad, she'd used to take Iris for walks. (*Slow down*, she'd shouted after Iris, whenever Iris had run off. *You'll start a stampede.*) But day by day, week by week, that pain had eased, until Iris had come to realise how much she liked being back in the old lane. It had made her mum and gran real to her again: the memories of them no longer something to fear, but cradle close. And although she had wept, the first time she'd visited their graves with Robbie – she'd sobbed – it had

225

probably been long overdue. As she'd sunk against Robbie's chest and let her tears go, she'd felt acceptance flow through her. She hadn't even known, until that had happened, just how fiercely she'd still been fighting the truth of her mum and gran's deaths.

Father Bannister often came out to see her when she was in the graveyard, always bringing her a slice of his housekeeper's apple cake, baked with preserves from his orchard. *To save you the effort of scrumping*, he'd say, chuckling at his own joke, no matter how many times he repeated it.

Sometimes, he called by The Heaton Arms in the evenings, and whenever he did, would stand everyone there a round, the Americans included – who, whatever Ambrose's views on their timing, were unquestionably fighting this war now, flying their raids in broad daylight, creating their own army of ghosts.

Iris had heard stories of fights breaking out between American, British and Canadian airmen over the different levels of dangers they believed themselves to be facing, but she hadn't seen any of that in Heaton. Although the odd jibe got exchanged about Brits not being able to target, and Yanks not being able to see in the dark, it was always done in jest, and never escalated. They all knew what each other did, and no one was interested in trivialising it. They just wanted to survive.

'Did you resent us for not being here?' a pilot from New York had asked Robbie, back in March, after Jacob had mentioned Robbie had flown in the Battle of Britain.

'Quite a few of you were,' Robbie had replied.

'Not as many as now.'

'True.'

'So?'

'No, I didn't resent you. Honestly, I didn't think about you. I thought about what we were doing, and carrying on doing it.'

'And now?'

'Now?' Robbie had shrugged. 'You're here, there's a war still to fight because of everyone who's spent the past three years making sure of it, and hopefully together we'll win it sooner.'

'Cheers to that,' the New Yorker had said, raising his pint.

They hadn't seen him again.

His plane had gone down over Munich the following day, and although chutes had been spotted, Prim's Clint said there'd been no notification of any of the crew being taken prisoner on the ground. The battered locals didn't particularly like bomber crew.

It could happen that they disappeared before getting processed.

They'd all been relieved that no one from 96 had fallen over Essen the night before. Although another V for Verity had been hit by flak, they'd managed to limp back to France before baling out, so stood a chance of being smuggled home by Mabel's friends in the resistance. Other than for them, every crew had returned, and Iris and Clare had taken it in turns to instruct them to absolutely pancake, which everyone, besides Ambrose, had enjoyed.

'Why are they still doing that?' he'd demanded of Sergeant Browning, appearing from nowhere in the control room.

Fred hadn't been there; he'd gone to Essen too, and had been aerodroming at fifteen before absolutely pancaking himself.

'Because it makes everyone happy,' Sergeant Browning had replied.

'It makes everyone happy, sir,' Ambrose had corrected him.

'It makes everyone happy, *sir*.'

'Hello, Queen. Absolutely pancake, over,' Clare had told *Bucks Boys*.

And Iris, who'd just told Henry in *Mabel's Fury* to do the same, had smiled.

'This isn't a game, Winterton,' Ambrose had barked. 'It's *war*.'

'Is it really?' she hadn't been able to help herself riposting. But she'd been tired after the long night, and impatient to see Robbie, and so very fed up with all of Ambrose's endless pettiness. She'd given up counting the number of times he'd now attempted to ground either herself, or Clare, or both of them, and it wasn't just them he did it to. He nitpicked at everyone (except Prim), handing out punishments for everything from badly polished shoes, to sloppy salutes, to untidy billets, to curfews missed by a minute. 'And here was me thinking I was doing all this for fun.'

For which impertinence, the crime of *being smart*, Ambrose had once again declared her grounded, *until further notice*, then he'd grounded Clare and Browning too, for protesting at how unfair he was being.

Robbie, his superior, had taken him aside though, straight after Iris had filled him in at interrogation, and had a word with him about the misguidedness of interfering with the morale of the crews, who probably wouldn't enjoy learning that their radio operators had been punished for keeping up their spirits by a man who, when all was said and done, tucked himself into bed every night.

'So now he hates you too,' said Iris to him, when he'd arrived at the cottage afterwards.

'I don't give a damn what he thinks of me,' Robbie had replied, tossing his cap to the floor, smiling as he'd joined her in the kitchen doorway. 'It might make life easier if you stop annoying him though.'

'But he *wants* to be annoyed,' Iris had said, leaning back against the door's frame, raising her face to his.

'And you love obliging,' Robbie had replied, running his hands around her waist. 'I can't keep going into bat for you . . . '

'I love it when you talk like a cricket captain.'

'I mean it. I can't. He's unimaginative but not stupid. Eventually he's going to guess that we're . . . '

'Up to mischief?' she'd said, unbuttoning his tunic.

'Exactly.' He'd kissed her neck. 'He'll start watching you too closely.'

She'd closed her eyes. 'He already watches me closely.'

'Closer, then,' he'd said, slipping her skirt from her. 'He might stop you coming here . . . '

'I'd never let him,' she'd said.

Which she wouldn't.

The time, all the elastic, timeless time that the two of them had now stolen together within the cottage's bewitched walls had become everything to her. Here, now, in Bettys Bar, she smiled, thinking back over it, their every touch and word and whisper replaying in her mind, making her sweltering skin tingle in anticipation of the next time they'd meet there.

Tightening her hold on Robbie, she glanced up at him as they reached the booth and slipped into the last free space left by the others, and could tell from the look he gave her – the enjoyment in his bright gaze, the promise – that he knew exactly where her mind was.

'I have no idea if this film's loaded,' said Jacob, bringing them back to the moment, frowning down at his birthday gift. He was sitting on the opposite side of the booth, between Clare and Beth. Tim was next to Clare, and Henry, Ames, Mabel, and Lewis were on the other side of Beth. The rest of Lewis's crew, and *Mabel's Fury*'s gunners, Danny and Gus, were already dancing. 'Should I open it up . . . ?'

'*No*,' they all choarsed.

'You'll expose it,' said Beth, a glutton for difficult men, taking the camera from him. 'Let me see what's going on.

Oh, these damn glasses.' She removed them, reaching into her handbag for a cloth.

'Here,' said Jacob, producing a kerchief from his tunic pocket and taking the glasses to clean them himself. 'There.' Carefully, he set them back on Beth's face, and if he was as oblivious as he was making out to the intensity with which Beth watched him do it, not to mention the colour flooding her cheeks, then it was high time he got some glasses too.

'It's definitely loaded,' said Beth, returning her attention to the camera, her glasses already fogging up again. 'Try taking a picture.'

'Drink?' said Tim to Iris, proffering one of the table's jugs.

'Absolutely,' she said, reaching for an empty glass, meeting his smile.

She'd spent a lot of time with him too, these past weeks, mostly back at The Heaton Arms, and here in Bettys: drinking, dancing, reminiscing.

'Do you still have that picture of your dad?' she'd asked him, as they'd walked home from Heaton one night back in January.

'I still have it,' he'd said, patting his chest pocket. 'I feel like he's keeping his eye on me when we fly.' He'd smiled ruefully. 'Foolish, probably.'

'Not foolish,' she'd said, reaching for his hand, just as she'd done when they were small children. 'Not foolish at all.'

'I wish we hadn't lost touch,' he'd said, looking down at their hands. 'If I could only go back and teach eleven-year-old me to write a proper letter. Or better yet, get on a train to visit you . . . '

'If we could only teach our eleven-year-old selves all sorts of things,' she'd said.

And, wistfully, he'd nodded.

Then, as the others had caught them up, he'd let her hand go.

'Thank you,' she said to him now, once he'd filled her glass.

'You're most welcome,' he said to her, and poured for Robbie too.

'*Salut*,' said Mabel, raising her own glass.

'To Jacob,' said Robbie, raising his.

'To Jacob,' everyone chorused.

And, as they all leant across the table, cheersing, Jacob held up his camera, clicking the shutter, blinding them with the flash.

'*Mon dieu*,' said Mabel, blinking.

'It works,' said Jacob.

'Please don't do that again,' said Tim.

'Take Beth for a dance instead,' said Clare.

'Yes,' said Iris. 'A birthday dance.'

'Do you want to?' said Jacob dubiously to Beth, like there could be any question.

'I'd love to,' said Beth, removing her glasses to wipe them again.

'Give them to me,' said Clare, grabbing them from her as she and Jacob left, scrambling over the rest of them. 'They'll only get in the way. Jacob, just make sure to dance nice and close to her so that she can see you.'

'And don't leave her to find her way back alone,' said Robbie.

'No, definitely don't do that,' said Beth.

'You'd better hold her hand,' said Ames.

'All right,' said Jacob, and, as though under duress, offered his to Beth.

But Iris didn't miss his smile as Beth took it. Or the tenderness with which he pulled her to him, carefully navigating her through the crowds for the dance floor.

'Why won't he just ask her out?' she said, turning to Robbie. 'All these dances, and he hasn't even taken her on a trip to the pictures.'

'He thinks it would be irresponsible of him to get into anything with anyone,' Robbie said, watching them go.

She watched him doing it, her eyes moving over his face, that she loved, and was as handsome as ever, but bruised by new shadows that hadn't been there at the start of March. The creases around his eyes – grooves formed from the intensity with which she pictured him staring out of the cockpit – had grown more pronounced too.

He looked so deeply tired.

All of them did.

Lewis – topping up Clare's glass – appeared closer to thirty than the twenty Iris now knew he was.

They should all be back at Doverley in bed, probably. Getting some rest for once.

'He thinks I'm irresponsible, being with you,' Robbie continued, turning back to her, his words sending yet another shiver of unease snaking down her spine.

'And what do you think?' she asked him, battling to ignore it.

'I think if I am, there's nothing I can do about it.' A smile played on his lips, pulling at the muscles in his cheeks. 'I could never resist you.'

'That's very good to know,' she said. 'And –' she leant towards him, whispering in his ear – 'I don't really wish you were an American.'

'I don't wish you were one either,' he whispered back.

Quietly, she laughed, threading her fingers with his.

'Will you dance with me?' he asked.

'I'll always dance with you,' she said.

And, together, they got up.

She didn't look back at the others as they followed in Jacob and Beth's steps to the dancefloor, so didn't register Tim's eyes on them as they walked away.

Clare noticed him watching them though.

'Look after that boy, won't you,' she said to Iris, much later that night, when, after Bettys' band had finished playing, and every cocktail had been drained, they'd all crammed back into their cavalcade of motors and returned to Doverley.

'Which boy?' Iris asked, crossing to their stained bureau, her mind still with Robbie, on whose lap she'd sat the entire drive home.

'Tim,' Clare said. 'You know, the one who uses up his sugar ration to carry a sweet for you on every mission, just to believe he'll survive. He loves you so.'

'Oh, no.' Pulling her dark hair loose of its grips, Iris dropped them into the bureau's top drawer and, in the mirror, watched a frown form on her face. 'We've only ever been friends.'

'He still loves you,' said Clare. 'I suspect he'd do just about anything for you if you asked him.' She sat on her bed, kicked off her shoes. 'So just . . . tread carefully.'

Iris didn't take Clare's words of caution seriously. Before she climbed into bed, she dismissed them as nonsense, and, telling Clare as much, pushed them from her mind.

Yet, the next morning, when Tim came to see her in the control tower – where she was on duty again, trafficking local circuits for those pilots who'd taken their planes up for a run – she found herself thinking of them.

There was no one else but them in the control room. Operations were officially off that night, and almost everyone was lying low, in their billets or the mess. Only four pilots had dragged themselves out to fly, all testing the repairs that their planes had undergone after Essen, and since it was such a small number, Iris was managing them alone. Sergeant Browning was reading his paper in the breakroom, on standby in case she needed him, and Clare had headed back to the attic to write to Hans.

233

Robbie, not flying, had gone to see his mother. Iris had visited Annabelle with him a couple of times now herself – once in February, then again at the start of March – and although Annabelle had been very welcoming, smiling as kindly, and shyly, as she always had (she'd remembered Iris's love of ham and cheese sandwiches), Iris didn't want to intrude on her time with Robbie too much. On both her visits, Annabelle had watched Robbie constantly, so obviously scared to miss a thing. Throughout the time they'd sat with her, she'd kept her hand on her son's arm – reassuring herself, Iris could tell, that he was still there, still with her.

'Will you tell me straight away if anything happens?' she'd said to Iris in February, when Robbie, fetching her another blanket, had left them alone. 'Anything official will take time to reach me, and I worry every day that I might be sitting here not knowing he's hurt.' Her helpless eyes had been full of dread. 'There's so much I haven't protected him from, it's unbearable that I can't keep him safe now. But if I could at least know that I'd know . . . '

'You will,' Iris had told her, somehow managing not to choke on the words. 'I'll tell you.'

'You promise?'

'I promise.'

'Guess who I saw doing something they shouldn't have been last night,' Tim said to Iris now, sitting in Clare's vacant chair.

'Who?' she asked, glad of his company.

Grateful too for the mug of tea he'd brought her. She picked it up, wrapping her cold hands around it, and took a sip. He'd even remembered to add a touch of sweetener.

'Eleanor.'

'Prim.'

'She didn't look that prim to me. Clint was giving her a leg up to climb through a window at the front of the house.'

'Really?' Iris laughed, picturing it. 'Did she make it?'

'Just about.'

'What time was this?'

'After three.'

'*Three?*' Her brow creased. 'What were you doing up at the house at three?'

'Walking. I couldn't sleep.'

'But you must have been exhausted.'

'I was. I am. I couldn't . . . switch off, I suppose.'

'Does that happen often?'

'A bit,' he said, with a shrug that made her frown more.

She shifted in her chair, studying him properly, and, as her eyes moved over the premature lines in his own rugged face, she replayed what Clare had said the night before. Not about him loving her – that was too uncomfortable – but the other thing.

Look after that boy, won't you.

It came to her that she hadn't been doing that. Not enough. For all she'd danced, and laughed, and chatted with him, she'd been so caught up with Robbie that she hadn't paused to question, until this moment, whether Tim, with his happy-go-lucky smile, was all right.

'You need to sleep,' she told him, softly, her thoughts moving to the photo he carried of his dad, and his impossible yearning for his protection.

'Plenty of time for that,' he replied, with another smile.

She didn't return it. It was a front, she realised.

A put-off.

Evasive action.

He was scared. Really scared.

Her old friend, who she'd played with, joyously, for years, was beside himself.

'Can I do anything?' she asked him, finally seeing those

sweets he took on his missions for what they really were: his lifeline home. 'Help, in any way?'

'You already do,' he said, and for a fleeting moment, his smile did falter. His dark eyes became serious. 'You help all the time.'

*

A deep fog set in that afternoon, and hung around for the following two days, meaning everyone at Doverley remained on the ground. They all whiled away long hours at The Heaton Arms, where Clare won a tournament of pool, Beth plucked up the courage to ask Jacob to the pictures herself ('Are you sure about this?' he asked her, with a pained look. 'Pretty sure,' she said), Mabel and Ames disappeared upstairs to Mabel's room, and Iris spent much more time with Tim, trying to keep his mind from everything.

'How is he when you go up?' she asked Robbie, the two of them watching Tim lose to Clare at pool.

'Fine. It's the anticipation he struggles with.'

'He's not sleeping. I'm worried he might start making mistakes.'

'Not a chance. He's too good.'

'I think he's probably due a rest.'

'Everyone's due a rest.'

She couldn't argue with that.

But nor did she, nor Robbie, have any interest in resting when they all returned to Doverley. Not doing that, *not wasting time*, they escaped to their cottage, wrapping themselves up by the kitchen fire, on the bed of blankets that Iris had long since stolen from Ambrose's stores.

'Do you remember when we used to talk about my mum?' she said, on the second afternoon of the fog, lying with her head in the warm nook of Robbie's neck. 'I asked you why you thought it was so bad to lift your skirts, and you said it was because you might catch a cold.'

He laughed, and she smiled, feeling the vibrations of it. She loved lying with him like this, whilst everyone else was far away, and the woods around them were so silent. It felt like they might be the only people in the world.

'I no longer consider you lifting your skirts to be remotely bad,' he said.

'No,' she said, feeling his hand move around the curve of her waist, leaning up to kiss him. 'Nor do I.'

He hadn't been her first. He knew that. Just as she knew she hadn't been his. Their pasts weren't something they'd dwelt on – why would they do that? – but nor had it surprised them that the other had one. They had, after all, spent the past three years living through a war. Iris didn't regret anything that was behind her, or behind him. It had brought them here, to *this*. And she never worried about what might materialise from their time together. Unlike her mum, she and Robbie both knew enough not to chance catching anything, least of all a baby.

She had started to wonder more about her father lately though, now that she was back: who he'd been, where he'd come from, how he'd died. She'd even summoned the nerve to ask Father Bannister if he knew anything about him, but Father Bannister had told her he unfortunately didn't know a thing. *It was before my time, I'm afraid.*

'The fog's clearing,' said Robbie, looking up at the open window above them: the same one Lord Heaton had once yelled at them through. 'I think we'll probably go up tomorrow.'

'Maybe not,' Iris said, without any real hope.

And the squadron did fly the next night.

They went on another operation to Essen.

It was a night like so many others that had gone before: long, and dark, and cold.

Yet, it was also different.

For Iris, it was different.

'The strangest thing just happened to me,' she said to Clare, once it had. 'I can't make any sense of it.'

Chapter Sixteen

Claudia and Iris

15 November 2018, Day 13 of the shoot

&

April 1943

I've been waiting for something like this to happen.

I can't make sense of it – there is no sense – but I've felt it coming.

That's the first thought I have when, down on the floor of the frozen base, all of us so nearly at the end of our first night shoot, eternalizing the last April departure of 96 for Essen, I open my eyes to the fraught faces of Ana, Nick, Naomi, Felix, and Emma peering over me.

Then, I let my eyes fall shut again, because my head really hurts, and it's all too much.

But all week long, ever since I stood in Tim's lounge watching him sleep and somehow *found* myself back in Bettys bar – there, actually *there*, all of it so strangely familiar, my heart bursting with love, filling Iris with my fear – I've felt as though I've been moving through my days and nights with a wall up ahead of me: hidden, unavoidable, but assuredly waiting for me to crash into it, like I've just crashed now.

I don't think I'm going to be able to work any more tonight.

That's the second thought I have.

The third is that that's a real shame, because we were set up and ready for action, and it's going to cost a lot of money to restage this shot.

Over in LA, someone is about to have their day ruined.

That's my fourth thought.

My fifth is that what's just happened could not have been more public, and I've failed, absolutely, at keeping my composure in front of everyone. *The Screen*'s anonymous source, who's been leaking more gossip to them all week – about the scenes we've filmed, and Ana's daily calls with the studio on our progress, and the ongoing discord over the ending – is going to have a field day.

The sixth thought that hits me is that I just hallucinated again, except I don't believe it was an hallucination.

I'm no longer convinced anything I've been experiencing has been fabrication.

The seventh thought I have is that it might finally be time I asked someone for help.

The eighth is that that person should probably be Nick.

And my ninth thought is that I'm not sure it can be Nick.

I've pushed him away so much this week, I no longer know how to pull him back.

*

It was last Friday, after we returned from seeing Tim, that I spent my first night back in the attic. Nick crashed out as soon as he'd hung up on another call with his lawyers (he's been having those all week, with the net that the clinic – who've now confirmed that my files weren't hacked, but leaked by a cash-strapped intern – have offered to compensate us with money that we don't need, won't compensate for anything, and which I don't want a cent of); I tried to sleep too, but I couldn't, so I left Nick a note, grabbed a spare blanket, and headed upstairs – in part because I was just too upset to go on lying next to him.

We'd argued a lot that evening, about a whole load of things, from his insistence on pressing ahead with the lawyers, to a cryptic text I saw pop up on his phone from an unnamed number, asking him if he'd changed his mind yet ('Changed your mind about what?' I asked him. 'It's nothing,' he said, swiping the text away), to his pause before agreeing with Tim that he thought I was the cat's pyjamas ('It was like you weren't sure,' I said. 'Seriously?' he said. 'You believe that?'), to his suspicion that I wasn't being open with him about what had gone on with Tim after I went back to his room for my phone.

'Nothing went on,' I said, reluctant, for obvious reasons, to get into Tim's warning that Felix is in love with me, let alone how, looking at his photo of the crew, I saw Robbie come to life, let alone how much I was still spinning out over that, and my moment in Bettys Bar. *Let alone* how crushed I'd felt when it had been over. 'He was half asleep. He told me my eyes are like Iris's.' *Windows to your soul.* 'That's all.'

'That's not all. You've been acting weird ever since.'

'I'm sorry you think I'm weird.'

'I said you've been acting weird.'

'I suppose if I was the cat's pyjamas . . . '

'Jesus Christ, *Claude.* I think you're the cat's pyjamas, ok?'

I hated that we'd ended the day like that, when only a few hours before we'd been holding hands. It was like a brief window had opened, making that possible for us again, and somehow we'd slammed it shut.

But that wasn't the only reason I went upstairs.

After days of being too intimidated to return to the attic after dark, I felt myself drawn, irresistibly, up there. Perversely, I *wanted* to discover if I could see those flares again, hear those planes. Ever since I'd left Tim, I'd been replaying my slip back to Bettys on repeat, and was craving more.

I needed another fix.

I saw no flares that night though.

I heard no planes.

No matter how intently I stared down at the set from the attic window, it remained silent, bathed in the fluorescent glow of Jeff's security lights.

Dejectedly, I wrapped myself up on Iris's bed, and dreamt dreams that began as scenes from the movie, then took a turn, filling with other actors, different lines, crowds in a pub, smoke in the air, the taste of boiled sweets, and homemade apple cake.

When I woke, I felt disorientated, giddy. It was as though I'd returned from a journey on which I'd left half of myself still travelling.

All day long on set, I continued to feel that part of me missing, except for during shooting, when, as Iris, I became secure in my own skin again.

Safe.

Off-camera, I know I was quiet, I'm aware I was withdrawn, and Nick wasn't the only one to throw a frowning look my way when, in our breaks, I sat apart from everyone, grappling with my dislocation at finding myself back in fifty per cent, worrisome, past-tense me.

She's another escape route for you, Mum said to me of Iris, back on Parliament Hill. *A fresh golden ticket to a different mind, a different world.*

Iris's mind doesn't feel different any more though.

Her world doesn't.

There are times when she feels more me, than me.

'That doesn't sound entirely healthy,' said Emma, when I confided in her about that much.

'It's helping,' I told her.

'Is it?' she asked, dubiously.

'It really is,' I said.

And, on-camera, it really has been. That day in Bettys, as Iris, I joked with Felix, I chatted with Emma, I teased and smiled with Nick, kissing him for the first time in longer than I'm ok thinking about – pressing my body against his with my nerves firing, and his heart hammering against mine – and what we canned was great, I know it was all great. 'Circle it,' Ana said, over and again, and I *enjoyed* myself. There was this one moment whilst we were all jitterbugging – Felix with me, Nick with Emma – when Emma landed on Nick's head, with such comedic inelegance that none of us could hold it together, and I laughed. I laughed so much. It felt *good*. They were such fun scenes. Caught up in them, swept up in Iris, I forgot everything else. I wasn't lonely, I wasn't scared, or failing. I was *happy*.

'You looked happy,' said Felix to me, when, the day finished, we walked behind Emma and Nick, back to our trailers. 'What about now?'

'Now?' I turned, meeting his dark gaze, and, thinking of all the long weeks we'd been at odds, found a smile, because he was there, with me. 'Now, I'm glad we're talking again.'

'Yeah,' he said. 'I'm glad about that too.'

Only, he didn't seem glad.

He seemed . . . edgy.

Preoccupied.

'Are *you* ok?' I asked.

'Me?' he said. 'Yeah, of course. I'm fine. Just tired from swinging you around all day.' He summoned a smile of his own.

I made mine bigger.

But we were both acting, and not particularly well.

He wasn't ok, I could tell.

We still weren't.

Not completely.

243

There was still this lurking reticence between us, and I hated it.

The filming at least has continued to go well all week. *Magically*, as *The Screen*'s source has said. Really, that part of things no longer worries me at all. It feels absurd, actually, that I ever struggled to believe I'd be able to make myself into Iris, when every day I've found myself morphing into her more completely than the one before. It's being here that's made that happen, I have no doubt about that. Back in rehearsals, Iris was purely a character to me: an elusive, ungraspable character; lines on a page, and nowhere to be found in that soulless LA room.

She was here.

All along, she was here: in her cottage; out in the woods.

Up in her bedroom.

'I don't want you to keep sleeping there,' Nick said to me on Saturday morning, after our first night apart. 'I'm afraid of what it's doing to you. Where it might take us . . . '

'This isn't about us,' I told him. 'It's about the movie. This is a job. I want to get it right.'

'You are getting it right. There's something else going on. Something else taking you up there . . . '

'No . . . '

'Yes.'

'*No*.'

'Then stay down here tonight. Please.'

I planned to.

But that night, after he fell asleep, I lay beside him, full of frustration that he'd once again called his lawyers, and sadness, so much sadness, over our kiss in Bettys Bar, and all the incredible moments we've now shared as Iris and Robbie, so effortlessly, when it just keeps being so bloody *hard* to be us.

I became sadder yet thinking about how great he was with

all the kids in Heaton, then, those women he was photographed with in those bars, who maybe he really *didn't so much as look at*, not even that one who kept cropping up. Maybe she was just a fan.

But what if he had looked?

What if I set him free to do that in the future, and give her, or someone like her, a chance?

Might he end up happier than I can ever make him?

Restlessly, I kicked off my covers, and stared at the ceiling, picturing the attic above.

I glanced sideways at Nick, then – wide awake and fearing I was on course to spend the rest of the night that way – caved to temptation, slipping from our bed, and creeping back upstairs.

He didn't say anything about it the next day when I returned to our room to shower.

Already dressed, he told me he'd leave me to it, and went to breakfast.

Watching him go, absorbing the anger in his set shoulders, the *disappointment*, I resolved that I wouldn't leave him again that night.

But I did leave him.

I haven't spent a night with him since.

And although I've felt like I've been betraying him every time I've left him, I haven't been able to stop myself. Because, although I still haven't seen any more flares from Iris's window, or that face again in her mirror, there have been moments – scores of them now – when, with my head on Iris's pillow, I've listened to the attic's silence and once again heard something very different: soft breathing; a rhythmic scratching; creaking pipes; clattering footsteps; the echoes of laughter.

In her bed, I've continued to have the most vivid dreams.

Two in particular keep repeating.

The first is brief.

I'm in a clinical-feeling hallway, looking at a middle-aged soldier through Iris's eyes: a colonel, I seem to know.

Go, I urge Iris, over and again.

You need to go.

The second, just as inexplicable, is even more haunting.

I find myself in a dimly lit room with a beautiful, faded woman in a wheelchair.

I'm looking into her eyes, and we're both crying.

She reaches up, touching my face, and says something that makes me cry more.

I don't know what that something is.

When I wake, with tears rolling down my own cheeks, I can never remember.

I have no idea who this woman can be.

If I've ever even known her.

Or why she leaves me feeling so desperately sad.

*

Iris spent most of that April afternoon before the squadron returned to Essen in bed. Robbie was busy at the base, so she'd decided she might as well try to bank some sleep. Clare was with her, in bed too, writing again to Hans.

It was his birthday.

'Twenty-seven,' said Clare, staring down at her pad. 'He was twenty-three when I left him. Soon, we'll have been apart longer than we had together.'

'It might not come to that,' said Iris. 'This war can't go on forever.'

'Can't it?' said Clare. 'What if it's with us now for always?'

Iris didn't reply.

The idea was too chilling to contemplate.

With a short sigh, Clare resumed her writing.

And Iris closed her eyes, listening to the rhythmic scratch of her pen, the groan of the attic's pipes, and the footfall of others in the corridor outside. This effort to sleep felt futile – she was too alert, too aware of the night ahead – but gradually, irresistibly, unconsciousness pressed down on her, with a weight so heavy, it might almost have belonged to another body.

She dreamt.

Kaleidoscope dreams: of the Heaton Arms, Tim's sweets, and Father Bannister's apple cake.

Then, Robbie's mother, beautiful and faded in her wheelchair.

She was crying, reaching out to touch Iris's own tear-stained face . . .

With a start, Iris woke.

Scrambling to sit, she pressed her hand to her beating chest.

'Are you all right?' said Clare, looking up from her letter.

'I'm not sure.' She swallowed. 'How long was I asleep?'

'A few minutes. Did you have a nightmare?'

'Yes.' Iris nodded. 'Yes.'

'*Will you tell me straight away if anything happens?*' Robbie's mother had asked of her back in February.

She'd just watched herself doing it.

It had been a dream though.

Just an awful dream.

Resolutely, determinedly, she pushed it from her mind.

*

The identity of that colonel, and the woman in the wheelchair, aren't the only unknowns I've wrestled with this week. Plenty more have been nagging at me.

Like, who that other woman was: the one with the Ploughman's in The Heaton Arms who I thought I recognised.

247

And, who Tim could have been talking about when he mentioned that *other* woman who showed him up to the attic.

And, whether he was speaking the truth, or was simply confused, when he said *Mabel's Fury* had already reached England before Robbie radioed Iris that final time.

Imogen hasn't been able to shed any light.

I finally met her on Sunday. She came up to Doverley for the Remembrance Service, which was beautiful, and poignant, and finished with Justin Holmes, who's playing Jacob – who didn't want to tempt fate by having his photograph taken that last morning before he disappeared – bugling a last post that caused all of us to stare into the clouds, my heart to ache, my throat to burn, and, seemingly, the entire world to stand still.

All I wanted, afterwards, was to go to the cottage. The force I felt tugging me there was huge. I didn't question what made that happen, or even try to fight it – there's only so much of that I can do – I simply knew I'd feel better if I went.

But I didn't go, because Imogen was there, even lovelier in person than on the phone, and I couldn't just leave her. Ana invited her to watch some of the filming, and since I wasn't involved in our next shot, I kept Imogen company, filling her in on Tim's revelation that Robbie made it back to England.

'What do we even do with this?' she said.

'I wish I knew,' I told her.

I've been racking my brains all week. Obviously, the only thing *to* do is solve the mystery of what happened, but I can't think how. No one can. Google's no use, it never has been, and, as Ana's pointed out, there's no point hiring more researchers either. We've had a whole crew of them working on the movie; if the truth was lurking in an archive somewhere, they'd have found it.

It can only come from Tim.

'Maybe you should talk to him,' I suggested to Imogen. 'He said you'd called . . . '

'What? No. I haven't spoken to him since his birthday.'

'Really?' I frowned.

She said you'd come, Tim said to me.

Was he confused about that, too?

Again, it's a question I can't answer.

Yet another frustrating unknown.

'Why don't you go see him again,' said Imogen. 'You've obviously been working some magic with him. Maybe he'll tell you more.'

I was planning to visit him tomorrow, on our day off.

I don't suppose I'll be doing that now though.

Gingerly, I raise my hand to my head, and think it might be bleeding.

*

It is bleeding.

'She needs to go to hospital,' says Nick.

'Do we call an ambulance?' says Emma. 'I don't think you're meant to move someone who's hit their head.'

'Isn't that more to do with the spine?' says Felix.

'I'm googling it,' says Naomi.

'I've got it,' says Ana, tapping. 'She fell more than a metre, right?'

'She fell about three,' says Nick.

'Then she needs an ambulance.'

'Are you sure?' says Blake, who appears to have joined us. 'That's going to get a lot of attention.'

'Fuck off, Blake,' says Nick. 'I'm calling one.'

'This is stupid,' I say. 'I'll be fine . . . '

'Ambulance please,' says Nick into his phone.

I feel like such an idiot, being the source of all this fuss.

It's not like Emma and I weren't warned about the stairs.

Iris came out on to the control tower stairs to watch the squadron depart for Essen, leaving Clare to manage take-off with Sergeant Browning. Folding her arms, she looked towards the laden planes, stationary and silent at their dispersal points, waiting for them to begin taxiing towards the runway. She shivered with apprehension, and the cold. The fog had entirely lifted now, exposing a starlit sky, and beneath it an April frost had set in, shimmering on the tarmac and the stairs. Piper was at the foot of them, getting tied up by the parachute rigger, Lydia, to stop her running after the planes. Browning would fetch her into the tower once they'd left, but not before. She liked to see them off too, and howled if anyone tried to prevent her.

And now here was Prim, coming up the stairs towards Iris, her blonde hair pinned beneath her cap, her legs clad in pristine nylons. She held on to the banister as she walked, stopping herself from slipping.

She didn't need to be down at the base yet. As an intelligence officer, her duties wouldn't start until interrogation, so she could remain in bed until dawn. But she always spent ops nights in the control tower breakroom, waiting for everyone to return. Annoying as she was, there was no disputing she cared.

'Shouldn't you be inside?' she demanded of Iris, joining her on the landing.

'I want to see Robbie off.'

'Well, I'm going in,' said Prim, pushing past her. 'It's freezing.'

Iris stepped aside, giving her room to pass.

And, in the same moment, as Piper let go a bark, the planes began to fire up their engines, their collective roar filling the night.

*

It was the noise of the planes that did it.

And the blaze of the flare path.

It hadn't yet been lit when Emma and I began climbing the stairs, passing Rusty, leashed at the bottom. The planes hadn't started up. We went slowly, our leather brogues as good as skates on the frosted wood. The temperature hasn't risen above zero for days now, and although the stairs had been gritted, they were still icy.

'Watch yourselves, please,' Jeff called after us. 'I don't want either of you breaking your necks.'

The shot we were about to film was the last one we had on for tonight. We've been working since sundown, getting everything for this sequence in the can: first, the squadron spilling out of their flight briefing; then, everyone in the parachute queues; then, the ground crew loading the incendiaries; then, Emma and I watching the boys head to their dispersal points. This final piece was meant to be of us on the stairs, and the planes taxiing to the runway. It's an effect-heavy shot, costly and labour-intensive, and the aim was to do it in one take.

'God, I'm ready for this to be over,' said Emma to me.

I nodded, but didn't reply, because that was when the stunt pilots started up our replica Lancasters' engines. We've only got three operating – nothing compared to the twenty-four planes that 96 often sent up – but even so, the noise was deafening.

Slowly, one hand on the railing, I pressed my other to my forehead.

My skin was clammy.

My head was splitting.

Below me, Nick and Felix were with the rest of their crew, done for the night and watching the moving planes. Ana, meanwhile, was up on a podium with a megaphone, giving

251

the extras working as groundcrew a final briefing on what she needed from them.

Reaching the control tower's landing, I tuned out, distracted by how woozy the lights were suddenly making me: brightening, then dimming, then brightening again.

'Claude?' said Emma, peering into my face. 'You ok?'

Which was when the pyrotechnicians ignited the runway torches.

Not answering Emma, I turned, drawn by the sudden whoosh of light.

At the foot of the stairs, Rusty went nuts, barking and straining to give chase to the flares, so much more excited by them than she was by that bird.

The flares didn't look the same as the ones I saw from the attic.

They were too uniform.

Too perfect.

I didn't have time to think about that though.

Everything else happened.

The guttural roar of the planes intensified, deafeningly, as though multiplying by . . . eight.

My eyes swam.

The world wavered.

And, through it all, cut the piercing screech of that bird, who was no way, no how awake.

That's when I started falling, tumbling backwards, my veins flooding with panic.

I saw Emma, staring after me, her eyes widening in alarm.

I heard Nick, above the roaring in my ears, shouting my name.

I opened my mouth, my throat filling with a scream.

But I didn't let it go.

My neck snapped back, throwing my stare to the starlit

sky, and I was no longer falling, but up at the top of the stairs again, with a blonde-haired woman whose fine-boned face felt instantly familiar. On my body, I wore a uniform still, only it wasn't tailored, the fabric was faded, and my legs were covered in woollen stockings rather than sheer tights.

I was about to fall all over again, I felt a rush of surety about that, and didn't want to do it twice, so I reached out, grabbing the blonde woman's arm.

*

'What are you doing?' said Prim, as Iris grabbed on to her.

'I'm not sure,' said Iris, frowning at her own impulse.

Releasing Prim's arm, she looked down at her feet, steady beneath her, not going anywhere.

They'd felt like they'd been about to, though.

As Prim had passed her, and she'd turned towards the noise of the planes, her whole body had flooded with adrenalin: the strongest sensation of somehow already being in the process of falling.

'I was about to slip,' she said.

'No you weren't.'

'I felt like I was.'

Prim narrowed her eyes. 'Have you been drinking Clare's brandy?'

'No.'

'I should hope not,' said Prim, carrying on inside.

Iris remained where she was, her frown deepening.

She really had felt like she'd been tumbling.

Slowly, she looked over towards *Mabel's Fury*, now taxiing towards the runway, and, reached up, touching her hand to her head.

She wasn't sure what made her do that, either.

Or probe her skull for a bruise.

There was no bruise.

Of course there wasn't.

She hadn't fallen.

And yet, as she pressed harder on her scalp, she was filled with a certain sense of a moment hurdled.

A pain missing.

*

'How bad's the pain?' Nick asks me, still on the phone to 999.

'I'm not sure,' I say. 'I can't really feel it.'

'You heard that?' Nick says, into his phone.

They heard it.

'The ambulance is on its way,' he tells me.

I open my mouth to protest again.

I don't need an ambulance, I intend to say.

But, 'Can you come too?' I ask Nick instead.

'Of course I'll come,' he tells me.

And I realise, as he tightens his grasp around mine, that, for the first time since last Friday, he's holding my hand.

*

'The strangest thing just happened to me,' Iris said to Clare, once the squadron was gone, Browning was fetching tea, and they were alone in the control room. 'I can't make any sense of it.'

'Sense of what?' said Clare, leaning back in her chair.

'Outside with Prim. I nearly fell, except I stopped myself before I realised it was even going to happen. Then it was as though . . . Well . . . ' She broke off, trying to think how to explain it. 'It somehow already had. Or –' she bit her lip – '*was*.'

She half expected Clare to dismiss her.

254

Scoff, like Prim had.

But Clare didn't dismiss her.

And it wasn't in her nature to scoff.

'Maybe it has happened,' she said, her fingers moving to her neck, lacing through the chain holding Hans's ring. 'Maybe it is.'

'What do you mean?'

'Oh, I don't know.' She frowned. 'Lately though, I keep wondering whether this is all as new for us as we accept it is.' She ran her thumb around the circle of Hans's band of gold. 'I find myself unsurprised by so much.'

'Because of your powers, you mean?' said Iris, which might have been a joke.

Except she didn't feel like joking.

'They're not powers,' Clare said, not joking either. 'Just a certain sense of . . . recognition, I suppose. Truth.' She looked across at Iris, her eyes still puffy from her earlier tears. 'I rather think we might have all fallen before.'

CLAUDIA BAXTER DOWN BUT NOT OUT

In breaking news, Claudia Baxter is under medical supervision after a fall on set last night. It's reported that she lost her balance at the top of RAF Doverley's reconstructed control tower – pictured here – and plummeted the full height of the external staircase.

'It was terrifying,' says our source. 'She didn't trip. Her whole face blanked out, and she just . . . dropped.'

'It's possible she had a stress-induced seizure,' says Odette Harrison, MD, a specialist in functional neurological disorders. 'That's entirely feasible, given the trauma of everything she's been going through, and the long hours she's said to have been working on set. Unfortunately, this fall won't have helped, and her doctors will need to undertake scans to rule out the possibility of a brain bleed.'

Nick Turner, pictured here heading into York Central Hospital with Claudia in the early hours of this morning, reportedly hasn't left her side since she was admitted. Claudia's mum, Alex Baxter, has also now joined them, but refused to comment on Claudia's condition when we approached her.

However, in a turnaround from her previous tight-lipped silence on everything Bomber Boys, director Ana Ashley has released a statement, via Twitter, reassuring fans that Claudia is recovering quickly, fully expects to return to work in the near future, and is extremely grateful for the wonderful care she's receiving from the NHS.

There's been an outpouring of love for Claudia in response, whilst a recent photograph of Claudia hugging a local woman in the Yorkshire village of Heaton continues to be reposted across social channels, with the accompanying hashtag, #leanonme, trending, and women coming forward to share their own experiences of miscarriage, and offer one another support.

Notoriously private Claudia doesn't, of course, do socials, so hasn't joined in.

And, according to our source, she's become increasingly antisocial with Nick, too. The word is, they aren't even sleeping in the same room any more.

They're in the same room now, of course, although we hope Claudia gets out of it soon, and can leave hospital asap with a clean bill of help.

You'll hear about it here first when she does.

Chapter Seventeen

Claudia

'Is this true?' Mum asks me, looking up from her phone.

We're in a curtained cubicle in A&E, and she's sitting by my bed. Nick's not here. He's out in reception, taking delivery of the clothes a runner's brought us. All we've got are the costumes we came in. Nick's spent the past ten hours in scrubs.

'Is what true?' I ask Mum.

'That you and Nick are sleeping in different rooms.'

I frown, which hurts my head. 'What are you reading?'

'*The Screen*,' says Mum.

Shit, I think.

Who the hell's told them that?

'Mum, come on,' I say, out loud, 'you know not to read that stuff.'

'So, it's not true?'

I sigh.

'Oh, Claude,' she says, heavily.

And I close my eyes, not because I want to sleep, but because I really don't want to be having this conversation.

I also feel very ready not to be in this cubicle any more. My CT scan was clear (so great, really, I'm so glad I've exposed myself to all that unnecessary radiation), and I've had two stitches in my scalp, which has stopped the bleeding. But I was sick in the ambulance, all over Nick's feet ('Oh good,' said Mum, when I told her, 'that's going to make your sister feel so much better about what happened on the plane.'), so I'm being kept under observation for a while longer.

'How long's a while?' I asked the nurse who delivered that news.

'That depends on whether you're sick again,' he said. 'Let's see if you can keep down this sandwich your mum's brought you.'

'What is it?' I asked Mum.

'M&S,' she said, like that was all I needed to know.

Opening my eyes, I tentatively take another bite (it's a chicken salad: my favourite when I was at school), and notice that Mum's no longer looking at me, but around the cubicle, her hands clenched in her lap.

'Are *you* all right, Mum?' I ask her, gently.

I haven't forgotten that the last time she was in this hospital, it was to pick me up after my nan and grandad died.

I think, actually, it must be breaking her in two, being back here.

I'm finding it disquieting enough, and I barely recall that day.

'I'm ok,' she says. 'It just feels very strange. Sad.'

'You shouldn't have come. You didn't need to . . . '

'Don't be ridiculous. Now come on –' she nods at my sandwich – 'eat that up so we can get out of here.'

*

I'm finally discharged at six, with strict instructions to rest for forty-eight hours, until Sunday night, and ideally not be left alone in case of any delayed symptoms. Mum declares she'll

259

stay and keep an eye on me whilst Nick's working, I tell her that's totally unnecessary, I have no intention whatsoever of not working, Nick tells me not to be crazy, of course I can't work, Mum tells him to ignore me, I'm concussed, then Nick calls Ana, who calls Jeff, who talks to Doverley's management, who make a staff room available for Mum in the house.

'Luckily I packed plenty of clothes,' Mum says as we leave the hospital via a secluded fire escape that Blake's recced for us, so avoiding the press outside A&E. 'I had a hunch you'd need me to stay.'

'I don't need you to stay,' I repeat, climbing into the waiting car.

'Of course you do.'

I don't protest further.

I haven't got the energy.

And besides, maybe Mum's right.

Maybe I do need her.

Now that she's here, I realise I'm glad she's going to stick around.

'You ok?' says Nick, holding the door as I buckle up, and god, he looks wrung out. He's spent the entire day on a plastic seat in my cubicle, where I'm certain he's been wrestling with memories too. Not about my grandparents, obviously, but the last time we were in hospital together.

I've been remembering that as well.

And I don't know if it's the thought of how much he was hurting then, or my guilt at how distant I've been from him – the lies I've told; the secrets I've kept – but I feel suddenly compelled to tell him how sorry I am, for everything.

You deserve better.

But I can't do that in front of Mum and the driver.

So, 'I'm fine,' I say instead.

And Nick gives me a strained smile, then closes my door, climbs in beside the driver, Mum gets in beside me, and we set off back to Doverley.

*

It isn't a massive deal that I've been invalided out for the rest of the weekend, not like it was when Emma was sick, and I take some comfort from that. Although we only have a fortnight left on the estate now, with a hard stop at the end – the National Trust need it back on 1 December for their festivities – the focus is still very much on finishing Emma's scenes, and she has several outstanding that I'm not involved in. Her final one needs rain, lots of rain, so is being saved until the weather cooperates. In the meantime, while I'm resting, she'll shoot a montage of pool matches with the boys (Clare was apparently incredible at pool), then another in which she pens Clare's un-postable letters to Hans, and, assuming that all goes to schedule, another night in Bettys Bar, with everyone except Nick and me.

We will both feature in that sequence, just back in Doverley's abandoned billiards room, with the idea that the noisy, boozy fun in Bettys will be intercut with much steamier, silent footage of the two of us.

My anxiety over filming that footage is something I think about at least once a day.

It's one of a trio of scenes scheduled for the last week of this month that I'm really, really dreading.

The second is the shot where I give Robbie the coordinates that lead him and the crew to their deaths.

The third is the one when I kill myself – which, like the second, I'm still hoping gets dropped from the script.

For the present though, I can't do anything about that, so I park it and, once we arrive at Doverley, leave Mum in Jeff's capable hands, gratefully acquiescing with her insistence that I go straight upstairs and make use of my rolltop bath.

'Remember to wear a shower cap,' she calls after me as, with Nick, I head for the stairs. 'You can't get those stitches wet.'

*

I don't see her again for the rest of the evening. She texts me while I'm still in the bath, saying her room's extremely comfortable, I'm not to worry about her, she's going to eat dinner with Felix then have an early night.

I suggest you do the same. Phil and the girls send their love xxx

'You pull that off,' says Nick, nodding at my plastic cap as he comes out of the shower, wrapping himself in a towel.

'My hair's going to get gross,' I say. I'm not allowed to wash it until these forty-eight hours are over.

'You could never be gross, Claude.' Exhaustedly, he runs his hand down his face. 'Want me to leave you in peace?'

'No, stay.'

It takes him aback.

I see that from the look he gives me, and, thinking of how incredible he's been all day, feel guiltier yet.

I'm sorry, I wanted to tell him in the car.

'I'm so sorry,' I say to him now. 'I know I haven't been making anything easy.'

'I'm not interested in easy,' he says, moving to rest against the vanity. His shoulders are coated with beads of water that catch the lights' glow. His face, despite his tiredness – despite the years I've spent looking at it – still gives me pause, pulling my eye.

It's a good face.

My favourite face, in fact.

Yet, even as I think that, I discover I'm picturing Robbie's too, and feel even worse.

'You deserve . . . ' I begin.

'Don't,' he says, cutting me off. 'I won't hear it.'

'But you do deserve better.'

'I don't *deserve* anything. I want you.'

'I think I've lost me,' I say, without knowing I'm going to, and my throat closes up, like it's trying to stop the words leaving, only they're already out.

And they don't seem to surprise Nick at all.

His expression moves in pain, but not shock.

'I lost me too,' he says. 'The difference between us, though, is I've wanted to find my way back to who I am.'

'I want to find my way back . . . '

'Do you?'

'*Yes.*'

With a sigh, he tips his head up, looking, sightlessly, at the lights above.

'What happened this morning, Claude? How did you fall like that?'

'I slipped . . . '

'You were standing still.'

'I still slipped.'

Slowly, he brings his gaze back down to mine. 'Did you want to do that?'

The question astounds me.

'No,' I say, appalled. 'Is that what you've been thinking?'

'No.' He frowns. 'I don't know.'

'Nick, I did not *want* this.'

'I was scared. You scared me. You keep doing it.'

'I don't mean to.'

'Then stop,' he says, and his low voice cracks on the *stop*. 'Please. Let me in.'

'I want to.'

'Then do it.'

'It's hard . . . '

'*Why?*'

'Because I'm frightened too.' This time, it's my voice that fractures. 'I'm so afraid I'm not enough for you. That I'm keeping you from how happy you could be.'

Setting his jaw, he draws a long, frustrated breath.

'You're enough for me,' he says. 'You've always been enough. But you haven't given me you in a long time.'

'I don't know where I am.'

'You're not looking.'

That stings. 'Yes, I am . . . '

'You're not . . . '

'I am.'

'You're *not.*' He shouts it, with a sudden ferocity that silences me. 'The only person you seem interested in finding is a dead woman.' His eyes, fixed on mine, fill with tears that I watch him fight to hold back. I can't bear it. Can't bear that I'm doing this to him. 'It's like you've given up on you, and that doesn't make me happy. It's breaking my heart.'

I don't know what to say.

It's breaking my heart too.

That's what I think.

But I still can't find my voice.

I really can't speak.

And I'm not holding back my tears.

They're out, gushing from my eyes as Nick moves towards me, kneeling beside the bath. And I'm not sure what I should do – if I should turn from him, as I'm used to doing, or towards him, as I want to – but while I'm still deciding, he rests his head against my plastic-covered one, holding my face in his hands, and his touch feels so welcome, so right, so *good*, that I stun myself by kissing him, which stuns him too – I feel that from his stillness – but then, he kisses me back.

And if, as I reach up, lacing my fingers with his, there's a moment when I sense the touch of that other hand I felt in Tim's lounge, in Bettys Bar, and kiss Nick harder – as him, and as *him*, the lines between my now and then, this love and that love, once again blurring – it's fleeting, gone in a gasp, and I don't allow myself to dwell on it.

Nick kisses me more, and for the first time since before we lost our son, neither of us attempts to push the other away. We cling to each other, not for any camera, or any script, but for us, as us, *in private*, and it feels so precarious, so delicate and unexpected, that I can't bring myself to ruin it by questioning whether it was entirely him I was with just now.

'I love you,' I say, looking into his luminous eyes, *windows to his soul*, and think only of how easy it suddenly is to pour my heart into those words. 'I want to give you me.'

'I want you to, too.'

'I want to believe it's enough.'

'You're enough . . . '

'I hope so.'

'You are,' he says, running his hand around my neck, down my bubble-covered back.

I'm still wearing my shower cap.

Remembering, I go to take it off.

'No,' he says, his eyes creasing in a smile. 'Leave it on.'

And, through my tears, I laugh.

He laughs too.

We laugh together.

Then we kiss again.

This time, we don't stop.

It really has been a long time.

A long, long time.

Almost a year.

We don't talk about that, afterwards.

We just lie together on our bed, silent and entangled, looking at each other, his hand on my waist, mine on his chest, both of us absorbing what we've just done.

I'm glad that we've let it happen.

Relieved.

Now that we have, it comes to me how much I've missed it. Missed him.

And I don't know what it will mean for us from here. I only know that it feels good, so very good, to be lying in his arms again like this, for now.

His eyes grow heavy.

I feel mine do the same.

'Please don't go upstairs tonight,' he says, bringing me back from the brink of unconsciousness. 'I won't sleep if I think you might. I need to sleep . . . '

'I know you do.' He's been awake for the best part of forty-eight hours. 'I won't go up.'

'You've told me that before.'

'I won't go. I promise.'

This time, I keep my word.

Rousing myself just long enough to swallow the painkillers I've been prescribed, I fall asleep easily, and, for once, feel no pull to the attic.

Perhaps, because I want to be where I am.

Or maybe because the painkillers are really strong.

Regardless, I wake only once before dawn, stirred by Nick's movement as he sits up, checking his phone. I blink, registering his blue-lit frown, then, groggily, drift back to sleep.

*

'What were you looking at last night?' I ask him, when, at six, his alarm goes off.

'When?' he asks, dragging himself up to sitting, looking back at me from the edge of the bed.

'I don't know. You were on your phone.'

'Was I?'

'Yes.'

He shrugs. 'I guess I was checking the time.'

'You don't remember?'

'No.' His brow furrows. 'Kind of.' Flexing his shoulders, he stretches, then stands. 'I was pretty out of it.'

He seems sincere.

But then, he is an excellent actor.

I consider pushing him further.

Asking him again about that unnamed text he dismissed as nothing the other day.

Have you changed your mind?

But before I can, he leans down, kissing me, and it's nice.

I don't want to ruin it.

'Go back to sleep,' he says. 'Make the most of having the weekend off.'

'All right,' I say, and let it go.

Still, as he heads into the bathroom, taking his phone with him, I'm left with a feeling of unease.

He never normally takes his phone into the bathroom.

He's hiding something, I'm certain.

Keeping secrets too.

Chapter Eighteen

I don't plan to share my own secrets with Mum.

When I do finally get out of bed and head down to join her in the emptied dining room for a late Saturday breakfast, I go intending to continue keeping it all to myself, just like I did yesterday in A&E. I never entertained the possibility of confiding in any of the staff there. I figured anything medically relevant would show up on my CT (and admittedly it was a relief when nothing did), then, after that, I just wanted to convince my doctor to discharge me. She was very nice, extremely capable and efficient, but also overworked, getting pulled in about ten different directions, and at no point was I tempted to add to her load.

I am tempted to confide in Mum though. I trust her, she's my mum, and I know she'd do anything in her power for me. But now that I've started to seriously contemplate leaning on her with this, I'm afraid, of so much. Like, how mad it will all sound to her. And, frightening her. And, being told I'm imagining everything, when I no longer believe I am. And, more than anything, of her trying to set me on a path to it all stopping.

I don't want any of it to stop.

I've realised that since my fall.

I'm not ready for it to be over.

I need it too much.

And I think Iris needs me.

Because what if I did stop her from falling in 1943?

What else might I be able to change, for *everyone*, if I can only work out what went so very wrong back then?

And I know, I *know*, how Mum will react if I admit to her that that's something I'm considering, so I really don't *intend* to tell her.

But she's seen through me my whole life, and built an entire career on extracting reluctant truths from the most closed of closed-box teenagers, so, given I'm not even that closed a box, but at least a quarter open, it honestly doesn't surprise me that, before the morning's through, she's got most of it out of me.

What she tells me in response though . . .

That surprises me a lot.

It becomes clear at breakfast, as she pours us both tea and fills me in on her evening, that she's already pieced a fair amount together.

Enough, anyway, to insist I tell her more.

It turns out she didn't only eat dinner with Felix last night. Ana joined them too.

Ana loves my mum, they've drunk a lot of champagne together over the years and have always hit it off. Felix isn't as close to Mum, or Phil ('It's oddly challenging to look a young man in the eye,' says Phil, 'knowing he's been watched by millions undressing my daughter.'), but they've crossed paths more than enough to be on decent conversational terms.

They certainly found plenty to chat about over dinner, all of it revolving around me, and how subsumed I've become by Iris; the solitary walks I've kept taking in the woods; the strange habit it's apparently been noted I've developed of peering into the sky, frowning at nothing.

Ana even took Mum up to Iris's room.

Told her about the flares she teased me for imagining on my first night here.

I assumed she'd forgotten all about that.

'She did,' says Mum, stirring half a sugar into her tea. 'At first. But –' her brow pinches – 'it's been preying on her, because of all the rest of it.'

'Well, it sounds like it made for an interesting conversation at least,' I say, irritable to my own ears. But it's horrible thinking of the three of them picking me apart like this whilst I was oblivious upstairs. 'Have Felix and Ana been talking to Nick too?'

'Yes,' says Mum, without apology. 'And Emma. They care about you, Claude. They're *worried* . . . '

'Please.' I hold up my hands, which are trembling. 'I can't keep listening to what a worry I am.' That banging's started upstairs again. I don't want to look at it, in case Mum notices. 'I really can't . . . '

'There's nothing wrong with being a worry, my darling, as long as you're open to help. But look at you. You're furious that the people closest to you even *want* to help.'

'I'm not furious.'

'Yes, you are. And Felix said you were extremely anxious about going into Heaton last week.'

'Of course I was anxious. I'd just had the details of my miscarriage broadcast across the globe.'

'You don't need to defend yourself. I'm not attacking you. Far from it. I couldn't have faced up to that. Not anywhere, and certainly not there.' She places her spoon on her saucer. 'I gather you're going to be filming in the village on Monday.'

'Yes.' The banging is really loud, louder than it's ever been before, and Mum hasn't so much as glanced at it. 'They're closing it all off for the day. It'll be fine.' I have no idea if it will be. 'Just some scenic shots.'

'Have you been into the village yet?'

'No, I haven't had time.' By an effort of will, I keep my focus on her. 'I've only been to Bramble Lane.'

'Where you hugged that woman.'

'Yes,' I say, distracted, briefly, by the thought of her kindness. I don't even know her name. I have looked for her among the women who've been standing shoulder to virtual shoulder online (and I'm pleased, I really am, that this mess has at least produced the silver lining of them being able to seek comfort in one another), but she's remained silent, so I guess is a social media recluse too. I've been worried that someone from the press, or village, might attempt to out her, but, thankfully, no one has. I'm sure she must be relieved too, and feel even more grateful, now I realize how private she obviously is, that she put herself out to help me the way she did. 'I actually want to find her,' I say. 'Thank her.'

'Maybe you could talk to her about it all. It might help you both.'

'Maybe.'

'Do you know whereabouts in Heaton she lives?'

'No.'

'It might be Bramble Rise.'

'Might be.' The banging seems to have paused.

Mum toys with her spoon. 'You really weren't curious to see Nan and Grandad's house?'

I shake my head. 'It's like you always say, they're not there.'

'And you honestly didn't go to the cemetery?'

'No, I'd have told you. But . . . ' I pause, wondering if I should go on.

'But?' she prompts.

271

'Well . . .' I frown, hoping I won't upset her. 'I did want to go, when I saw it. I *want* to.'

She considers it for a moment, her expression unreadable.

Then, with a slow sigh, she nods.

It amazes me that she doesn't try to dissuade me.

'Let's go after this,' she says, shocking me more. 'As long as you feel up to it.'

'I feel up to it,' I say. 'But do you?'

'Yes. It's time.'

I frown. 'You're sure?'

'I'm sure.'

'All right,' I say dubiously.

And, for a few seconds, we're silent.

I study her, trying to wrap my head around her suggesting this, after so many years.

Absently, she reaches for the pot, pouring more tea.

She stirs in the milk.

Forgets her sugar.

I open my mouth to remind her.

Then, the bloody banging starts again.

I set my teeth, once again resisting the urge to look up at it.

'Did you remember Bramble Lane?' Mum asks.

'Not at all.' I take a breath, willing the banging away. 'It's strange, actually. I was expecting it to be quieter. More open. I could have sworn there used to be fields behind our house.'

Carefully, she stirs her sugarless tea. 'Fields?'

'Yes. I remember chasing sheep with Nan.'

'You never chased sheep with your nan,' she says.

And is it me, or has her voice turned weirdly tight?

'Yes, I did,' I tell her.

'No. She was asthmatic. Very allergic . . . '

'But I remember . . . '

'You didn't chase sheep with her.'

'But there were fields behind the house, yes?'

God, will this banging ever stop?

And what's even causing it?

It sounds like hammers.

Lots of hammers, knocking on nails.

Into what though?

Wood, my subconscious supplies.

And, from nowhere, I remember what Tim said about Doverley's wood rot, and how half of the first floor disintegrated in 1943.

It had to be replaced . . .

Is that what I'm hearing?

Have I really just asked myself that question?

And did Mum just say something else?

She's definitely looking at me like she's expecting an answer.

'What's that?' I ask.

'I said, what makes you think there were fields behind the house? It was right in the middle of the estate.'

'It's how I remember it,' I say, and the banging stops again.

Instinctively, I glance upwards at the silence.

I can't believe I've done that.

'What's got your attention up there?' Mum asks me, quick as a flash, and this time there's no doubting the tightness in her voice. 'You've been trying not to look ever since we sat down.'

'No I haven't . . . '

'I'm afraid you have.' She narrows her eyes in a penetrating glare. (She's very good at those.) 'What's going on?'

Nothing, I could say.

It's absolutely nothing.

But her eyes on me don't waver.

And I never have been able to lie to her.

'You really haven't heard it?' I say, and it's like a pressure valve opening, just letting that question go.

'Heard what?'

'The banging,' I say, my heart pummelling at this leap I'm taking.

Mum continues to stare.

For an uncomfortable length of time.

'Claudia,' she says, and oh god, she's used my proper name, 'I'm going to ask you a question, and I want you to answer it honestly. Have you been hearing any other noises?'

I swallow, drily. 'What do you mean?'

'I think you know what I mean.' She leans towards me, and my heart quickens all the more. 'When you've been looking up at the sky, have you been hearing something there?'

It's my turn to stare.

Does she know?

Can it really be possible that she *knows*?

'Claudia,' she persists. 'Have you heard a . . . bird?'

She refuses to tell me how she's guessed about the bird.

'Not until you've done some more talking,' she says, and, pushing away her unsweetened tea, suggests we fetch our coats and leave for the cemetery.

'Are you really sure about this?' I ask her. 'You've never wanted to go before.'

'No,' she agrees, 'but I think we need to go now.'

'Why?'

'Let's get there first.'

'Mum, come on . . . '

'No, I'm not saying anything else until we're there.'

'Why?'

'I'll tell you when we're there,' she repeats, in a definitive tone that lets me know there's no point pushing her further.

So, with a frustrated sigh, I tell her I'll see her outside in five minutes, then head back to my room to layer up.

It's been cleaned in my absence: the bed made; the bathroom reordered. Nick's obviously been and gone too; he's left a note on my pillow telling me to please make use of it and get some more sleep. I touch my fingers to the paper, picturing him here in his costume, and – replaying his kiss this morning, everything yesterday – wish I hadn't missed him.

You're enough for me, he told me last night, and it made my heart swell.

I feel it happening again now, remembering.

I think I might actually be starting to believe it.

Believe him.

Perhaps that's why I'm feeling so guilty that, in the space of one barely eaten breakfast, I've opened up to Mum more than I have him. Because how many times has he implored me to confide in him? And how many times have I remained silent, hurting him more, when he's been hurting so much already? I have no idea, it's too many to count, and it makes me really ashamed that I've done that to him.

Him, who at the start of all this drove from York to Highgate at a moment's notice, just because I called to ask him to dinner with my family.

Him, who invited Phil and my sisters along with him flying, didn't flinch when Lisa vomited on his feet, but joked with her about it, then took Hannah and her friends out in London, even though it was undoubtedly the last thing he felt like doing that night.

Him, who I've scared enough with my behaviour that he's been agonising over it with my friends, called Mum when I fell, then sat in a plastic chair by my side all day long yesterday, holding my hand, silently panicking that I'd deliberately thrown myself down that flight of stairs.

Him, who believes I'm beautiful when I'm wearing a shower cap, and can still make me laugh, even when I'm crying.

Him, who today has used his break from a full-on day filming to check on me, and leave a note on my pillow.

Him, whose face I've always loved more than any other, until I saw Robbie Grayson's, and who really does deserve so much better than to share heart-space with a man who died nearly eighty years ago.

Him, who, whatever his own secrets, I need, finally, to be transparent with about that, and everything else I've been holding so close.

I'll do it tonight, I decide, shrugging on my coat.

Then, pocketing his note, I head back downstairs, buzzing with apprehension, and impatience too, determined to get to the bottom of whatever it is Mum knows, and hasn't been telling me.

Chapter Nineteen

I lead the way into Heaton, following the same route that Nick took with Emma, Felix and me last week, out through Doverley's hidden gateway, and across the frosty, sub-zero fields. I don't tell Mum everything as we walk, circumnavigating the huddling cows, clambering over first one wooden gate, then another, our feet crunching down into puddles of ice. But step by step, question by question, I do tell her a lot. By the time we approach the village, the church's steeple coming into view in the pale-blue sky, she knows almost all of it: from the moment of my arrival at Doverley, when I somehow knew to skip that uneven front step, to the hours I've lost in the ruins of Iris and Robbie's cottage, to the onslaught of memories that have increasingly filled my conscious and unconscious thoughts: of darkened nights, and cold moons, and smoky pubs, and uninsulated control towers, and apple cakes, and boiled sweets, and that nameless colonel, the woman in her wheelchair, and so, *so* much.

The only thing I don't go into is how convinced I've become by the slips I've found myself taking, not only into Iris's memories, but her world. I'm not sure why I keep that to myself when I say so much else. Perhaps I'm still too afraid of being dismissed, which probably isn't fair – Mum doesn't attempt to trivialise anything I tell her – but nonetheless, I remain silent on all that.

I think about it though, our entire walk through.

I'm still thinking about it as we approach Heaton, swapping the frozen fields for the gritted country road into the village. Out loud, I talk to Mum about my trip to see Tim Hobbs, and how I felt as though I was visiting an old friend, and inside I replay those haunting moments I experienced in his lounge: first, seeing Robbie come to life in that photo, as though I really had been behind the camera's lens; then, finding myself in the thick of the noise and heat of Bettys Bar, holding on tight to that hand around mine.

Robbie's hand, I'm certain.

That woman was there in Bettys too, I've since realised: the same one I saw when I fell, whose arm I made Iris grab, and whose fine-boned features have remained with me since: so incomprehensibly familiar.

'Will you visit Tim again?' Mum asks, drawing my attention back to the moment.

'I was planning to yesterday,' I say. 'I can't stop thinking about him.' I picture him now, all alone, just his memories for company. *It's always happening*, he said of the war. *Always.* 'I hated leaving him. He was so frail . . . '

'He is one hundred.'

'But he's got no one, Mum. And I think he's really scared about whether we're going to do his past justice with this movie. *I'm* scared about that. It's all just . . . make-believe.'

'What else could it be?'

'I don't know.' I stare out at the glittering road. 'The sets feel too pristine though. The base is too compact. Our costumes are so tailored, and we're all made up perfectly, all the time . . . '

'Claude, you're actors . . . '

'Right. And this'll be a movie. A brilliant one, maybe. But

278

still just a . . . *movie*. A one-hundred-and-thirty-three-minute cinematic recreation of something that I see really . . . I don't know . . . ' I search for a word ' . . . *differently.*'

Mum sighs. 'I wish you'd never come here.'

'I don't.' I turn to her, pouring into my stare how much I mean this. 'I want to be here. I've always wanted it. From the moment I picked up the novel. It's only now this has happened that I've realized the . . . *ownership* . . . I've always felt for Iris. Even when I was struggling in rehearsals, I could feel her . . . '

'Waiting for you,' Mum says, finishing my sentence for me. 'Yes, I know.'

She lets go another deep sigh.

And, silently, we keep walking, reaching Heaton, crossing the green for the churchyard and cemetery.

To my relief, the village is almost as deserted as it was last week. The weather's obviously keeping everyone inside. Although there are a handful of people out – a couple walking a dog on the other side of the war memorial; a trio of kids kicking a ball on the brittle, whitened grass – they're all too caught up in their own mornings to look our way.

I fix my own attention on the church as we draw closer, thinking again of that man who used to stare at me during Sunday morning services, with his hard blue eyes. I still can't work out who he might have been, but I'm unsettled enough by the emotions he stirs up in me that, as Mum and I enter the churchyard, I ask her if she has any idea who he was.

She doesn't answer me.

Not straight away.

My question clearly upsets her though, because she dips her head, pinching the top of her nose with her fingertips.

'Mum?' I say, frowning. 'Who was he?'

'I don't know,' she says, in a tone that's flat, and tense, but not, actually, particularly surprised.

279

Just as with that bird, I realize I must have spoken to her about this man before.

'You used to be terrified of a blue-eyed man,' she says, confirming it. 'No one ever brought you to this church though. So far as I'm aware, you've never set foot inside it.' We come to a halt at the cemetery gate. 'There were these two little boys you kept asking for, as well, wanting to know where they'd gone. One in particular, you fixated on, insisting that he was looking for you. Waiting. It made you so . . . *desperately* . . . sad.'

'What about that bird?' I say, the question leaving my cold lips quietly.

'Yes, you used to talk about the bird too. Not much to me. I wasn't here. You know that.' Her eyes, overly bright in her cold face, strain with guilt. It's not the first time she's looked at me like this. I'm not sure she'll ever forgive herself for leaving me as much as she did back then, no matter how many times I tell her she needs to.

I try to do it again now.

'Mum, stop. You're too hard on yourself . . . '

'No.' She shakes her head. 'You needed me. You really needed me, and I was no use to you. I was young, heartbroken, afraid of everything, letting you down most of all, and you weren't . . . Well . . . ' Her brow pinches. '. . . *straightforward.*'

'Oh.' I grimace.

'No, don't look like that.' She reaches for my hand. 'You were gorgeous, and sweet, and precious. But you weren't like other children. You saw the world differently to the rest of us. You *heard* it differently. That bird you used to talk about, it was alive to you. Nan thought, the way you described it, that it might have been a hawk, they used to have them here when she was a child, but she could never hear it. No one could.' She places her other hand around mine. 'I remember, on your fourth birthday, I took you out for a walk, and you kept pointing at the sky, asking where the bird was, but I couldn't tell you, and you just started ... *wailing*.' She widens her eyes, remembering. 'I realise now how frightened you must have been, but then, I didn't know what to do. I thought you were going to make yourself ill, so I lied to you, said I'd seen it flying away, but you didn't believe me. You just kept crying.' She pauses, studying me. 'Do you remember?'

'No.' I try to, delving into the depths of my mind, but I can't find anything there. 'I don't.'

'And what about here?' She nods in at the cemetery.

I turn to look, my eyes moving over the slumbering space, taking in the trees, the patches of green where their branches have protected the earth from the frost, and all the graves, disordered and unplanned, squeezed together over the centuries. 'Yes,' I say, feeling a stirring of recollection. 'Yes.'

Then, 'Where are Nan and Grandad?'

'They're not here,' Mum says. 'They never have been.'

Slowly, barely aware of my own movement, I turn back to face her.

She stares at me, her face taut with emotion, her breath, seemingly, held.

'What?' I say, numbly.

'They were cremated. I scattered their ashes up on the peaks.'

'But . . . ' I frown. '*What?*'

'I'm so sorry.'

'I remember us burying them . . . '

'You don't, my darling. You just don't.' She forces the words out in a strangled rush. 'I know you've always thought you do, and I tried when you were little to convince you that you didn't, but you got so upset. Hysterical.' She gives me a helpless look. 'In the end it just felt kinder to leave it. Then, the lie . . . *grew* . . . '

'They really weren't buried?'

'No.'

'What about the funeral?'

'I didn't take you. You were too little, had been through too much . . . '

'Mum –' I place my hand to my head, fighting the absurdness of what she's telling me – 'this can't be right.'

'It is, Claude.'

'Then why are we here?'

'Because you ran away here, the day before the accident. Grandad found you curled up among the graves, fast asleep, your face all swollen with tears.'

I stare, appalled.

'I know,' says Mum. 'I know.'

'Why have you never told me?'

'Because I didn't want to. It was awful. Traumatic. Then the crash happened, and that was . . . *god* . . . ' She exhales a white puff of breath. 'So much worse. I've never wanted you to come here again. Until this bloody movie, I never thought you would. But now . . . Now . . . ' She fills her cheeks with another deep breath, letting it go. 'Now, I wish I'd asked my dad which of these graves he found you by.'

'Why didn't you?'

'It didn't feel relevant. You were four years old, and had run away to a cemetery. That was all I cared about. But . . . ' Her forehead creases. '. . . I've been wondering if you might know.'

'Mum, I don't remember doing this . . . '

'I think you should go in anyway,' she says, and in one quick movement, opens the gate. 'See if your feet will tell you the way.'

'Mum, come on . . . '

'Just try,' she says. 'I'm with you.'

So, partly because she's asked me to, but mainly because I need to know, I do try.

And my feet do know the way.

They take me the length of the graveyard, around the church, to an overgrown patch of grass where two simple headstones stand crookedly side by side, nestled beneath the latticed branches of an apple tree. The stones are weathered, coated in moss, but their simple inscriptions are still visible.

Catherine Winterton, reads one. *b. 1900 d. 1933*

Bernadette Winterton, reads the other. *b.1860 d. 1933*

I've seen pictures of both headstones before.

Just as with Bramble Lane, they've featured in their fair share of social media posts.

I've never really felt much, looking at those posts.

Not like I feel now, shivering in this cemetery on this cold, frozen day, certain, right in the core of my pounding heart, that I do know this place.

I have been here before.

Mum's turned unnaturally still beside me, staring at the headstones too.

'Did you have any idea?' I ask her, the words sticking in my throat. 'Suspect . . . ?'

'No,' she says. '*No*. I was worried you were using Iris to run away again, but no more than that.'

'You're sure?'

'I'm certain. My god . . . I never, ever, *for a moment*, entertained the possibility that anything you've told me about this morning might be waiting for you here. Not in my wildest dreams.' She shakes her head. 'I didn't want you to come back because this was such an unhappy place for you, and you've been unhappy enough. But I was hoping you'd get through it, be too busy to remember too much . . . '

'But I don't remember anything about me. Only Iris.'

'Oh, Claude . . . '

'Do you believe me?' I ask, discovering as I do how much I need her to.

For it to not only be me who does.

'I don't know,' she says. 'This is well above my pay grade. But . . . oh . . . *god* . . . ' Tipping her head back, she stares at the sky. 'I actually don't know if I can say this . . . '

'Say what?'

Silence.

'Mum, come on . . . '

'All right.' She scrunches her hands into balls. 'All right.' She pulls in a quick breath, obviously bracing herself.

I'm still trying to work out what she could possibly be finding so hard to get out, when . . .

'I think you need to talk to Eleanor Norland,' she says.

I frown.

The name means nothing to me.

'Who's Eleanor Norland?' I ask.

'She lives over there,' says Mum, gesturing at the Georgian houses on the green. 'She's retired now, has been for years, but she was a psychiatrist. Your nan took you to her.'

'I don't remember . . . '

'Yes,' she says, nodding grimly. 'You do. She used to give you those Rich Tea Biscuits. You couldn't manage her name, so you called her Ellen. Mrs Ellen.'

I could be angry.

I could be bloody furious.

I am, at first.

'Have you heard of the term gaslighting?' I demand of Mum, who my whole life through has sworn blind to me that Mrs Ellen never existed.

'I haven't been gaslighting you,' she insists. 'I've been trying to protect you.'

'From what?'

'Too much . . . '

'What, though?'

'If you'll let me speak, I'll tell you.'

'Fine,' I say. '*Fine*. Go ahead, please.'

And she does go ahead.

Not in the cemetery.

'I don't want to do this here,' she says. 'Let's head back to the house.'

So, we head back to the house, crossing the green, then the fields, and as we walk, she explains herself, and gradually my anger seeps from me.

Because although I still hate that she's lied to me, I do understand her reasons.

They're good reasons.

Devastating, but borne of love.

And to my disbelief, they're all to do with my father.

She has talked to me about him before. Not much. She's always claimed she didn't know enough about him herself.

'He wasn't the type who could allow anyone to know him well,' she once told me. 'That was his shield. His superpower. He needed it, the way he grew up.'

His mother had died not long after having him, and his father was disinterested, so he spent all of his childhood in care. He started at UCL the same year Mum did, studying philosophy too. The two of them met at a party, and Mum was apparently like a moth to a flame when he singled her out.

'He was an extremely troubled, extremely beautiful young man,' she said. 'I wanted to fix him, of course. But he didn't want to be fixed. I doubt he believed he could be.'

She fell pregnant with me quickly, he panicked, dropped out of his course, packed his bags and left London without a word to Mum of where he was going, only to show up at Nan and Grandad's house the afternoon I was born, with a teddy bear that I've still got, and pictured myself one day giving to a child of mine.

'I have no idea how he knew you'd come,' Mum's said. 'I was stunned. And really just so angry. But I let him hold you, and he was . . . *spellbound*. He thought you were absolutely perfect.'

Not so perfect however that he stuck around. Instead, he vanished again, that same day, after my grandad came home from work and tore a strip off him. He couldn't cope with hostility, Mum says. He'd grown up around too much of it. None of us ever saw him again, this damaged, troubled, untouchable father of mine. He died not long after. Mum's never been able to find out how.

Or so I thought.

But, as Mum and I return to Doverley, she confesses that there are things she *hasn't* told me about my father.

And the last time I saw him was not the day I was born.

'He used to telephone the house on your birthdays,' she says, as we reach the fields. 'He was always desperate to hear how you were.'

'What did you tell him?' I ask, squinting at the horizon. For the first time in days, there are clouds there. The rain everyone's relying on for Emma's final scene looks to be on its way, and it sends a rivulet of foreboding trickling through me. 'That I wasn't straightforward?'

'Not just that,' she says. 'I told him everything about you. And that he should come and see you for himself. But he wouldn't. I think he was afraid to let you know him. I suspect he . . . well . . . *felt*, somehow, that his time was running out.'

I frown. 'Was he sick?'

'Not so far as I was aware, no.'

I stop, confused. 'Then . . . ?'

'He was like you, Claude.' She turns to me, her face pained.

'Not the same. He never spoke of having anyone else's memories. Not to me, anyway. But he believed, utterly, that these lives of ours keep rolling around on constant repeat. Layers of existence that have just the slightest variations.' She eyes me. 'Sound familiar?'

Slowly, I nod, my mind filling and spinning with the dreams I had when I arrived at Doverley, of Nick and me acting out Iris and Robbie's reunion all those different ways.

Also, what Imogen told me of Tim's own confusion over where it happened.

He was completely convinced by whatever account he was giving me, she said, *even if he'd told me something totally different the week before.*

And Tim's unforgettable words about the war.

It's always happening. Always.

Mum talks on, describing how my father pictured this life we're in as one of infinite others playing out in a boundless theatre of time: stages upon stages of existence, stacked in a dimensionless tower. 'Your dad's theory was that most of us never experience anything beyond the limits of our own stage,' she says. 'Some might get glimpses. A strange dream maybe, or murmuring of déjà vu, but no more than that.' She sighs. 'He believed he was different, of course. That his other stages helped him. *Guided* him.'

'And did you believe him?' I ask, looking up and around us, the hairs on the back of my neck rising as I picture it, this theatre of time: all our pasts, and presents, and tomorrows sharing this space, our earth and air, unfolding over and over and over.

The idea makes such perfect, instant sense to me.

It really is like I've had it all explained to me before.

'I was captivated by him,' says Mum. 'At first. Then I got scared. He never seemed to be entirely here, was always at least half somewhere else.' Briefly, she closes her eyes. 'It absolutely petrified me when you seemed to be starting down the same track. Your nan was straight on it, took you off to Eleanor. God knows how she and Dad afforded the fees, but you went every fortnight. Ate your biscuits. Chatted away. You loved going.' She gives a forlorn shrug. 'I think it was because she was so calm with you, where the rest of us just panicked. God –' she expels a choked sound – 'it's so damn easy to deal with other people's children, and so bloody hard when it's your own.'

'What about my dad?' I ask. 'Did he ever get help?'

'I doubt it. He really did view it all as a gift. He never claimed to be able to predict the future, certainly not in any precise way, but he depended on the instincts he said came to him, for where he should be, what he should do. He said *that* was how he knew to come to the house the day you were born, and I didn't believe him. Who would believe a thing like that? But . . . Oh . . . ' Her eyes brim. 'I don't know how to tell you this.' Wretchedly, she stares at me. 'I never wanted to tell you . . . '

'Tell me what?' I ask, although I don't know why.

I don't think I want to know.

'That he was with you,' Mum says. 'In the car.'

'What car?' I ask, and again, I'm not sure why I do.

Because I really don't want to know.

But I've already realised.

My plummeting heart has too.

'You mean the crash,' I say, and my voice no longer sounds like mine.

Miserably, she nods.

'Was that when he died?' I ask.

'It was. I'm . . . *beyond* . . . sorry. I don't know why he was there, it's taunted me for twenty-nine years, and it will taunt me until the day I die. But he was lying across you when that tractor driver got to you. A branch had come through the windscreen.' Her tears spill free. 'He stopped it . . . '

Mutely, I stare.

I open my mouth to speak.

Then I close it again.

I can't speak.

Can't absorb this.

Someone was watching over you, that tractor driver told me when he pulled me from my car seat, not a scratch on me.

He must have shielded my eyes.

Shielded me.

I don't remember seeing any of it.

'Did I know he was my father?' I force the question out.

'I don't know,' Mum says. 'You've never spoken about it. You didn't speak at all for nearly three months afterwards.' More tears run down her cheeks. 'We stayed up here. I thought that was the best thing for you, and you were just . . . *silent*. I was terrified you were never going to speak again. I kept taking you to Eleanor, but she couldn't get through to you either. Then we sold the house, moved down to London, and within days you started talking again.' She draws a ragged breath. 'It was like as soon as I'd got you away from here, you could forget. Not just the accident, but everything you used to get so upset over. That man, those boys, that bird . . . And I wanted that for you. It made you *happier*.' She shakes her head. 'Eleanor said I was letting you bury it, that it would come back to haunt me, haunt you, but I didn't listen to her. I didn't want you to know your dad had died doing that for you. I didn't believe anyone should have to carry something like that, let alone a four-year-old child. Let alone *you*.' She's really crying now. My brave, strong mum is in pieces. 'By the time you were old enough for me to speak to you about it, I'd kept it from you for so long, I didn't know how to unpick the secret. *That's* why

289

I've been so terrified of you coming back here.' She wipes her cheeks. '*That's* why I haven't wanted anything about your nan and granddad's accident coming out.' She presses the heels of her hands to her eyes. 'I've been so scared of what it will do to you, finding this all out.'

'Mum, come here,' I say, wrapping her in my arms, holding her close, for myself as much as her. 'It's all right.' *It's not*, my inner voice screams. *It's not*. 'I don't blame you . . . '

'You should.'

'I don't. You did your best for me. No one could have done better. Look at me.' I pull away from her. 'Look at this balanced, functional human being you've raised.'

She laughs, cries more, and places her hand to my face. 'He loved you, Claude. Whatever his faults, he really loved you. More than life.'

'Yes,' I say, my own tears breaking free. 'Yes . . . '

'I love you too.'

'Well, I know *that*.'

She smiles.

Then, resting her head against mine, she locks my eyes with hers.

'What do you think?' she says. 'Do you want to see Eleanor?'

'I don't know if I want to,' I say. 'But I think I probably need to.'

'Yes,' she says. 'I think you probably do too.'

*

I head upstairs as soon as we reach the house. Mum doesn't want me to, she says she's worried about leaving me to myself, but my stitches are throbbing, and I'm desperate to lie down, close my eyes, and at least try to begin processing everything she's told me.

I want some time alone, I say.

I need it.

But Nick's in our room when I get there, sitting on the edge of our bed, his phone in his hands.

I stall, taking in his grim expression, and feel my every muscle tense in sudden certainty that something else not at all good is about to come my way.

I'm tempted to turn away, walk back through the door, and keep walking, not have to face up to this, whatever it is.

But I stay where I am, trapped in the beam of his stare.

I can't tell what he's thinking. He's got his contacts in, dark and brown, obscuring his eyes, stopping them from being windows to anything.

He's wearing his air force blues.

Coldly, I register that, and that he's left shooting to come looking for me.

Not to leave another message, though.

Not this time.

Whatever he's got to say, it's obviously serious enough that he needs to say it in person.

'Why aren't you working?' I ask, and it amazes me how calm I manage to sound.

'I've got a half hour,' he says, and doesn't sound calm at all. He *sounds* like he's trying not to choke. 'Justin's on with Emma.'

I glance down at his phone, my memory once again throwing up his frown last night.

Also, that bizarre text.

Have you changed your mind?

The smiling face of that woman he was pictured with over the summer.

And, still, everything from this morning continues to churn through me, on a loop.

Someone was watching over you, that tractor driver said to me. *It was my dad*, I think, *my dad*.

'Something's happened,' I say, out loud. 'What's happened.'

'I didn't want you to have to deal with it,' says Nick, and, dropping his phone, stands, coming towards me. 'I've been trying to shut it down. Get rid of it.'

'Get rid of what?' I say, and now I feel like I'm choking.

But I really can't deal with this.

Can't handle a new nightmare.

I'm already juggling too many.

He was lying across you when that tractor driver got to you.

'What's happened?' I repeat.

'Nothing,' says Nick. 'That's the only thing you need to remember. Nothing has happened. I need you to trust me. I really, really need you to do that.'

'No one says that before anything anyone wants to hear.'

'No.' His face is rigid with control. 'I know.'

My phone pings.

'Ignore that,' says Nick.

Another ping.

Then another.

I reach into my pocket, my fingers brushing his note, closing around my phone, at once desperate, and terrified, to pull it out and look at what's happening on the screen.

It buzzes again.

Then, it starts ringing.

'Claude, silence it,' says Nick. 'You've always got it on silent for me. Silence it now, please.'

'Just tell me what's going on,' I say, not silencing anything.

'It was that night I took your sister and her friends out,' he begins.

And, thinking of Hannah, realising where this is going, I want to silence him.

292

But since I can't, I do my best to tune his words out.

I watch his lips move, feel his hands take a hold of my arms, but don't listen to what he says.

Not properly.

I can't.

Because it's worse than a nightmare.

It's *real*.

Very, very real, and happening to us.

It's happening to me.

But I really have had enough.

I can't take any more.

So, I close my eyes, breathe deep, and will myself into being somewhere else.

Somewhere not here.

Somewhere not now.

Somewhere, then.

Into the silver light of a late summer's dawn. A fading moon above me.

A friend by my side.

It's hot. Blisteringly hot, for all it's so early.

Autumn's coming though, it's just around the corner, and I can't bear that either.

Time, my mind whispers, *is running out.*

Chapter Twenty

Iris

August 1943

Time is running out.

Iris more felt than heard the whisper of those words, like a shadow coming over her. And she didn't know if they really might be a warning from another life, *another fall*, or were simply borne of her own fear in this one, but what did it matter anyway?

She couldn't see that there was anything to be done about it.

Except wait.

Wait, and hope.

Like she was waiting and hoping now, staring out of the control tower window, into the silver light of the late summer's dawn.

The fading moon was full, just as it had been for Iris and Clare's first shift at the station, when the boys had flown to Milan. Tonight, the squadron had been sent to the Baltic coast, and Iris and Clare were once again at their desk, Sergeant Browning at his chalkboard, the three of them poised for them all to start returning.

They were just missing their old group captain, Fred. But he, tragically, wasn't with them any more. He and his crew had disappeared over Essen, the same night that Iris hadn't fallen down the control tower stairs. No notification had been received that any of them had been taken prisoner, so they were all missing presumed. Iris thought of them every day, hoping they'd somehow made it to safety. She thought of them now, as she sat twitchily beside Clare, and of Fred's kindness most of all. His wife had taken their daughter to live with her parents in Kent. And maybe Fred *would* find his way back to them there, surprise them by suddenly appearing.

It did happen.

Sometimes.

Pulling at her hot collar, Iris checked the time.

Almost five.

God, she hated it when the moon was full.

HQ had declared its light essential for the accuracy of this raid, though. The target had been a Nazi weapon plant; the rumour was they were building pilotless rocket bombs there – missiles devastating enough to win them the war – so nothing less than its total destruction would do. Several hundred crew had been sent to see to that, and *Mabel's Fury* had led the attack as Master Bomber. There'd have been no swooping in and getting away for them on this raid. Instead, they'd have had to circle the target for the entire operation, coordinating it through a new high-frequency transmitter, dodging flak and fighters until it was complete.

It hadn't been done before.

No one knew what the chances might be of survival.

If there was any chance at all.

Robbie and the others had been away training for the best part of a month. They'd only returned to Doverley last night, straight from a briefing at Bomber Command, with barely time to refuel before they flew off again. To Iris's fury and frustration, she hadn't been able to get to them before they went. Get to *him*. Ambrose, with typical timing, had appeared in the control tower to supervise take-off, and been impossible to escape. All Iris had seen of Robbie since July had been for a snatched, delirious weekend in London, two weeks ago now, when they hadn't gone to a show, or eaten chocolates in any interlude, but had barely left their hotel room, which Robbie had booked for them at The Savoy.

He'd spent a chunk of June away too, on a period of enforced rest. Tim's high-up uncle in Bomber Command had ordered it for the entire crew at the entreaty of his sister – Tim's mother, who'd used to fill Tim's pockets with those sweets, and who, at the start of June, Iris had written to, by then much too worried about her old friend, not to.

He doesn't seem to be sleeping at all any more, she'd told Mrs Hobbs. *I don't think he can be eating either. He's lost a lot of weight, and although he tries to pretend that he's coping, he's jumpy, distracted, and his hands shake, much more than the usual. I think you should visit.*

Mrs Hobbs had arrived the morning *Mabel's Fury* had returned from another sortie to the Ruhr, from which three of the fifteen crews that 96 had sent, hadn't come back (including the last ever V for Verity; it had been scratched from use now); she'd taken her son out for lunch, visited a payphone, and within twenty-four hours, Tim, Robbie, Jacob, Henry, Ames, Gus and Danny had been packing their bags, off to a convalescent hotel in Hampshire.

If only they never had to leave, Mrs Hobbs had written to Iris. *Thank you, dear girl. He's all I have left in this world. I'm sure his papa would want me to thank you, too – I'm certain he'd tell me off for all those pantomimes I should have taken you to. I really do feel so terribly about that now. Please accept the apologies of a very silly woman.*

'I hate her,' Robbie had said to Iris when they'd met in the cottage before he'd left.

'No, you don't,' she'd said, wrapping her arms around him.

'In fact, I do. And you might as well know that I'm seriously reconsidering my feelings about you.'

'You need this,' she'd told him. 'All of you need this.'

She'd really thought they had.

That it would do them good.

But Tim as well as Robbie had written to her whilst they'd been gone, saying what torture it was, being reminded what safety felt like, knowing the life he must return to. *I know you meant well, Iris, but I wish you hadn't done it.* And although he, Robbie, and everyone, had returned from that restful fortnight looking younger, healthier, *refreshed* ('Iris, darling, can you please talk to Tim's mum about me?' Lewis, in his tartan slippers, had said), they'd been put straight on to battle duty, sent once more to Essen, and come home ten years older again.

Then, in no time at all, they'd been made into master bombers and sent off to learn how to do even more perilous work.

Time hadn't raced, only dragged, whilst they'd been away, and although the summer days had mostly shone bright and warm, like this one promised to be, Doverley had felt relentlessly bleak without Robbie in it. To make matters worse, at the end of July, the house had started to fall apart, causing devastation in the administrative offices, many of which had lost their ceilings. Now, there were workmen all over the place, their relentless hammering putting paid to any chance those of them on nights might have of catching up on sleep ('I've finally discovered some sympathy for Prim,' said Clare), whilst Ambrose had become even more bad-tempered, shouting at everyone, poor Beth most of all, who was in enough of a state as it was, with Jacob gone so long.

She'd seen him in London too, the same weekend Iris had

spent in The Savoy with Robbie. Jacob hadn't reserved a room at any hotel though. Instead, he'd taken Beth to stay with his parents at their home in Barnes.

'I know where I'd rather be,' Iris had said to Robbie, as, unlocking their door, he'd swept her up, carrying her into their room, making her dissolve into laughter.

'I know where I'd rather you were, too,' he'd replied, kicking their door shut.

'It was all very proper,' Beth had told Iris as, together, they'd caught the train back north. 'Separate rooms, whist after dinner, all that. But they were lovely. And really, it's terribly optimistic of Jacob, isn't it, taking me there?'

'Any talk of a proposal?' Iris had asked, thinking of Prim, who was expecting American Clint to pop the question, *any day now*, and talked constantly of the exciting new life waiting for her in Denver, just as soon as the war was over. (Assuming it did ever end.)

'No,' Beth had replied, biting her lip on a smile. 'Not yet. And you?'

'No.' Iris had shaken her head. 'I've told him he's not to.'

Don't, she'd said, back in the Savoy, when, rolling over sleepily on the pillows, he'd pulled her warm body to his, and told her that he had something he needed to ask her. *Not until this is all over. It's just tempting fate, otherwise.*

It's not tempting anything, he'd protested.

Please, she'd insisted. *Let's wait until the end of your tour.*

That's a very long wait, he'd said.

And it was.

Grounded for all these weeks, he and the crew were still barely halfway through. Plenty of 96 were further along, and had knocked off a quick series of operations through August, when the truncated summer nights had made for shorter raids, mostly into Italy, who everyone hoped would soon surrender after the toppling of Mussolini back in July. Lewis and his *Bucks Boys* had only to fly three more times, including tonight, before they'd be done.

'Here's to lucky three,' Lewis had said the night before in The Heaton Arms, taking a swig from his watered-down beer.

'Where are they?' said Clare now, moving to the window, her arms folded tight. 'Where?'

'They'll be coming,' said Browning stoutly. 'They're on their way.'

The squadron had sent a full quota of crews up the night before. Browning had the code names of all twenty-four of them on his chalkboard, blank space beside them, awaiting the time of their return.

It was another seventeen agonising minutes before the first descending plane flickered into view, and the call of their operator ended the control room's terrible silence.

'Hello, Tower, Percy here. It's good to see you.'

'Hello, Percy, it's very good to see you,' said Clare. 'Absolutely pancake, over.'

'All right,' said Browning, marking them, *Harlow's Heroes*, off on his board. 'One down, twenty-three to go.'

And, over the following half hour, plenty of those twenty-three did come back.

To Iris's quaking relief, *Mabel's Fury* came back, at two minutes before six: intact, smoke-free, its lumbering weight touching effortlessly down on the runway.

Clare had given them their instruction to land, since Iris was busy with another crew. But hearing her do it, *Hello, Oscar*, knowing that she would now get to see Robbie again – speak to him, touch him, *be* with him, if only for one more day – she very nearly broke down.

Time is running out.

Not yet, she thought. *Not yet.*

299

She couldn't be too euphoric though.

They were only the sixteenth plane to return, and that worried her.

It worried them all.

They'd been expecting *Mabel's Fury* to arrive last. They'd had to remain over the target longest, after all.

But they couldn't be the last.

There were still eight planes missing.

'They'll come,' said Browning, gripping his chalk. 'We'll wait.'

They did wait. None of them went to interrogation that morning. They remained in the control tower until the sun had fully risen, flooding their glass-walled room with its rays.

But there were no further calls to their switchboard.

No more elated requests to land.

Only the telephone trilled: Prim, ringing from interrogation.

Grimly, Browning listened to her.

He nodded.

Hung up.

Turned to Iris and Clare.

'Don't,' said Clare, guessing what he was about to say.

Don't, Iris thought, knowing it too.

But Browning spoke anyway.

'They all went down.' His Scotch voice was gruff, straining with his effort at control. '*Heaven Sent* baled over the North Sea. They're safe, they've been picked up by one of our patrols. All the others were taken over the target. There were fighters everywhere.' He turned, looking up into the serene summer sky. 'Picked us off like coconuts in a shy.'

'Were there . . . ?' began Clare.

'No,' said Browning. 'No chutes. Not that anyone saw.'

Mutely, Clare shook her head.

And, slowly, Iris stood.

She went to the chalkboard, touching the names of the seven crews they'd lost.

Then, the blank spaces they'd each left.

Forty-nine lives, reduced to an empty square.

Her fingers came to a rest on the gap beside Q for Queen.

Bucks Boys.

She pictured Lewis's smile, his floppy hair, and felt a pain in her chest so sharp, she couldn't breathe.

Where are they? Clare had said.

They weren't anywhere, any more.

They were gone.

'We heard them,' said Tim, waiting for Iris outside the control tower when she finally left it.

She was by herself. Browning had already returned to his billet, and Clare had volunteered to be the one to tidy up from the long night: cleaning the mugs, filing the logs. Wiping the chalkboard. 'Go on,' she'd urged Iris, 'Robbie will be looking for you.'

All Iris wanted was to find him, but she stopped short when she saw Tim, the pain inside her growing as she took in the state of him. His eyes were wild in his haunted face. His skin, pallid. And the sweet, which he pressed absently into her hand, was hot, damp with his horror.

'Lewis left the transmitter on,' he said. 'We heard them. All the way down.'

'Oh, Tim.' She choked, pulling him to her, too desperate to comfort him, attempt to comfort herself, to give a damn about whether it was or was not appropriate. She heard them too, Lewis and his crew, as clearly as if she'd been in *Mabel's Fury* herself, their terror shattering the still summer's morning, filling her ears.

'They didn't bale,' Tim said, into her neck. 'They couldn't get to their chutes. They were burning. Everything was burning. They were all so scared.' His body shuddered. 'They were so bloody scared.'

'Shh,' she said. 'Shh.'

'I feel something coming, every time we go up. I know it's coming. I just don't know when it's going to come for us . . . '

'Shh,' she repeated, automatically, trying not to let his words in. They were panic, she told herself.

Simple terror.

Not truth.

Yet, as Tim clung to her, she replayed her own sudden foreboding, only a few hours before, *time is running out*, and held him tighter, clinging to him too.

Then, at the sound of an approaching truck's horn – more bombs, on their way – he pulled back, jerkily wiping his eyes.

Gently, she reached up, doing it for him, and he caught her hand, squeezing it with a tremoring smile.

'Rob's at the house,' he said. 'He had to telephone HQ, give them a full report. He wanted me to tell you he'd meet you in the woods after.'

'And you?' said Iris, as desperate as ever to run to Robbie, but equally reluctant to leave him alone. 'What will you do?'

'I'll try and sleep.'

'Do that,' she said. 'Please, Tim.' She was still holding his hand. 'You must try.'

*

Every airbase had a team responsible for packaging up the belongings of those who didn't come back: emptying their lockers, changing their sheets, preparing their billets for the next intake. They were called the Committee for Adjustment, and everyone did their best to avoid them, hating to be reminded of what they stood for. But there was no escaping them that morning. They were already everywhere when, leaving Tim at his billet, Iris set off for the woods. She saw them, sombrely carrying crates full of blankets, books, forgotten lucky mascots – a pair of tartan slippers – and became so overcome by the waste of it, the never-ending waste, that she had to stop, bending over in the long grass, clutching her stomach, fighting to get her gulping, raging grief under control.

It was Prim, of all people, who came upon her.

'Here,' she said, laying her hand on Iris's shoulder, proffering her a kerchief. Her own eyes, reflecting the bright morning light, were red. Calm now, she'd obviously wept too. 'Go and find Robbie,' she counselled Iris, just as Clare had. 'Neither of you will feel better until you do.'

He was already at the cottage when Iris reached it, standing outside in the leafy, dappled sunshine. His face was as pale as Tim's had been; his blue eyes shadowed by the night.

He didn't smile, when he saw her.

Just moved, as she moved to him.

'How have you kept coming back?' she asked him, her cheek to his beating heart. 'How?'

'I don't know.'

'Tim told me you heard them . . . '

'Yes.' Just a single word.

So much pain within it.

'I can't bear it,' she said. 'I don't want you to go again.' She looked up at him, pouring into her stare how much she meant it. 'Ever.'

'Iris, we—'

'No.' She shook her head. 'Don't you dare tell me you have to.'

'Iris . . . '

'You need to wear your chutes. Always . . . '

'Iris . . . '

'No, I mean it. What use are they damaged? You need to keep them with you. Keep them safe . . . '

'Iris, please –' he held her face in his hands – 'it's all right.'

'It's not.' Tears burnt her eyes. 'I'm scared, Robbie.' Her voice fractured on the admission. 'I'm so scared . . . '

'I know. But we're here. For now, we're here.'

'It's not enough.'

'It has to be.'

'I want now to be forever.'

'So do I,' he said. 'So do I.'

And then they were kissing: hungrily, urgently, backing each other into the cottage, clutching to one another like they might truly hold fast to life itself.

The August morning was only growing hotter.

Close and still.

There was no risk of either of them catching cold as, together, they stole the only escape they could.

They weren't careful about that.

For once, they weren't careful about anything.

They were in too much of a rush.

Too desperate to be together again, after their long separation, and forget, however fleetingly, the war they were trapped in, and which kept on, and on, closing in around them, tighter every day.

Time is running out.

They fell asleep that morning wrapped in each other. When they woke, the goshawk's call fracturing the soft, enveloping silence, neither of them had moved, it was mid-afternoon, and they had to rush to get back to the house and base before they were missed.

Clare was up in the attic when Iris got there, sitting at their bedroom window with Hans's box of letters on her lap. She wore a cotton summer dress. Her fair hair was loose on her shoulders. Her skin was bathed in golden sunshine.

Iris would remember that image of her, always.

Going to her bed, she sat heavily down on it. She felt exhausted, despite her long sleep, and disorientated, unanchored by fear and grief.

'I've been torturing myself with whether Hans might have been up there,' said Clare. 'I'm scared it was him who killed Lewis and the boys.' She looked down at his letters. 'I want to write to him. I've been trying to all day, but can't seem to find words.' A tear escaped her. 'I don't feel like he's here any more.'

'Clare, you can't know that.'

'Can't I?' said Clare, closing Hans's box, laying her hands atop it.

'No,' said Iris.

Clare didn't reply.

She rested her head against the window, her eyes moving to the base, and the eight empty dispersal points lining the distant perimeter.

Iris would remember that too: how lost she was, staring down at it all that afternoon.

How resigned.

She'd try to guess, over and over again, what else she, so silent and contemplative, had been thinking.

What else she might have been sensing.

I rather think we might have all fallen before.

Whether she had, even then – even if only subconsciously – *known*.

Chapter Twenty-One

Claudia and Iris

21 November 2018, Day 19 of the shoot

&

October 1943

It's a mild, grey Wednesday morning, with a forecast of heavy rain.

I'm not working.

Everyone else is.

Last night, we reshot the scene I messed up when I fell, and today – Emma's last on set – they're all preparing to film her finale, which I can't bring myself to watch.

Mum's back down in London. She went on Sunday, reluctantly, but I told her I needed her to let me get on with things.

'Promise me you'll stay offline,' she said.

'I'll stay off,' I said.

And I have, by and large, kept away from all that.

I've pored over that photo of Nick kissing that woman more than enough.

I don't need to keep doing it.

He moved into Mum's room on Sunday so that I could have ours to myself. I haven't been sleeping there though.

I've been sleeping in the attic.

And now I'm here, in the drawing room of this house on the green, reeling from my realisation that the woman I've come to see is none other than the woman I noticed staring at me in The Heaton Arms, eating her Ploughman's lunch. Not only that, but it's hit me that I've seen her other places too, in other *times*: back in Bettys, and up at the top of RAF Doverley's control tower stairs. She was younger then, of course, with blonde rather than white waves in her hair, but still unmistakeably her, with the same knife-sharp cheekbones, piercing eyes, and pointed chin. I can't get over it. Can't believe it's taken me this long to realise.

I've told her that I saw her before I fell.

Too electrified to keep it to myself, I mentioned it as soon as I arrived.

'I grabbed your arm,' I said, as she showed me into this drawing room.

'Really?' she replied, in much the same way as she might have responded to me passing comment on the weather.

She was eighteen in 1943.

She's ninety-three now.

When I used to visit her, thirty years ago, she was in her sixties, and doesn't look like she's aged a day since: a living, breathing advertisement for the age-defying powers of cold cream, and always wearing a sunhat.

She's asked me to call her Ellen.

'Let's do away with the Mrs, shall we?' she said, gesturing for me to sit in the armchair I'm currently ensconced in. 'I'm not married, and –' her lips twitched – 'it's always been doctor anyway.'

She was a WAAF at Doverley during the war.

'The last of us left,' she said, settling herself into the chair opposite mine. 'I'd be grateful though, Claudia, if we could keep that between us. I've no interest in being hounded for my memories by voyeuristic strangers. I was very clear with Tim that he was to keep me out of his stories to Ms Hale. I've had many ambitions in my life, but featuring as a character in a novel has never been one of them.'

In spite of everything, I found myself smiling at her candour.

'You're in touch with Tim then?' I asked her just now.

'Yes, very much so.'

'Were you friends with Iris?'

'You don't recall?' she says, deadpan.

And I study her, trying to work out whether she's making fun.

I don't think she is.

She's really not the teasing kind.

I find I'm remembering more about her, the more we talk. Nothing detailed. But her mannerisms feel familiar. Her forthrightness does. I'm pretty sure she was like this with me even when I was four, and I think it was probably her directness that I liked most about her. How seriously she took me.

I can't decide whether I like her now.

Instinctively, I trust her, but I haven't immediately warmed to her.

She's very buttoned up.

Proper.

'Iris and Clare used to call me Prim,' she says, in such a close echo of my thoughts, that laughter bursts from me.

It comes out strained.

Nervous.

Hand to my mouth, I swallow it, and Ellen arches a perfectly drawn brow.

'That can't have been very nice,' I say.

'No,' she agrees, 'but we got off on the wrong foot. With Clare, I never found my way back.'

'What was she like?'

'Clare? I really didn't know her. But –' she frowns – 'I did want to. She was the kind of person it felt very cold, being on the outside of. I suspect that it was rather wonderful, having her for your friend.'

'Yes,' I say, thinking of Emma, and how much I'm going to miss knowing she's around, once she's gone.

'She was fun,' Ellen continues. 'And sad. And much too young.' She sighs. 'I wept for her when she went.'

Slowly, I nod and, hearing the first drops of rain pattering the room's windowpanes, turn to them, staring out at the bleak morning.

They'll be getting started at Doverley.

I feel a weight of resignation pull through me at the scenes they're about to immortalise.

'Was there anything that anyone could have done?' I ask Ellen.

'Countless things,' she replies. 'But no one did them.'

'But—'

'They didn't do them, Claudia,' she repeats sharply, with a firmness that startles me. 'There's plenty we'll never know about the past, and only one thing we can be completely certain of.' She gives me a hard look. 'We can't change it.'

*

Clare's birthday dawned cold and bleak, the leaden clouds blanketing Doverley promising heavy rain. They wouldn't be going out to celebrate that evening. Ops were scheduled on, despite the bad weather, and despite the boys having only just returned from Frankfurt. *Mabel's Fury* was once again on battle orders, and both Iris and Clare had been rostered on duty as well.

They'd worked on Iris's birthday the month before, too. And on Robbie's. For his twenty-fifth, he'd flown to Turin and back. Later that morning, Iris had driven with him to visit his mother, helping her out into the autumnal sunshine for the picnic she'd arranged – of champagne, and ham and cheese sandwiches – and after, Iris and Robbie had spent the night hidden away in a B&B, both of them on twenty-four-hour leave passes that Robbie had extracted from Ambrose, who'd undoubtedly worked out the lay of the land between them now, but neither of them cared any more. Perhaps it was reckless of them, but time had come to feel so finite that they couldn't waste it worrying about detection. And Ambrose still had no idea about the cottage so, as long as they were seen to be toeing the line elsewhere, there really wasn't a great deal he could do.

'If you'd only marry me, there wouldn't be anything he could do anyway,' said Robbie. 'I'd enjoy telling him that.'

'I'm not going to marry you just so you can put Ambrose in his place,' she said.

'Marry me because I love you, then.'

'Please,' she said, 'not yet. I can't talk about this yet.'

Frankfurt was rumoured to be the target again that night. Robbie had returned from it at five that morning, it was now just gone ten, and in eight short hours he'd be on his way back.

The target was almost always somewhere in Germany, now that Italy had finally surrendered.

How have you kept coming back? Iris had asked Robbie after that terrible raid when Lewis, and all those others, had fallen.

I don't know, Robbie had told her.

But he and the boys – still spearheading every attack they were sent on as master bomber – now had only eight sorties left to go.

Iris wasn't relaxing.

She couldn't allow herself to hope.

She was too scared to do that.

310

Especially now.

Filling her lungs, she leant against the frame of her bedroom door, staring down at the letter she'd just collected from her pigeonhole, her veins coursing with a thousand different emotions, joy, tentative joy, murmuring through them all.

She hadn't told Robbie that she'd visited a clinic.

He didn't know that she'd caught a bus to York the week before, and had been watching the post ever since, waiting for this letter to come.

She wouldn't tell him until his tour was over.

It would distract him.

Put too much pressure on him.

All he needed was to carry on doing as he had been, and *keep coming back.*

'Anything for me?' said Clare, who'd returned from breakfast ahead of Iris, and was on her bed, cradling a mug of what smelt like medicinally laced cocoa.

'Just a bit,' said Iris, saving her own news for another time – this was Clare's day, not hers – and moving to hand her the stack of cards she'd collected from her pigeonhole. 'Ambrose asked me to pass on his felicitations too.'

'Really?'

'Of course not,' said Iris, tapping her on the head with her cards.

*

'I'm pretty sure I did change the past,' I tell Ellen. 'I think Iris would have fallen if it hadn't been for me. I reached for your arm . . .'

'So you've said.'

'You don't remember it?'

311

'Vaguely, maybe. It was more than seventy years ago. But if Iris did that . . . '

'She did . . . '

'Then she was always going to have done it.'

'How can you know?'

'Because, Claudia, she already did.'

'I don't think it's as simple as that.'

'No, I can tell.'

We fall silent.

I study her, so still and composed.

She studies me.

She doesn't check her wristwatch, or consult a notepad.

She hasn't got a notepad.

This is no therapy session we're having.

I'd just like to meet, I said to her on Monday, when I called her using the number Mum gave me. I did it whilst I was here in Heaton, on a break from shooting our village scenes. The entire centre was cordoned off, but a lot of locals turned up to watch from behind the barriers, plenty of paps and reporters with them, yelling their intrusive questions between takes. We all ignored them, of course, and the filming went off without a hitch. It was nothing too complex – snippets of dialogue; a couple of atmosphere shots – and I managed not to show myself up again, but I wasn't remotely fine. I was reeling, cracking from the inside over Nick, and Mum, and Felix too – who really hasn't been helping – my stitches throbbing, by eyes darting from the church, to the graveyard, to this house on the green. *I need to try and understand some things,* I told Ellen. *I'd be grateful for your time, if you don't mind.*

Not at all, she replied. *I've been waiting for your call.*

'I've been fascinated by your career,' she says to me now. 'It's enthralled me that you've chosen to spend your life slipping realities, when you were such an expert at it as a child.'

'Did you ever suspect whose reality I was slipping to?'

'Did it occur to me that you might be inhabiting the past life of Iris Winterton?' She gives me an incredulous look. 'No, Claudia. You were a confused, quiet and cautious child. I knew Iris as a headstrong, capable, and frankly sometimes rather rash young woman. I never once connected the two of you. And I'm a scientist. In the business of facts. It took me a long time to entertain the possibility that there might be some truth in the things you told me.'

'But you did entertain it?'

'I had to. You were so convinced about it all. And I did a great deal of research, talked with colleagues, people I respect, and found other cases like yours. Not many.' She raises her slender hands. 'But enough to be able to push my cynicism aside and consider that your visions mightn't be hallucinatory.'

'They're not. They're real . . . '

'Well, that's the troubling thing about hallucinations, Claudia. They're extremely good at seeming that way. No –' she fixes me with a stern glare, stopping me from interrupting – 'I'm not trying to dismiss what you've been experiencing. I'm simply stating the obvious, which is that hallucinations would be by far the most plausible diagnosis. And you really are under a great deal of strain . . . '

'That's not why this is happening. It's being here. It's opened me up.'

'I'm sure it has. But I'm equally certain you arrived already open *to* it. You were an exceedingly lonely and vulnerable little girl.' Her face softens, just as it did when she spoke about Clare, allowing me another glimpse of her heart, beating beneath her cashmere jumper. 'Your grandparents did their very best for you, but you had no real-life friends, and you missed your mother desperately. You craved escape. An alternate reality.

And,' she says, her eyes holding mine, 'I don't doubt you need one now. Perhaps even more than you did then.'

'I haven't *chased* this.'

'Haven't you?' She raises a dubious brow. 'You keep on sleeping in Iris and Clare's room, which I have to tell you is inexplicable to me. That attic is the most cold and uncomfortable home I've had . . . '

'It doesn't feel uncomfortable to me.'

'No, because you're so unhappy. And I'm sorry for that. I really am deeply sorry, Claudia.' She leans forward in her chair, so earnest in her sudden sympathy that I have to look away. 'But perhaps if you weren't,' she says, 'perhaps if you hadn't come back here heartbroken, you might not have found this all waiting.'

'I'm glad it's been waiting though. I've needed it . . . '

'That's my exact point.'

I open my mouth to argue, then, finding nothing to say, close it again.

I feel like I've been aced in a game of tennis.

'You told me you've been having dreams,' Ellen says.

'Yes.'

'Would you like to tell me about them?'

'I'm not sure where to start,' I reply, feeling increasingly like I am in a therapy session: the most draining one of my life.

'Wherever you like,' she says.

So, with a deep breath, I begin with the two I've had most often: of that colonel, and my own warning to Iris to go, *you need to go*; then, that woman in the wheelchair who touches my face.

'Can you think who she might have been?' I ask.

'Can you?' says Ellen, which isn't answering my question.

I don't press it though.

I'm too preoccupied remembering the emotion I've seen in the woman's eyes.

The deep grief, but also hope.

'I've got no idea who she is,' I say. 'She keeps telling me something that makes me cry, but I can't ever hear her.'

'That's dreams for you,' says Ellen. 'What else have they shown you?'

'So much,' I say, and go on, describing smoky pubs, ice-coated windows, blinking switchboards, sticky sweets, tart apple cake, and a smiling boy in tartan slippers.

Ellen becomes very still when I mention him.

Stiller yet when I talk of the other time I saw her: not in a dream, but life, just as I saw her outside the control tower, only this time inside Bettys Bar, all done up and sitting with a man in a USAAF uniform.

'And have you had any other such . . . *episodes*?' she asks me tightly.

'A couple,' I say, and tell her about them too: first, Robbie's face coming to life in Tim's photograph; then, the absolute vividness with which I was transported on Saturday night out of my and Nick's room, and into the burgeoning warmth of a clear summer's dawn.

'I was desperate to warn Iris,' I say. 'Make her realise how close the end was coming.'

'She needed no warning,' says Ellen. 'There wasn't a single person among us who didn't live with the proximity of death hanging over them. Except perhaps Ambrose.'

'Ambrose?'

'Our adjutant. He never seemed to care about anything, except making life more unpleasant than it already was. Such a nasty little man.' She gives a mirthless smile. 'I was happy he didn't get a mention in the book.'

'You have read it, then?'

'I have.'

'Did you like it?'

'No. It made me extremely angry.'

'Really?'

I wasn't expecting that.

In what way? I'm about to ask.

But she talks on, saying Ambrose's omission from *The Bomber Boys* is, to her mind, the strongest point in its favour. 'To my enduring regret, I pandered to his ego. I was silly and naive enough to believe I should do that.'

'What about Iris? Did she pander to him?'

'Not at all. Ambrose despised her for it, of course. Robbie too, for always being in her corner. Not that he'd have been anywhere else.' She smiles again, more truly this time. Achingly so. 'I was desperately envious. We were all a little in love with Robbie Grayson.' Her eyes glimmer. 'You of course know what it is to court a man who's admired like that.'

I blink at her abrupt change in subject.

Shift in my seat.

'I'm not sure that Nick and I are courting at all any more,' I say.

'No?' She sounds genuinely surprised.

Clearly, she's not one for browsing gossip columns.

'You seemed to be getting on so well when I saw you in The Heaton Arms.'

'That was the general idea.'

'I am sorry, Claudia. You really must be in a great deal of pain.'

Miserably, I nod.

Because she's not wrong.

I am in pain.

And so is Nick.

Other than for on set, we've barely spoken since Saturday night. He told me by text that he's dropped the case against the clinic in Los Angeles (*I'm sorry, Claude, it shouldn't have taken this for me to be able to hear you*), and I suppose that's something. Apparently, no one's really talking about my misshapen uterus online any more either. They're all too busy discussing Nick's *naughtiness*, back at the start of this month, when he came to stay in Highgate, played chauffeur to Hannah and her friends, opened a tab for them in that London bar, and was pictured kissing a twenty-four-year-old woman. *Not* the same one I've been obsessing over all these months. No, it turns out Nick's been telling the truth about her. One of her friends confirmed that this week, tagging her (lou93) on a repost of Nick's kiss that's gone viral enough to hit the papers, quipping (with multiple laughing emojis) that Nick obviously has a thing for London girls. *Too bad you never could persuade him to try homegrown, Lou. Hahaha.* And, god, I wish I could claw back the emotion I've wasted since summer, staring at her face.

Now I have another's to taunt me.

Chelsea, she's called, and Nick was caught kissing her within touching distance of my sister.

Hannah didn't see it happen. She was turned away from them, laughing with a friend. The first she knew about any of it was on Saturday night, when Chelsea posted the photo on her socials, and Hannah's phone lit up with people demanding to know what kind of a sister she thinks she is.

I feel sick to my stomach that she's been dragged into it all.

'I'm fine,' she's told me. 'It's you I'm worried about. Nick too.'

Chelsea is the older sister of a girl called Elodie who Hannah's been at school with since primary. I've never liked Elodie, she's a total user, and I've told Hannah countless times to kick her to the kerb. But when Elodie heard that Nick was driving Hannah and the others to the bar, she turned up too, bringing Chelsea with her: all buxom and doe-eyed, with a plumped-up pout and thick, lacquered eyelashes.

'Just Nick's type, basically,' said Felix, when, breaking the no airmen in the attic rule, he came up there to see me on Sunday morning, sitting on Clare's bed. 'Come on, Claude. You know there's no way he wanted any of this.'

I do know that.

I believe completely that Nick had no interest in kissing Chelsea. You can tell, if you look at the photo closely, how stunned he is. He's told me he was too shocked to immediately react, and pushed Chelsea away the instant he made sense of what was going on. But how, *how* could he have been so stupid, getting himself into that situation in the first place?

'It's 101,' I said to Felix. 'He should have had his wits about him.'

'Like us, you mean, in Sicily?'

'That was different.'

'Not that different. We fell afoul of a camera angle, so did Nick.'

'We were *acting*, Felix. It wasn't real.'

'It wasn't real for Nick either, but you're punishing him anyway.'

'I'm not *punishing* him . . .'

'You are. Just like you punished me. And it hurts, Claude. It *hurt* me. So much that I actually started to question whether it had all been as platonic for me as I'd thought. No.' He held up his hands, seeing my widening eyes. 'No need to panic. I'm not about to declare my undying love . . .'

'Right,' I said, still panicking a bit anyway.

'Seriously, Claude, it's fine. I've always known it's just friends for us. I realised that when we auditioned for *The Go-Between*.' Fleetingly, a smile lifted his leaden expression. 'It was you telling me about your laxative commercial.'

In spite of myself, I smiled too, replaying his laughter. 'You snorted Sprite out of your nose.'

'You acted constipated for an ad that got pulled.'

'At least it did get pulled.'

'Yeah,' he said, 'small mercies.'

And, as we fell silent, our smiles fading, I looked across at him – my friend, my brilliant friend, for all these years – feeling worse than ever for the pain I'd caused him.

You turned so cold, so fast.

'I'm sorry,' I said again. 'I was thoughtless. Self-obsessed.'

'Yeah,' he agreed. 'But you were also in hell, and I shouldn't have flinched. Not the way I did.' He exhaled. 'I've been feeling like I've stumbled into Tim's story, becoming this point on a triangle I've never wanted to be part of.' He gave me a weary look. 'I hated having to convince Nick of that. I hate that I ever came between you.'

'If it hadn't been you, it would have been something or someone else.' Such a miserable truth. 'I really am sorry, Felix. It's been scaring me that we'll never get back to how we were.' I frowned, thinking of the niggling tension that had persisted between us, like an unshakeable virus, reappearing every time I'd started to hope it might have gone away. 'I love you way too much for that.'

'I love you too, you idiot,' he said. 'But . . . *god –*' he closed his eyes – 'I'm the one who's sorry.' He pulled in a breath. Shook his head. 'I have to tell you something.' He sounded so suddenly abject, I genuinely feared he might be ill.

My trepidation grew as he jerked to his feet, pacing the small room, all too obviously summoning the courage to go on.

'Felix,' I said, 'what's wrong?'

Warily, he eyeballed me.

'Just say it,' I said.

And, with a pained grimace, he did.

'I'm the one who's been speaking to *The Screen*,' he blurted. 'I'm their anonymous source.'

I didn't react.

I couldn't.

I felt stupefied.

So, *this* was why he'd been acting the way he had?

Not because of me, at all, but because he'd been hiding . . . *this*?

Oh my god, I thought.

Oh my God.

'The reporter, Kate, called me a couple of hours after we had that row in your trailer,' he said, 'reminded me I owed her a favour.' He talked on, telling me that not every photo taken of us in Sicily was from when we were acting. There were others too, which *The Screen* have been sitting on, of us having dinner at this little place we used to go to on the rocks. 'Obviously we weren't doing anything wrong,' he said, 'but they looked fairly intimate, and I knew they'd fuel the fire, so when Kate showed them to me back in August, I convinced her not to print them and said in return I'd help her out with the inside track on this shoot.' He tugged his hand through his hair. 'I didn't think about what I was promising. I just wanted to kill those photos. When she called again, I should have told her to forget it, but I was still really angry over everything with you, not thinking straight, and I couldn't see a way round it. So, I . . . talked.'

'Right,' I said, the anaesthesia of my shock already fading, anger taking over as I replayed everything Kate had written. 'You *talked*. Nearly got Emma fired. Said Nick's casting was a publicity stunt. That I might . . . *shatter*, was it?'

'She twisted my words. Paraphrased, left stuff out . . . '

'Yes, that's what they *all* do.'

'I'm sorry. I am . . . '

'Felix . . .' I was incredulous. '. . . you told them Nick and I were sleeping in separate rooms.'

'No.' His face hardened. 'That wasn't me. They had no quote

for that. *The word is*, was all they said. Kate must have got it from one of the staff. I refused to comment when she asked me . . . '

'You refused to comment?'

'Yes.'

'Why couldn't you have said it wasn't bloody *true*?'

'God, Claude, I don't know. I screwed up.'

'You one hundred per cent did,' I snapped.

And yet, even in the hot haze of my fury, I understood why he'd done it.

I was grateful that he'd done it.

I didn't need to see those photos of us, dining by candlelight on the shores of the starlit sea, to know I never wanted them to get out.

I just couldn't bring myself to say that to him. Or admit to myself what a hypocrite I was, for still being so mad at Nick.

I was too caught up in my own righteous indignation.

'Does anyone else know?' I asked.

'No.'

'You need to tell them.'

'I will.'

'When?'

'Soon. Just . . . please,' his eyes implored me, 'let me do it in my own time, ok? Let it come from me.'

'Fine,' I said, grudgingly. 'Don't take too long though.'

'I won't.' He exhaled, sat back on Clare's bed. 'I can't tell you how glad I am that I've finally told you. Even if you hate me forever, at least you know.'

I won't hate you forever.

Again, I didn't say it.

I wish now I had.

I wish I'd told him I could never hate him, and that it was all right, he'd done what he had with the best intentions.

321

But I remained silent.

Cold.

'I'm sorry,' he repeated. 'I really didn't come up here to drop this all on you.'

'Why did you come?'

'Because it's killing me, seeing you and Nick in all this unnecessary pain.'

'That's not my fault.'

'It's not Nick's either. Fine, he let his defences down, screwed up too, but only because he's a really decent human and probably wasn't imagining anyone would stoop so low as to do something like this. So, give him a break, hey?'

I didn't agree to do anything.

I asked Felix to leave me alone.

And, with a sigh, he did, whilst I remained in the attic, furious at myself and him now, as well as Nick, but still Nick most of all, growing evermore incredulous, the angrier I got, that he'd been so careless as to let Chelsea near him, for long enough that Elodie had snapped her picture.

It was Elodie who got his number off Hannah's phone. Chelsea's been texting him ever since – Nick's shown me her messages – asking to see him again, *I bet I'm a lot more fun than Claudia*, eventually threatening to go live with her photo unless he gave in.

Have you changed your mind?

'Why didn't you tell me?' I asked him on Saturday.

'I almost did,' he said. 'The night we got here.'

I remember it.

It was after Ana's welcome dinner. He grabbed me as I came out of the bathroom.

What is it? I asked him.

I'm glad you're here, he said, *that's all.*

'I couldn't bring myself to make you more unhappy,' he's

322

now told me. 'And I was scared, Claude, that you wouldn't believe it had been nothing. You've been so convinced I've got it in me to cheat. All I've wanted is for us to have this time here to have another go.'

'It was Nick, wasn't it, who gave you your BAFTA for *The Go-Between*?' Ellen says, her voice pulling me from my miserable thoughts.

'You saw that?'

'Yes. I was on the edge of my seat for you.'

'You were?' Through my upset, I manage a smile, touched. 'Thank you.'

'I imagine it was a very happy night.'

'It was.'

Nick had won best actor the year before, for his part in a 1920s underworld thriller, so was on stage to present best actress. He grinned as he pulled the card from its envelope and leant towards the mic, announcing my name.

We hadn't met before. Felix hadn't yet had the chance to introduce us.

But we'd had our eye on each other, even then.

I'm in awe of you, Nick said into my ear, his hand closing around mine as I joined him on the stage: his touch, his voice, making my already racing heart pump.

'You nearly tripped over,' says Ellen.

'I did,' I agree. 'He caught me.'

'You both laughed. You couldn't stop. You could barely get your acceptance speech out. Every time you looked back at him, it set you off . . . '

'Yes,' I say, heavily.

I feel no urge to laugh now.

I want to cry.

We were friends first, for years. I used to tease him, actually, for his playboy ways. I know he was never untrue to his girlfriends, he just had lots of them, and I suppose I must have been jealous, because I'd roll my eyes and accuse him of being a brat-pack poster boy, which he was always infuriatingly amused by. ('It was either laugh or cry,' he's since said.) Then, three years ago, we wound up on the same flight to London from LA, got drunk in my suite, and that was that.

'It used to be really easy between us,' I say. 'Then it got so . . . hard.'

'I do understand,' says Ellen. 'I was let down once. Very badly. By a man who wore a USAAF uniform, and used to take me to Bettys.'

'I'm sorry,' I say, taken aback, as much by the intimacy as her corroboration of what I told her I saw back then.

And I am sorry.

I don't like to think of her hurt.

'It was decades ago,' she says. 'I've had time to heal. But, Claudia, you're very raw. You're not in a good state at all. So please be extremely sure, won't you, before making any decisions about what your life should look like.'

'I have no idea what my life should look like,' I say, and, expelling a ragged breath, tip my head forwards, sinking it into my hands. My scar still hurts. I run my finger over it, remembering Nick kissing me in my shower cap, and have to bite my cheeks to keep them under control. 'I love him,' I say. 'I love him so much. But I can't give him what he needs. And it feels like we'll never be able to be us. We'll always have the press watching, waiting for us to slip up. And lately . . . lately . . . ' I swallow. 'Lately, it's seemed like all we've had is bad. I can't sentence us to a lifetime of that, and I can't see our way out.'

'So, you've been finding another one. Retreating into Iris.'

I don't respond.

'Things were by no stretch easy for her,' Ellen says. 'They were hard. Insurmountably hard, in the end.'

'Do you know what happened to her?' I ask.

This time, she's the one who doesn't reply.

Slowly, I raise my eyes back to hers.

'You said the novel made you angry,' I say. 'Was it because of the ending?'

She remains silent.

She's not going to answer, I can tell.

Not yet anyway.

And there's no doubt in my mind any more that she at least is one hundred per cent treating this as a therapy session.

I don't mind though.

I'm not upset with her.

Just increasingly grateful, really, really grateful actually, that she – who was on the edge of her seat for me when I got my first BAFTA, and listened to me as a child, *heard* me back then – still cares enough about me that, at the age of ninety-three, she's invited me into her home so that she can try again to help me.

Outside, the rain grows heavier, drumming against the windows.

'What are you thinking about?' she says, at length.

'I don't know,' I say. 'Everything.'

'Can you give me something specific?' she asks.

So, I do.

I give her my father's theatre.

*

'I miss him,' said Clare, staring down at her pile of cards, holding Hans's ring in her fist. 'None of these are from him, I can't feel him at all, and I miss him so much.'

'Oh, Clare,' said Iris. She was in bed, feeling nauseous, and failing to sleep. The workmen downstairs were making their usual stop-start racket, waking her every time she came close to drifting off. 'He could still be here, missing you too.'

'He's not here.' She pressed his ring to her chest. 'But I do believe I'll see him again.' She tipped her head back against the eaves. 'Perhaps I might not even have that long a wait.'

'What do you mean?' said Iris uneasily.

'Do you remember when we talked about us all having been here before?'

'Yes,' said Iris, edgier yet. She still often thought of her non-fall down the stairs – every time, in fact, that she felt that returning presence within her, filling her with an urgency, to do what, she only wished she could guess – and didn't at all like what she now realised Clare was saying. 'It was a rumination, Clare. An idea . . . '

'It's become more than that to me,' said Clare. 'I really don't think any of this is final.' She looked to the rain-drenched window. 'I'm sure it's just an act, in an endlessly repeating play.'

'A long act, let's hope,' said Iris, sitting up now, hating the finality in her friend's tone.

'I suspect that's already decided,' Clare replied, in the same accepting way. 'But the end doesn't scare me, not if it takes us back to our beginning.' Her cheeks moved in a smile. 'I want that. Even with all the pain, it helps, believing Hans and I will find one another again. Have our time again.' Her voice scratched with emotion. 'I need to believe that's all waiting.'

'Clare, you don't know he's gone . . . '

'He is.'

'You can't give up.'

'I don't want to . . . '

'Then don't. Sleep instead. You're exhausted.'

'I can't sleep,' said Clare, turning again to the window, frowning at the rain outside.

'Try at least.'

'There's no point,' said Clare.

Then, 'I think maybe I'll go for a walk.'

*

'I take it you know about my father,' I say to Ellen.

'I never met him, Claudia. Never spoke to him.'

'But you know that he was . . . '

'In the car with you?' She nods. 'Yes, my dear. I do know about that.'

'Mum said he couldn't see the future . . . '

'None of us can do that.'

'Maybe not,' I say, although nothing would surprise me any more. 'I do believe he couldn't. Otherwise, he'd have stopped the crash from happening, wouldn't he?'

'I'm sure.'

'Mum said he believed that his other existences fed him instincts for the things he should do, the places he should be. I'm certain he must have been following one of those instincts when he got into the car with me, even if he didn't know what it would cost him.' Those words are very hard to say. The idea of what he did for me, *gave* for me, gets no less painful for the amount of time I've now spent thinking about it. 'I keep wondering whether he'd have done it if he *had* known. Mum said he loved me more than life, but—'

'You were his child,' Ellen interrupts. 'I absolutely believe he would have still chosen to protect you. As for what he knew, has it not occurred to you he might have sensed it was his time?'

'No,' I say, because I don't want to think about anyone having a set *time*.

Not my father.

327

Not my grandparents.

Certainly not Robbie, and Iris, and the rest of them.

'I do keep wondering about his instincts though,' I say. 'We all get them. Thousands, maybe hundreds of thousands, in our lifetimes. Anticipation, excitement, dread, caution . . .'

'Hope,' proffers Ellen. 'Courage.'

'Yes,' I say. 'All that. Most of us don't question where they come from. But my father did. He *knew*. When Mum described his theatre to me, I could see it.' I close my eyes, seeing it again. 'So many infinite stages of time and existence, hovering over one another, each lit by its own house lanterns.' I open my eyes, meeting Ellen's focused stare. 'Have you ever stood on a stage?'

'I have not.'

'You can't see out. Not easily. Not when the lanterns are bright, and trained on you. They block everything beyond. But that doesn't mean it's not there. You can hear it, if you listen. The coughs. The shuffles. A whisper.'

'And you believe these whispers are where our instincts come from?' Ellen says.

To my relief, there's no scepticism in her tone.

No resistance.

Just desire to understand.

It gives me the courage to go on.

'I do,' I say. 'I feel it now, everywhere, this sense of being amid layers of time. I'm sure that even if most of us aren't consciously listening to those layers, we still always are. And we react, like my father knew he was reacting, trying different paths, making changes, no layer exactly the same.' I draw breath, my mind moving to Tim, and all the different variations of his own past that he told Imogen. I see my own dreams too, of Nick and me enacting those variations, and picture us still doing it, on other stages. 'I believe that for some of us, our lanterns can flicker off. We get to see beyond our own layer, and steal glimpses, however fleeting, of the infinity we're part of.'

I look to Ellen, watching a crease form in her brow.

She's thinking, I can tell.

Processing.

'Do you have a theory for why this only happens for some of us?' she asks.

'My father thought it was a gift.'

'Does it feel like that to you?'

'It's started to.'

'Because you think you can help Iris.' She phrases it as a statement rather than a question.

It doesn't surprise me.

I realised she'd worked that much out from the moment she told me I couldn't change the past.

'You can't,' she repeats now. 'Or certainly no more than this version of you might have already intervened. It's all already happened, my dear. However infinite a theatre we might be a part of, however many acts we might yet have to play, in this present, in *our* present, the past is sealed . . . '

'But . . . '

'No, Claudia. Don't forget, I was there, physically there. Whatever you hope you might yet do to reverse what's gone, my memories aren't going to rewrite themselves. You do not have that power.'

'Then why does Iris keep pulling me back into her?'

'I don't believe it's that way round.'

'I do, though. She needs me . . . '

'It's you who needs her.'

'*No.*' I all but shout it. 'From the moment I arrived here, my lanterns started flickering off, I know now it happened when I was a child too, only it's not *my* other stages I keep finding myself on. It's Iris's. Even when I'm not in her, I hear her world.

That bird. Those planes. The hammering. I follow *her* instincts. Then, when I slip into her, I see . . . *everything.* It's not false. It's not imagined. It's as though we're the same person . . . '

'You are absolutely not the same person. You are you. Solely you.'

'But . . . '

'No, listen to me now. You are *you.*'

'Then why is this happening?'

'I don't know,' says Ellen, and I can hear how much it perplexes her. 'I did consider, when you were a child, that you might have an old soul. Incredulous as it makes me to say this, I'm wondering now if we all might carry some essence of those who are gone, with traces of other existences behind us, and in front of us, even if most of us don't realise it.' She frowns, turning it over. 'Maybe you and your father are right, too. Maybe we're all ever-present, with our souls, and fragments of souls, living eternally in parallel, doing better, finding our way back to those we've loved, so we can love them again. I hope so. It's a wonderfully comforting idea. But, Claudia –' her unblinking eyes hold mine – 'this is your existence. You belong on *this* stage.' She shakes her head. 'Nowhere else.'

I don't try again to argue.

A sudden pelt of rain lashes the window, distracting me.

It's really pouring now.

Absolutely sheeting.

Emma will be acting Clare's last scene.

I want to stop it.

I want, so fiercely, to do that.

But whatever Iris was doing, in this crucial moment of her friend's life, I've never had any sight of it.

Was there anything anyone could do? I asked Ellen.

Countless things, she said, *but no one did them.*

'You can't seriously want to go out in this,' said Iris as Clare stood, pulling on her jacket.

The rain outside was getting heavier.

Absolutely sheeting.

'I need some fresh air,' said Clare. 'And to get away from this wretched banging.'

'You'll get soaked.'

'I'm not worried about that,' said Clare, making for their bedroom door. 'I'll take Prim's umbrella.'

*

'Where were you when Clare died?' I ask Ellen.

'Barely fifty yards from her. I was coming out of the ops room. I'd stayed back to finish my reports, and I saw her. She saw me too, and started towards me.' She speaks quietly, remembering. 'She had my umbrella. I think she felt badly about it, and was coming to give it back.'

'And Tim?'

'Yes, he was there too. He struggled with sleep, and was on his way off for a walk. Clare had had the same idea. Then, out of nowhere, that Messerschmitt was swooping right down over the base.' Her expression becomes distant. 'He strafed Clare, and several groundcrew too, before our gunners shot him down.'

Silently, barely aware of my own movement, I shake my head.

'They were all gone,' says Ellen, and I see her heart clearly now: in her brimming stare, her clenched hands. 'Extinguished, in a second.' Her lips tremble in a heartbroken smile. 'On this stage, anyway.'

I want to say something.

I can't speak.

'She wouldn't have known anything about it,' Ellen goes on. 'I promise you that. I discovered, years later, that her fiancé had been killed only a few weeks before. It would be . . . *wonderful,* yes . . . to think that by the time I got to her, she was on her way back to him.' She swallows. 'I ran to her, the instant she fell. Tim did too. But she'd already left us.' Dipping her head, she presses her fingers to the corners of her eyes. 'It broke Tim.' Her shoulders move in a shallow breath. 'He simply couldn't stand it.'

'The other day, he said the war is always happening.' I force the words out, past the mass in my throat. 'It upset him so much. I think all he could see of it was the pain. The fear . . . '

'Well, there was plenty of that.' She drops her hands from her eyes. 'Love too, though. So much love.' She gives me another small smile. 'Don't forget that.'

'What happened to Iris?' I ask her again. 'The book's wrong about her, isn't it? That's why it made you angry.'

'Of course it's wrong. It's fiction. A story. Tim should never have permitted it . . . '

'But what happened?'

'You need to ask Tim.'

'I've tried.'

'Try again.'

'Do *you* know what happened though?' I say, and hear how entreating I sound.

But I need, so desperately, for her to tell me that she does.

To believe there's a hope that I might yet find out.

Because I haven't given up on being able to do something about this at least, no matter what Ellen might say about us all having our time. No matter her insistence that we can't change this present's past.

Rationally, logically, I accept that I probably should.

But there's been nothing rational or logical about anything I've experienced here.

And I can't give up on anything.

'I don't know what happened in that plane,' Ellen says. 'But I do know what didn't happen on the ground. I know what Iris didn't do, and I'm certain of what she doesn't deserve. That at least *can* be fixed. So, visit Tim. Talk to him like you've talked to me. Make him tell you.' She leans back in her chair. 'Help him make amends at last.'

Chapter Twenty-Two

Claudia

I can't visit Tim today, impatient as I am to.

I've stayed with Ellen too long and am late getting back to make-up, who I'm with for an hour, having my hair pinned and my face painted so that I can ruin it all for the cameras in the aftermath of Clare's death.

Iris never actually held Clare in her arms, like I'm about to hold Emma. She does it in this movie because that's the way Imogen wrote it in her book: Iris sprinting to the rainswept scene, where she has to be dragged away from her friend's body by Robbie. I feel no nerves about whether I'll be able to pull off her tears. Frankly, I'm so full of them, it will be a relief to once again let them go. But I do feel extremely unsettled by Ellen's revelation, just before I left her, that Imogen's version of this event is, like her ending, pure fabrication.

Because in this instance, Imogen wasn't the one who made it up.

Tim was.

He told Imogen that this is what happened, so we all have asterisks covering our scripts reminding us that we're not allowed to change any of it.

'It was Tim who had to be prised off Clare,' Ellen said to

334

me in her living room. 'Everyone came out of their billets when the firing started, and Robbie made straight for Tim, pulling him away so that the stretcher bearers could get to Clare. Tim thrashed out, sobbing his poor heart out, but Robbie held him fast, quietening him, and got him back to their billet before he could make any more of a scene. I think it was then that he accepted how dangerously frayed Tim had become.' She frowned sorrowfully. 'I'd been aware of it for a while. You could always tell in interrogation. These days of course, someone in his state would be signed off, given understanding and time to heal. Back then, he just had to keep going, or he'd have been discharged with LMF. *Lack of Moral Fibre*.' Witheringly, she sighed. 'It was a different time, it cast a very long shadow, and Tim's still carrying a great deal of shame. It didn't surprise me at all that he's had himself portrayed as such a stoic in the book.'

He really has. There's not so much as a hint that he's struggling to cope with anything in Imogen's writing.

Of all the crew, it's only Jacob, the bomb aimer, who's shown to experience any kind of debilitating fear.

'But you see that's wrong too,' said Ellen. 'To me, he never seemed scared, so much as pragmatic. A realist who was resigned. He was very much in love actually, with a woman called Beth Twinton, who came to be a dear friend to me. He refused to discuss the future with her. It maddened her, but after he was killed, she discovered he'd left her a great deal of money. She used it to set up a school near his parents' home in Barnes, which I'm sure would have made him happy. He'd been their only child, and Beth lost her parents in the Blitz. Jacob was doubtless hoping they'd look after each other. He really never believed he'd survive.' She sighed. 'Like poor Clare.'

'How did Iris find out about her?' I asked.

'Robbie told her. I took him up to her and Clare's room.'

'He was there?' I said, and even as I did, pictured him, kneeling on the floor beside the bed I've been sleeping on, waking Iris: his face wet from the rain, his eyes looking into hers.

I can picture him now.

Hear his voice.

Iris.

Iris . . .

'I was next door,' Ellen told me. 'Her sobs came through our wall.' She pressed her hand to her chest. 'Like I've said, I wept for Clare myself. Wept for them all.'

Within a couple of hours, I'm sobbing too, in the mud beside Emma's prone body, the rain soaking through my woollen uniform, dripping chillingly down my neck.

Nick is pulling me, not Felix, away.

I fight him, but he keeps a hold of me.

He wraps his arms around me, fast.

'Iris,' he says.

Iris . . .

I hear them both.

I turn to Nick, and I see them both.

Two rain-drenched faces, flickering in and out of my focus.

'I can't bear it,' I say.

I know, that other voice tells me.

'I know,' Nick says. 'It's all right . . .'

'It's not.'

We're here, says Robbie. *For now we're here.*

It's not enough, I think.

And, with a slow blink, it's only Nick I see.

Only his eyes that I look into: the wrong colour, but full of a love that might well be award-worthy, but which I do also believe is real.

Love isn't our problem though.

I realise it never has been.

And it's not enough.

Because it's everything else that's destroying us.

It's always been everything else.

Nick knows that too.

He can't bear it either.

I feel that in the way he's holding on to me.

I see it in the pain that's snapping in his stare.

Neither of us want to be doing what we're doing, acting out the dying days of this other doomed love story, but we keep going anyway for the cameras, for the crew, until Ana calls, *cut*, Naomi circles what we've done, and, stepping away from Nick, I let him go.

*

Emma stays with us for one more night.

We don't have a big send-off.

'Who in hell feels like that?' she says, when, wet to our bones, we head back to our trailers together for the final time.

But later, after I've finished my other scene for the day – packing away Clare's belongings on the set of our bedroom – we do have a farewell just the two of us, up in Iris and Clare's actual room, dressed in our pyjamas, dressing gowns and thick socks, eating dinners we've carried up from downstairs, drinking from miniature bottles of medicinal brandy.

It's not the first time we've eaten together this week. I haven't braved the dining room since Saturday, and Emma's been keeping me company – always in my room, up until now. We've talked a lot, including about our plans for after this. Mine's to finally have a break, while she's looking at taking the lead in a fantasy, shooting in New Zealand, with Felix again. Her new agent, at my agency, is handling the negotiations.

337

'I just hope Felix doesn't try to get me fired again,' she says – not coldly, not *unkindly*, but with a wry smile, a lot more magnanimous than I, to my prevailing shame, managed to be about what he did.

You need to tell them, I snapped at him, back on Sunday. *Don't take too long.*

He did it this morning, while I was with Ellen, and the rest of them were together, about to start shooting.

'I found myself hugging him,' Emma told me, when she and Ana caught me up on it all before our scene earlier.

'So did I,' said Ana. 'After I ate him for my second breakfast, obviously.' She raised a brow. 'But he was so *woeful* about it, and we all know there's not a malicious beat in his heart. Blake's actually thrilled. He wants to use Felix now.'

'What about Nick?' I asked, feeling even more like crap in the face of their generosity, and selfishly hoping Nick would make me feel better by having been even more unforgiving. 'How did he react?'

'He hugged him too,' said Emma, with an apologetic pout. 'Said he appreciated him. I think they were both trying not to cry. There was a lot of back slapping.'

'You gotta throw him a bone, Claude,' said Ana. 'He won't be ok with himself until you do.'

'I'm looking forward to NZ,' Emma says now. 'It'll do me good not to be in a part that breaks my heart. And I *know* you need to give yourself this rest.'

I don't disagree.

She's right, of course.

I've found myself opening up to her more, these past nights. I haven't told her everything I've discussed with Ellen and Mum – it's too much – but I have spoken about my dad, my grief over what he did for me, and Nick as well: all the pain I feel for us. She's been great, not trying to fix anything, just listening, and

338

it's finally dawned on me that I should have leant on her much more than I have, long before now. But instead, I spent all my time in the woods, and up in this attic. Alone.

That's why I wanted to bring Emma here tonight. Everything today has made me confront how idiotic I've been, cutting myself off from friends, when so many others had theirs taken away.

And I think Clare would enjoy the idea of us together in this room, drinking brandy in her honour.

Do you believe you're all carrying parts of them? Ellen asked me before I left her this morning. *Does Nick hold the essence of Robbie in him? Does Emma hold Clare? Felix, Tim?*

Tim's still alive, I pointed out.

Does that matter? Perhaps you're all living their new stories, and have found your way to each other for them, as well as yourselves.

Perhaps, I said. *I honestly have no idea.*

I have considered it though.

I've thought about Felix's adamance that he won't repeat Tim's triangle.

My own growing friendship with Emma.

And, most of all, Nick, who was drawn back here long before we started shooting, using it as *his* escape from the pain of now that he just couldn't tolerate. I've turned over the ease with which he's taken to flying, and how at home he's become in this place, finding his way to the village through Doverley's old gateway, opening it with a knack that made me spin when I watched him do it. I've observed him everywhere else too – around the sets, the base, my attention caught constantly by the pull of his eyes, *windows to his soul* – and found myself wondering plenty.

What I am certain of is that he hasn't pondered these possibilities himself.

339

The lanterns on his stage are alight, and he is purely now. Purely here.

So is Felix.

So is Emma.

And maybe Ellen's right.

Maybe they don't need to be anywhere else.

Or maybe, *maybe*, they're not needed anywhere else.

By anyone else.

Emma sits on Clare's bed, ducking to avoid the eaves, and raises her bottle to mine.

'To Clare,' she says.

'To Clare,' I echo. 'To both of them.'

'May they be drinking better brandy than this, wherever they are.'

Smiling, I clink my bottle to hers, and we down them; swallowing, gasping, laughing.

Faintly, I hear whispers beyond us: of other gasps.

More laughter.

Perhaps, if I turned to the mirror, I'd catch a glimpse of two further forms: shadows moving in the glass.

But I don't turn to the mirror.

I make room on Iris's bed as Emma moves, sitting beside me, wrapping me in her arms.

'Promise me we'll do this more,' she says. 'Promise me we'll do it lots.'

'I promise,' I say, hugging her back.

You were an exceedingly lonely and vulnerable little girl, Ellen told me earlier.

You had no real-life friends.

'You're gonna be ok, Claude,' says Emma. 'It's all gonna be ok.'

*

She's already left by the time I wake the next morning, off to catch her plane home. It's Thursday, 22 November, and by the end of this weekend we'll also have said goodbye to the last extras remaining with us. This time next week, the rest of us will be packing to leave too. We have just seven days of filming left, including another night shoot this evening, and only one day off remaining – tomorrow – which I'm determined to spend with Tim.

I call Roger from my trailer at bang on 9 a.m., telling him I need to talk to Tim about the night *Mabel's Fury* went down. I've decided to be candid about that now. I can't afford not to be. We're almost out of time, and increasingly it's looking like Imogen's ending is the one we're going to be going with. As things stand, I'll be shooting Iris's final words to Robbie next Thursday morning, mistakenly giving him the coordinates that lead *Mabel's Fury* into the sights of a Nazi warship. Over in LA, special effects will create the moment that that ship's guns destroy *Mabel's Fury*'s engines. And, on Thursday afternoon, the boys will film the panic of their final moments as they realise that they're going down with their parachutes damaged. They'll jettison all their equipment, shedding weight in a desperate bid to reach England, until, realising how hopeless it is, Nick, *Robbie*, will fix the plane's steering to keep it flying straight, and he and the others will jump, parachute-less, through the escape hatch, freeing *Mabel's Fury* of their own weight too, so that Tim – unconscious, *bleeding out since Berlin* – might have a chance of gliding to land.

The next morning, I'll wade into the North sea.

Even now, a location team's out, confirming arrangements for the beach we're using.

'I need Tim's help,' I tell Roger. 'I spoke to a friend of his, Eleanor Norland, and she's certain he can give it to me.'

'Can you hold for a minute?' Roger says. 'I'll talk to him.'

'Absolutely,' I say. 'Thank you.'

And I do hold.

I hold for several minutes, pacing my trailer, trying to guess what Roger and Tim are saying, growing more agitated the longer the classical music playing into my earpiece goes on.

Then, 'Claudia, I'm sorry,' comes Roger's voice: embarrassed, awkward. 'Tim's not feeling up to visitors tomorrow.'

No, I think.

'Please,' I say out loud. 'I won't keep him long . . . '

'I'm afraid it's not going to work. Maybe try again over the weekend?'

'Tomorrow's my last free day,' I say heavily.

'I'm sorry,' he repeats.

So am I.

But I'm not giving up either.

As soon as I hang up on Roger, I reach for my script, tear free the final pages, grab a pen, and, on the back of this scene that Ellen said Tim should never have permitted, I write to him, begging him to let me visit. I don't take my time over what I say – I don't have time – but write from my heart, without inhibition, hoping to touch his.

You believe that the past is always happening, I scribble. *So do I. After the weeks I've spent here, recreating this beautiful, terrible chapter of time, I believe it utterly.*

I carry on, talking of my father, just as I did to Ellen, relaying his certainty that none of us ever truly go, but remain always present, fated to live these lives we've been given over and again. I tell him of all I've seen and heard of Iris's world, and finish by entreating him to help me understand her end. *Turn off the lanterns illuminating my stage one final time, I beg you. Let me see what you saw on this November night in 1943 so that I can try to make it right.*

Then, folding my hastily scrawled note up, I seal it shut with

342

garment tape, and head out of my trailer into the morning's glare. The skies have cleared, the temperature's once again plummeted, and the glinting fields around me are buzzing, hectic with everyone getting ready for this next scene we're about to shoot, back in the control tower. The actor playing Sergeant Browning is coming out of make-up, ready to go, but it's not him I look at.

I look at Nick, who's sitting on the step of his own trailer, cradling a cup of steaming coffee, wearing jeans and a sweater – he's not working until this afternoon – staring right back at me.

I hold tight to my letter, and consider asking him to deliver it for me.

He'd do it, I know.

But I can't ask him.

Can't keep trying to depend on him.

I'm afraid it will only disappoint and hurt us both more.

So, I give Nick a pinched frown and head for Felix's trailer, since he's not working until later either and I need, belatedly, to show him I do still trust him.

That I know I can depend on him.

'Don't you dare,' I say to him, when he opens his door and, seeing me, draws breath, without doubt to apologise again. 'You've said it too much. So have I. But I keep messing up, and I really am sorry for being so awful.'

'I deserved it.'

'You didn't. You were trying to help.'

'Pretty ineptly.'

'It doesn't matter. I shouldn't have let it matter. You're one of the most important people in my life, and I haven't deserved *you*, but –' I grimace – 'I do need a favour.'

His eyebrows shoot up. 'A favour?'

'I know, it's rich, but –' I hold out my letter – 'can you please take this to Tim?'

He frowns. 'Is this about the ending?'

'What else?'

'Claude –' he shakes his head – 'it's getting very late in the day for this. Maybe give it up. Focus on—'

'Please,' I say, cutting him off before he can say, *you*. 'I'm asking you to do this for me, as my friend. Watch Tim read it, if you can.'

He sighs, but doesn't protest further.

He doesn't go alone to Tim's home, either.

Nick drives him there.

'He offered,' Felix tells me, once he's back and comes to find me on the soundstage, just as I've finished my scene and am re-entering reality. 'He saw us talking, asked me what was up, so I told him.'

'If I'd wanted to tell him, Felix, I'd have done it.'

'He's trying to make things right too. And we both watched Tim read your letter.' He gives me a suffering look. 'About fifty-five times.'

'Did Tim show it to you?' I ask, and hold my breath.

'No,' says Felix.

I let my breath go.

'You made him cry, though.'

'Oh God,' I say, pressing my hand to my head.

'Yeah, I felt pretty ordinary about it. Roger mentioned you called earlier, wanting to see Tim. That Tim said no . . . '

'Has he changed his mind?'

'Nick told him he should. He laid it on actually, saying how much you've been through, and that it will mean everything to you if he agrees.'

'Really?'

'Yeah.'

I sigh, aching over him doing that for me.

And, however inadvertently, for them.

He's trying to make things right, Claude.

'What did Tim say?' I ask.

'Nothing. He fell asleep, like last time. But I'd keep an eye on your phone if I were you. Nick was pretty persuasive. Your letter obviously packed a punch too. I think between the two of you, you might have convinced him.'

I do keep an eye on my phone.

I keep an eye on it all day long, checking it between takes as we decamp to the fields, filming Clare's send-off: Joshua bugling another last post, the rest of us toasting Clare with brandy, just as Emma and I toasted her last night.

I leave it on loud when I return to my room for a nap before nightfall, but don't nap, because I'm waiting for it to ring.

I'm still waiting for it to do that when I'm sitting back in make-up, ahead of the night's shooting.

But it's not until I'm down at the base, getting into position with Nick and the others for our first take, that it lights up with Roger's name. We're at *Mabel's Fury*'s dispersal point, by the plane's model replica, and about to film Iris and Robbie's final goodbye, seventy-five-years – almost to the minute, in linear time at least – after they uttered it.

They were surrounded then by the rest of *Mabel's Fury*'s crew, just as Nick and I are surrounded now.

Tim was there.

They were all of them still there.

The runway flares would have been burning.

Effects have them burning here: too uniform, too orderly, but nonetheless glowing with smoky, mesmerising heat.

The dark sky above is moonless.

And although the starlit night is a still one, a strong, icy wind is blowing, care of huge, industrial fans.

Rusty, held on a leash by her wrangler, is barking.

345

Trucks are motoring all around, full of extras: groundcrew, servicing the other model planes.

It all feels devastatingly familiar to me.

Not real, but real enough.

Apologies for the late message, Roger's said in his. *Please do come by at 9 tomorrow. Tim's told me he'll extinguish your lanterns, if that makes any more sense to you than it does to me.*

'Thank you,' I say to Nick, joining him under the vast shadow of *Mabel's Fury*'s wing. 'He's said he'll see me. Felix told me you helped.'

'Not really. All I did was tell Tim I can't stand to see you crushed again.' He gives a short shrug. 'I guess he can't stand the thought of that either.'

I nod, and feel my hand tense with the urge to reach for his.

I don't give into it.

He doesn't reach out to me either.

But his eyes, glinting with cold, hold mine.

And for a second, all is silent.

All is still.

'All right,' says Ana, slicing through that fragile moment of peace between us, scattering it. 'Let's get going.'

The scene doesn't take us long.

It's not a late night.

The perfect, heartrending aptness of this goodbye that Iris and Robbie share has, unlike everything following it, never been in dispute, and the words, the emotion, come readily to all of us.

I live it here.

I live it then.

'You'll guide us in,' Nick says.

You'll guide us in, Robbie says.

Their faces, their voices, morph, filling my sight, my senses.

'Get us home.' *Get us home.* 'Do you believe it?'

Do you . . . ?

Silently, unable to talk, I nod.

I nod.

'No.' He shakes his head. 'Say it, please.'

I need to hear you say it.

So, I say it.

'I believe it.'

I believe it . . .

And Nick smiles.

Robbie smiles.

I breathe, *I breathe*, my chest feeling as though it's about to explode with everything I'm containing within it.

And Ana calls *cut*, wrenching me back to here, to now. But I know it's all still happening. I *feel* it still happening – within me, around me: such boundless pain and fear and love and longing pulsing on, on and on and on, in the gusting cold; the smoky, frozen night. I raise my face to it, pulling in another deep breath, filling myself up with this goodbye that I want more than anything to have never ended, and which I can't, I just *can't*, accept was the end.

Everyone heads to the dining room for a late dinner as soon as we're done.

'Will you come?' Nick asks me.

'You should come,' Felix says.

I don't.

I'm not hungry.

And there's only one place I want to be.

The attic's atmosphere feels more charged than ever as I make my way down the dark, creaking corridor: its whispers, louder; its layers, very close.

I don't lie on Iris's bed, when I reach her room.

I don't look in her mirror.

I go to her window, where I don't so much see as *sense* the world around me shiver. I stare down at the security-lit set, so hard it blurs, and feel no alarm as the planes and buildings plunge into blackness, becoming dark shapes in a darker sky, only a certain conviction that the air I'm breathing no longer belongs to the night of 22 November 2018, but the dawn of this day in 1943.

I can't be sure what's happening – whether I'm in a past that's already happened, or a moment that hasn't yet been decided – I know only that I'm about to break under the weight of my own trepidation.

Do something.

The words sound in our minds.

He needs your help.

Help him.

Closing my eyes, I press my fingers to the window frame.

Help him.

I feel a chill on my face.

The icy touch of a tear, snaking down my skin.

I bite the insides of my cheeks, another tear falling.

How do I help?

I don't know.

I still have no idea what to do.

And now, I hear a different voice: neither Iris's, nor mine, but a young man's.

Familiar, somehow.

They couldn't get to their chutes. They were burning. Everything was burning.

My eyes snap open, a rush of adrenalin coursing through me as it comes to me that I do know something.

I know that when *Mabel's Fury* was found, seven damaged parachute packs had been left inside it.

Wherever Robbie, Jacob, Henry, Ames, Gus and Danny were

when they disappeared into thin air, they did it without those parachutes strapped to their backs.

I know this.

I *know* it.

But I've left Iris.

I'm terrified I've done it too soon.

I remain at her window, staring down at the base, willing myself to return to her, but Jeff's security lights remain stubbornly on, and I stay maddeningly here.

Hoping, *hoping*, that she heard.

Chapter Twenty-Three

Iris

22 November 1943

It was a moonless night, and the darkness blanketing the windswept base was almost complete. The only light came from the runway's flare path, its burning torches shimmering in the gusty air. Iris, once so captivated by these torches' sinister beauty, paid them scant attention as she came to a halt on the control tower's frosted stairs. Rather, it was the squadron's Lancasters that stole her focus, all of them taxiing into position for take-off: their cabins full of men, their bellies packed with bombs.

All day, ever since she'd woken to the deep darkness before dawn – shocked into consciousness by a force of panic so strong she'd had to fight for breath – she'd been dreading this moment. She hadn't known for certain when she'd woken that Robbie would be flying tonight, yet she had *known*. And, alone as she'd been as she'd moved to her window, staring down towards his billet, she'd felt a presence: that shadow stealing over her, *into* her, just as it had so many times now, no longer whispering, but insisting, that time really was almost out.

Do something.

Now, at another belt of icy, petrol-scented wind, she reached up, holding her cap firm. Down at the foot of the stairs, Piper strained to escape her leash, watching the planes too. Barking, Iris was sure. She couldn't hear her.

She heard nothing but the guttural roar of the Lancasters.

They were going to Berlin.

Not all of them would come back. Desperately as Iris wished it could be different, she knew that it wouldn't. Not tonight. And although she'd learnt by now not to trust that a full quota of crews might ever return from a sortie so deep into the Reich, she'd also never known who'd be the ones to fall.

Never, in her heart, been so agonisingly sure it would be them.

Tonight's mission was meant to be the last of their tour.

Against every odd, they'd made it through forty-four operations, so nearly at the end.

So very nearly safe.

She watched them pull to a juddering halt at the head of the runway, her eyes wide, stinging in the cold.

Had Robbie reminded everyone to wear their parachutes?

He'd promised her he would, but she was scared he'd been humouring her.

Terrified that, in the close confines of the fuselage, they'd all left their chutes off, no matter how that had ended for Lewis and his crew.

They all had extras now anyway.

Iris had decided that they should when she'd been standing at her window this morning. At breakfast, she'd persuaded the parachute rigger, Lydia, into sneaking them out of the store for her. One of the drivers had agreed to play taxi, running Iris and the chutes out to the plane. And Prim – who'd stunned Iris when she'd snuck Robbie up to her room after Clare had been killed – had stunned her again by insisting on coming along too, helping Iris to stow the chutes in *Mabel's Fury*.

'Let me do it since Clare can't,' she'd said to Iris, a little stiffly – she was, after all, Prim – but with kindness in her eyes.

She didn't talk any more of going to Colorado after the war.

She wasn't expecting Clint to propose.

They all knew now that Clint had already done that once, to his wife: a woman called Cynthia, who was currently back in Denver raising her and Clint's three children.

Cynthia's friend, an American Red Cross worker, had broken the truth about that to Prim last week, at Bettys, intercepting her as she'd been dancing with Clint. It had been Clint, rather than Prim, who the woman had aimed her rage at, but Prim – dressed in her very best frock – had still looked as though her world was ending.

Iris – only in Bettys herself because Robbie had persuaded her to be (*Clare wouldn't want you to bury yourself. I wouldn't. Please remember that, won't you?*) – had pulled Prim away. Robbie had driven them home, where Iris had taken Prim up to the attic, given her a dose of Clare's medicinal brandy, and put her to bed, knowing that Prim wouldn't want her to say another word about it in the morning.

Prim still hadn't talked about it.

But Iris often heard her crying, through their shared wall.

She wasn't doing that now. She was already in the control tower, ready for the night's vigil ahead.

Clare's replacement was inside as well, managing take-off with Sergeant Browning.

Shortly, all too shortly, Iris would join them, helping to direct these crews before her on their way.

And, in the morning, she'd bring the lucky ones back.

Absolutely pancake.

She still gave them that foolish instruction.

352

'Don't stop,' Henry had said, when she almost had after Clare went. 'We all like it too much.'

Robbie had told her just now that he rather than Henry would be the one to call the control tower tomorrow, letting her know they were coming.

'I'll be doing it before you know it,' he'd said. 'You'll guide us in. Get us home. Do you believe it?'

Silently, unable to talk, she'd nodded.

'No.' His brow had creased in a frown. 'Say it, please. I need to hear you say it.'

So, she'd said it.

'I believe it,' she'd forced out, knowing only that she'd wanted to. So very, very much.

He'd smiled, reassured.

It was something, at least, that she'd been able to give him.

And now, before her brimming stare, *Mabel's Fury* jerked back into motion. Iris's colleague inside had clearly issued the command. *That's a green for go. Proceed to angels ten and vector ninety to Idaho.* Gripping the stair rail, Iris followed its thundering silhouette as it gathered speed, nose lifting, Robbie pulling back on his throttle.

She hadn't told him her secret.

Their secret.

At the thought, the baby in her stomach fluttered, and her eyes fell shut.

When she opened them again, *Mabel's Fury* was airborne, rising slowly, then disappearing, fast, into the black sky.

Her tears, contained for too long, broke free, snaking down her frozen face. Hastily, before anyone could see, she wiped them away.

Then, dragging her gaze from the void *Mabel's Fury* had left, she turned, heading up the rest of the control tower stairs.

You'll guide us in, Robbie had said.

Get us home.

She pulled the tower door open, not ready, by no stretch ready, but resolved at last on facing all that this night was about to ask of her.

Chapter Twenty-Four

Claudia and Iris

23 November 2018

&

23 November 1943

When I wake the next morning, it's to another deep frost, and the tentative, almost too painful to acknowledge hope that the past has somehow changed whilst I've been sleeping, the ending to our movie already rewritten. But nothing's been rewritten (*of course it hasn't*, I'm sure Ellen would say), and, when I check my phone for emails, the only one I find pertaining to the end-scene still waiting for me is from Ana, with a Google map link to the beach that's been selected for Iris's death.

Sorry, Claude. I don't want this either.

There's an email from Blake too, asking Nick, Felix and me for another meeting. *Felix, I need to weaponise you.* Ignoring it, I run to my room, where I shower, dress, and, pocketing Nick's keys that he insisted I take last night, head off in his car to see Tim.

*

He's ready for me when I reach him, sitting once again by his lounge window. He's dressed smartly, in a pair of slacks, woollen jumper, and blazer, and has his thick white hair tamed

355

into a vintage side-parting. He's obviously gone to an effort, and seeing it – seeing *him* again, so frail and vulnerable, fighting to be strong – I'm overcome by the same rush of tenderness I felt towards him the last time I came to visit. It's stronger than ever now I'm thinking of what Ellen said about him falling apart when Clare died; his fear, and shame, and the war's *long shadow*. I want to go to him, press his hands into mine and find the words to make it better for him, somehow. I feel such an overwhelming instinct to look after him.

Silently, he smiles – a slight, sad smile – like he's guessed what I'm thinking.

And perhaps he has.

He's read my letter after all. *About fifty-five times.* He knows more than most about the inner workings of my mind. And Ellen paid him a visit yesterday, spoke to him about a lot of what we discussed. She said on Wednesday that she'd try to, and left me a voicemail while we were filming last night, confirming she'd managed it.

'Did he believe any of it?' I asked her, returning her call on my drive here.

'I think so,' she said. 'It's obviously been a great deal for him to absorb, which isn't easy for him. He really is fading quickly.' She paused, and I pictured her frowning. 'He didn't show me your letter. He still refused to confide in me about any of it. He insisted it's only you he'll talk to, so yes, I think he must believe you hold a link to her. I'm certain he needs to unburden himself.' She sighed. 'Don't let him lose courage, will you?'

Removing my coat, I sit on the sofa I shared with Nick and Felix. It feels empty without them; cold, and overly large.

The coffee table before me has no tea or baked goods on it, just an old leather album, which I eye, curiously.

'Is this yours?' I ask Tim.

'I'm its caretaker,' he says. 'It should have been Jacob's. He took most of the pictures.'

'During the war?' I say, heart quickening at the idea; the possibility that there are photos, of all of them, contained in this album's pages.

'Yes, during the war.' His eyes move to the framed picture of the crew on his bureau. 'That was the last shot of Jacob's film. It was a long time before I could bring myself to have it developed.' Slowly, he brings his gaze back to mine. 'Ellie told me you have memories. You said in your letter you've seen our past . . .'

I nod. 'There's so much I haven't seen though. So much I can't find.'

'But what if you're not meant to? What if these lanterns you speak of are with us to protect us? *Shield* us from those things it's not ours to witness?'

'I don't want to be shielded.'

He gives me a pained look. 'Are you sure?'

'I'm sure,' I say, and, suspecting that his courage really is now wavering, at this eleventh hour, I will him the strength to go on.

And, with a laboured breath, he does.

'I know myself what it's like to live at the mercy of an unbiddable mind,' he says. 'Even when I was a young man, mine gave me knowledge I had no desire to hold. Warnings, of events looming, with nothing to help me know what to do about them. No specifics. No markers. Just . . . *instincts*.' He swallows. 'You said your father was the same.' His voice catches. 'Noah . . .'

'Yes,' I say. 'Noah Reeves.'

'Reeves,' he echoes, and blinks, clearly upset.

About my father?

I don't ask; he keeps talking, giving me no chance.

'I've been told my mind is failing,' he says. 'I've felt, these past years, as though it's crumbling. Not so much with my lanterns going off, as my stage's walls coming down.' He takes another rasping breath, but doesn't reach for his oxygen: determined to keep going, I think, now that he's made himself start. 'The memories I hold have always been my memories alone. But they haven't always looked . . . the same.'

I nod again, and don't consider asking how many of the memories he shared with Imogen were fabricated. Even knowing that there are things he's concealed, and twisted, I still trust that most of what he passed on was rooted in truth – however many variations of that truth he might have lived.

His memories, for the most part, haven't been false, I'm certain.

They're just from different stages.

Different acts, but not different stories.

'What about that night?' I ask. 'Have you always remembered that the same?'

'Yes,' he says, flatly. 'Nothing about that has ever changed.'

'And you do remember it?'

'I can't forget it,' he says, and drops his gaze to the album on the table, which I'm by now certain is full of the friends he lost. 'I couldn't show this to Imogen,' he tells me. 'The faces in it have always felt too . . . precious . . . too fleeting, to share with someone who didn't love them as I did. But please –' he raises his wavering hand, gesturing at the album – 'I'd like you to look.'

'You're sure?'

'I'm quite sure.'

And, pulse racing, I get down on my knees, pulling the album towards me, opening it, finding photograph after photograph of the base as it was then: sprawling, and bleak, packed with people who smile and laugh, despite what they're living through. The original Piper features plenty: chasing a football with boys in shirtsleeves; lying on her haunches at the steps of Billet 4B; looking dotingly into the face of a bespectacled WAAF who crouches in long grass, stroking her neck.

That WAAF appears in a lot of the photos too, happy and smart, with an adoring expression of her own, that she gives time after time to Jacob, behind the camera.

Beth Twinton, my mind, and logic, supplies, and I feel such pain for her, knowing she lost this man she loved, and who loved her too, so much so that he always had his lens pointed her way, and wrote her into his will.

'Did she ever meet anyone else?' I ask Tim.

'No one like Jacob,' he says.

I want to ask him about Iris and Robbie: whether I'm going to find any pictures of them here.

But I don't.

I'm too afraid of him dashing my hope.

Silently, I keep turning the pages, finding a shot of Gus and Ames in a smoky, spartan Heaton Arms, then another picture of the two of them with Henry and Danny, in deckchairs outside their billet. Behind them, in the billet's doorway, is the shape of a figure that I think might belong to Robbie, but he's just a silhouette: the tantalising suggestion of life, rather than life itself.

Impatiently, I turn to the album's final page.

And, 'Oh,' I exhale, taking in the photograph there, of a packed booth in a packed bar, the crowd crammed into it reaching across the table, cheersing their brimming glasses. Only the glasses are in focus. The people – the men in uniform; the women in dresses – are blurred with movement. But I can just about make out Tim, *a young Robert Redford*, and Ames too, with his arm around a slight, striking woman whose eyes are closed for the flash. *Mon Dieu.* I see the edge of Beth's face, and the polka-dot sleeve and curls of another (Clare? If only she'd move into the shot), then a floppy blond head that makes me think of tartan slippers.

And a couple.

A dark-haired couple who cause my every nerve to tremor, and my breath to freeze in my throat.

They're turned towards one another, their shoulders touching, the lines between their bodies indistinct, like they'd been made, specially made, to fit together like this.

'It's the only picture I have of the two of them,' says Tim, knowing just who I'm looking at. 'The only picture I still have of her.' I raise my gaze to his. His face is heavy. His dark eyes full of grief. 'Rob had another. He kept it with him, in his flight jacket.' His voice rasps. 'It disappeared too.' He breaks off, chest heaving, and this time he does reach for his mask, sucking air from it. 'She took that photograph,' he says, once he can talk again, looking back at the picture on his bureau. 'You know that.'

'Yes,' I agree.

'Jacob didn't want her to.'

'No, I remember.' *He thought it was tempting fate*, Tim told me on my last visit. 'You said it didn't change anything though.'

'How could it have?'

'I don't know,' I say, even as I find myself caught in a fresh wave of grief at the idea.

'It couldn't,' Tim insists, consoling me, just like he did before.

I suspected then that he might also have consoled Iris.

I feel even surer of it now.

That she, at least, survived that night.

'She didn't want to take it,' he repeats. 'I persuaded her.' He shakes his head. 'I was terrified of her and Jacob's superstition. And it was the last flight of our tour. So, I told her to be a sport, give us our picture.' He closes his eyes. 'She did it for me.'

Silently, I absorb it.

I look from Tim's embattled face, to his strained expression in the picture, and for the first time see the fear he's fighting to contain beneath his handsome, *stoic* facade.

How have I not noticed it before?

I don't know.

But, in a rush of clarity, it comes to me that, whoever else he might have consoled about this photograph, he's also been trying to console himself.

'She was so uneasy, she nearly dropped the camera,' he says, his eyes once again open, staring at his friends. 'Then, she took the shot too soon. No one was ready. See how Rob's smiling? He was trying to cheer her up. He made a joke . . . '

'A joke?' I say, replaying that glimpse I've held on to of him, coming to life. His lips moving, about to speak. 'What did he say?'

Even now, I half fear Tim will clam up, claim he can't remember after all.

But there's none of that today.

'He said, "Clarence, come on, you're only worried because you're going to have to finally give me an answer tomorrow."' He gives me a desperate look. 'He'd asked her to marry him. She told him she'd only talk about it after our tour.' His eyes fill. 'She wouldn't talk to him about it that afternoon either. She said to him, "Oh, do be quiet, Robbie," but she was laughing. He had such a knack for making her laugh.' He fumbles for his mask. 'I was jealous.'

'Is that why you pretended you couldn't remember who

took this?' I ask, getting up and moving to crouch beside him, helping him with his mask. 'Were you afraid Imogen would guess how you felt?'

'I think she guessed anyway,' he says, through the plastic.

'Yes,' I agree, 'I think she did.'

Tremblingly, he pulls the mask away.

'I don't know why I lied about it,' he says. 'There's so much I've hidden, I got myself mixed up with where I should start, and where I could stop. And I've been so ashamed. So . . . *terribly* . . . ashamed.' He stares at me. 'I took everything, from all of them.'

'What do you mean?' I say, my mind racing to keep up.

'It was my fault.' The words choke him. 'It was all my fault. And I've tried to fool myself that by sharing their story I might make myself near to them again. Repay them, by making them live again, here. Now. But I can never repay them.' His face strains. 'I've *hurt* them. I've hurt Iris. Let Imogen make it her fault. Ellie's been so angry about it, but I never meant for it. Never . . . ' His eyes implore me to believe him.

I don't know what to believe.

I still don't know what actually happened.

So, I ask Tim again to tell me what he remembers.

And, this time, he does.

*

'You're pregnant, aren't you?'

Iris looked up from her untouched mug of tea, stunned.

Prim looked back at her, calmly.

They were alone in the breakroom. The others on duty were all elsewhere, trying to sleep. The overhead lamp buzzed. The blackout blinds tapped against the windows, gusting in the cold draught, bringing the scent of ice, petrol, and salt. It was

362

just after one in the morning. A sea mist had blown in from the coast at eleven, and had been getting thicker the last time Iris checked. She was resisting the urge to keep looking, trying to trust that it would blow away again in time for everyone's return.

'It's in the hands of the gods,' Browning had said as he'd gone off to rest. 'Nothing any of us can do. Get some shut-eye, Winterton. That's an order.'

She'd ignored that order.

So, here she was, staring at Prim.

Trying to think what to say.

'How did you guess?' she asked her.

'You keep touching your stomach,' said Prim. 'And it's getting a little round. Be careful, won't you? Ambrose is just waiting for an opportunity to dismiss you. I suspect he'd relish the chance to overrule Robbie too.'

'I know.'

'Why on earth haven't you got married? Any fool can see it's what you both want. I have to say I'm rather disappointed in Robbie.'

'He doesn't know. I haven't told him.'

'What?' said Prim, eyes widening. 'Whyever not?'

'I didn't want him to have to worry about anything else.'

'But he wouldn't have been worried.' She sounded incredulous. 'Have you even met your beau, Iris?'

'Yes, Eleanor . . . '

'You can call me Ellen, if you like. Or Ellie. Anything, frankly, but Prim.'

'All right.' Iris grimaced. 'Sorry.'

'No you're not.'

'I am, actually, *Ellen*. And I have met Robbie.'

'Then you should know you'd only have made him happy, telling him this. You must do it the first chance you have.'

She folded her arms, and her woollen stockinged legs. 'Don't cheat him of happiness. Iris. Iris! Are you even listening to me?'

'Shh,' said Iris, moving to the door, opening it to the dark, uninsulated corridor, letting more cold air in. 'I thought I heard something.'

'Heard what?'

'That,' said Iris, running now, at another beeping. 'Someone's trying to radio in.'

*

'We never got to Berlin,' Tim says. 'I made a stupid mistake, a rookie mistake, and didn't allow proper provision for the wind.' His eyes empty as he leaves me, reliving it. 'There was a flak field near Frankfurt. We all knew to avoid it. But it was a dark night, and I was in a panic. *Blind panic*, they call it, don't they?' He doesn't pause for me to respond. 'Rob asked me to request another rest leave, after we lost Clare. I didn't want him and the boys to finish their tour without me though.' His scarred cheeks work. 'I fooled myself that I could keep going for them, keep switching my fear off up there.' Wheezing, he once again grapples for his mask, shakily lifting it to his face. I do my best to hold it steady for him, but I'm shaking too. 'By that night, I'd directed us through one-hundred-and-four sorties,' he says. 'All I needed was to bring us home from that last one. It was our third tour. I doubt we'd have been asked us to do another. Even Bomber Command had its limits. But the wind was strong, and I was in too much of a rush to get us home, so I didn't allow proper provision.' His face works. 'I didn't allow *proper provision*.'

I lay my hand to his arm, trying to calm him.

'I led us straight into that flak field,' he says. 'They coned us with their lights, and Rob was a good pilot, but he wasn't good enough to get us out of that. They tore us apart. God –' he closes his eyes – 'the hell of it.' He takes a shallow breath. 'I got hit.' Weakly, he touches his ribs. 'We lost all but one engine, and nearly lost Danny too, out the rear-turret. Ames dragged him in. Knocked his chute out though. A lot of the others were damaged.' He swallows. 'There were extras . . . '

'Extras?'

'Yes.' His eyes peer into mine. 'You know about them?'

'No.' Slowly, I shake my head. 'I just . . . hoped.'

'Ellie's always said we had Iris to thank for them.'

Even as he speaks, my mind fills with that voice I heard at Iris's window last night.

They couldn't get to their chutes. They were burning. Everything was burning.

It felt familiar.

I couldn't place why.

I can now.

It was Tim's voice, of course: younger, clearer, full of panic, but unmistakeably his, sounding in Iris's memory.

Was he the reason then, that she smuggled those extra chutes aboard?

Or did I play a part?

I don't know.

I really don't.

But what I am becoming crushingly convinced of is that it doesn't matter.

'The chutes didn't do any good, did they?' I say to Tim.

'They might have,' he says. 'The boys could have bailed over Frankfurt, taken their chances on the ground. But I was in a bad way, I'd never have survived the fall, and they knew that.' His eyes brim. 'Somehow, Rob and Ames got our fires out, and us away. We turned back to England still a mission short of our full tour, with one engine running, failing electrics, and all our bombs and incendiaries jammed in our bay doors.'

*

'They're not releasing,' said Robbie, his voice crackling over the weak connection. He'd brought *Mabel's Fury* back to England, but was still some distance away: close enough to radio, but not nearly close enough for Iris to be able to hear the plane's engines, or see its lights blinking through the thick fog.

They'd been trying to jettison their bombs all the way home. Robbie had ordered Jacob, Ames, Gus, Danny and Henry to bail out whilst they'd still been over France, but they'd refused to abandon him and Tim, and, with little fuel left, they'd now sunk too low for their chutes to have enough time to open up and save them. Robbie couldn't take them low enough to chance a jump, not with all their bombs ready to detonate at a touch; even if they survived the fall, the plane would explode within a second, obliterating them, and who knew who else on the ground.

Their only hope was to try again to offload their bombs over the water so that Robbie could attempt to bring *Mabel's Fury* into land.

They had enough fuel remaining for one last go.

And what if that doesn't work?

Iris hadn't asked Robbie that.

She knew the answer.

They all knew the answer.

And maybe, on a calmer, clearer night, he and the boys might have a slim hope of surviving a leap into the water.

But the November seas were high, the temperature perishingly cold, and no patrol boat would be able to find them in this visibility.

Not quickly enough.

So, no, she didn't waste their time – their racing, disappearing time – by asking him that foolish question.

She had only one thing she needed to say to him.

Do it the first chance you have, Prim had told her.

Don't cheat him of happiness.

'Robbie,' she said, gripping her hands into fists, fighting her panic, her grief, 'can you still hear me?'

Her earpiece fizzed with static.

'Robbie?'

Nothing.

'Robbie, please . . . '

'Iris,' he said, his voice travelling to her from his pitch-black cockpit, much fainter now. 'I hear you. Can you hear me? Iris?'

'I hear you,' she said, and not risking so much as a pause for another breath, let their secret go. 'You're going to be a father, Robbie.' Tears burned her eyes, her throat. 'We're having a baby, so you have to come home.'

More crackling.

Had he heard?

Had he?

'Robbie,' she said, frantic. 'Are you there?'

Silence.

'Robbie . . . '

Then,

'Iris,' he said, and she could tell he was smiling. 'That's the most incredible news.'

*

367

'The boys only gave up when our last engine did,' says Tim, his voice raw. 'We were gliding, still close to land. It was all so silent, except for the wash of the waves. On a clearer night, we'd have been able to see the coast.' He pauses, and I can tell he's picturing it: the swirling white air beyond the cockpit; his friends, *brothers*, looking at one another, accepting their time had come. 'They took the chutes,' he says, 'even though they knew they'd do no good. I couldn't manage to go with them. They were . . . wretched . . . about leaving me.' His lips tremor. 'Rob tried to take me anyway. He pulled me all the way to the forward hatch. But I told him to leave me, that I'd rather die quickly, than drown slowly. He said that he couldn't leave me to die alone, but I made him, told him he had to fight, for Iris. For their baby.' He inhales, breath scratching. 'He should never have been in that plane. I forced him into bombing. I thought we'd be safe together. But I killed him.' He lets go a racking sob. 'I killed them all.'

Helplessly, I stare at him.

I want to find the words to comfort him.

But I can't.

It's all too unbearable.

Too hopeless.

'I don't know what happened,' Tim says. 'I've never been able to make sense of it, but as soon as Rob went, the bombs dislodged, falling too, and the plane must have leapt up, gained enough height to clear the coast, because the next thing I knew I was crashing into land.' Wheezing, he fights another sob. 'I don't remember being found. But when I came around in hospital, it felt like a punishment. I couldn't bring myself to talk about any of it, and everyone assumed I'd forgotten. It was too easy to let them.' With a trembling fist, he wipes his face. 'Fifty-five-thousand men were killed flying for Bomber Command,

and six of them were my very best friends.' His face folds. 'I've been drowning slowly ever since.'

'Oh, Tim,' I say, still with no idea how to go on.

And he hasn't finished anyway.

'Iris and Ellie never told anyone we hadn't made it to Berlin. They didn't want me to have to fly my last mission, once I was better.' He wipes his cheeks again. 'I've known for a long time I need to set this record straight. Even before Imogen wrote her book. And I never imagined she'd think of making it Iris's fault.' He reaches for my hand, gripping it with surprising strength. 'I need you to believe that.'

'Surely you could have asked her to change it . . .'

'I never read her damnable ending. The book was already in print by the time Ellie got a hold of it and told me what had been done. I didn't even talk with Imogen about the ending. I didn't want to remember, and I was terrified of Imogen realising that I did.' His whole face droops. 'I feel sometimes that I've spent my entire life afraid.'

'You weren't afraid last time I saw you. You said then that you were already over England when Robbie radioed Iris.'

'Did I?'

'Yes. Felix thought you wanted it out.'

'I do.' He nods. 'I'm glad I've done it.'

We fall into silence.

Outside, the weak winter sun shines.

Sightlessly, I look at it, torturing myself with the thought of Robbie, and all of them, disappearing into the black November sea, with their own bombs plummeting around them: I see them alone and cold, drowning, slowly, their lanterns blinking off, then illuminating again, returning them to warmth and safety; their mother's arms, and fresh years of life.

It's a wonderfully comforting idea, Ellen said.

I want to find comfort in it.

But I'm struggling to feel anything but the pain Tim feels. The fear.

'Would you stop it all from ever happening if you could?' I ask him.

'No,' he says, without consideration, letting me know he's asked himself the question before. 'I'd never be so presumptuous. And there was happiness back then.' (*Love too*, said Ellen. *So much love. Don't forget that.*) 'I couldn't steal that from them. And if you're right, and we do keep going, then maybe we'll one day learn to do better. Although . . .' His voice softens. '. . . I don't know where that would leave you or your picture.'

'I don't care about the picture.'

'I do. Very much. Like I said, we need to set the record straight. But, Claudia –' he looks into my eyes, his own once again filling – 'I care about you more. A great deal more. Your father, too.'

'My father?'

Silently, he nods.

I frown, confused.

Why do you care about my father? I almost ask.

Why do you care about me?

But I don't say anything.

I'm thinking back to his upset before, speaking of his unbiddable mind, and my dad's being the same.

Noah, he said, in that sad, strained way.

'Did you know him?' I ask.

'Just wait,' he says. 'I'll get to that.'

*

'*Will you tell me straight away if anything happens?*' Robbie's mother had asked Iris, back in February.

'*I'll tell you,*' Iris had promised, knowing, even then, that the day would come when she'd be forced to keep her word.

She hadn't forgotten it.

Her dreams hadn't let her.

She was grateful for that, at least: that she'd never taken a moment for granted.

Moving mechanically, she'd left Doverley at dawn for Annabelle Grayson's nursing home.

'Where are you going?' Ambrose had demanded of her, emerging through the cold morning mist to intercept her as she'd left the tower.

'To where I need to be,' she'd said, and, ignoring his orders to stop, carried on.

She'd caught the first bus to York from Heaton, then another to the home, where she hadn't had to tell Annabelle anything, because the instant Annabelle had seen her in her doorway, her entire being had crumpled, and she'd known.

'Is there any hope?' she asked Iris, as Iris knelt before her.

'There's always hope,' Iris said, offering her that comfort at least.

But there wasn't hope.

Robbie was gone.

She knew it.

She felt it, in the hollow he'd left inside her: a space she hadn't even been aware that his presence on this earth had been occupying.

A space that, here, now, kneeling beside Annabelle, she felt Robbie's fluttering child turn and reach into, as though searching with its miniscule fingers for the touch of a father it would now never know.

'I'm pregnant,' she told Annabelle, wanting to give her that comfort too. 'He knew.' Her eyes swam. *That's the most incredible news.* 'He was happy.'

'Of course he was,' said Annabelle, her own tears falling, laying her hand to Iris's face. 'You always made him the happiest. It was your effortless gift to him.'

'He made me happy,' said Iris, crying more. 'Always.'

'He'll do it again,' said Annabelle, her stare full of grief, but faith too. *Hope.* 'He'll find you again. You'll find each other. I believe it. And until then, you'll have your child.'

It was as Iris was leaving that Annabelle insisted she take her wedding band.

'Robbie's father was different when he gave this to me,' she said, pressing it into Iris's hand. 'I received it in love, please take it with mine.' Her swollen eyes glinted. 'This world is far too judgemental a place. Don't let it judge you. Not more than it already has.'

'I won't,' said Iris, more tears breaking from her. 'Thank you.'

'What will you do now?'

'Go back to Doverley, I suppose. Face Ambrose's music.'

It was what she intended to do.

But Lord Heaton was in the home's entrance hall when she got to it. She recognised him easily – he hadn't changed, other than that he was wearing his silly show colonel's uniform in place of faded tweeds – and, feeling no inclination whatsoever to speak to him, she walked past him.

'*Get out of there this instant*,' he'd yelled at her, the last time he'd spoken to her. '*My god, is that you, Iris Winterton?*'

'Is that you, Iris?' he said again now, pulling her to a halt.

And perhaps on another day, in another set of circumstances, she'd have been surprised that he still knew her.

'You're the image of your mama,' he proclaimed, which might have surprised her too: that he remembered her mother.

But she had no capacity for surprise.

Nor could she muster the energy to care when Heaton told her that he'd just been visiting his sister.

'What's brought you here?' he asked.

'It doesn't matter,' she said, since what would it mean to him?

'You're a WAAF at Doverley, I believe?' he said.

That did take her aback.

'How do you know that?' she asked.

'Gosh, I'm not sure.' Was he blustering? 'I must have heard it from someone.'

She frowned, and was about to ask him who he'd heard it from.

Then she realised she didn't care.

'I say,' he said, peering at the tear stains on her cheeks. 'Are you quite well?'

'No,' she said. 'And I must get back.'

'Let me take you?' he offered. 'I have a driver. He's bringing the car around now.'

'It's fine, honestly.'

'Please, my dear. I'd . . . like . . . to help you. You really don't look well.'

She was about to protest again.

Then, she stopped.

Her mind was whispering again.

Go, the whispers told her.

You need to go.

She didn't want to listen to them.

Not again.

Not any more.

And yet, they kept on.

On and on.

Go.

'All right,' she found herself saying to Heaton. 'If you're sure.'

'I'm sure,' he said. 'It's the least I can do. Driver won't be a tick.'

'Road accidents still happened, even in wartime,' Tim tells me. 'It was foggy, icy, and the bus Iris should have been on skidded off the road. Everyone was killed. But because of Heaton, Iris lived. She broke her wrist when Heaton's driver swerved to avoid the bus, but that was it.'

I only half listen.

I'm remembering that other dream I've so often had: of me, in Iris, talking to that colonel.

Go, I've kept telling her, on and on.

You need to go.

I've always believed, until this moment, that I was trying to make her run away.

But I wasn't.

I wasn't doing that at all.

I was making her stay.

My head spins with the realisation.

I stare into Tim's face, picturing the colonel again, wondering how, *how*, I knew to make Iris go with him.

An instinct from another of my own stages?

The warning memory of a parallel me, failing to help her before?

I'm too distracted to think.

Because whatever the truth of that, there's one thing I no longer have any doubt about: I *did* help Iris.

Just like I stopped her from falling down those stairs.

And although I still don't understand where this connection between us has spun from, I'm now thinking of my father again, how he saved me from my own death on these Yorkshire roads, and wondering whether Lord Heaton and Iris were connected too.

'Were they any relation?' I manage to ask Tim.

'Heaton and Iris?' He nods. 'I suspect so. Iris's mother worked for Heaton during the first war, when she fell for Iris, and he owned the cottage they lived in. Iris would never have had it though. I think she much preferred the idea of a father who'd had no choice but to abandon them. She loathed Heaton. Even more so once he saved her life. Certainly at first.' Breathlessly, he tells me she was taken to hospital after the accident, where a doctor set her wrist, and reported her pregnancy to Doverley's adjutant. 'Ambrose had her dishonourably dismissed.' He sinks his head back against his chair. 'He was a . . . vengeful . . . creature. But Beth and Ellie didn't let him win. They got a hold of Iris's file, destroyed her records. Ambrose was killed himself, by a V2 rocket. We bombed that factory.' He closes his eyes. 'Lewis and his boys went down that night.'

He's starting to drift.

Seeming to realise, he jerks his eyes open, and pushes himself on, saying that Iris moved to East Grinstead, where he was in a burns hospital. 'She got a job in their office,' he says. 'Ellie had the idea that the vicar in Heaton should give her a wedding certificate and reference. Not with Robbie's name on it. That would have been too risky.' He breathes in, out. 'She took her gran's maiden name instead.' Another breath. 'Reeves.'

For a beat, I stare, stunned all over again.

Then, 'That was my father's name,' I hear myself say.

Except my voice doesn't feel like my own.

My lips don't.

'Yes,' says Tim.

And my brain works, doing the sums.

My father was born in 1965, the same year as my mother.

Iris would have been forty-seven.

Too old, surely, to be a mother again herself.

Not without the kind of help that didn't exist back then.

But . . .

Was she too young to be a grandmother?

I look to Tim, my heart pounding faster than ever, my mind fighting what I suddenly want to be true, much too much.

'I've watched you in the pictures for years, thinking you had a look of her,' he says. 'I told Imogen that. It's your eyes.' *Windows to your soul.* 'Your smile.' He smiles himself, with infinite sadness. 'Until I read your letter, I never imagined it could be anything but coincidence.'

'But it's not a coincidence?' I say, desperately.

'No.' His dark gaze swims. 'It's not.'

*

The baby was a girl.

She arrived, in the maternity wing of East Grinstead's cottage hospital, eight-and-a-half months after the sultry August morning Iris and Robbie had been so careless in their cottage, and a month before D-Day, filling the sun-filled dawn with her cry.

Iris held her. She held her for hours, looking into her eyes, *windows to her soul*, wondering if it was possible that she might actually be feeling the first shattered parts of her heart starting to knit back together. Life, the entire business of living, still felt overwhelming – more so, now that she had this child, *their daughter*, to look after – but she was, at last, grateful that she was still here to do it.

Happy, even, that when Heaton had offered to drive her home that morning, she hadn't said no.

Tim came to see them that afternoon, arriving with the first clang of the visiting bell. He'd only recently had another graft, and his face was shrouded in bandages.

'I don't want to scare her,' he said, cradling Robbie's daughter in his arms.

'You won't scare her,' said Iris.

'She's perfect.'

'Isn't she?'

'What will you call her?'

'Clara,' said Iris, watching her watching Tim: intent, but not afraid. 'For Clare, but different enough that she'll only ever be herself.'

'Clara,' Tim echoed, his voice thick with tears. 'It suits her.' He touched his finger to hers. 'And if she'd been a boy? Would you have called him . . . ?'

'No,' Iris said. 'I couldn't have had him thinking he had to replace him.'

'No one could.'

'No.'

And for a second, they were silent.

Listening for his voice, even knowing it wouldn't come.

Across the ward, another baby cried.

Over by the door, an orderly arrived, wheeling a tea trolley.

'Iris,' said Tim, drawing her gaze back to his, so dark and sorry, staring out from his bandages. 'Whatever you need from me, it's yours. Always.'

He hadn't told her what had happened in *Mabel's Fury*.

He wouldn't, Iris knew that.

Just as she wouldn't press him to, even though she was certain he'd forgotten nothing.

What would the point be in that, other than to cause him more pain?

He'd lost his photo of his father that night, along with everyone else.

It had melted, next to his heart.

Look after that boy, Clare had said to Iris, the night of Jacob's birthday.

'You never have to give me anything,' she said to Tim now. 'Just keep being my friend, please. And I'll do my very best to be yours.'

*

'I loved her,' Tim says. 'I loved her to distraction. So, I was her friend. As good a one as I knew how to be.'

Haltingly, he tells me the rest: how, after the war, Iris moved with Clara to York, near Robbie's mother, whilst he went overseas with the foreign office, returning to visit as often as he could. Ellen visited Iris too, and so did Beth Twinton. He doesn't go into a lot of detail, but from what he does say of those years they all had together – full of birthday teas at Bettys, seaside holidays, country walks, frozen Guy Fawkes nights, school plays, and summer picnics – I can tell how happy they were.

And also, how guilty that makes him.

'Clara was wonder itself,' he says. 'She was fun, and stubborn, and warm, and smart, and very cheeky. Rob would have been so proud of her.' He stares down at his mask. 'I never forgot that every moment I had with her, with both of them, was a moment I'd stolen from him.'

'I'm sure that's not how he'd have seen it,' I say, hating that he's believed this, for all these years.

'It's the way it was,' he says.

He finishes his tale with devastating brevity. Iris died in 1962, the same year Robbie's mother went. Clara had started at Oxford – just as Iris and Robbie had hoped to – and, during her first term, whilst Tim was posted in Brussels, Iris discovered she had a tumour at the base of her skull. 'The doctor's said if they'd caught it sooner, they might have operated, but it started to grow, too fast, and then . . . she was gone.' More tears blur his eyes. 'She went peacefully. Clara and I were with her, and I don't doubt it broke her to leave Clara behind, but, at the end, it really was as though she knew she had a welcome waiting.' His chest heaves. 'I'm sure she did.'

'Yes,' I say, gripping my hands into fists, trying to keep myself under control.

'She asked me to look after Clara,' says Tim, 'but Clara didn't want to be looked after. Not by me, not by Ellie or Beth. She wanted her mum, and she'd lost her, which made her so . . . angry.'

I nod, understanding that.

'I'd lost her too.' His voice catches. 'I'd lost her, and I knew I didn't deserve to be the one of us still left, so when Clara kept asking me to leave her alone, I did the worst thing possible and gave in.' He draws another rasping breath. 'She went back to Oxford, and I went to Brussels, where I drank too much and told myself she'd call when she was ready.' His shoulders slump. 'She never called. I think she was too ashamed. Things were said, and I don't think she forgave herself for them.' He bows his head. 'I should have told her there was nothing to forgive. But I let her push me away, when I should have pulled her in. Iris and Rob would have pulled her in.' He grips at his mask. 'Ellie tried to warn me. She told me to pull myself together, get on a plane, that Clara didn't need time, she needed me. But I wouldn't hear it. Couldn't believe it. Then Clara . . . ran. She left Oxford, turned from everyone who cared for her, leant on a man who wasn't good, when she'd only ever deserved the world, fell pregnant with your father, then died too.' His eyes spill. 'She died, all alone, and she didn't need to, but she went anyway.'

I don't ask what happened to her.

I already know that my father's mother, ill with pneumonia when he was born, died in hospital two days later.

So very young, Mum said. *She really must have been desperately low, not to have sought help.*

It's always hurt, thinking about her.

It torments me now.

Because she's no longer a stranger to me. She was Iris and Robbie's child, who I helped to save when I stopped Iris getting on that bus in 1943.

Except, it wasn't only her I saved.

I saved my father, too.

I saved myself.

With a visible effort, Tim keeps talking, saying that because he had no legal link to Clara, no one contacted him when she died, and, although he sensed something was wrong, it was years before he uncovered what had happened to her, or that my father even existed. 'No one would tell me where he was, though. I had no rights, there weren't computers like we have now, no web. I tried, I tried and tried, but I couldn't find him.' Miserably, he looks at me. 'I felt there was something waiting for him, but there was nothing I could do.' His face strains. 'It never occurred to me, until I got your letter, that he might have known something was waiting for him, too.'

'Oh, Tim,' I say, holding his trembling hands fast in mine. 'I am so sorry.'

'Why?' he says, woefully baffled.

'You've spent all these years torturing yourself.'

'I failed them. I failed your father . . . '

'You never met my father,' I say, releasing his hands, pulling his frail body into my arms, desperate to console him, for myself, and for all of them. 'How could you have failed him?'

'Because I did.' His body shakes. 'I failed them all. I've never told anyone about him. Not even Ellie. It's hurt, too much.'

'I'm so glad you told me,' I say.

And I am.

My heart is breaking, but it's a relief, beyond words, to know the truth at last.

To understand, finally, this thread, between all of us.

I'm not sure how long I hold Tim for.

I feel no urge to move.

Nor, it's clear, does he.

But as our embrace goes on, I become conscious of a weight that's stolen over me, not entirely unfamiliar, *so heavy it might almost belong to another body*, and, for the first time, wonder at the possibility of another's presence within *me*.

In my arms, Tim's body loosens, and I think he must feel it too.

Do you have a theory for why this only happens for some of us? Ellen asked me.

My father thought it was a gift, I told her.

Does it feel like that to you? she asked.

It's starting to, I said.

It does now.

'Thank you,' says Tim, when, at length, he pulls away from me, keeping a hold of my hand. 'Thank you, so much, for listening.'

'Tim,' I say, 'thank *you*.'

And he nods, his dark eyes shining into mine.

For a moment, we're silent again.

Then, 'You've still got questions, I think,' he says.

'A couple,' I agree.

'Then, please, ask them.'

'You're sure?' He looks so tired.

'I'm sure. Ask.'

So, I do.

'You told me last time we spoke about a woman who showed you up to the attic,' I say. 'Was it Iris?'

'No. It was Ellie. I lost touch with her after Clara went, but when I retired, I moved back here, and we became friends again.' Briefly, he smiles, and the warmth of it fills the room, lifting the sadness that's been weighting the air, just a fraction. 'She's been a very . . . loyal . . . friend.' His chest whistles. 'I couldn't tell Imogen about her. She didn't want to end up in her book.'

'Was it her who warned you I'd pay you a visit?'

'No,' he says, and it doesn't escape me that he knows immediately what I'm talking about.

She said you'd come, he told me, before I left the other week.

I assumed at the time that he meant Imogen.

Until Imogen told me she'd never said any such thing to him.

'Who was it?' I ask him.

He doesn't immediately respond.

He closes his eyes, for so long that I fear he might be falling asleep.

'Tim?' I whisper.

'It's all right,' he says, sluggishly, 'I'm still here. And yes, that was Iris.' His lips move in another smile. 'Your great-grandmother.'

He falls silent again: remembering, I can tell.

And, in the space of a slow blink, so do I.

A walk down Doverley's driveway.

The scent of autumn: dying leaves, smoke, and damp.

My arm, looped with Tim's.

My eyes fixed on the profile of his young, troubled face.

'How do you know?' I hear him say, back then.

'It was during the war,' he tells me now. 'A couple of days before our last flight. She was trying to persuade me into trusting I'd survive it all. She told me that I had to.'

382

'*You can tell our story.*' Iris's voice fills my ears, and just as last night, I can't be sure whether I'm recalling, or being. I no longer care. '*Maybe they'll make a picture of us all.*'

'She loved the pictures.' Tim smiles. 'She had all sorts of ideas about who could play us. She liked the idea of Rita Hayworth for Clare. I said she should consider Ingrid Bergman for herself.' His eyes glimmer. 'You must have been told how much you resemble her.'

'Once in a while,' I say, and smile too, through the ache in my cheeks.

'*Perhaps the actress will pay you a visit,*' comes Iris's echo.

'She joked that the actress would come to see me,' says Tim. 'She told me that I had to get through the war, because you'd need me to help you.' His face trembles with emotion. 'It's you I need to help me, though.' His gaze holds mine. 'Can you? Please? Make it right, like you said in your letter?'

'Of course I can,' I say, and don't need to ask him how he wants me to make it right.

It's not what I wanted when I wrote him my letter.

It's cutting me in two, accepting that I really can't save any of them.

But I have now accepted it.

I've seen it: the final truth I've been searching for, and which Ellen was at such pains to convince me of.

On this stage, for *our* present, what's past is past. The only true agency I now have is in shaping what comes next.

And I can give Tim some peace at last.

Rewrite his ending.

'How should we start?' I ask.

'With a swim,' he says, so quickly I can tell he has it all worked out. I think perhaps he has for decades. 'All of them together. Not alone.'

'Not alone,' I agree. 'Then, a boat?'

'A German boat.'

'And a kind officer?' I guess.

'Yes,' he tells me, his body sagging with relief. 'He takes the boys prisoner. But Ames escapes and finds his way to Mabel in France.'

'They remain hidden,' I say, burying my knowledge of Mabel's true end, just before D-Day, care of a Gestapo noose. 'Safe.'

'Safe,' Tim echoes. 'Rob and the others get taken to a camp in Germany. They're liberated in 1945.'

'Like Fred,' I say, thinking now of 96's first group captain, who went down during the Battle of the Ruhr, and came back from the dead at the end of the war, delighting his wife and daughter by suddenly appearing in Kent, at his wife's parents' home.

'Just like Fred,' says Tim, letting more tears go. 'Rob comes back to England, looking for Iris and Clara.'

'I can see him now,' I say, my own eyes stinging with the vividness of the image. 'Iris has taken Clara to Doverley, to see the cottage . . . '

'Yes,' Tim says, unsurprised that I know about it.

And I see the cottage too: not in ruins, crumbled by weather and time, but still whole, its front path dappled by soft spring sunshine.

'A little girl in the village tells Robbie where they are,' I say, thinking of my gran as a child in Heaton, certain she'd want to play this role. 'He sets off, and finds them in the cottage's garden.'

'He surprises them,' says Tim.

And neither of us go on.

We don't need to put words to what Robbie says next.

We both know.

I can't hear it, because it never happened.

But I imagine it.

That low, fun voice.

The hint of Yorkshire in his accent.

All the boundless life and love.

Hope too, of a different future, for all of them, all of *us*, ahead.

Hello, Clarence.

A LAST-MINUTE PLOT TWIST
AT DOVERLEY HOUSE

It's official: Iris Winterton and her bomber boys are getting a sparkling new ending.

We're offering no clues as to what that ending's going to be. We don't have any. But Bomber Boys *author, Imogen Hale, arrived at Doverley House late yesterday, and has been working with a team on-site since, rewriting the movie's closing scenes.*

'It's all very sudden,' said our anonymous source. 'One minute, we're planning to go ahead as per the novel, the next, that's off and everything's changing.'

We have of course tried to uncover what's triggered this sudden about-turn, but our source either couldn't, or wouldn't, say.

But they've assured us that everyone believes the new ending is going to be a very good thing.

'It's given the whole team a lift,' they've said. 'We're all buzzing.'

And when will we mere mortals find out what this new fate for Iris and the boys looks like?

'When you buy a ticket and see the movie,' our source said.

Chapter Twenty-Five

Claudia

W*hen you buy a ticket and see the movie.*

That was pure Blake.

All of it was him.

He gave Felix those words he took to *The Screen.*

Felix was waiting for me yesterday when I arrived back at Doverley from Tim's. It was midday already. Not wanting to leave Tim alone, I'd called Ellen from his room, telling her everything – quietly, since Tim really had fallen asleep by then – and hadn't set off myself until she'd arrived in a taxi, ready to be with him when he woke.

'So now we know,' she said, as I greeted her at Tim's door. 'I do see it.' She looked into my eyes, her head to one side. 'You have nothing of Robbie, though. Nothing at all.' Her cheeks moved in a smile. 'He really must be somewhere else.'

'I hope so,' I said.

With a sigh, she looked across at Tim. 'How peaceful he seems. I fear he won't stay with us much longer now. He's done what he's been waiting to.'

I hated leaving them.

But I'd had things to do too.

I telephoned Imogen on my way back to Doverley, filling her

in on Tim's revelations, getting her on board with the rewrites ('Oh my god, of course,' she said, '*of course* we'll change it for him'); then, I called Ana, briefing her as well ('*Yes*, Claude, *yes*,' she said. 'I love this. I love you'); and, that done, I disintegrated, sobbing so uncontrollably that I had to pull over, my head on Nick's steering wheel, overwhelmed with pain at all of it, and for myself too; the complete disarray of my stage that I need to somehow wrestle into order if I'm ever going to have a hope of functioning, let alone living on it again.

'I see Tim got his own back,' said Felix, opening the door of Nick's car, pulling me into a hug.

It felt good.

So good, I cried more, just at the relief of it.

He'd been on his way to the library when he'd spotted me approaching, and came down to see me instead. Blake and Nick were in the library waiting for him. It turns out another of *The Screen*'s journalists had followed him and Nick to Tim's home yesterday, and contacted Blake for comment.

That's what Blake's meeting request had been about.

'We'd better go up,' I said.

Which we did.

'What's happened?' said Nick, catching sight of my face, getting to his feet.

'Has anyone seen you?' asked Blake, worriedly.

'Only Felix,' I said. 'Now, listen . . . '

And I brought him and Nick up to speed too.

I left nothing out.

Not even about my father.

I trusted them not to take it any further than that room.

I *wanted* to trust them.

Pain, I'm finally learning, loses some of its power once shared.

'You've had a big morning,' said Blake, with a long exhale.

'What do you need?' asked Nick.

'A lot,' I said.

Then it all moved really quickly. The meeting grew; Ana, Naomi, Jeff and several others arriving, Ana dialling in Imogen, and waking a whole heap of people in LA, who forged a plan for the rewrites. Blake, meanwhile, called *The Screen*, offering them Felix's exclusive on the news of our revised ending, in return for them not digging any further into Nick and Felix's visit to Tim.

'They just wanted to say hi,' he told the journalist. 'So leave the guy be, hey? Hasn't he given enough?'

*

'You're not going to make it Tim's fault, are you?' Nick said to Imogen, when she arrived last night. 'Surely we can save him from that, second time around?'

'Absolutely we can,' she agreed. 'We will.'

The other writers arrived from LA first thing, and have been hard at it all day while the rest of us have been tying up our last scene in The Heaton Arms, on the eve of *Mabel's Fury*'s final flight. I've been reshooting some other takes too, laying the ground for Iris's tear-filled admission to Robbie that she's pregnant: a hand to my stomach; a moment of nausea.

'How you doing, Claude?' Ana's kept asking me.

'Fine,' I've told her.

'You're not fine,' Nick said, our mics off between takes. 'And you don't need to be. No one expects that.'

'What about you?' I asked him, looking into his dark, bloodshot eyes. 'Are you ok?'

'No,' he said. 'This whole thing's killing me.'

He's still staying in Mum's old room.

Give him a break, Felix told me.

I want to.

389

I really, really want to.

But every time I think about doing it, I remember how painful it's all got, and I'm still trying to get my head around how to change that story for us.

But this story at least has now been fixed, the writing team have hammered it out, and we on the cast have been given our new pages.

Over the next five days, the boys will stage their flight to Berlin. They'll make it all the way there, just like in the novel, and will be hit by flak. Tim will still be injured, and the plane's electrics will be damaged, preventing Jacob from discharging their bombs, so Robbie will turn back to England with them stuck in the bay's doors.

On the control tower set, I'll receive Robbie's call, and tell him he's going to be a father.

The boys will circle back to the coast.

Six of them will jump.

Back in LA, a team in special effects will create the moment the bombs fall too, sending *Mabel's Fury* leaping upwards, high enough that Tim glides back to England, crashing into land.

Then, this coming weekend, after we're packed up here, all the crew except Felix will take a swim in the North Sea, and find their way to that German boat, and its kind officer.

The movie's final scene, just Nick and me, won't happen until well into the new year.

And it won't take place at Iris and Robbie's ruined cottage in the woods, because I still haven't told anyone about it.

Tim and I agreed that I shouldn't.

'It belongs to them,' he said, 'and you now, too.'

Instead, a location team has already been tasked with finding us another cottage of some sort, with a sloping thatched roof, winding front path, and pretty, bloom-filled garden.

That's going to take them a while.

Even when they do find it, we won't be able to shoot immediately.

Not whilst it's winter, and the trees are so bare, the days so dark.

No, that last scene, sun-kissed and full of light, life and hope, needs to wait for spring.

*

No one expects these last days to be easy, and they're not. The revised scenes, unrehearsed, packed with new lines and new blocking, take relentless hours to get right, and making them perfect becomes an all-consuming task. We split – me in the control tower, the boys on the cutaway – practising, filming, practising, filming again. Every day, we work longer, pushing deep into the night, drained from lack of sleep and the emotion we're expending, but continuing regardless, propelled by the sense that this is something special we're doing. Something not true, but right.

As it should have been.

And, to my mind at least, maybe, *maybe*, one day, will.

I barely see Nick, except for an unbearably tense session on Tuesday morning when we finally shoot Iris and Robbie's passionate encounter in the billiards room. It's a closed set. We don't have to stage these stolen moments of intimacy in front of a lot of people, but we still do enact them under the scrutiny of Ana, the camera operator, and sound recorder. I never like doing these scenes ('Does anyone?' says Nick), and the way I've always got through them in the past is by viewing them emotionlessly.

Or, with the help of Felix making light.

But Nick doesn't make light.

And I can't view any of it emotionlessly.

'That's what's made it so good,' says Ana to me afterwards, with a big hug.

But it is only Nick I see as I kiss him, and say Robbie's name. Only his touch I feel.

Only his voice I hear, telling me he loves me.

And I cling to him, knowing that I'm really clinging to us, wishing so many things, and most of all that I knew how to stop it all feeling so much like a last, hopeless goodbye.

*

He doesn't say goodbye to me when, first thing on the final Friday of November, with everything we need to have done at Doverley somehow suddenly *done* – all in the can, along with our blood, sweat and tears – he leaves the estate, speeding up the driveway along with everyone else heading to the coast for the weekend's shooting.

Felix has gone too.

'For moral support,' he said.

'Fine,' Ana told him. 'But you're not billing anything.'

I'm all alone at Doverley. The trailers have gone, all the sets inside have been taken down too, the rigs and props removed. Even the base has been dismantled and towed away: another episode of this estate's history consigned to invisibility.

I watch Nick's car disappear into the drizzle from Doverley's uneven front step. I'm breathless. I saw him heading out from our room and raced down to catch him. Now that I haven't, I don't consider calling him to say what I need to.

It hurts too much that he's left like this, without saying anything.

I'll be glad to leave Doverley myself now. It feels empty without him here any more.

Hollow and very lonely.

Phil's on his way to collect me though. He insisted on taking the day off to come, and has just given me an updated ETA that's two hours away. We're going to stop in Cambridge on our way home, for lunch with his mum and dad. It will be lovely. It always is with them. I'd be looking forward to it a lot more if I wasn't feeling so poleaxed by Nick having given up on us, just as I've realised that I can't let myself do any such thing.

Turning from the bleak morning, I head back into the house, and upstairs to finish packing. It doesn't take me long; I collect my last bits from the bathroom, keeping that shower cap, and stow it all in my case, along with my copy of *The Bomber Boys* – pausing, as I always have and always will, to look at Robbie's smile.

You're only worried because you're going to have to finally give me an answer tomorrow, Tim told me he was about to say.

I have no memory of it.

Or of Iris's laughter in response.

Oh, do be quiet, Robbie.

There's so much I haven't seen, not only of then, but of Iris's years with Clara after the war.

And perhaps Tim's right.

Perhaps my lanterns really are protecting me from those things that are not mine to recall.

Or perhaps my role in my great-grandmother's life finished the moment I saved it, stopping her from catching that bus.

Or maybe I'm simply no longer searching for what's passed because I'm ready at last to be here again, moving into my own unknown tomorrows – which, unlike all of them, I have the privilege of being able to count on stretching ahead of me, hopefully for decades yet to come.

But, before I go to those tomorrows, I return, one last time, to the attic.

I haven't been up this week. I haven't been able to bring myself to return. And I've been angry at myself for never bringing Nick.

Iris would have brought Robbie, I'm sure.

She wouldn't have hesitated.

Wouldn't have wasted their time.

Stepping over her and Clare's creaking threshold, I go to their bureau, and, putting Iris's hairgrip back where I found it, feel my body loosen in release.

I'm done with it all, at last.

I lay my palm on Clare's nail polish stain, and look into the mirror, deep into my own hazel eyes staring back at me.

Then, in the enveloping silence, I head to the window, my focus settling on the damp expanse of trodden grass where the base and planes have all stood.

I see nothing else.

This is your existence, Ellen told me. *You belong on this stage. Nowhere else.*

For the first time in as long as I can remember, the thought doesn't intimidate me.

I really have needed Iris. Ellen's been right about that too. I was numb when I arrived here, afraid to let myself feel anything, but in Iris, I've *felt* – fear, grief, happiness, desire, love, *so much love* – and it's opened me back up, crumbled *my* walls.

Silently, I thank her.

I thank all of them: these ghosts who will never be ghosts, all of them living their own eternity of lifetimes.

Closing my eyes, I place my fingers to the cold window, picturing a dark head, a polka-dot sleeve, and feel a brush of warmth encircling me.

And, in the distance, over above the woods, I hear that hawk, calling.

One final time.

*

I hadn't intended to come to the cottage again.

Just as with the attic, it's felt too hard.

It's been more than a week since I last sat by this gatepost I crouch beside now. Then, I was still frantically grappling for a way to change the unchangeable, and I had no suspicion when I got up to go that I might be doing it for the last time. I thought I preferred to leave it that way: to have farewelled this place as I found it, without plan, or ceremony.

But I'm happy, now I'm here again, that I gave in to my instinct to come. I've grown to love this beautiful, wild, ageless place.

I love it most this morning.

I saw this piece of paper by the gatepost, weighted by a rock, the moment I entered the clearing, and knew instantly who it was from.

I trembled as I bent to pick it up.

I'm trembling now as I read it.

I've known about this place for a while, Nick's written. *I came looking for you when you were out walking, a couple of days after everything broke about our son – who, by the way, will always be Louis to me, just like we said we'd call him if he was a boy. I've wanted to tell you that, but I've been afraid it would make you sad. When I saw you here, crying, all I wanted was to comfort you, but I was afraid then of making you sadder too.*

I've come here a lot now myself. Done a lot of thinking. I think you'll come back here today, and if I'm wrong, then you'll be upset that I left like this, so I'll call later to explain. But I don't think I'm wrong. And I didn't want to talk this morning. We've tried talking, and it keeps not working, so I thought it would be easier to write.

Look where that got you with Tim.

I'm not walking away from us. All this week, we've been giving Iris and Robbie a second chance, and I'm not about to give up on the possibility of ours. It's like I keep saying, I'm not interested in easy. Just because something's hard, it doesn't mean it's wrong. But you need a rest. We both do. So, can we please take one, pause to breathe, and see where it takes us?

We've got time. As much as we want.

Let's use it.

Shakily, I reach for my phone, and really do need to get back to the house for Phil, but I want to do this first.

I want to do it here.

I don't call Nick.

Like him, I write.

I'm not giving up either, I tell him, just as I intended to when I raced down from our room to catch him earlier. *And I want to be able to breathe again. I want to breathe with you. Let's take ourselves somewhere good.*

It's a minute before he replies.

I watch my phone, imagining him pulling over, looking down at his screen, not frowning, like I've seen him frown at his phone so often lately, but smiling: a slow, warm smile that lifts his face that I love, more than any other.

I see dots, and smile too, knowing he's typing.

We'll go somewhere good, he says. *A new beginning.*

No, I tell him, *we've had our beginning. This can be our middle.*

A long middle, he replies.

Yes, I say. *A very long middle.*

I like the sound of that.

396

Chapter Twenty-Six

Claudia

April 2019

A cottage of some sort, Oxfordshire

I've driven myself here today, for this last scene.

It's a beautiful day, clear and bright, sweet with the scent of cut grass, wild meadow flowers, and the first whispering promise of summer to come.

I haven't seen Nick yet.

He was already in his trailer when I arrived, and I headed straight to mine to get ready. It's all been a rush as I was late arriving. I brought Lisa and Hannah with me from London – they're on their Easter holidays – and Mum guilted us into letting Stewart tag along too. ('Oh, go on, girls, he'll love a day in the countryside, and he's so much better behaved these days.') He's not better behaved at all, I had my concerns from the start, and sure enough we lost him to a rabbit, for a fraught half hour, when we stopped to walk him at Cherwell Services. He looked pretty downcast when he finally reappeared, his tail literally between his legs, so my guess is the rabbit got the better of him.

Lisa and Hannah have taken him for another walk now to tire him out, and Ana's here with me, running me through a briefing ahead of the shoot, which will be the very last for this movie. She's been working flat-out ever since we left Doverley, getting everything else finished: from the boys' sea swim ('How was it?' I asked Nick. 'Pretty cold,' he said), to the bittersweet scenes showcasing Iris, Robbie and Tim's childhood, to the entirely bitter sequences at Bomber Command HQ, re-enacting the death sentence decisions that were taken there. Ana's kept me updated, but I haven't considered joining her to watch the filming myself.

I've remained in London, resting.

In December, Nick headed back to Montana to spend time with his own family, catch up with old friends, and rest too.

I haven't seen him since then, but we've talked, lots, getting better at it the more we have, finally sharing everything it used to feel so impossible to put words to: no more secrets. The hole our son, *Louis*, has left in us is no less, but it is something we now carry together.

And I've told Nick about what I experienced at Doverley. At no point has he tried to dismiss it, or rationalise any of it away; he's simply listened, *heard*, making me feel the very opposite of alone.

We've spoken about plenty of other, less weighty, things too. Like, Felix and Emma on their shoot in New Zealand, and how often they've kept mentioning each other whenever we've caught up with them on the phone. And the repairs Nick's helped his parents with around the family's farm; the horses he's reacquainted himself with, and the long rides he's taken at dawn. I've filled him in on the variety of cooking courses I've been doing with Phil – the sourdough, gnocchi, gyoza and macaroons we now know how to make – and my long walks with Stewart, lunches with Imogen, then the trips I've made back to Yorkshire to visit Ellen and Tim (still with us; 'I want to see this picture of yours,' he keeps insisting), and Georgie as well: the woman who hugged me, and who Ellen gave my number to.

We've become close, actually.

Mum was right: it has done us good to talk about everything.

'You're looking well,' says Ana to me now, as we head to my trailer door. 'Sleep suits you.'

I don't disagree.

It does suit me.

I've been enjoying getting more of it.

Each evening in Highgate, after dinner with my family, I've kissed them goodnight, gone up to my room, talked with Nick, and climbed into my old bed, where I've slept deeply.

Not dreamlessly.

But I've dreamt as me.

And a lot of him.

I'm pretty apprehensive about seeing him again, after all this time.

I follow Ana out of the trailer with my hand to my ribs, pressing against the bubbling there, and, in my pale-blue tea dress, feel a bit like I'm heading to a school dance.

But it's one I'm excited to be at.

I'm ready for it.

I'm really, really ready for this.

*

I only briefly catch sight of him, before I get into position.

I don't know if he sees me, but I see him, in uniform, heading around the back of the cottage, surrounded by crew.

Lisa and Hannah are sitting behind Ana.

'Where's Stewart?' I call out to them, anxiously.

'Sleeping,' Lisa calls back. She's been coming out of herself more lately. I've collected her from her school gate most days, done some work with her drama class too, and Mum reckons it's been helping. I hope so. 'Nick put him in his trailer.'

'All right,' I say, with a deep breath, and a smile.

I have a new co-star for this scene: a sweet little one-year-old called Bess, all dark curls, dimples and chubby creases, who I join in the garden, getting down beside her on the lawn. Her mum remains with us until the last moment, entertaining Bess with a squeezy giraffe, then I take over, with a 1940s rattle, as we're counted in.

She's a total pro, and plays along beautifully: laughing, clapping, reaching for the rattle. I won't pretend it doesn't hurt, being with her like this, but the pain is bearable. What's passed has passed; I've made my peace with that now, and feel full of what might yet be.

Nick's getting close, walking around the garden's fence, up to the gate.

I still don't see him, my focus is all on Bess, but I know he's there.

My heart knows it too, beating, *beating*.

Losing interest in the rattle, Bess totters to her feet, grabbing at my hair.

I laugh, taking her hand in mine, extracting it, and my stomach flips in anticipation.

The catch on the gate clicks.

Dipping my chin to my shoulder, I turn towards it.

I do that because I'm meant to, but also because I want to.

And because this scene – pure fiction for them, for now – is very real for us.

My eyes lock with his.

He stares at me.

He looks younger.

Rested.

Sleep suits him, too.

Heart bashing, I stand.

He takes a step towards me.

I remain rooted to the spot.

It's our scene in the control tower breakroom, all over again, except now there are two of us who his attention moves between: from me, to Bess, back to me.

It's only me he touches though, running his arm around my waist, turning my legs liquid.

Only me he holds as, slowly, he dips his head, lowering his mouth to my ear.

And I know the words that are meant to be coming, but also that it doesn't matter what Nick says, because it's been decided that this final, whispered line of Robbie's should be left to the viewers' imaginations.

For me, it will always be, *Hello, Clarence.*

That's not what I hear now, though.

Not in this story.

Not in our story.

'I think you're the cat's pyjamas,' Nick says, in a voice that's low, deep, pure Montana, and only his. 'I always have. I always will.'

And I smile, looking into his eyes, that are the wrong colour, but which unequivocally make my heart sing, then I pull him towards me, kissing him.

'Cut,' calls Ana.

But we don't listen.

We don't cut.

Not yet.

Neither of us are ready to leave this scene.

WHERE HAVE
NICK AND CLAUDIA GONE?

The New York premiere for The Bomber Boys *last night was everything we could have hoped for: glamour, glitz, and a star-studded turnout. What's more, the movie – already slated as frontrunner for awards across all major categories – was even better. (Read our full review <u>here</u>.) Everyone has given the performance of their career, and that ending is everything.*

No surprise the mood on the red carpet was jubilant.

But there were two noticeable absences from the celebrations.

Neither Claudia Baxter nor Nick Turner were in attendance.

No one was saying where they've got to either.

'That's their concern,' said Ana Ashley.

'Leave them alone,' Felix Jade told us.

'I'm sure you'll hear about it when they're good and ready,' added Emma Jameson, who was sparkling on none other than Felix Jade's arm. 'I really wouldn't hold your breath.'

Epilogue

Claudia

December 2019

I haven't brought my dad's bear to the hospital with me.

I didn't have time to go home and fetch him.

Nick and I were both in our hotel room, getting ready for the premiere, when the call came, much sooner than we'd been expecting, telling us it was time.

Frantically, we headed straight for JFK.

It's a long flight from New York to Los Angeles.

We were really scared, through all of it.

It felt like history repeating.

Only it was different, because we were together.

And even though she's come early, it's not too early.

She's ok.

We're with her.

I didn't know how this was going to work. I've been terrified to trust it. Petrified that this child would somehow look at me, us, as interlopers.

Strangers.

'Come on, Claude,' Phil's kept saying. 'You know better than that.'

He and Mum are already on a flight over from London with Lisa and Hannah. Nick's parents are on their way from Montana too. They'll all be here soon.

But for now, it's just us three, here together.

Nick's holding her, so tiny, so perfect, and I'm right beside him, my finger held firm in her clinging grip, which I know is just a reflex – I've read all the books – but it feels like a lot more than that.

We haven't named her.

Not yet.

We've got time.

For the moment, we're silent: not talking, just becoming.

Us.

And I'm not scared any more.

She's not looking at either of us like we're strangers.

It really does seem as though she, so calm, and peaceful, and trusting, knows who she's with.

And the longer I look at her, I know that I know her too.

She blinks.

Her mouth moves in a silent o, nose scrunching, and my heart overflows.

Hello, you, I wordlessly tell her, pressing my lips to her forehead, closing my eyes at the sensation of her little fist tightening even harder around mine. *I've been waiting for you. We've both been waiting.* I open my eyes, looking deep into hers, so round and huge, windows to her soul, and feel my cheeks lift in a smile. *I think we might have met before.*

Author's Note

It was years ago that I first read Martha Gellhorn's *The Face of War*: a collection of articles from her time as a war correspondent. One of these articles is entitled *The Bomber Boys,* and chronicles Martha Gellhorn's night at a RAF bomber base in November 1943. It's a piece of writing that, once read, never leaves you. Two WAAF radio operatives feature in it, anxiously waiting for the base's operational crews to return, then instructing them to *pancake* and *aerodrome* as their names are checked off on a chalkboard. The entire article lived in my mind as I wrote *Every Lifetime After,* not least the two unnamed WAAFs, who became Iris and Clare.

More inspiration for this novel came from stories I've found of World War Two ghost planes: not only the tragic mysteries of crews and planes that disappeared without trace during the conflict, but also the reports of people who, much more recently, have glimpsed propellor-driven planes in the empty night sky – just as Claudia hears them in the dark silence of Doverley.

For Claudia, this is because her lanterns extinguish, and she's permitted to see layers of existence beyond that which is now. This idea of time running in infinite parallels is one I've always been fascinated by, but the concept of Claudia's lanterns really took shape for me when I read *The Last Enemy* by Richard Hillary, a fighter pilot who wrote his autobiography before he was tragically killed, training to fly bombers in January 1943. In his book, Hillary relays a discussion he's had with a close friend, Denise, who is grieving for another pilot called Peter Pease. Denise tells Hillary that she doesn't fear death, or loss, because she believes that all of us are ever-present, fated to meet again. She says she sees this world we're in as a brightly lit room that we can't see out of, except in scarce moments when we get to turn off all the lights, take up our window coverings, and steal a glance at what's beyond. I loved this idea, which, over time, evolved into Claudia's stage, the dimming of her father's lanterns – Tim and Clare's too – and the blacking out of her own.

This all happens for Claudia in Doverley and Heaton. Both these places are fictional, but I have done my very best to be faithful in my representation of the era, the workings of a RAF bomber station, and the day-to-day existences of those who served in them. Likewise, in the present day, I've tried to create as realistic as possible a portrayal of a movie set. For anyone who is interested in reading more about the world of films, I thoroughly recommend, *Making Movies* by Sidney Lumet. And, for those who'd like to delve deeper into the history of the RAF during World War Two, I found several books invaluable. I've already mentioned *The Last Enemy* and *The Face of War,* but also recommend: *Bomber Command* by Max Hastings; *Lancaster* by John Nicol; *First Light* by Geoffrey Wellum; and *The Guinea Pig Club* by Emily Mayhew.

Acknowledgements

As with any novel, writing *Every Lifetime After* was a labour of love involving a huge amount of work – all human, no AI – which, in this case, spanned years. Never has it felt more important to acknowledge that than now, with the creative industry under such immense threat from the under-regulated use of AI. The human heart, mind and soul forms the essence of all stories, and that should never be forgotten or lost. I hope that as long as readers like you choose to read books written like this, it never will. So, first and foremost, I would love to thank you for picking up my book: you're the reason I write, and your support means everything.

I couldn't write my books without the brilliant, talented people who help bring them to life. I've been lucky enough to work with my editor, Manpreet Grewal, and agent, Becky Ritchie, for close to ten years now, and would be nowhere without their amazing insight, experience, and cheerleading. I want to say a huge thanks, too, to Priyal Agrawal at HQ, who is such a wonder to work with. Thank you also to Donna Hillyer, the entire team at HQ, and of course to Alexandra McNicoll, Lucy Joyce, Jack Sargeant, Euan Thorneycroft, and everyone at AM Heath.

Iona Grey, thank you, thank you, thank you.

And, always, thank you to my husband, Matt, and to our children, Molly, Jonah and Raffy. We've definitely all met before.

ONE PLACE. MANY STORIES

Bold, innovative and
empowering publishing.

FOLLOW US ON:

@HQStories